D0274189

MONSTER
IN THE CLOSET

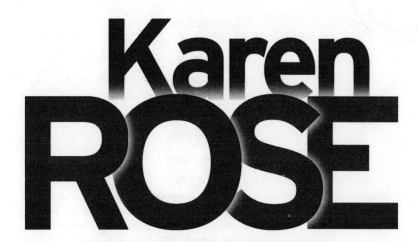

Karen ROSE

MONSTER
IN THE CLOSET

HEADLINE

Copyright © 2017 Karen Rose Hafer

The right of Karen Rose Hafer to be identified as the Author of
the Work has been asserted by her in accordance with the
Copyright, Designs and Patents Act 1988.

First published in 2017 by
HEADLINE PUBLISHING GROUP

1

Apart from any use permitted under UK copyright law, this publication
may only be reproduced, stored, or transmitted, in any form, or by
any means, with prior permission in writing of the publishers or,
in the case of reprographic production, in accordance with the terms
of licences issued by the Copyright Licensing Agency.

All characters in this publication are fictitious and any resemblance
to real persons, living or dead, is purely coincidental.

Cataloguing in Publication Data is available from the British Library

Hardback ISBN 978 1 4722 4462 8

Trade Paperback ISBN 978 1 4722 4461 1

Typeset in Palatino by Avon DataSet Ltd, Bidford-on-Avon, Warwickshire

Printed and bound in Great Britain by Clays Ltd, St Ives plc

Headline's policy is to use papers that are natural, renewable and recyclable
products and made from wood grown in well-managed forests and other
controlled sources. The logging and manufacturing processes are expected to
conform to the environmental regulations of the country of origin.

HEADLINE PUBLISHING GROUP
An Hachette UK Company
Carmelite House
50 Victoria Embankment
London EC4Y 0DZ

www.headline.co.uk
www.hachette.co.uk

To my readers all over the world – thank you for loving the characters who live in my head as much as I do. I wrote this book as a sort of 'Valentine' to you.

To all the fathers who love their children without reservation, including the stepfathers who step up to be the dads they don't have to be, but are. May your children treasure the blessed gift they've been given.

To my sweet husband, Martin, who has always been the most amazing dad to our daughters.

BAINTE DEN STOC

WITHDRAWN FROM DLR LIBRARIES STOCK

Acknowledgements

Terry Bolyard, for helping me to reconstruct my villain.

Amy Lane, for inspiring me to write something that I hadn't planned to.

Erica Ridley and Roy Prendas, for naming Tavilla's gang. ¡Gracias!

My lovely editors, Claire Zion and Alex Clarke, for embracing this surprise book.

Beth Miller and Caitlin Ellis for all the hours of editing and more editing.

Robin Rue, for loving it at first sight.

Sonie Lasker, for once again advising me the best way to knock a big guy on his . . . posterior section.

Geoff Symons, for generously sharing his forensic expertise, including blood spatter.

Prologue

Baltimore, Maryland,
Wednesday 22 July, 2.45 P.M.

Jazzie Jarvis slowed her steps as she struggled up the third of the four flights of stairs to their apartment. Sweat streaked her face and the weight of her backpack nearly bowed her in half. Mama had forgotten to pick her up. *Again.*

Most days it didn't matter if she forgot. It was hot walking home from day camp, but Jazzie could manage that. The problem was the heat combined with her full backpack. She'd sweated all the way home.

At least the sweat hid the tears she hadn't been able to hold back. Because Mama hadn't just forgotten to pick her up. She'd forgotten about the art fair. *And I reminded her over and over.* She'd promised that she'd come. *She promised.*

But she hadn't. Jazzie had stood at her table for more than an hour, eyes fastened to the door, all her projects from day camp arranged perfectly. The clay pot she'd painted and glazed and fired all by herself, the sketches she'd worked so hard to get just right. The pretty piece of rock that she'd sanded until it shone like a diamond. All of it had been there, waiting for Mama to see.

But Mama had forgotten to come and Jazzie had barely managed not to cry as all the other moms and dads walked by, smiling at her, complimenting her. Pitying her because she was the only one whose mama hadn't come. All the other moms and dads had helped their kids pack up their stuff and carry it to waiting cars.

1

Fancy cars because it was a fancy day camp. Exclusive. *Expensive.*

Aunt Lilah, Mama's sister, had paid for it because Jazzie's mama didn't have the money anymore. Not since her dad had left them. Jazzie didn't miss him. *He wouldn't have come to see my art anyway,* she thought bitterly. He'd worked all the time when he'd lived with them. They'd never really seen him. Not even on Sunday, because that had been his golf day, when he entertained clients.

It had always been Mama who'd come to school, who'd attended concert recitals and award ceremonies. But Mama hadn't been . . . herself, not for a long time.

Not since her dad had left. Maybe even before. Her little sister Janie was too young to remember when they'd been happy. Jazzie could barely remember it herself.

So while all the moms and dads were packing up their kids' art projects and leftover supplies, Jazzie had packed her own, keeping her chin stubbornly up. Her eyes burned, but she was not going to let anyone see her cry. Especially not the rich kids who sneered because her mama drove an old car with a crappy paint job.

Jazzie had been one of the rich kids once. Before her father left. They'd had a nice house, a nice car. Lots of clothes. Plenty of food. They still had food because Uncle Denny, her father's brother, wouldn't let them go hungry. That hurt Mama's pride, but she'd allowed it, because she wouldn't let them go hungry either. Jazzie and Janie would have school clothes, too, because of Aunt Lilah. They wouldn't be fancy or have designer tags because Aunt Lilah was . . . What was the word again? *Oh, right. Frugal.*

Not cheap. Not selfish. Just careful. Which was what Mama was learning to be, because now she had to work and she didn't make much money. Now they lived in a crappy little two-bedroom apartment on the fourth floor of a building with a broken elevator. An apartment they had to share with her grandma.

Jazzie's lips curled in a sneer of her own because she did not like her father's mama. Grandma could be hateful sometimes. She was the one who called Aunt Lilah selfish and cheap. All because Grandma was stupid. She'd borrowed too much money and lost her house. All for Jazzie's father, who broke all his promises.

2

'Asshole,' Jazzie muttered under her breath, more than a little proud she hadn't stuttered, even a little. 'Ass. Hole,' she repeated firmly, enunciating the way her speech therapist had taught her to do, because *asshole* had a lot of sounds that she had trouble with. She figured her therapist wouldn't have approved of the word, but Jazzie didn't much care. It was a damn good word, well worth practicing because it came in handy. Often. Especially when she thought about her father, which she'd done a lot in the last few months. Ever since they'd had to leave the house that had always been her home.

Mama had tried so hard to keep the house, but she couldn't make enough money as a secretary. It wasn't her fault. That was all on her dad, who according to Grandma could do no wrong and would be back soon to take care of them again. 'Soon' had stretched into almost three years.

That was a long time when you were only eleven.

Jazzie grabbed onto the banister and pulled herself up the last stair. All she wanted was to curl up on the sofa, watch cartoons, and let the A/C cool her skin.

She stopped on the landing. The front door to their tiny apartment was ajar, and Jazzie could feel it. The . . . wrongness of it. The heavy dread she could actually taste. And it tasted bad. *It was . . .* She wanted to cry. *Toilet smells.*

Not again, Mama. Not today. Jazzie was so tired, so hot, but she knew she'd have to clean Mama up. She didn't want Janie to see their mama this way. Ever.

Her shoulders slumped, her eyes filling with new tears. *Dammit, Mama.* Sometimes her mother was so sad. She and Janie tried to cheer her up, but nothing they did was ever good enough. Some days Mama didn't get out of bed at all. And some days she came home from work early and drank until she fell asleep on the sofa. Those were the days the drapes were pulled so no light could get in. Dark days, in more ways than one.

Those were the days that Jazzie gathered the empty bottles and threw them away, then cleaned her mama up, covered her with a blanket, and tried to make it look like she really was just napping

3

and not passed out drunk. Jazzie didn't want Janie to know about any of that. Her little sister was only five. She didn't understand the dark days.

This was going to be one of those days.

Jazzie would see to her mama, then call Aunt Lilah to pick up Janie from day care, because Mama wouldn't drive when she was drunk. Because Jazzie would never let her. Which meant finding her car keys and hiding them. Again.

I'm running out of places to hide things. Something needed to change. But Jazzie didn't know what that thing could be.

She carefully pushed the door open enough to slip through. It was dark in the apartment, but she'd known it would be. Still hauling her backpack, she tiptoed into the living room, not wanting to wake her mother – because drunk Mama was not very patient. She picked her way around the furniture, some of the only things they'd kept from the house. It was fancy furniture that didn't look right in this shabby little room, but it was familiar. Mama liked to sleep on the sofa most nights, probably because she had to share a bedroom with Grandma. Jazzie figured she had it good with only having to share with Janie.

The wingback chair in the corner was Jazzie's and always had been, even before they moved here. The chair had come with them from the old house. Cuddling deep into it made her feel protected. And behind it had always been a good hiding place when her parents had fought. She'd hidden behind the chair a lot in the old days. *So maybe we weren't so happy after all.*

She stumbled as her foot hit something unfamiliar. Grabbing the arm of the sofa, she managed to stay upright, just as she heard a sound. A loud sound. Rustling and banging and thudding. And then a man's voice, swearing.

Someone's here. In the coat closet. Jazzie's breath froze in her chest. *What do I do? Oh God. What do I do?* She opened her mouth to shout for her mama, but snapped it closed again. *No. Just hide. Back away and hide.*

Her eyes had grown used to the darkness, and she took a step toward her bedroom. *I can hide under the bed.* But more crashing

4

sounds came from the coat closet and the door started to open. Her heart pounding, Jazzie dropped to her knees and crawled behind the chair, grateful for the darkness. She'd hidden so many times. No one could find her if the room stayed dark.

Don't let him turn on the lights. Please.

The man in the closet began to curse again, his voice muffled. But she could hear the words. Foul, mean words. And . . .

Oh no. Oh God. She knew that voice. What was *he* doing here? *Where's Mama?*

She concentrated on breathing silently . . . until her eyes focused on the floor in front of the sofa. *A shoe.* She'd tripped on a shoe.

Her breath came faster. Harder. So hard it hurt her chest. *Mama's high-heeled shoe.*

And it was still on Mama's foot.

Horrified, she kept looking, because she couldn't stop. *Mama's skirt.* The good suit she wore to weddings and award ceremonies at the school. She'd dressed up.

She was going to come today, Jazzie realized. Mama hadn't forgotten. But she was lying on the floor. So still. *She's hurt. She's hurt and I have to help her.*

He hurt her. Again. Rage exploded inside her and she wanted to hurt him back. Wanted to hit him and kick him until he left them alone. But he was bigger and stronger. And meaner. So she stayed where she was. *Just wait. Wait till he leaves. Then you can help her. You can call 911. Then Aunt Lilah.* Aunt Lilah always knew what to do. *Just wait. Wait till he's gone.*

She chanted the words silently, in her own mind. Her mother was so still. *Let her be okay. Please let her be okay.* She'd fallen between the sofa and the coffee table, and Jazzie couldn't see her face from where she was hiding. Couldn't see her mama's chest to see if she was breathing. *Say something, Mama. Anything. Please.* Hoping to see a twitch or hear a moan, Jazzie kept staring at the skirt of her mother's good suit.

Which . . . was dark. It wasn't supposed to be dark. Mama's good suit was white. It was supposed to be white. But it wasn't. It was almost black. Big spots of black.

Stains. *Oh God. Oh God. Oh God. No. No.* Bloodstains. Mama was covered in blood. Jazzie covered her mouth with her hand because she could feel the scream clawing up her throat. *And he'll find me. He'll hurt me too.*

Don't look. Don't look. She closed her eyes tight, not wanting to see any more of her mother there on the floor. But she heard another loud crash and the smashing of glass.

Mama's things. Her keepsakes. Their Christmas ornaments. He was breaking them. Coats were flung from the closet, landing on the floor in a heap. He was looking for something. *What? Why?*

'Fucking bitch!' he snarled. 'Where is it? Where did you put the fucking money?' A big box was thrown out of the closet, landing in another clatter of glass, and Jazzie scooted further behind the chair, her mind racing, thinking about all the things in her backpack. The pot. The clay pot she'd made for Mama. She could hit him with it.

But that was stupid. He was tall. She couldn't hurt him. She couldn't get away.

It got suddenly quiet. Maybe he was gone. She risked a peek around the chair as a new round of cursing came from the closet. No. He was still here. *Just a little while longer. Hold on, Mama. I'll call for help soon.* From here she could see past the coffee table. She squinted into the darkness to see if her mother's eyes were open, and—

No. Nonononononono.

That . . . *thing* on the floor. It couldn't be her mama. It couldn't be . . . a person. But it was. She knew it was. *Mama.* A sob filled her chest and she pressed her hand harder to her mouth. *Oh God, Mama. My mama.*

The closet door flew open all the way, slamming against the wall, and he burst into the room.

Jazzie froze. He was tall, just like she remembered. But skinnier. He looked wilder. Even meaner. He kicked the pile of things he'd thrown on the floor, then bent down and stared at the . . . the thing on the floor. Her mama.

'What did you do with the goddamned money?' he thundered, then kicked at the . . . the thing. *At Mama.* 'Tell me!'

6

Do not make a sound. Jazzie held her breath, trying so hard not to whimper.

'Holy shit,' he muttered. He stood up and backed away, his eyes wide and suddenly scared. 'She's dead.' He swore again, this time sounding more confused than angry. He was coming back to himself. Jazzie remembered him doing that whenever he'd yell at her mama. Whenever he'd slap Mama hard and make her cry.

He backed up a few more steps, stumbling over the pile of coats on the floor. 'Oh my God. I killed her,' he whispered, and looked at his hands. 'Oh shit. Shit, shit, shit.'

He drew a deep breath, then let it out. 'Stay calm. Just stay calm. You can fix this. You got this.' He took another few breaths, then swore again, more quietly this time. 'Wash your hands. Clean the drain. Get your jacket. And get the fuck out of here.'

Jazzie rocked herself behind the chair. Her face was wet. Her teeth sank into her palm and her body shook like she was sick. But she didn't make a sound. Not a single sound.

She knew what would happen if he found her.

She heard water running and then smelled something harsh. It made her nose tickle and she scrunched up her face so that she wouldn't sneeze. Bleach. That was the smell. Grandma kept it under the sink. She was always cleaning with it.

He reappeared, his hands now clean. He grabbed a hoodie, while she watched, utterly numb. Using a towel from the sink, he wiped down the tables and the lock and the door handle and the door itself before shoving the towel down the front of his hoodie. Then he was gone, the door shut tightly behind him.

Jazzie didn't move. Couldn't move. Couldn't breathe. She just sat and rocked and stared and told herself that it was just a dream. A bad, bad dream.

One

Hunt Valley, Maryland,
Saturday 22 August, 12.50 P.M.

'Heels down, Janie.' Taylor Dawson stood in the middle of the training ring, focused on the five-year-old girl sitting astride what was the most gentle, patient horse Taylor had ever known. Janie's back, already too stiff and rigid, tightened further, her little hands clenching the reins as a frown thinned her lips.

Taylor knew the child's frown was not directed at her, but almost wished it were. A perfectionist in little zebra cowboy boots, Janie was angry with herself. Angry that she'd had to be corrected by anyone. That she wasn't already perfect.

Taylor swallowed a sigh. *Been there, done that.* Looking quickly to her right, she met the worried eyes of Janie's big sister, who stood on the other side of the fence, watching Janie with an eagle eye. Taylor gave the girl an encouraging smile. Jazzie did not smile back, her expression a mix of poorly hidden desperation and stoic determination. At eleven years old, she'd become her little sister's keeper. Her protector. Her staunchly silent protector.

Because Jazzie Jarvis had not spoken a single word, not in the two weeks Taylor had been interning for Healing Hearts with Horses. According to Maggie VanDorn, Taylor's boss, Jazzie hadn't spoken in the two weeks before that either – not since finding her mother's broken body in a pool of her own blood, her face nearly unrecognizable.

It'll be okay, Taylor wanted to promise. *For both of you.* But she couldn't promise that. Nobody could. Janie and Jazzie had

9

been through a hell no child should ever endure.

Taylor suppressed a shudder. How did anyone come back from that? Adults didn't come back from that kind of trauma. How could two little motherless girls begin to cope? To heal?

But if it could happen anywhere, it was here. Healing Hearts with Horses had been providing therapy to traumatized children for over a year now, and already had a slew of success stories. Taylor knew this because she'd very thoroughly researched the program, including its founder/president Daphne Montgomery-Carter *and* her staff, before submitting her application.

In addition to her philanthropy, Daphne was a full-time prosecutor for the city of Baltimore. Somehow she managed to raise money for the program in her 'spare time', lending a hand to the therapy sessions whenever she could. All the day-to-day details were left to Maggie VanDorn, an accomplished horsewoman and licensed therapist, who had years of experience working with child victims of violent crime.

Janie and Jazzie had a good chance for recovery here – if they'd let themselves relax and have a little fun. Getting Janie to actually breathe while on her horse would be a good start, but telling a new rider to remember to breathe often made them even more stressed.

Getting Janie to sing would get her to breathe without her knowing she was doing it.

'Hey, Janie!' Taylor called. 'Did you know that Ginger likes music?'

Janie turned her head to stare at Taylor suspiciously. 'Horses don't like music.'

'Ginger does. She loves it when I sing to her. Especially when I'm riding her. She just chills out like you're giving her a massage.' It wasn't exactly true, but it wasn't necessarily a lie either.

Taylor was good at telling not-exactly-truths that also weren't lies. She'd perfected the skill at the feet of the master of lies and deceit. *Thanks for that, Mom.*

Pushing her own bitterness aside, she smiled at Janie. 'Do you know any songs?'

A wary nod, but no reply, which was no surprise. Unlike Jazzie, who'd remained mute, Janie did speak sometimes. Their files said that Jazzie had been shy before their mother's murder because she had a painful stutter, but Janie had been a champion talker, never meeting a silence she couldn't fill. Now Janie was withdrawn, her communication reduced to sentences of four or five words. *Well, duh*. Who wouldn't be withdrawn?

'Do you know "The Wheels on the Bus"?' Taylor asked, and grinned when Janie rolled her eyes. It was a beautifully normal gesture from a kid who'd forgotten how to behave like a child.

'That's for babies,' Janie said sullenly.

And you're oh-so-old, Taylor thought sadly, but forced her lips to remain curved. 'Fair enough. How about "Twinkle, Twinkle, Little Star", then? Do you know that one?'

'Yeah,' Janie muttered. 'Everybody does.'

'Good. Help me out, then. Let's make Ginger happy.'

Taylor began singing the song loudly and off-key, because the universe had not gifted her with any musical ability. She made it through the song once solo while Ginger patiently plodded around the training ring, Janie still rigid as a board. The second time, though, Janie began to sing as well.

Taylor didn't ask any more questions, immediately launching into 'You Are My Sunshine', hoping Janie knew that one too, gratified when the little girl followed her lead. After the second time through that song, Taylor began to see the desired effect. Janie's shoulders softened, her posture relaxing a fraction. She was singing with a studied focus, like she did everything else, so she wasn't enjoying it, but she was breathing and that was a good start.

Taylor searched her mind for the songs she'd sung with the kids at the campus day care where she'd volunteered as an undergrad, quickly eliminating all those that were either violent – like the old woman who swallowed a fly and eventually died – or those that mentioned a mommy, and came up with . . . *nada. Shit*.

But Janie solved the problem herself, filling the silence with a gritty, muttered, angry version of 'Let It Go'. *Thank you, Disney*, Taylor thought.

She heard the gate open and close, the footsteps behind her too heavy to belong to Jazzie, who was too afraid of the horses to approach them anyway. It was Maggie VanDorn, then. The manager of the program was an efficient older woman with a big heart and years of experience in social work. Maggie pressed a cold bottle of water into Taylor's hand.

'Good thinking, getting her to sing,' Maggie murmured.

Taylor's lips curved at the praise. She'd learned that Maggie never said anything she didn't mean. 'She's still not enjoying herself, but she's breathing.'

'Joy takes time.' Maggie sighed. 'Lots of time. And speaking of time, Janie's session is over and you need to take a break. You've done four sessions back-to-back and it's time to get out of the sun for a while.'

'I'm fine,' Taylor said dryly. 'I'm from California, remember? I grew up in the sun.'

'Be that as it may, take a break,' Maggie insisted. 'I don't want to have to replace you because you got heat stroke. Your face is redder than my heirloom tomatoes.'

Taylor put up her hands in surrender. 'Okay, okay.' She drank most of the bottle of water, then splashed the rest in her face. It *was* hot here, she had to admit, a lot hotter than back home in Northern California, where the temps rarely climbed above eighty year-round and the humidity was non-existent. This suburb of Baltimore had been eighty degrees by breakfast and the high was supposed to be ninety-nine. The air was so muggy, she was beginning to wish she had gills.

'Let me get Janie down and cleaned up,' Taylor said. 'Then I'll take her and Jazzie back to their aunt.' The aunt whose eyes were a constant mix of grief and fear and fury.

Lilah Cornell had lost her sister and gained responsibility for her two nieces all in the same day. A former prosecutor who'd worked with Daphne, she was now on the fast track in the attorney general's office, which meant she worked long hours, nearly seven days a week.

All that had abruptly changed when her sister was murdered,

but no one on the farm had heard her complain. Lilah did have help at least. The girls' father was no longer in the picture, but his mother, their grandmother, had been living with Janie and Jazzie at the time of the murder. Grandma Eunice had watched the girls while her daughter-in-law was at work. After the murder, she'd moved with them to Aunt Lilah's posh but very small apartment, which had been a major adjustment for all of them. Maggie had mentioned that Lilah was looking for a bigger place, which only added to the little family's general stress.

But both Lilah and Eunice seemed to be good women who loved the girls. Lilah accompanied them for their Saturday therapy sessions, while Grandma Eunice brought them during the week.

Taylor pointed at the farmhouse, to the large window that provided a view of the training ring – complete with audio courtesy of discreetly placed microphones. 'Lilah's waiting in the lounge.'

Daphne and Maggie had converted the dining room of the farmhouse to a sitting area where parents and guardians could monitor their kids. Healing Hearts was all about transparency. The program prided itself on making the children and the adults feel safe.

Maggie's nod was briskly approving. 'I'll take care of Ginger. She's done for the day. We'll use Gracie for lessons this afternoon.'

'Yes, ma'am.' Taylor approached Ginger and Janie, smiling when she heard the little girl still singing softly. Janie had released her iron hold on the reins and was stroking Ginger's neck.

No smile bent Janie's lips, but the little stress lines around her mouth had disappeared. No child should have stress lines. But kids like Janie did. *So did I. I still do.*

Taylor cleared her throat. 'Ginger likes you.'

A solemn nod. No words of reply, just a look of bruised exhaustion in Janie's eyes, like she was so tired of being scared but had resigned herself to it. Taylor recognized that look too. She'd seen it in the mirror often enough.

'Time to dismount and get a cold drink, okay?' Taylor held her hands out, ready to catch the child if she fell, but Janie executed a flawless dismount, then stood motionless for a few hard heartbeats, staring up at Ginger. Then she stunned Taylor by throwing her arms around the horse's neck and leaning up to Ginger's ear.

'I like you too,' Janie whispered.

Taylor quickly looked over her shoulder to Maggie, whose eyes held a satisfaction that was tender and fierce all at once, underscoring that Janie had made a breakthrough. *And I got to be here for it*, Taylor thought, her eyes stinging.

Taylor didn't delude herself into thinking that she'd made the breakthrough with Janie. Maggie VanDorn had done all the work, really. But it didn't stop her from feeling a little of Maggie's satisfaction. This could get addictive. *Except that I'm not going to stay.*

She hadn't come to Maryland intending to actually work the full internship or even to stay more than a few days, but the Healing Hearts clientele had sucked her in more quickly and completely than she'd anticipated. It was going to be hard to walk away once she'd gotten what she'd come for.

Baltimore, Maryland,
Saturday 22 August, 1.05 P.M.

Gage Jarvis snugged the tie against the collar of his crisp new shirt, nearly sighing at the feel of quality linen against his skin, of the silk tie between his fingers, all slippery smooth.

How long had it been since he'd worn a tie? Hell, since he'd worn a dress shirt?

His hands faltered on the Windsor knot. He knew exactly how long. Two years, nine months and fourteen days. The day he was fired from his job at Stegner, Hall, and Kramer. Of course they'd told everyone he'd resigned to 'pursue other interests', but he'd been fired, for doing the same damn thing every other lawyer in the firm did. Pretentious, sanctimonious, holier-than-thou assholes. *Judging me. Me.* He'd been the top junior partner, had brought in more business than all the others. Almost put together. Which the partners had lauded, until Valerie made her little phone call to the cops. *Domestic violence.* The fucking bitch.

Hell, he hadn't even hurt her that bad that time, either. And he wasn't sorry. She'd had it coming, like she always did. He could have hurt her a lot worse.

He could have done what he had done a month ago. Beaten her until she didn't get up. Ever again. *Shoulda killed her two years, nine months, and fourteen days ago. Would have saved everyone a whole lot of trouble.*

She'd recanted back then. Withdrawn her complaint. But it was too little, too late. The partners had ordered his office searched, had found his stash in his desk drawer. Hidden, of course, but they'd found it easily enough because they hid their stashes in exactly the same place in their desk drawers.

So he'd done a little coke. So what? So had everyone else. They needed it just to wake up, because the hours were grueling, the competition fierce. Too many partner wannabes and too few positions. Fucking asshole senior partners had to retire or die before any of the slave-labor junior partners were given the proverbial key to the executive washroom. Because Stegner, Hall, and Kramer still had those keys, and Gage had wanted one.

And he would have gotten it, if it hadn't been for Valerie's malicious lies. And her sister's, too. *Can't forget about Lilah.* No, he never would. Valerie would never have made that call to the police on her own. Lilah had made it for her.

Ruined my stupid fucking life. One of these days he'd see his sister-in-law humiliated and cast out, just like she'd had him ruined. But at least Valerie had been taken care of. That would have to be good enough. For now.

Because I'm back. Back in his city, ready to reclaim the life he'd had. *No, not the life I had. A much better one.*

Because he had a new job. A better one than he'd had at the old firm. Soon he'd have an expense account again and could wine and dine and . . .

He realized he was scowling into the dressing room's full-length mirror and abruptly smiled at himself. *That's better*, he thought, massively grateful that he'd never done meth like the Romano kid had. Gage might have a few track marks and a bit of a sniffle, but his teeth were still nice.

15

He regarded his reflection with a satisfied nod. The suit, while not quite up to his old standards, was a giant leap above what he'd been wearing for the last few years. It was a decent fit – not great, but not as bad as it would have been a month ago – and the white shirt made his tanned skin look even darker. The tan he'd come by honestly, courtesy of the two and a half years he'd spent combing the beaches of Florida. It had helped him look . . . not so dead. He'd been gaunt there at the end. He was still too thin, but at least he didn't look like a walking corpse anymore.

Laying low for the last month had been a pain in the ass, but he'd used the time to start getting his body back into shape, and it had paid off. He looked stronger, and almost healthy. Younger. Dyeing his hair and growing a beard had been a practical necessity at first. After Valerie . . . well, he hadn't wanted anyone to know he was in town.

Now, he really liked the beard. He gave his jaw a stroke with his thumb. Just enough stubble to make him look like a pirate. Sexy as shit and just a little bit wicked.

His hands stilled once again, then fell to his sides briefly before buttoning one of the buttons on the suit because he was twitchy.

And wicked. Yes, he was. He wasn't proud of some of the things he'd had to do since his life skidded off the tracks. But he was back now. He gave the suit coat a little tug and brushed a speck of lint from his lapel. This morning had been the end of it. The very last thing he'd had to do.

This morning he'd snipped off the loose ends, putting Valerie and her damned – *still open* – murder case to rest. He hadn't wanted to do it that way, but Baltimore PD had left him no choice. It had been a month since Valerie got what was coming to her, and he'd all but hand-delivered a suspect into BPD's hands within days of the murder, but the lazy bastards hadn't moved yet. Hadn't arrested the guy.

What the hell had they been waiting for? A fucking engraved invitation?

Clearly they'd had doubts. But BPD's doubts were no longer his problem. He'd waited as long as he could – he'd given them a month, for Christ's sake – but he had to report to his new job on Monday, and he was not restarting his career with a murder charge hanging over his head. So he'd helped the process along. Wrapped it all in a tidy bow and left it for them to find.

He stared at the mirror, his jaw hard and unyielding. All right. It hadn't been all that tidy, he admitted to himself. There had been unintended collateral damage. But there'd been no witnesses and he'd had his face covered, just in case. He'd listened to the police radio and there were no BOLOs. So no one had seen what he'd done today.

He had no regrets. It had been necessary. As soon as he'd turned up in the city, he'd have been swarmed by fucking cops. Now the slate was clean. He could 'arrive', stop by to see his mother, and when she asked where he'd been for the last month, he had the perfect story all ready.

Rehab. Naturally. Thanks to his brother, he even had a location and people to vouch for him. He'd been in rehab in Texas.

She'd believe it, of course. She was always ready to believe the best of him.

She was a fool. But then, most people were.

Luckily, I am not.

Which meant that he had to see Valerie's daughters and make the appropriate noises of grief now that he was back in town. He huffed, irritated. It would be expected. It would be weird if he did not. So he'd bite the bullet and see the bitch's spawn.

He'd even take care of them. Financially. Once he was flush again, which would be a good long while. Until then, Aunt Lilah could foot the bill. She had custody, after all.

A sharp rapping on the changing room door had him sucking in a startled breath.

'Sir?' It was the sales clerk, a dapper man with silver in his hair. Gage had picked him because he'd never seen the man before. He didn't want anyone to know he'd been here. He didn't want to have to tie up any more loose ends.

He let the breath out carefully. 'Yes?' he asked, his voice level.

'I was just checking to see if you needed anything else.'

'No.' Gage shrugged out of the coat and slipped the tie from his neck. 'I'll take it all,' he said, trying to decide if he'd wear the suit out of the store, or if he should change back into the clothes he'd been wearing – a polo shirt and chinos, perfectly clean and almost new, bought at a local thrift store. It had irked him at the time, buying used clothing, but it was better than what he'd packed in his duffel when he left Miami. He hadn't owned anything that wasn't either threadbare or covered in not-safe-for-work graphics, castoffs from the T-shirt shop on the boardwalk where he'd done odd jobs for under-the-table cash.

'Excellent,' the clerk said happily. 'And how will you be paying today?'

Gage eyed the chinos and his mouth curled into a smile. His pants pocket was full of twenties, converted from the wad of smaller bills he'd appropriated that morning while presenting BPD with a suspect they could no longer ignore.

There had been unfortunate collateral damage, true, but there'd also been a very fortunate monetary reward.

'Cash,' he said.

I'm back. I'll have it all. And I'll never let anyone take it away from me, not ever again.

Hunt Valley, Maryland,
Saturday 22 August, 1.10 P.M.

Taylor accompanied a silent Janie into the barn so that she could put away her riding helmet and wash her hands and face. Jazzie was waiting outside and took Janie's hand firmly, leading her to the main house. Neither girl said a word.

Until they walked inside. Taylor took a moment to let the A/C wash over her, trying not to groan about how good it felt to get out of the heat.

'Miss T-Taylor?' The words had come from Jazzie's mouth, tentatively uttered. It was the first time Taylor had heard Jazzie's voice.

Trying to hide her shock and maintain her cool, Taylor hunched

18

down a little so that she could look Jazzie in the eye. At five-nine she tended to tower over the children. 'Yes, Jazzie?'

Jazzie's eyes were stark, her swallow audible. She glanced at her sister, then back at Taylor. 'Th-th-*thank* you,' she whispered.

Moved, Taylor had to remind herself to exhale. Her lungs had momentarily frozen.

'You're welcome,' she whispered back. Then she followed her gut and put her arms around Jazzie's thin shoulders. 'I lost my mom too, not so long ago, and it *hurt*. It hurt so much.'

Which was the gospel truth, because even though Donna Dawson had lied to her for her entire life, Taylor had loved her. 'I miss her every day. I miss her voice and her smell and the way she'd smile, and especially the way she told me she loved me. Sometimes I miss her so much that it feels like a giant's sitting on my chest, squashing all the breath out of me. Like I'll never breathe right again.' She considered her next words and again went with her gut, saying what she wished someone had said to her. 'And sometimes I kind of wish the giant would squash harder because then I could see my mom again.'

A sudden stiffening of Jazzie's shoulders told Taylor that she'd hit a nerve. A heartbeat passed, then two, then Jazzie's arms were around Taylor's back, squeezing tight. She buried her face in Taylor's shoulder, her little body shaking with sobs that cracked Taylor's heart in two.

Taylor went down on one knee for balance and rocked the child, stroking her hair. 'Go ahead. Cry all you want to. It's totally okay.'

After a few minutes Jazzie's sobs quieted but she didn't pull away. Taylor kept on stroking her hair, remembering how much she herself had needed a gentle touch after her mother died. How grateful she'd been when her dad had put his own grief to the side to comfort her.

'I know you hurt,' she murmured in Jazzie's ear. 'I know Janie hurts. It's okay to hurt. Do you hear me?' She waited until Jazzie nodded. 'Good, because that's important. It's okay to hurt. But I'm still really glad that Janie finally had some fun today. It means the giant sitting on her chest got off for a minute and let her breathe. Maybe you got to breathe a little too, watching her. But later, if the giant comes back, don't you worry. It doesn't mean either of you did anything wrong. It doesn't mean that today didn't count, that it wasn't important. The giant will come and go, but eventually he'll stay away a little longer before coming back. And then you'll be able to breathe again. And then it won't hurt so bad.'

Jazzie nodded again before pulling away. She took a step back, her eyes down, clearly embarrassed by her outburst. Taylor gently nudged her little chin up so that Jazzie met her eyes.

'I cried a *lot* when my mom died.' Taylor swiped her thumbs gently over Jazzie's cheeks. 'And I was twenty-two.' *And my mother wasn't brutally beaten to death. I had a chance to say goodbye.* Jazzie and Janie hadn't gotten that chance. 'So don't you be embarrassed about crying, okay?'

Jazzie nodded, sniffling, her dark eyes rimmed with red. Taylor pulled one of her business cards from her pocket. 'It's a little bent up, but it's got my number and my email on it. You can text me if you or Janie need anything, okay?'

Jazzie put the card in her pocket, then turned and walked to where Janie and their aunt waited. Lilah pressed her palm to her heart, her face as wet as Jazzie's had been. 'Thank you,' she said, giving Taylor a shaky smile before taking her nieces by the hand and leading them out.

Alone in the quiet, Taylor slowly straightened, her heart in her throat. *I helped. A little.* It felt way too good. *So even if my whole convoluted plan goes to hell in a handbasket, I'll have this moment.*

A footstep behind her shattered the moment. She had a split second to detect the sensation of body heat at her back before twelve years of personal defense training kicked in, her father's voice taking over her conscious thought.

One to the solar plexus. She drove back with her elbow, coming into contact with something solid. Hearing a grunt, she whirled, fists clenched, her eyes registering the tall man as her right fist took an upward swing. *Two to the jaw.*

Ignoring the pain exploding in her knuckles when they encountered the granite of the man's jaw, she followed through as she'd been taught. *Three to the chest.* She pushed forward, palms flat, striking a hard set of pecs.

A vicious curse uttered in a deep, unfamiliar voice filled her ears as pain burned up her arm to her shoulder. *Four, run like hell.*

A scream frozen in her throat, she started to turn, *to flee,* but was stopped short by the solid thump that vibrated the floor under her feet. The man had landed squarely on his ass, his palms held out in a gesture of surrender even as he blinked up at her in stunned disbelief.

The fear retreated slowly as she stood there, not taking her eyes off him, the adrenaline steadily leaking out of her like air from a tire puncture. Her conscious brain began to kick back in, coolly logical. *You're safe. You're here. At the farm. You're at the farm.*

A new, different kind of panic swept over her. *Oh my God. What did I just . . . ? Who did I just . . . ?* A whimper rose in her throat, fortunately blocked by the scream that was still stuck there, so all that came out was the sound of her own heavy breathing.

The man lumbered to his feet, rubbing his jaw and watching her like one would watch an injured animal. Taylor supposed that was fair enough.

He was tall, taller than her by a good six inches. His shoulders were broad, his blond hair cut short. He appeared to be about her age, but his eyes looked far older. He had the face of a model, all chiseled and handsome and . . .

And she'd hit him. *Oh my God.* She realized that her mouth was hanging open, and she snapped it shut. This time the scream let the whimper slide past and she covered her mouth to stifle the sound.

'Whoa, there,' he said quietly. 'I didn't mean to startle you. I'm very sorry.'

Wait. Taylor frowned. Had he really told her to 'whoa'? Horror morphed into irritation. *Really?* It wasn't just the word that was so irritating. It was the deep voice he'd used to deliver it. It was the voice she herself used to quiet skittish horses.

I'm not a horse, buddy, she wanted to snap. But he had apologized and she had come to this farm for a reason and meeting the locals

21

was part of the plan. *So don't screw this up.* She lowered her hands to her sides, shaking out her still-throbbing fingers.

She looked up with an attempt at a smile and found herself staring into eyes that were the prettiest shade of blue she'd ever seen. Just like—

Holy shit. She was back to horrified as she realized exactly who she was staring at. His pretty blue eyes were the same color as those of her employer. This was Daphne Montgomery-Carter's son, Ford Elkhart.

I hit the boss's son. I am so fired. But cutting into the horror was the knowledge that Ford had just returned from the week-long camping trip that had served as a bachelor party for Dillon, one of the farm's stable hands. It was what she'd been waiting for.

The travelers had returned. *All of them.* Her gut did a queasy flip. *It's showtime.*

Two

*A*re *you all right?* The flash of anger in the dark eyes that stared up at Ford had the words freezing in his throat. Then the eyes flickered in recognition, after which they and the pretty face that went with them went carefully blank, devoid of any expression at all.

Stop standing here looking like an idiot, he snapped to himself. *Say something*. He gave himself a little shake, and glanced down at her hands to make sure she hadn't resurrected the clenched fists. She had a mean right hook. 'You must be Taylor Dawson. The new therapist.'

Her nod was as wary as he felt. 'Until Maggie fires me.' Her sigh was nearly soundless. 'I am so sorry. Did . . . did I hurt you?'

He could feel his cheeks turning five shades of red. 'Only my pride that you actually just asked me that.' He smiled, relieved when her lips twitched. 'Nobody's firing anyone. That was my fault. I know better than to walk up behind someone. Especially here, where we have so many people who have been on the receiving end of violence.'

'You did startle me,' she admitted quietly. 'Still . . . I need to 'fess up to Maggie.'

'Not if we do a do-over.' Ford stuck out his hand. 'Hi, Taylor. I'm Ford Elkhart. You must be the new therapist.' He released the breath he was holding when she shook his hand firmly before dropping hers to her side again. 'It's nice to meet you.'

Her grip had been strong, but her skin was soft. And Ford was

23

stunned that he'd noticed. It had been a very long time since a female had left him this nervous. That the last time had ended so epically badly wasn't something he was going to think about right now.

Taylor smiled, little more than a curve of her lips, but it was genuine. 'I'm not a therapist yet. Just an intern. I'm not licensed yet.'

Which he'd known, of course. Getting knocked on his ass had flustered him. That, and the way her eyes lit up when she smiled. 'I know. My mother told me that you're between undergrad and graduate school. Daphne is my mom.'

Her smile grew into a grin, a teasing sparkle lighting her dark eyes. 'I know. Your mother talks about you. A lot.'

Ford felt his cheeks heat again. 'Hell.'

A chuckle soothed his irritation. 'She's proud of you and she doesn't care who knows it.' The smile dimmed, the sparkle giving way to a flash of sadness. 'Be glad she's here.'

Ford frowned. Found himself hesitating over his next words before freeing them from his mouth. 'Your mom isn't. I heard you talking to Jazzie.'

'We lost her a year and a half ago.' She grimaced. 'Cancer.'

'I'm sorry,' he murmured. 'My mom had cancer too. It was scary, but we were lucky.'

'We weren't,' Taylor said flatly before drawing a breath. 'I need to be going. I'm on my break. Maggie will be annoyed if I'm late getting back.'

'I don't think she'll mind too much,' Ford said quietly, stepping aside to let Taylor pass. 'She looked thrilled with Janie's progress today. Janie's been coming here for a month and today was the most relaxed any of us have seen her. So I think Maggie will think you've earned your break.'

Taylor's dark eyes narrowed. 'You were watching me?'

He felt his cheeks grow even warmer. 'Yes, for the last part anyway. My mother said you were out there with Janie, and I have to admit to being . . . curious.'

He'd come to the lounge to observe Janie's session but had found himself staring at the tall young woman with the dark braid spilling down from the back of an Oakland Raiders cap. She was graceful and energetic all at once. He hadn't been able to take his eyes off her. And when Janie had hugged Ginger . . .

Well, Janie's aunt Lilah hadn't been the only one wiping away tears. Normally he would have left the room before Janie and Jazzie returned, because he hated the thought of distressing them, but he'd stayed – and he was so glad he had. Janie wasn't the only sister who'd taken a leap that day. Jazzie's leap was . . . giant. Standing in the shadows, he'd seen the raw trust in her eyes and the emotion on Taylor's face.

Taylor studied him. 'Curious about what?'

'About the intern who has Maggie and my mom so pleased.' He shoved his hand in his pocket to keep from rubbing the back of his sweating neck. 'Anyway, good job. I've volunteered here from the beginning. The Jarvis sisters have been two of the tougher nuts to crack.'

'They miss their mother,' Taylor murmured, the corners of her mouth drooping sadly. 'I can't even imagine what those little girls went through, finding her body.'

'And knowing her killer's still out there,' he said grimly. There had been an investigation, but no arrests so far.

'Yes, I read that in the file.'

'Janie doesn't seem to worry about it, but Jazzie's old enough to know.'

Taylor closed her eyes, her sigh weary. 'To know. To be afraid. To always wonder if he's lurking, waiting to jump out from behind a tree to drag them away.'

There was something in her tone, something that hinted at a first-hand knowledge of that fear, and her reaction to his presence suddenly made a lot of sense. He was about to ask her, but she opened her eyes abruptly and the look he saw there had him veering away from the question.

Hunted, he thought. She looked hunted.

'I can't even imagine that kind of fear,' she said quietly before he could say another word, and he knew she was lying. She didn't have to imagine. She *knew* that fear. But for now he didn't challenge her, because she seemed to need the lie.

'But you do know how it feels to miss your mom,' he said.

'Yes, so I've been channeling that. So far, so good.' She tilted her head, the sunlight picking up the red highlights in her hair. 'Why did you hide in the shadows?'

'I wasn't hiding. I was keeping myself out of Jazzie's way.' Ford sighed. 'She gets scared around men.'

Taylor sucked in a sharp breath. 'Was she assaulted?'

Ford shrugged. 'She won't say one way or the other and it's not in her official file. But the men around here have learned to give her space. She's a lot stronger than she looks. And she's got a great right hook,' he added ruefully. 'Just like yours.'

Taylor blinked in stunned surprise. 'She hit you too?'

'Not me. My brother, Cole. He startled her in the barn when she was watching over Janie. Jazzie's only eleven, but she's a mother hen. She never leaves Janie's side.'

'I noticed. What happened with your brother?'

'It was the girls' first time coming here and both of them were a bundle of nerves. Janie was crying and Jazzie was trying to comfort her. Cole was just trying to help, but he crowded her – unintentionally – and she swung at him. Knocked him back a step or two. I'm not sure who was more shocked – Cole, Janie, or Jazzie herself. I don't think she meant to hit him, let alone wallop him like that. I don't think she believed she could.'

'Well, that part I get.' Taylor rolled her eyes. 'I didn't expect to hit you either. I only met Cole once, before you all went on your camping trip, but I remember him being about your size. How did Jazzie even reach his jaw?'

'He'd leaned down to talk to her, thinking he was doing the right thing. He didn't think about why she'd gotten so scared so fast. Cole's big, but he's still a kid. He's only fifteen.'

Again her eyes widened. 'Fifteen? He looks twenty.'

'I know. Poor kid. It used to get him into trouble at school. Teachers expected more from him and kids poked fun at him because he looked like he'd failed a few grades. Now he's in a better school and nobody bothers him. I think he'd forgotten that he can be so intimidating.'

26

'I don't expect he'll be forgetting it again any time soon,' Taylor said dryly.

Ford found himself grinning. 'I don't expect that he will. And neither will his brother.'

She rolled her eyes, embarrassed. 'God. I still can't believe I did that.' Then a frown wrinkled her brow. 'Why didn't Maggie tell me about Jazzie's fear of men?'

Ford fought back a frown of his own. If Maggie hadn't said anything, it meant that she didn't fully trust her intern. Which made him want to kick himself for spilling it. He'd have to tell Maggie that he'd let the cat out of the bag. He didn't relish that conversation.

Then again, if Maggie didn't trust her intern, she hadn't told his mother about it. If Maggie had, Daphne wouldn't have been so effusive in her praise.

'Maggie's a lioness about protecting the kids' privacy,' he said. 'If it wasn't in the official file from Children's Services and if Jazzie hasn't actually said anything, then Maggie would keep that to herself until she found the right time.'

'That sounds like Maggie,' Taylor agreed. 'Thank you for telling me. I've been focused on getting Janie comfortable in the saddle, mainly because Jazzie hasn't wanted to participate and I haven't wanted to push her, but I'll nudge her a little harder on Monday. She needs this as much as Janie.'

'Um . . .' He hesitated, not wanting to shove his other foot into his mouth. Hoping he wasn't about to surprise her yet again. 'Not on Monday. The program's closed.'

She looked at him blankly for a second before she remembered. 'Oh, right. For Dillon's wedding. Dillon asked me to come,' she added uncertainly.

Ford ground his teeth, abruptly annoyed with her. She looked like she didn't want to go, or was at least uncomfortable that Dillon had asked. 'But?' The word came out of his mouth too fast, too hard, and too short, but he couldn't help it, dammit. 'He makes you uncomfortable?' *If anyone's mean to Dillon, they'll answer to me.* That went double for Dillon's fiancée, Holly. Nobody messed with Holly.

Both approaching thirty, Holly and Dillon had Down syndrome. They'd fought hard for their independence and Ford would be damned before he allowed anyone to hurt them, especially on their wedding day. That included the farm's newest intern, regardless of her dark eyes and pretty face.

Taylor's eyes registered startled understanding before narrowing. 'You think it's because he has Down syndrome, don't you?' Her jaw went hard and tight. 'Don't even *bother* denying it.' She turned on her heel, leaving him with his mouth open as she made her exit.

It took Ford a second to process her words. Another second to process that she was walking away. And a third to realize that he didn't want her to go. *Not like this.*

'Taylor. *Wait.*' He caught up to her before she got to the lounge door. He slapped his palm to the door, keeping her from opening it. 'I did think that, and I'm sorry.'

She froze, her hand gripping the doorknob so tightly that her knuckles turned white.

Ford swallowed. He'd scared her again, the last thing he'd wanted to do. Clearly remembering that right hook of hers, he pulled his palm away from the door, making himself as small and non-threatening as he could.

'I'm sorry,' he repeated quietly. 'I've seen too many people hurt Holly and Dillon, and I just reacted. Holly's older brother, Joseph, is my mom's husband, so technically Holly's my step-aunt, but she's more like a sister to me. I'm more than a little protective. We all are.'

Taylor's shoulders sagged, but she didn't give up her hold on the doorknob. She didn't yank the door open and bolt either, though, and that was encouraging.

'My youngest sister, Julie, has cerebral palsy,' she said, keeping her gaze squarely on the door in front of her. 'She's twenty, but she has the learning capacity of a fourth grader. We love her. Just the way she is.'

Ford felt even worse now. 'We love Dillon and Holly the same way. I shouldn't have judged you. I hope you accept Dillon's invitation and come to the wedding.' He forced his lips to curve.

'Holly works for her sister's bakery. The cake is going to be amazing.'

Taylor slowly released the doorknob, wiped her palm on her jeans, then gripped the knob again, much less forcefully. When she finally looked up, her expression was politely distant. 'Just so we're clear, I hesitated because I didn't want to be a wedding crasher. I met Dillon a few days before you all left for your camping trip. I haven't met Holly yet. I didn't want to be in the way. But if my staying away will hurt Dillon, I will be there with bells on. Now, if you'll excuse me, I have to get back to work.'

The door closed behind her and Ford let out the breath he'd been holding. 'Shit,' he muttered. 'Way to go, Elkhart.' If Taylor quit, his mother would be upset, and Ford would walk over hot coals to avoid that. But even more importantly . . .

If Taylor quits, I would be upset, he admitted in the quiet of his mind. But there was no way he'd let anyone else know the new intern had grabbed his attention so completely.

Because she'd be going home at the end of her internship. California, his mother had said. Clear across the damn country. Nothing could come of any relationship, even if she was interested. Which, thanks to his own bumbling mouth, she wouldn't be. There was no use in even considering it. Or her.

But he *was* interested, though he was going to keep his interest to himself, because everyone would make a big deal of it due to the fact that he hadn't had a date in almost two years. Not since . . .

His brain stumbled. *Say it, you coward. Say it out loud.* Since . . .

'Kimberly.' He spat the name into the silence, cursing his ex once again. For hurting him. Betraying him. Setting him up to be kidnapped, for God's sake. But mostly for making him afraid to get close to anyone new.

Ford closed his eyes. He was afraid. Not of the physical pain. He'd handled that. It was the humiliation that had followed his rescue. The pity. He hated the pity. It was better now, but there were still whispers.

Poor Ford. Such a nice young man. Shame he had to go through all that. Wish he'd find himself a nice girl. Poor Ford.

If he dated an intern only to have her walk away at the end of her term, the whispers would become actual words once more. *Poor Ford. He got his heart broken again. He has such bad luck with the ladies.*

And that was *so* not happening again. So as pretty as the new intern was, she was off limits. That was all there was to it.

Baltimore, Maryland,
Saturday 22 August, 3.05 P.M.

Detective JD Fitzpatrick pushed through the doors to the autopsy suite, swallowing back the snarl that had twisted his face the moment he'd received the call to come to the morgue. *One job.* He'd asked Hector to cover one fucking job while he was gone. All he'd had to do was to tail Toby Romano.

And keep him alive, he added acidly in his own mind. Hector hadn't covered that one job very well. Which was why JD had detoured to the morgue instead of going straight home to his wife and kids. Lucy, Jeremiah and Bronwynne would have to wait. Once again.

Because Toby Romano was laid out on a stainless-steel autopsy table, his skin cold and gray. He wasn't even twenty years old.

JD avoided looking at the three men standing around the table, using the moments it took to suit up to silently grieve a young man who should not be dead. Who'd never really had a chance to live. The kid had been on a bad path from the moment he'd drawn his first breath, still connected to his drug-addicted mother. *Could have been me. So damn easily.* But JD had had an aunt who'd taken him in. Toby hadn't been so lucky. Now he never would be.

JD donned the paper cover-up and mask, wishing he hadn't left town in the middle of this case, then forced himself to remember that he was more than the job. That he had a family and friends – which had meant keeping his promise to attend at least part of the camping trip that had served as Dillon's bachelor party. Friends kept their promises.

JD closed his eyes as he pulled on a pair of gloves. He'd promised Toby Romano safety. Not to the man's face, because Toby hadn't

30

even known he was in danger. But he had promised himself the young man would stay safe.

Goddammit, Hector. I asked you to do one fucking thing. One mother-fucking thing.

Once again JD swallowed back the snarl, reminding himself that Hector was a fine cop – an experienced detective – and had never shirked his duties in the year they'd worked together. The man cared, and he'd supported JD a hundred percent since the case started. Whatever had happened, JD had to believe Hector would have a good explanation.

He turned to the three men standing silently next to Romano's body. Neil Quartermaine, the medical examiner, appeared weary. JD's boss, Special Agent Joseph Carter, normally unreadable, flicked a strained warning glance toward Hector. Because Detective Hector Rivera looked absolutely devastated.

JD approached the group warily. There was no reason for Hector to look so wrecked. Yes, this sent them back to the drawing board in their search for Valerie Jarvis's killer, and yes, Romano was dead, but Toby had been JD's confidential informant. Hector hadn't even met him before this case began.

Something else had gone down. Something big.

'What happened?' JD asked, his gut wrenching when Hector's eyes slid closed. It couldn't be the little girls. Joseph would have told him that up front. Still, his eyes darted from gurney to gurney, looking for a sheet-covered body that was . . . child-sized. But there were none. 'The Jarvis girls?'

'No,' Joseph assured him. 'Jazzie and Janie are fine. They're at the farm today, in fact.'

JD held himself rigid, even though he was sagging with relief on the inside. 'Then why the hell is Hector looking like he lost his best friend?' Hector flinched. 'I'm sorry, man,' JD added more gently. 'Tell me what happened.'

'Romano lost his tail last night,' Hector said quietly. 'Went into a bodega and out the back door. The officer called it in as soon as he realized. We searched for Romano, but the guy was in the wind. We put out a BOLO, but got nothin'. I finally told Officer

31

Mancuso to go to the alley where Romano'd been sleeping and just wait for him. We figured he'd come back when he got tired. It was his habit.'

'Yeah, it was his habit,' JD said evenly, making an effort to keep the bitterness out of his voice because Hector looked so damned tortured, but . . . *Goddammit*. Toby Romano had been an important link – JD's only link – to the murderer of a mother of two. The mother whose beaten body had been found by her daughter. Now Toby was dead and JD was out of leads. *And running out of time*. 'Did Toby come back to his alley?'

Hector shrugged. 'Not under his own power and not until dawn.' He pointed to another body on a gurney, a male about twenty years older than Toby. 'It looks like that guy dumped him in the alley. Romano had OD'd. The second guy may have been going through Romano's pockets – they were all turned out. As best we can tell, Officer Mancuso confronted the second guy, but was not prepared for him to have a knife.'

It was JD's turn to flinch. 'Oh no,' he murmured.

'Yes,' Hector said, his voice now harsh. 'Officer Mancuso got off two shots. Both hit John Doe over there, but Mancuso was bleeding already. John Doe took Mancuso's service weapon, shot him in the head with it, and ran. Doe collapsed a block away, bled out.'

'And Officer Mancuso?' JD asked carefully.

Joseph Carter shook his head. 'He didn't make it,' he said gruffly. 'He had no brain activity when the EMTs brought him in, but they tried to bring him back. Hector was sitting with the officer's wife in the surgery waiting room all morning. They got the news about fifteen minutes ago.'

'You knew him well?' JD asked Hector as gently as he could.

Hector's nod was curt. 'Yeah. I was his trainer. He was a damned good cop.'

JD's shoulders sagged. *Fuck it all*. 'I'm sorry, Hector.'

Another curt nod. 'So am I. I'm sorry Darren Mancuso is dead and I'm sorry your guy OD'd on my watch.'

'Toby was a junkie,' JD said sadly. 'Started using when he was still a kid. I knew him when I was in Vice. He was a meth-head. It

32

was a matter of time. But he was my link to Valerie Jarvis's killer. I'm back to square one.'

'Maybe he really *was* Valerie Jarvis's killer,' Joseph said in that damned unreadable tone of his. The one that made it unclear if he really believed what he was saying, or if he was playing devil's advocate.

JD frowned. They'd had this conversation too many times already. 'He couldn't have been, Joseph. He was on the other side of town the day Valerie Jarvis was murdered.' Beaten to death in her own living room, her face unrecognizable.

'His alibi didn't cover all of the time-of-death window Quartermaine gave us.' Joseph's voice was so mild that it grated.

JD glared at him. 'You know part of that window is accounted for.'

'Not if you can't get her to talk,' Joseph snapped.

Neil Quartermaine spoke up. 'What are you talking about? How is part of the Jarvis woman's time-of-death window accounted for?'

JD drew a breath, let it out. 'We're keeping that quiet. Need-to-know only.'

Quartermaine gave him a sour look. 'You have *got* to be shitting me. You guys have never shut me out before. Why now?'

Because the life of an eleven-year-old girl depends on it. But JD kept that to himself, just as he'd done for the last month.

'Your case just changed, JD,' Hector murmured. 'We have a dead cop. There'll be an investigation. IA will get involved. I don't think you can keep the kid's secrets any longer.'

JD wanted to tell Hector he was wrong, but he knew better. Hector had been one of the few he'd trusted with all the details of this case. Only Hector, Joseph and Brodie, their crime-scene investigator, knew everything. Everyone else got only what information they agreed to release. That included cops. And MEs.

Joseph glanced at the wall of drawers that held victims' remains. 'Officer Mancuso will be put in one of those drawers once his wife says goodbye. We need to make a change here, JD. Our plan isn't working.'

No, it wasn't. *Dammit.* JD looked around. 'Who's here, Neil?'

'At the moment, right here? Just us,' Quartermaine said, his irritation clear. 'Three other pathologists are working today, but they've gone out to lunch. What's this about?'

'Valerie Jarvis was beaten to death four weeks ago,' JD began.

'I know,' Quartermaine snapped impatiently. 'I did her autopsy.' He looked away, his jaw clenching. 'I'm sorry. It was a difficult one. Her face . . . was just gone.'

'I know,' JD said quietly. 'It was my crime scene. Some things you just can't unsee. And when I think about her kids seeing her that way . . .'

'That's all I could think about after finishing her exam,' Quartermaine said with a sigh. 'I'm sorry. Continue, please.'

JD was actually reassured by Quartermaine's outburst. The man was a damned good ME, meticulous and sharp-eyed. Almost as good as Lucy had been when she'd had Quartermaine's job, before Jeremiah was born. That a brutal homicide had affected him demonstrated that he retained his connection, his commitment to the dead. His humanity.

'Nothing to be sorry for. It appeared to be a robbery gone wrong. The house had been thoroughly searched. Torn up. Valerie's sister, Lilah Cornell, went searching for her after Valerie didn't pick up her younger daughter from day care. Janie, who is five, was with her aunt when she discovered Valerie's body. According to her aunt, so was Jazzie, the older daughter, who is eleven. All that's in the police report. What isn't in the official report – yet – is that we found drying bloody footprints at the scene, leading from the body to behind a chair in the corner. They matched the size and shape of Jazzie's shoes.'

'Oh hell,' Quartermaine whispered. 'She got home first? She found her mother?'

'We think so,' JD said. 'Her aunt found her hiding behind the chair when she got there a few hours later.'

Quartermaine's throat worked as he swallowed hard. 'I didn't think I could imagine worse than those two girls finding their mother, beaten like that. But imagining the older one alone with that body for hours? Yeah, that's worse. Still, why the secrecy?'

JD grimaced. 'Because we think we have a leak somewhere in the system. If that little girl saw something . . . I can't let it get out. The killer left believing no one had seen him. If he finds out?'

'He'll come back for the child,' Hector said heavily. 'We all saw the mother's body. We know what he's capable of doing.'

Quartermaine gave a short nod. 'Yeah, we know. But why do you believe there's a leak?'

'We put in the preliminary report that there was an estranged husband and we were looking for him,' JD said, 'because a man caught on the Jarvis apartment security video was about the right height. The husband's name is Gage Jarvis and he has a history of domestic abuse. We put a BOLO out on him. Within twenty-four hours, we had an alibi. A sheriff's deputy out in Texas called to say that he'd seen Gage on the day of the murder, but no one had seen him the day after or any time since. We kept the BOLO active, and two days later, one of the items stolen from the Jarvis apartment shows up in a pawnshop. A brooch. Worth about fifty bucks. On the shop's security camera, selling the brooch, is Toby Romano, looking carefree. He told me he'd found it on the ground where he slept. He got ten bucks for it and used it to buy meth.'

'You believed him?' Quartermaine asked carefully, and JD shrugged.

'I believed he didn't kill her. I didn't believe he'd found the brooch on the ground. There was some connection to the killer. I just never found out what it was.'

'If Romano had killed the woman,' Hector said, 'he probably wouldn't have sold the brooch in a pawnshop with a camera. He was smart enough to ditch us, so it's clear he was too smart to incriminate himself like that.' He looked down at the body on the table with a sigh. 'He'd have traded it or taken it to a seedier shop, done a back-alley sale.'

'Exactly,' JD said with a nod. 'We think someone set him up to take the fall. He's about the same height as the man we saw on the camera in the Jarvises' apartment lobby. But Romano was playing basketball with some friends during the last half of the time-of-death window. His pals vouch for him. Of course, they're junkies too.

So . . . alibi by junkies versus a Texas sheriff's deputy. It's clear which one you're going to want to believe.'

Hector grunted. 'The alibi from the deputy is damned convenient.'

JD shrugged again. He'd been around and over it so many times. 'The deputy's got a good rep out there. We'd need evidence to accuse him of lying.'

'Like the little girl telling what she'd seen,' Quartermaine murmured. 'I take it she isn't talking?'

'Would you?' JD asked soberly.

Quartermaine flinched. 'No. I'm amazed the child isn't catatonic.'

'She nearly was,' Joseph said with a sigh of his own. 'We got her into Daphne's equine therapy program, hoping we'd shake something loose. So far, nothing. The child hasn't spoken since finding her mother.'

'And we don't have much else besides flimsy alibis and a hocked brooch,' JD admitted. 'No physical evidence in the apartment itself. Valerie's killer was smart. He poured bleach all over the kitchen, where he washed up and wiped down the surfaces he'd touched. Mostly I've got my gut, which is saying that it doesn't make sense that Toby would beat the woman to death. I've known him for years and he's never been violent.' He sighed. '*Was* never violent,' he corrected himself. 'He had no connection to Valerie Jarvis that I could find. And the beating . . . it was personal. Her killer broke every bone in her face. He broke her fingers, one of her arms, and several ribs. This was a crime of passion. Of rage.'

'And the husband?' Quartermaine asked. 'You said he had a history of domestic abuse. I found evidence of old breaks in Valerie's arms. All that was in my autopsy report.'

'I know. Valerie filed a complaint against him almost three years ago, but withdrew it. He disappeared shortly thereafter, leaving his job. His boss insisted that Gage left for personal reasons. That he'd been given a stellar recommendation and would be welcomed back.'

'But you didn't believe him?' Quartermaine asked, his brows quirking up.

'No. The boss was way too smooth, which didn't surprise me, since he was the senior partner of Stegner, Hall and Kramer.

Ritzy criminal defense firm,' JD added when the ME looked confused.

Hector's jaw tightened. 'They're notorious for representing anyone with enough money to pay, including known drug kingpins. The prosecutors' office suspects they've bought off jurors in the past, but they've never been able to prove it. Gage Jarvis was one of their up-and-comers before he "quit". He had a rep for getting his clients off when it looked like the prosecutors had a slam dunk, and he was one of the firm's most productive junior partners.'

Quartermaine made a sour face. 'And if it got out that he'd been fired, they'd have a shitload of appeals or civil suits because all the other firms would smell blood in the water.'

'Exactly,' JD said grimly. 'Plus Gage Jarvis specialized in defending murder suspects, so he'd know how to frame an innocent man.' He looked down at Toby Romano. 'I don't think Toby killed Valerie Jarvis. I've been watching him for weeks to see if he met with anyone who might have been involved. Or to see if he tried to pawn or trade any other items stolen from the apartment. Or if someone tried to deepen the frame, since I hadn't arrested him yet. I thought Valerie's killer might try to corner him, but I didn't expect him to OD on meth.'

'He didn't,' Quartermaine said, surprising him. 'He OD'd on coke. There was meth in his system, but it was only a fraction of what he'd have needed to OD.'

JD frowned. 'Toby Romano didn't use coke. To my knowledge he never had. It was too pricey for him.'

'Unless he sold some more stolen items,' Joseph said. 'That he just happened to find on the ground beside him.'

Quartermaine checked his notes. 'He had some items on him when he was brought in. A watch and a pair of earrings were sewn into a hidden pocket inside the waistband of his pants. We took an inventory by X-ray and sent it all to Agent Brodie in CSU. She opened the pouch and confirmed the items were on the list of things stolen from Valerie Jarvis.'

'Does that account for everything that was stolen?' Joseph asked.

JD shook his head. 'It's hard to say. Valerie's jewelry box had been emptied, but her sister said she'd been selling stuff off to pay the bills. The victim had once owned many valuable pieces, but Miss Cornell was pretty sure they'd all been sold long ago.'

Quartermaine pointed to the still-covered body of the second man. 'Well, John Doe had one of the items, too – a wedding band that had belonged to the victim's mother. It was gold plate. Not worth a lot.'

'He must have found it in Romano's pocket before Officer Mancuso stopped him from searching,' Hector said.

JD shook his head. 'Why wouldn't Toby hide the ring with the other items?'

'Maybe he was planning to sell it for more coke,' Joseph said. 'Maybe he showed it to John Doe there, and John Doe decided to take it from him.'

'But it was worth less than the brooch,' JD pushed back. 'It doesn't make sense.'

Quartermaine's brows had crunched, like he was thinking hard. 'But other things might. Things you need to know about John Doe,' he said, lifting the sheet from the man's face.

JD sucked in a startled breath. 'Wait. I know him. His name's . . . Clyde? No. No, Cleon. He's a dealer. But not Toby Romano's.'

Three

Gage flinched at the knock on the door of his room, his back going ramrod straight as his fingers fumbled the slide of the Glock he'd been cleaning. Recovering quickly, he began to methodically – and quickly – reassemble the gun while tilting his head toward the door to better hear the rattle of the doorknob in case his visitor got a little impatient.

He was on alert, his senses acute. Hyperaware. He glanced at the cupboard where he'd hidden the stash he'd found.

He wasn't expecting anyone. He'd already paid his rent for the week. In cash, of course, because it was that kind of place. No lease, no credit check, no signature, no trail.

His neighbors kept their heads down, just like he did. Nobody wanted anybody else to know they were there. Because it was that kind of place.

His landlord never came inside this building, probably because of the rats. Gage couldn't say he blamed him. He'd lived in places like this off and on for the past few years, once his money had run out. At least the rats in Baltimore were smaller than the ones in Florida, where they truly were the size of chihuahuas.

The landlord collected the cash at the back door on Mondays, between seven and eight a.m. 'Be there with the green or be evicted by eight fifteen' was his motto. Gage didn't even know the guy's real name and he didn't care.

Gage racked the Glock's slide as he sidled up to the door. There

39

was no peephole, because the tenants rarely, if ever, had visitors. Other than the landlord, only one other person knew he was there.

'Yeah?' he grunted, lowering his voice.

'It's Denny,' came the quiet reply. 'Open up.'

His brother, Denny, was that one other person and had only come to see him once before – the day Valerie got what was coming to her. That had been the only time Gage had physically seen Denny in the month that he'd been home.

Well, if you didn't count all the times Gage had planted himself down the street from Denny's house so that he could observe his brother's routine and, importantly, his family's. One never knew when such things might come in handy.

Especially since Denny was the only one who knew what Gage had done that day. Denny probably wouldn't tell, but Gage knew he could turn that 'probably' into 'definitely' with the right threat. A man's family was an easy target.

And if Denny got brave all of a sudden? Then he'd die. It was as simple as that.

Holding the Glock at his side, Gage opened the door enough to be sure that Denny was alone. He was, so Gage let him in, sliding the pistol into the back of his waistband.

'Arms out,' Gage snapped before Denny could say a word.

'What? Why?' Denny demanded.

'Just do it.' Gage stared down at him until Denny complied, sticking his arms straight out with a roll of his eyes. Gage ignored him, focusing on patting him down, making sure he carried no weapons. He even checked Denny's ears. 'Damn wires are getting so small.'

'Really, Gage?' Denny said, exasperated and angry. 'I'm not wearing a fucking wire. I got you your alibi, for God's sake. I'm not going to turn you in.'

Gage couldn't care less if his brother was annoyed. Hell, Gage couldn't care less if his brother was *breathing*. But Denny *had* gotten him the alibi, so that counted for something.

At least his brother wasn't a complete waste of skin.

Gage wished for the ten millionth time that he hadn't called

Denny in a near panic after leaving Valerie's place that day. He'd instantly regretted it. In hindsight, he could have handled it himself. Denny had loaned him some money, enough that Gage could rent this place and feed himself for a few weeks. He'd then tried to help Gage look innocent, but had fucked the situation up even more, which was typical of Denny. Having a deputy sheriff in Texas voluntarily call to say he'd seen Gage on the day of the murder had made BPD suspicious.

Still, Gage had an alibi and he'd built the rehab story around it to account for where he'd been in the interim. He'd say that it hadn't been a fancy rehab facility this time, because he'd been penniless and homeless. This time rehab was in the home of a friend, a junkie who'd gotten sober. He'd gone online and researched the towns in the vicinity of the deputy who'd given him the alibi. He'd found one such do-gooder – a junkie turned mega-church pastor who'd been very helpful once Gage had paid him a personal visit. He'd had to steal a few old clunkers for transportation, but it had been worth it.

It had taken a week of his time and most of the money he'd taken from Valerie's jewelry box, but it was worth it. One cleverly picked hooker to seduce the former junkie and get him into her hotel room plus about a hundred photos Gage had snapped on his phone of the two going at it like weasels on the hotel bed made for one very desperate mega-pastor.

He'd thought Gage wanted his cash, and Gage had taken some of it. But what he had really wanted was for the preacher to vouch for him, to spin a tale of Gage's detox and recovery. A reformed junkie would have all the lingo right, so his description would be spot on.

There would be no medical records and no money trail for prosecutors to follow. The combination would stand up in court were he ever to face a grand jury. There was plenty of reasonable doubt. He'd defended and won cases that were far flimsier than his.

He stepped back, satisfied that the only thing Denny carried was a few extra pounds. 'Why are you here?' he snarled, and his brother shook his head.

'I always forget how much of an asshole you really are,' Denny said, actually marveling at what everyone else in the universe already knew to be fact. Everyone except their mother. She'd never believe Gage to be anything but an angel.

'Why are you here?' Gage repeated, even more annoyed.

'Why are *you* here?' Denny hurled back.

Gage looked around the shabby little room. It barely fit a twin bed, and the bathroom was so small he had to practically straddle the toilet to pee into the bowl. He deliberately misunderstood the question. 'Because it's all I can afford right now.' Until he got his first paycheck. Which would hopefully be in two weeks.

Denny's eyes narrowed. 'Don't get smart with me, Gage. Why are you still in this city? I gave you an alibi.'

'And I'm grateful,' Gage said mildly.

'So be grateful in another city. Another state. Better yet, another fucking country!'

Gage raised a brow. 'There are fucking countries? Hell, that's where I want to go. God knows I haven't had any in a while.'

Denny's nostrils flared, his breathing sharp and hard, like a bull ready to charge. 'For God's sake, be serious.'

Gage leveled him a look – the one he'd given as a defense attorney to clients who were guilty as hell but not properly grateful that he'd taken their case. The one he'd given as a customer to the dealers who'd tried to rip him off. And, at the very end, the one he'd given to any other addict foolish enough to try to take his cot in the Miami shelter where he'd finally hit rock bottom.

That look had had the same effect then as it was having on Denny right now. His brother visibly paled and took a step back. But to Denny's credit, he wasn't pissing his pants. Not yet. His little brother was meeting his stare with one of his own, level and . . . honest. Above all else, Denny had been honest.

Wrangling that alibi from the Texas lawman must have cost his brother a part of his soul. Because Denny was also a loser. Which was why his brother worked at a Legal Aid office when Gage had been a junior partner of the most prestigious firm in the city.

Still, Denny had grown a backbone in the two years, nine months, and fourteen days that Gage had been gone. Which was a shame.

Good thing I shadowed his family. Not-so-idle threats might be required.

'I will ask you once again,' Gage said with quiet menace. 'Why are you here?'

Denny drew a trembling breath, but he didn't look away. 'The man you framed for Valerie's murder died today.'

Gage raised a brow. 'Really? How?'

Denny continued to hold his gaze steady. 'OD'd.'

Gage shrugged. 'He was a junkie. ODs happen.'

Denny's jaw tightened. 'A second man was found dead a few blocks away. Gunshot wounds. I heard that they think he was a dealer.'

'The junkie shot his dealer?' Gage asked innocently.

Denny's nostrils flared again. 'No. A cop shot the dealer. The dealer knifed the cop, stole his gun, and blew his brains out. They're all dead.'

Gage shook his head. 'A sad ending for all, but law enforcement officers live with risk. It's part of the job.'

Denny's eyes flashed such fury that Gage was tempted to back up a step, but of course he did not. 'You motherfucking bastard,' Denny whispered. 'You killed them all, didn't you?'

'Of course not,' Gage lied baldly. Then smirked. 'What did you want me to say?'

Denny was shaking his head in disbelief. 'You *killed* a fucking *cop*, Gage. What the hell is *wrong* with you?' He was still whispering, so Gage wouldn't have to kill him.

Not just yet, anyway.

Gage didn't blink. 'I have no idea what you're talking about. And neither do you.'

Denny's shoulders sagged. 'I hoped. I really, truly hoped that I could look in your eyes and see truth. But I only see lies. All lies. Just like it's always been.' He looked around the room, saw the new suit hanging on a peg next to the door. 'And what's that? You told me you were broke, that you needed cash for food. Yet you buy a new suit. From Brooks Brothers? I can't afford Brooks Brothers. What idiot would extend you credit?'

Another shrug. 'I didn't ask for credit. I used cash.' Because killing a dealer had its bonuses. Cleon Perry had had more than five hundred bucks stuffed in his pockets and another two grand stashed in the broken-down Chevy that Gage had appropriated.

He'd netted twenty-five hundred bucks, and that didn't count the sizable stash of coke Cleon had been carrying with intent to distribute. Too bad he died first.

Leaving it all to me.

'If you have no further accusations, you can go. I'll pay you back the money I borrowed when I get my first paycheck.'

Denny stared in disbelief. 'Paycheck? You got a job?'

'I start on Monday.'

Denny's mouth worked, but for a few seconds no sound emerged. 'Monday?' he finally managed. 'Who on God's green earth would give *you* a job?'

Gage was getting really pissed off. 'Cesar Tavilla.'

Denny stumbled backward until his back hit the door, his knees buckling, horrified panic filling his eyes. 'You're going to work for an El Salvadoran gang boss?'

Gage shrugged. 'I imagine he prefers to be called the head of his family's business empire. "Gang boss" is so pejorative, don't you agree?'

Denny blinked hard. 'What are you going to do for him?'

'Legal work. I'll defend his people when they find themselves falsely accused by BPD.'

'Falsely accused by BPD?' Denny echoed in a small voice. 'How . . . how did you get this job?'

It hadn't been easy, actually. 'I crossed paths with Mr Tavilla in a bar in Miami.' Because he'd heard that the man was in South Beach on vacation and had followed Tavilla's entourage, waiting until he could get close enough to talk to him. All while making it look like a chance encounter, of course. Getting close had been the hard part. Tavilla's entourage had included several bodyguards. 'We got to talking and he remembered that I defended his son a few years back.' Because Gage had reminded Tavilla explicitly that his son might have been on death row had it not been for him. 'And that I

44

saved his life.' Cocky little bastard. Tavilla's son had always been a fuck-up and always would be. 'And that he owed me a favor. He asked me if I wanted a job. I needed one, so I said yes.' Because he'd run out of the money he'd stashed away in offshore accounts in case he was ever audited. Money that nobody had known about but him. 'So, in summation, little brother, that is why I have a suit and that is why I'm still here.'

'But why *here*?' Denny cried. 'Why not go somewhere else to find a job?'

Rage flashed abruptly. 'Because,' Gage snapped through clenched teeth, then caught himself, drawing a breath and smoothing his expression. 'Because,' he continued calmly, 'this is *my* town. They forced me out once, but they'll soon see that they made a big mistake. They'll see exactly what they let slip away because they were stupid.'

'Who is *they*?' Denny demanded.

Gage gave him a pitying look. His brother was not the brightest bulb in the chandelier, for sure. 'Everyone in this fucking city. But mostly Stegner, Hall and Kramer, the fat-assed bastards. My clients paid their salaries, but they didn't appreciate anything. They forced me to quit and *I lost everything*. They'll be begging me to come back to the firm and I'll just laugh in their wrinkled old faces. *This* is an opportunity that they'd kill for, but it's mine.'

Denny shook his head, eyes flashing with bewildered fury. 'You came back to impress your old firm by getting a job with a *gang boss*? You killed your wife and framed an innocent kid for the crime so that you could go to work for a murdering *criminal*? A fucking *drug lord*? You killed three people today. One was a cop. Dammit, Gage. I *lied* for you.'

'And I said I was grateful,' Gage said mildly. 'Now, I need to get a few things done today. I'm meeting my new boss for dinner tonight. I hate to be rude, but you need to leave.'

Denny didn't move. 'Who *are* you?' he whispered, his voice breaking. 'This is going to kill Ma.'

Gage just looked at him. He really didn't care who it killed. His mother had outlived her usefulness when she mortgaged her house to pay for rehab he hadn't wanted to attend. Now she had no house and no money, so Gage had no use for her. 'Time to go, little brother.'

Denny shook his head slowly. 'Your wife. You beat your wife to death. Why?'

Gage shrugged again. 'I told you. She stole from me.'

That answer had seemed to satisfy Denny a month ago, but it wasn't satisfying him today. 'What exactly did she steal, Gage?'

'My house – the one I *paid for* that strangers are living in. I never saw a penny.'

Denny's face went florid with a sudden burst of rage. 'You sonofabitch. Your wife was forced to leave her home because *you* ran away and stopped paying the mortgage because *you* snorted all your money up your goddamn nose! You were gone for almost three years! Valerie didn't steal from you, Gage. She was *foreclosed on*. She declared *bankruptcy*.'

Gage knew that *now*. He hadn't known it when he'd first arrived back in Baltimore, tired and hot and hungry after hitchhiking from fucking Florida and just wanting to sleep in his own goddamned bed in his own goddamned house that he'd paid for. But there were strangers living there now. An old guy with a red Ferrari in the garage and a barely legal, smokin'-hot wife who lounged by the pool – *that Gage had paid for* – wearing not much more than a piece of string.

Seeing strangers in the home *he'd paid for* . . . His temper had simply snapped and he'd found Valerie in her little apartment. She'd told him there was no money from the house, but he hadn't believed her.

If she hadn't lied to him so many times before, he might have. But Valerie was a serial liar. So he'd hit her to make her talk. And then she'd threatened to call the cops and he'd hit her again. Knocked her to the floor, to her hands and knees. And then? She'd laughed. Kneeling on the floor like a dog, she'd looked up and laughed. *At me*. At what he'd become. So he'd hit her again and again. And again. Until she hadn't laughed any more.

It was only due to years of practice that he kept his voice icy and his emotions hidden. 'If she'd needed money for the mortgage, she should have asked St Lilah. The woman's loaded.' Because Lilah Cornell was a penny-pinching, man-hating, power-hungry bitch, who thought she was something special because she worked for the attorney general.

Gage wanted to laugh. His new boss had the AG's office in his pocket. *Huh. That means I'll have Lilah up against a wall. Maybe literally.* He was turning that optimistic thought over in his mind when Denny took an unexpected step forward, his eyes flashing once again.

'If it weren't for "St Lilah", your daughters would be *homeless* because you *killed* their *mother*. And Ma, she gave up her house, sold it, so that she could take care of them, because Valerie worked all the damn time. Ma cooks their food and washes their clothes. Did you know that?'

He did, actually. And he knew that their mother hadn't sold her house. She'd been foreclosed on too. Stupid woman. Gage hadn't asked her to mortgage the place to send him to rehab. He hadn't needed rehab, because he was not an addict. The idiot woman had paid for the whole thing in advance.

None of that money was refundable. He knew, because he'd checked. He'd wanted the cash. Which he would have snorted up his nose. Which was his goddamn business.

'No,' he lied smoothly, because Denny obviously didn't know that Ma had lost the house. If he had, he'd have been a lot madder. Gage fleetingly wondered how she'd kept that detail from Denny's notice. *Hm.* The old woman might not be as stupid as he'd thought. 'I didn't know that. That's nice of her.'

Denny was staring at him like he'd sprouted antennae. '*Nice of her*? Goddammit, Gage. Do you even hear yourself? We are all taking care of *your children*. Because *you are not*. Because you *killed their mother*. My God. If it weren't for Missy and me, your daughters would be going to bed hungry, because we pay their grocery bill. Did you know that? Times are tight. Missy and I count every penny. But we feed our children, Gage. And now we feed yours.'

But they were not Gage's children. Which was really the crux of the whole matter, wasn't it? He inclined his head. 'Again, I am grateful.'

'*Grateful*? You're *grateful*?' Denny took another step forward, his shoes nearly touching Gage's, his eyes wide and furious even though he continued to speak in harsh whispers. 'Have you even *seen* your daughters in the month that you've been back? Do you *know* what they're going through? Do you even *care*? Did you know that they found their mother? Did you know they have nightmares *every night*? How can you have done this to them? How do *you* sleep at night?' Tears filled his brother's eyes. 'Do you have a fucking *soul*?'

'I suggest you step back, Denny. I may have no soul, but I do have a temper and you are dangerously close to making me lose it.' He cocked a cool brow. 'And you know what happens when I lose my temper.'

Denny didn't step back. Instead, he leaned closer. 'Are you threatening me?' he hissed.

Gage's control on his temper thinned. 'It appears that I am. Get out. Just *get out*.'

'Or what? You'll kill me too? Shoot me? Knife me? Beat me to death?' Denny's fists were clenched and he was slowly drawing them up, as if he really planned to throw a punch.

Oddly, it was the sight of Denny's fists that calmed Gage down. Who the fuck was this stranger? he wondered. *Not the brother I knew.* If Denny had been like this all along, Gage might have had more respect for him. He smiled at Denny, and it was not a nice smile. 'Maybe all of the above. Or maybe I'll just focus on Missy. After all, she's so small. Her bones are so fragile.' And then he had the pleasure of seeing his brother turn sheet white.

'You stay *away* from my *wife*!' Denny snarled as he lunged for Gage.

Gage reached for the pistol at his back and had it pressed to Denny's throat before his brother could lay a hand on him. Denny froze, his gaze fixed on the pistol.

'Or what?' Gage mocked, just to be an asshole.

Denny took a giant step back, feeling for the doorknob behind him. 'Or I'll do what I should have done weeks ago. I'll turn you in.'

Gage tilted his head, curious. 'Why didn't you?'

'Because Ma still thinks you're redeemable. That you're *worthy*.' He spat the word. 'Because I didn't want her to have to visit you in jail for the rest of her life. Because I thought you'd leave and she'd never have to know you were even here. I gave you an alibi – I lied for you – because knowing what you really are would break her heart, and I won't do that to her.'

Gage smiled. 'Then you won't tell her now,' he said calmly.

Denny's eyes narrowed. 'Just watch me.'

Gage wasn't impressed. 'You'd be disbarred. You'd lose the pathetic career you have.'

'*I don't care.* Because *I* value my family more than my precious job. I promise you, Gage, if you touch one hair on Missy's head, if you even look at my sons, I will turn you in so fast your head will still be spinning when you get a needle in your arm.'

Gage rolled his eyes. 'Don't be dramatic. Maryland doesn't have the death penalty.'

Denny leaned forward once more. 'I didn't say the state would do it.' He left, slamming the door behind him.

Gage stood very still for a long moment, staring at the door. Then he shook his head. Denny would never tell. Sure, his brother had learned to posture. Bluster. Bluff, even. But he'd never tell.

If Denny had really been all that brave, he'd have an actual job instead of schlepping it down at Legal Aid. He'd have made something of himself.

Like I did before. Like I'll do again.

Baltimore, Maryland,
Saturday 22 August, 3.25 P.M.

JD studied the dead man's face. 'Yeah, that's Cleon Perry, all right. Dealer, wannabe pimp. General scumbag. Served some time for possession and distribution when I was with Vice.' He looked at Hector, who was staring at the corpse, a muscle ticking in his taut jaw.

Because this was the man who'd killed Hector's friend.

Hector jerked a vicious nod. 'He's right. Cleon Perry.'

JD knew Hector had also done a turn in Vice before being recruited into the Violent Crimes Enforcement Team, Joseph's small joint FBI/BPD task force. He was surprised that Hector hadn't recognized Cleon at the crime scene.

'You didn't know it was him?' JD asked. 'I mean, you found him, right?'

Hector shook his head. 'I was in the ambulance with Darren Mancuso. I stayed in the hospital with his wife until . . .' He took a step back, his fists clenched at his sides. 'But that's Cleon. I never arrested him, but I knew him. Wouldn't have made him as a killer.'

'None of us would have,' JD said, risking a squeeze to Hector's shoulder. 'Never seemed the type to knife a cop. He was always more of a runner.'

'I know,' Hector said grimly. 'Guess he changed his MO.' He drew a deep, unsteady breath. He was holding himself together, but barely. 'Motherfucker.'

There was silence for a moment, then Quartermaine cleared his throat. 'I submitted his prints, but I haven't gotten any matches back yet. For now, I'll assume you are both correct and this is Cleon Perry. Okay, so Mr Perry here was shot once in the shoulder. Bled a lot. Soaked through his clothes.' He looked up at them. 'Was there a trail of blood leading to his body?'

'No,' Joseph answered quietly. 'Officers found him during a search of the neighborhood, in the next alley. He'd crawled behind a dumpster and died, Mancuso's gun stuck in his waistband. There was a trail of blood at that scene. He'd apparently sat down, back to the alley wall, then crawled to the dumpster. Maybe he heard sirens and thought he could hide. But Mancuso's backup got there fast.'

'Just not fast enough,' Hector said bitterly.

Quartermaine sighed softly, but pressed on. 'There should have been blood along the path Perry took from the first crime scene to where he died, a block away. He was bleeding profusely from the shoulder wound alone – the first shot from the officer's gun – but the second shot should have left even more blood. Give me a minute.'

50

He walked to the computer on the countertop and pulled up several picture files. 'I know your CSU team took photos, but my techs took a few, too.'

JD, Joseph and Hector gathered around him, watching as he quickly tabbed through the photos. 'Ah. This one. Look at the trail of blood. The second shot was to Perry's thigh. Hit his artery. See this pool of blood? He lay there for at least a minute, bleeding from both wounds. You'll want your blood-spatter expert to confirm this, but if he crawled under his own power, there should be arterial spurts along this path from the pool of blood to the dumpster. They should be longer at first, then shorter, landing closer to his body as he crawled.'

'But there aren't,' JD said, processing all the details. 'Just this wide swath of blood. He didn't crawl. He was dragged.'

'That'd be my conclusion,' Quartermaine agreed. 'There was very little blood behind the dumpster. He'd mostly bled out here.' He pointed to the pool of blood. 'I think he was shot where you found him, both times. In fact, I don't think he was conscious when he was shot in the leg, or if he was, his blood pressure had dropped dangerously low. The blood pooled steadily. No indications of any spurts at all.'

'So he was not shot in the alley where Officer Mancuso died. Perry was killed in the alley where he was found, then the gun was put in his waistband and he was dragged.' Joseph turned back to Cleon Perry's body, studying the man's hands with a frown. 'No defensive wounds. Mancuso had them. He fought back. What about the knife Perry used to stab Officer Mancuso? Where is it?'

'It was found on his person. Agent Brodie has it now. She'll have to tell you if they lifted any prints from it.'

Joseph took out his phone and started to text. 'Asking her now.'

'What about gunshot residue?' JD asked.

'Perry tested positive,' Quartermaine confirmed, 'but that only means he held the gun at least one of the times it was fired. Both shots were fired at fairly close range, but the leg wound was made with the gun almost touching his skin.'

Hector's eyes narrowed. 'The shot fired when he was already

51

unconscious. You're saying that someone put the gun in Perry's hand, pointed it at his leg, and pulled the trigger.'

'I said that I only think he was unconscious,' Quartermaine cautioned. 'I have no evidence to support that. But . . . essentially yes. What you just said.'

JD let the scene play in his mind. 'If there was no trail of blood where Toby and Mancuso were found, Perry was not shot there. If he wasn't conscious when he was shot the second time, and he did all his bleeding where he was found, is it even likely that he was ever in the alley with Mancuso?'

Joseph checked his phone when it buzzed. 'Brodie says the blood on the blade matches Mancuso's type and she did find Perry's prints on the knife's hilt. Perfect ten-point matches. No smudges. The rest of the hilt was wiped clean.'

JD drew a breath, let it out. 'Perry was framed too.'

Hector's face creased into a snarling frown, like he didn't want to be thinking that Perry hadn't done it. Because it meant his friend's murderer was still out there. 'Why? Why would anybody pick Cleon Perry to frame? He's just a two-bit dealer. So low on the totem pole that nobody even tries to take over his territory. He's no threat.'

'Maybe that's exactly why,' Joseph said thoughtfully. 'Nobody will miss him. Nobody will seek revenge. He just disappears. A footnote.'

Hector scowled. 'And the SOB who killed a mother, a twenty-year-old addict, a two-bit dealer and a decorated cop walks away free.'

JD tried to line it all up in his mind. 'So . . . Toby is framed for Valerie Jarvis's murder, but I don't arrest him. Sometime last night he shoots himself up with enough coke to kill him. Any idea on his time of death?'

'Four to six hours before Officer Mancuso and Cleon Perry died,' Quartermaine said.

'That would have been helpful to know up front,' Joseph snapped, annoyed.

'Like I could get a word in edgewise,' Quartermaine returned sarcastically. 'I was going to tell you, but JD starts going off on how Toby Romano never did coke.'

'Which he didn't,' JD said firmly. 'So let's—'

'I've got a question,' Hector interrupted. 'Toby Romano was no weakling. Neither was Cleon Perry. How'd this cowardly fucker get close enough to do these things to them? Did he tie them up?'

'Unlikely,' Quartermaine said. 'No ligature marks. But Toby also had ketamine in his urine. Not much. Certainly not enough to give him much of a high. Ket and coke are often taken together, but if the ket was given first, it would have sedated him. At least enough to pump him full of coke.' He brought up another file on the computer, the screen now filled with numbers. 'Same with Perry. I'll run some more tests to see how it would have been administered.'

'So . . . can I go back to thinking this through now?' JD asked.

'Not yet,' Quartermaine said. 'I have a question. You said when you first recognized him that Cleon Perry wasn't Toby's dealer. How did you know that?'

'Because I've been watching Toby ever since he was caught selling the brooch, and he buys from somebody else.' JD remembered too late that Toby was laid out on the table right behind them. '*Bought* from someone else. And before you ask,' he added, because Quartermaine's mouth had tightened disapprovingly, 'no, I did not arrest Toby or his dealer, but I have enough photos of their transactions to go back and get him later. Toby's dealer is not terribly covert and he always deals from the same street corner.'

Quartermaine's nod was reluctant. 'Just do it soon, okay? I get enough addicts on my table. The thought of a known dealer walking around free to peddle his poison to kids . . . Just arrest him soon.'

'After we arrest the bastard who killed a cop,' Hector growled.

'Yes,' Quartermaine murmured. 'You can continue thinking it through now, JD.'

JD raised an eyebrow at the doctor, then said, 'Okay. Toby shoots up with coke, even though he wasn't a coke user. He dies and somebody dumps his body in his normal spot but doesn't expect a cop to be there. There's a scuffle, Officer Mancuso draws his weapon, and somebody – most likely not Perry – knifes him.' He glanced at

Hector, who closed his eyes. 'Sorry,' JD murmured. 'Where was Mancuso stabbed?'

'Up under his vest,' Joseph answered. 'Long blade. Just sliced his gut open. The gunshot was to the side of his head.'

'He was already down on the ground when he was shot,' Hector said quietly. 'Cowardly fucker to shoot a man when he's already down.'

JD wholeheartedly agreed. 'Same kind of coward who'd beat a woman until she was unrecognizable.'

'You really think it's the same guy, then.' Hector didn't phrase it as a question, but JD answered anyway.

'Yeah. Toby had pawned one of the pieces stolen from Valerie Jarvis's apartment, but I didn't even bring him in for questioning for the murder. I knew he hadn't done it. His pawning the item in a shop with a camera was too damn tidy. So Valerie's killer must have gotten tired of waiting. He had to make it so obvious that Toby had murdered Valerie that we'd have to come to that conclusion. It would have been more believable if he'd also planted the murder weapon on Toby, but he couldn't have done that.'

'Because he beat Valerie with his fists,' Quartermaine said quietly. 'Which Toby couldn't have done.' He turned back to Toby's body and gently lifted the young man's hand. 'No scarring.'

'It's been a fucking month,' Hector said bitterly. 'It would have healed.'

'I took photos of Toby's hands as soon as I got the report from the pawnshop,' JD told him. 'That was only two days later. They weren't even swollen. They should have been cut up and scabbed over. Traces of the killer's blood and skin were found on Valerie during autopsy.'

Hector's eyes narrowed. 'Enough to get a DNA sample?'

'Yes,' Quartermaine said. 'The results came back a few days ago.'

'So we can prove it wasn't Toby's blood on Valerie Jarvis,' Joseph said.

Quartermaine nodded. 'But you don't need DNA for that. The blood type's no match.'

'The DNA didn't match any in the database,' JD said, 'but that just means her killer isn't in the system.' He hesitated, then sighed. 'It didn't match Jazzie's DNA either. No overlap whatsoever.'

Joseph frowned. 'You didn't tell me that.'

Quartermaine looked surprised. 'You had the kid tested?'

'Her aunt gave me a hair sample.' JD glanced at Joseph. 'I just got the results. I was going to tell you, then this all happened first.'

'So the killer was not Jazzie's father.' Hector's voice was terse as he brought the conversation back to topic. 'Or at least not her biological father. Is Gage Jarvis the stepfather?'

'No,' JD said. 'His name's on her birth certificate. If he found out he wasn't her biological father, it could be motive for Valerie's murder. Either way, when we find an actual suspect, we can do a DNA comparison.'

'But first we need to find an actual suspect,' Joseph said pointedly.

'So let's think this through,' JD snapped back. 'Like I've been wanting to. Okay? Okay. So somebody kills Valerie and tries to make it look like Toby did it. But I don't arrest Toby and time passes and somebody gets impatient. He wants us to believe that Toby did it so he sets him up with more items stolen from the apartment. Toby ODs on coke – not his usual drug. Somebody dumps him in the alley, but he doesn't expect Mancuso and knifes him, then shoots him to make sure he's not ID'd.' He paused a moment, thinking about what had to have happened next. 'Did Mancuso get a call into dispatch before he confronted whoever was dumping Toby's body?'

Hector nodded. 'He called for backup, then called me, which was why we got to him so fast. Said he saw a guy in a hoodie, about six feet tall. Couldn't tell much else.'

'The shootings of Mancuso and Perry happened within minutes of each other,' JD continued. 'This guy didn't have time to really make a plan, which says a lot, because he came up with a good one on the fly – except for no trail of blood in the first alley. So Perry's in the next alley, unconscious. Let's backburner the why for a few minutes. The shooter runs to Perry and shoots him with Mancuso's gun, because he suddenly needs someone to take the fall for the cop's murder. He puts another stolen item in Perry's pocket to connect him to Toby and sticks the gun in Perry's waistband to connect him to Mancuso. This way it looks like there were only three people involved – Toby, Mancuso and Perry.'

'Okay,' Joseph said slowly. 'I can buy that. But why Perry was there in the first place is still a big question.'

'True.' JD scratched at his face under the mask he still wore. 'That's a damned good question. What if he hadn't been?'

Joseph's brows crunched. 'What do you mean?'

'I mean, what if Perry hadn't been there? Dead or alive?' JD chuffed out an impatient breath. 'If you can't think forward, think backward. For now, leave Officer Mancuso out of it entirely. He was an unexpected development. Unplanned. What would we be thinking right now if we'd found only Toby Romano's body, OD'd and holding on to more items stolen from Valerie Jarvis?'

'That he'd been in the Jarvis apartment on the day of the murder,' Hector supplied. 'That he'd lied to you about only having one item that he'd conveniently "found", so he'd probably lied about other things. We'd want to conclude Romano killed Valerie Jarvis.'

'We might close the case on the basis of Romano alone,' Joseph said grimly, understanding sharpening his eyes. 'He didn't need Cleon Perry to frame Toby Romano. Perry was there for another reason.'

Hector shrugged. 'Cleon Perry was a coke dealer. Romano was pumped with coke. His killer had to get it from somewhere. Maybe he bought it from Perry and planned to kill Perry to keep him quiet, but later.'

JD nodded. 'But Officer Mancuso surprised him and he had to change his plan.'

'There'd be huge pressure to find and arrest a cop killer,' Joseph agreed. 'This way, it looks like it's all tied up with a neat little bow. Both bad guys are dead. We can close the case. Walk away.'

'Why?' Quartermaine pressed. 'Why go to so much trouble to make you close the case?'

'Because if we close the case, we won't investigate anyone else,' Joseph said quietly.

JD nodded. 'And our initial suspect – Valerie's estranged

husband Gage Jarvis – is never investigated. What do you want to bet that Gage magically materializes in the next few weeks?'

Joseph's eyes narrowed. 'If he does, we need to be ready to grab him. And if Gage Jarvis is not involved, we still have a killer out there – he's up to four victims, including a cop. And if he finds out there was a witness hiding in Valerie Jarvis's apartment that day?'

Hector blew out a breath that puffed out his mask. 'He'd kill that little girl without losing a minute's sleep.'

JD's gut tightened painfully. 'We won't let that happen.'

Four

Taylor was almost finished brushing Gracie, her afternoon lesson horse, when Dillon made his feeding rounds. He broke off a flake from the hay bale, putting most of it into Gracie's trough. The rest he hand-fed the gray mare that was almost as gentle as Ginger. Out of all the horses on the Montgomery farm, Ginger and Gracie were Taylor's two favorites.

Dillon scratched Gracie's nose and the horse leaned into him. 'Hey, sweetheart,' he said softly, forcing her to lean even closer to hear him. He kissed her muzzle. 'Did you miss me?'

'She certainly did,' Taylor said, and Dillon jumped, pressing his hand to his chest.

'Crap, Taylor!' he exclaimed. 'You scared me to death.'

Taylor moved out of Gracie's way when the horse shuffled backward, startled by Dillon's outburst. 'I'm so sorry, Dillon. I thought you saw me.'

Dillon drew a deep breath. 'No, I didn't. But it's okay.' He grinned. 'Heart's still beating.'

Taylor's eyes popped wide. 'Do you have a heart condition?' It wasn't uncommon in individuals with Down syndrome. She wanted to kick herself. *Holy shit. I nearly gave the bridegroom a heart attack.*

'I did.' He tugged the V-neck of his T-shirt down a few inches to show a scar. 'I had surgery when I was five. The scar goes down to my belly button. But the doctor says I'm fine now. I was only teasing.'

Taylor nodded, trying to calm her own racing heart. 'Good enough.' She leaned against a support pole, partly because her legs were shaky and partly to decrease the difference in their heights so that Dillon didn't have to look up so far to meet her eyes. He was about five-four with his boots on – average for an adult man with Down syndrome and obviously tall enough to do his job, because he did it so well – but Taylor still felt like she towered over him. 'I'd hate to give you a heart attack before the wedding.'

He grinned at her. 'Holly would kick your ass. She could, you know. She's a blue belt.'

'That's amazing. I wish I'd taken karate in a real school. I never got a belt.' And . . . she hadn't meant to say that. *Shit.* She was disclosing personal details all over the damn place today. *You're just rattled.* It had been a rattling kind of day. Jazzie's outburst and then . . .

Ford. She drew a breath. *Yeah. Him.* She liked him. *Don't even think about it. You can't have him.* She was going home. As soon as she got what she'd come for. *Probably.*

Dillon was tilting his head, looking confused. 'Where did you take it, then?'

She blinked, stalling for time so that she could remember what they'd even been talking about. *Oh. Right. Karate.* 'My dad taught me what he knew.' She gave him a rueful smile. 'He worries about me, especially all the way out here all by myself.'

Dillon frowned. 'You're not by yourself. You're with us.'

'But I'm not at home. This is my first time away from home.'

Dillon nodded knowingly. 'My mom and dad worry about me too. But they let me go. Let me have my inde . . . independence.' He stumbled over the word and she was quiet while he forced it out. 'They let me live alone. And now I'm going to live with Holly.' His smile returned, pride in his eyes. 'We have our own apartment.'

'Good for you,' Taylor said with a hard nod. 'For both of you. I've never had my own apartment.'

'You still don't,' he pointed out. 'You live in the big house with Maggie.'

Taylor's lips twitched. 'True enough. But until two weeks ago,

I'd never been away from home without my dad or my sister Daisy. Or my mom, when she was alive.'

Sorrow had Dillon's mouth bending down. 'I'm sorry, Taylor.'

'It's okay. She's not hurting anymore. I'm starting to remember her before she got sick, so that's a good thing, right?'

'Right.' He scrunched his brow, thinking. 'If you want, you can go to karate class with Holly. Maybe you can still get your belt.'

She should have told him that she'd be going home at the end of the internship. But she didn't and she wasn't sure why. 'Maybe after you and Holly get back from your honeymoon.'

His grin was devilish. 'Yeah.' He drew out the word and waggled his brows.

Taylor threw back her head and laughed, and Dillon laughed with her. She slipped from the stall and made sure the door was latched. 'You're naughty, Dillon. I like that.'

He gave her a slow wink. 'Holly does too. Are you coming to our wedding? She wants to meet you.'

'I am, absolutely. I still have to get a present. I hope something's left on your registry list.' She held up a finger to silence him when he opened his mouth. 'And I hope you're not planning to tell me that I don't have to bring anything. My mother brought me up better than that. If I showed up to a wedding without a gift, she'd come down from heaven to haunt me.'

If indeed that was where her mother had ended up. Taylor wasn't so sure.

'Then I won't say that.' He walked her to the barn door, his expression going a little shy. 'I heard about what happened with Janie and Jazzie today. That's really nice, Taylor.'

Taylor's cheeks heated. 'I didn't do anything special.'

'You're nice. They both know that. Kids and horses know,' he said wisely.

'Thank you,' she said softly. 'Holly is a lucky lady.'

He grinned again. 'I know. I tell her every day, too. Gotta go home now. She hasn't seen me since before the camping trip.'

The camping trip that nearly every male in the place had attended. 'Did you guys have fun on the trip?'

'Oh yeah. It was amazing. Ford and Cole came, Grayson and JD too. And Clay was able to be there for the last few days.'

Taylor's cheeks heated at the first name, but her heart started to thunder in her chest when she heard the last one. *Finally*. Finally someone had mentioned his name in a way that allowed her to ask her questions.

Except Dillon winced a little. 'Even Joseph came.'

Worried at Dillon's tone, Taylor shoved away the tingle of awareness she'd felt at the sound of Ford's name. And the sheer terror at Clay's. 'You . . . you don't like Joseph?'

Dillon shrugged. 'I like him fine, but . . . Well, once he caught Holly and me . . . well, you know. We were on the couch at her parents' house and . . .'

It was Taylor's turn to wince. 'Ouch. Awkward.'

'Yeah.' Dillon exhaled heavily. 'Joseph still frowns at me sometimes.'

'Holly's his little sister. I guess that's to be expected. But he's good to you?' FBI Special Agent Joseph Carter was Daphne Montgomery's husband, and the only time Taylor had met him was during her interview. He'd gone over her background check with a fine-toothed comb, his eyes like lasers. She'd honestly wondered if the man had X-ray vision or something. But he hadn't seemed mean. Just terribly cautious. He reminded her of her dad in that respect. Given the vulnerability of the kids in the program, she'd appreciated Joseph's caution.

She'd also appreciated the care her father had put into building her identity so that even a determined federal agent hadn't been able to find a single hole. *Thanks, Daddy*. She'd tell him when she called home to check in tonight. She'd promised him she'd check in with him twice a day to let him know she was okay. It was the least she could do for making him worry.

'Oh, Joseph's good to me,' Dillon said blithely. 'He and Daphne gave me this job. I make good money here.'

'You should,' she said, relieved that he wasn't really afraid of Joseph Carter. 'You work hard. You're amazing with the horses. You earn every penny.'

His smile was pleased. 'Like I said – you're nice. Not everybody talks to me like you do.'

'Or gives you a heart attack?' she teased, but she understood what he meant. It made her insane when people babbled in baby talk to her sister Julie. Julie hated it too. *Focus, Taylor. Ask the questions you came for.* But in a way that didn't make Dillon either suspicious or uncomfortable. 'I met Ford today, and Joseph when he interviewed me, but who are the others?'

Of course she knew who they were. She'd researched everyone associated with the farm, reading every article that popped up. Some of the names had more background information than others. Of course, the person she was most interested in had the least information.

'Well, Cole is Daphne's stepson and he lives with her in her other house.'

'Mercy. How many houses does Daphne have?' she asked, knowing that answer as well.

'Only two. She lives in the house close to Baltimore, because she works there. Maggie lives here. Maggie told me once that Daphne bought this farm because she wanted to start the therapy program, even though she didn't know it yet.'

'Daphne told me that too. When I interviewed.' Taylor had sensed within Daphne a kindred spirit, a woman who under-stood what it was like to be a scared little girl. Of course Daphne's trauma had been quite real. Taylor had always considered her own trauma real, too. Until she found out that her whole life had been built on a single colossal lie. 'I didn't know that Cole was her stepson, though. She called him her son.'

'She and Joseph adopted him, so he's Cole Carter now. Cole is Ford's half-brother.' Dillon frowned. 'They have the same dad. The dad's not nice. But Ford and Cole are.'

Ford's dad was Travis Elkhart, a wealthy judge who lived in Virginia. Elkhart and Daphne had divorced when Ford was younger. There was no record of any animosity within the family, but those things often didn't make it into newspaper articles.

'Ford taught me how to ride,' Dillon went on, 'and Cole and I work out at the gym. I used to not be able to even lift a hay bale. Now I can throw 'em. Not as far as Cole, though.'

'Maybe I need to work out too,' Taylor said ruefully. 'I can carry bales, but I can't throw them.'

Dillon frowned again, this time in puzzlement. 'But it's not your job to throw bales. It's my job.'

'Then I'll gladly let you do all the heavy lifting,' she said with a smile. She hesitated, feeling guilty about pressing Dillon for information. But it was necessary. At least she wasn't putting on an act with him. That would have been cruel and Taylor liked to believe she wasn't capable of such a thing. 'What about the other people who went on your camping trip?'

'Oh, right. Well, Grayson is my friend. He works out with us sometimes.' Dillon's eyes grew round. 'He can bench more weight than all of us. It's crazy. He's a lawyer like Daphne. He's her boss. He and Joseph are like brothers, so Grayson is Holly's brother, too. He's also married to Paige, who teaches karate to Holly. So we're friends.'

'And the other two? JD?'

'Well, JD is a cop. Detective Fitzpatrick. He works with Daphne and Grayson sometimes. He's married to Lucy.' Dillon grimaced. 'She used to cut up dead people.'

'You mean she was a medical examiner?'

Another grimace. 'Yeah. Ick.' Then he brightened. 'They have a little boy, Jeremiah, and a new baby girl named Bronwynne. Holly and I babysit them sometimes. They're sure cute.'

'I saw Detective Fitzpatrick's name in Janie and Jazzie's file. He was the detective investigating their mother's murder.'

'I know.' Dillon sighed. 'JD has to see dead people all the time. I couldn't do that. I'd be too scared.'

'So would I.' *And the last man in your camping party?* she wanted to ask. But she held her tongue while Dillon tilted his head, concentrating.

'Oh, yeah,' he said. 'Then there's Clay.'

Finally. This would be the information she'd come all the way from California to hear. *Clay Maynard.* 'I've heard his name. He's Daphne's security manager, right?'

63

'Right. Clay is a good guy. He does all the cameras and alarms.'

'To keep the children safe,' she murmured.

'Yes. That's important. The kids *have* to feel safe,' Dillon said forcefully. 'That's our most important thing here.'

'Is Clay good to the children?'

Dillon looked at her like she'd asked if the Pope was Catholic. 'Well, yeah. He loves kids. Cordelia is his little girl.'

Taylor kept the frown from her face, a habit born of hours of practice. 'He has a little girl?' That hadn't been in any of the articles she'd turned up. Because Taylor had looked. Because she'd always wondered.

Breathing through her stunned surprise, she admitted to herself that the knowledge hurt. He had another daughter. *Cordelia.*

She made herself think rationally. *Of course he has a family.* She didn't truly think he'd spent all these years alone. *Cordelia.* She'd seen that name recently. *Oh, right.* 'She must ride here,' she said, hearing the weakness in her voice. She shored it up, so that the next words came out without a quiver. 'I saw her name on one of the saddles.'

'Cordy's part of the program.' Sadness flickered in Dillon's eyes. 'She got scared once by a man with a gun. She has nightmares still.' He sucked in a breath, his expression abruptly stricken. 'Nobody's supposed to know about the nightmares. Don't tell anyone I told, please.'

'I won't, of course. But why is it a secret? I thought she came here for help with the nightmares.'

'She does, but she doesn't want her mom to know.'

Taylor didn't even try to control her frown, because despite being dismayed that Clay had a daughter, she was angry on the child's behalf. No child should be afraid to seek comfort from her nightmares. 'Why not? Did her mother threaten her?'

'Oh no. No.' Dillon wagged his head. 'Stevie – that's Cordy's mom – she didn't threaten Cordy. Not ever. See, Stevie used to be a cop. It was her fault that Cordy got taken by the man with the gun. He really wanted Stevie.'

'Oh.' Taylor exhaled quietly. 'He used Cordelia as a pawn.

A tool,' she clarified when Dillon looked uncertain. 'A tool to hurt her mother. So her mother feels guilty.' Taylor wondered if her own mother had ever felt a speck of guilt when she'd been the frightened child. 'And Cordelia doesn't want her mother to feel even worse.'

'Yeah. That's it exactly. Cordy loves her mom,' he added with a shrug. 'So she doesn't talk to her mom about the nightmares because it makes her mom sad. Only Maggie knows. And me. And Clay, too.'

'Cordelia trusts Clay?'

'Of course! He's her dad. Well, not her real dad. Her real dad died before she was born. Clay married her mom – you know, Stevie – about a year ago, and now he has a family. Which is good, because Clay *deserves* a family,' he added, adamant.

'Why?' Taylor asked, and tried not to hold her breath for Dillon's answer.

'Because he lost his little girl. He can't find her. Her mama hid her away.'

'Why?' she asked again, her voice cracking.

Dillon didn't seem to notice. 'I don't know. All I know is that he goes looking for her, every chance he gets. He was there looking for her right before our camping trip. He gets so sad when he comes back because he still can't find her.'

Taylor's throat grew tight. 'Where?' she managed to ask.

'On the Eastern Shore. Camping's fun there. Bugs are bad, though.'

She shook her head. 'No, not camping. Where did he go searching?'

'Oh. In California. I don't know exactly where. He probably told me, but I'm not too good with maps. Maggie would probably know and— Oh crap.' He smacked his forehead. 'I was supposed to tell you that Maggie wanted to see you in the office. Gotta get home myself, though.' He threw a wave over his shoulder. 'See you around, Taylor.'

'Good night, Dillon.'

She stared after him, shaken by his words. Clay had been looking for his daughter. *All this time.* She swallowed hard. But he wasn't going to find her in California. *Not right now anyway.* 'Dillon? Thank you.'

He turned around, brows hiked high. 'For what?'

For helping me know that coming all the way out here wasn't stupid or foolish. But she couldn't say that. 'For making me feel so welcome and for inviting me to your wedding. I was scared to come here, but you've helped me with that.'

His eyes widened. 'You were scared? Of us? And I helped? How?'

'Sure I was scared. It's my first time so far from home. Away from my family.' She wasn't lying to him. Those had been true fears. Just not the biggest ones. 'You made me not be so scared. So thank you.'

Chest puffed with pride, Dillon walked back to where Taylor stood, leaned up on his toes, and wrapped his arms around her neck in a warm hug. 'You're welcome. You have friends here.' He pulled away, his smile delighted. 'Like me.'

'Like I said – Holly's lucky. Go home, cowboy. Kiss your girl.'

She watched him go, then closed her eyes, leaning wearily against the post. Phase one was complete. She'd heard what she'd come three thousand miles to hear from a reliable source. Dillon knew right from wrong and good from bad. He'd said Clay was a good man.

Everyone else associated with the farm who she'd met so far had been friends of Clay. They'd say he was a good man out of loyalty if nothing else. Dillon, on the other hand, seemed more concerned with Cordelia's welfare than with her stepfather's.

Taylor had detected no deceit in Dillon. *Not like my deceit radar is foolproof, though.* Her own mother had lied to her for years – *years* – creating an emotionally damaged adult who'd been terrified to go anywhere alone. Who'd always been watching for the boogeyman hiding behind a rock, under the bed, in the closet. Who'd jumped at shadows. *But that's not me. Not anymore.* Taylor knew that it was well past time she took her life back.

Now for phase two – meeting Clay face to face. That would take a little more courage. He'd been her nightmare for so many years, his face the one she'd learned to fear. To hate. And even though her mind was slowly accepting the truth, it didn't mean the fear and hate magically disappeared.

She only hoped it didn't take too much time. Her internship was only for six weeks, and two weeks were already gone.

Speaking of which, she still had a job to do for the length of time she remained. And if Maggie had heard that she'd struck Ford Elkhart, that time might be very short.

Pushing away from the post, she straightened her spine and made her way to the office. 'Hey, Maggie. Dillon said you wanted to see me.'

The older woman sat behind an ancient scarred wooden desk, her booted feet propped up on the corner. 'Come in.' She gestured to the fridge. 'Get a drink and have a seat. We need to talk.'

Hunt Valley, Maryland,
Saturday 22 August, 3.55 P.M.

Ford came out of the shadows of the corner of the barn nearest the office door. He hadn't intended to spy on Taylor again, yet he had. He'd actually been looking for her so that he could tell her to go and see Maggie when he heard Dillon's alarmed yelp and Taylor's sincere apology.

Ford had almost revealed himself, but changed his mind at the last minute, not wanting her to think that he thought Dillon needed to be protected from her. Instead he'd stayed and listened, and now he couldn't be sorry that he had. He'd learned more about Taylor Dawson in a few minutes of eavesdropping than he could have in hours of searching online.

Taylor had never left home before, for one. She'd been frightened to come here, which could partially explain her response when he'd startled her earlier.

He'd also heard her ask Dillon more questions about Clay than all the rest of them put together. With the exception of making sure that Joseph was good to Dillon, she'd focused on Clay, and that didn't sit well with Ford. Clay was his friend, and Ford protected his own.

They'd had reporters sniff around the farm a time or two, but mostly they were looking for news leads on the kids, not the staff. If Taylor Dawson was a reporter looking for some kind of an angle, she could take herself back to California. As fast as possible.

Except . . . Joseph had vetted her, and the man did not make mistakes. Anyone coming through the farm's gates underwent thorough background checks, and Taylor would have been no exception. Joseph protected the kids, but he also protected Ford's mom, and Ford appreciated that. He hadn't exactly liked the broody FBI guy at first sight, but he'd warmed to him pretty quickly because Joseph loved his mother and would lay down his own life to protect her. That was a helluva lot more than Ford could say for his biological dad, who was, as Dillon so understatedly described, not nice.

Travis Elkhart was a selfish sonofabitch who'd cheated on Daphne, divorcing her without a dime – or health insurance – when she'd discovered him with his secretary. Travis Elkhart had used Ford as the bargaining chip, agreeing to non-disputed custody only if Daphne didn't fight for alimony – or health insurance.

Which would have been a death sentence, because her breast cancer had been serious.

Luckily Ford had perfected the art of eavesdropping at a young age and knew things about his father that Travis did not want anyone to know – specifically about the woman dressed in black leather wielding a whip over his father who'd been licking her boots.

The memory made Ford shudder. Some pictures you couldn't erase from your mind.

Luckily Ford had had his camera phone on him when he'd stumbled on the scene, unbeknownst to the participants. And luckily Ford's grandmother Elkhart had been blackmailable. Instead of getting nothing, Daphne had gotten a generous settlement, had retained her health insurance and had gone on to do amazing things with her life – including the founding of Healing Hearts, which had helped so many kids already.

Ford would allow no one to threaten his mom or the program.

Which pulled his thoughts back on track. *Taylor Dawson. Asking questions. Potential wolf in the henhouse.*

Except . . . she'd sounded so lost. And her voice had broken when she'd asked Dillon where Clay had searched for his daughter. In California.

In California. Holy shit.

His gasp echoed in the quiet of the barn. *Oh. My. God.*

Ford froze as the possibility struck him squarely in the face. *Her eyes.* Taylor's familiar dark eyes. Now he knew where he'd seen them.

In Clay's face.

It could be a coincidence, he told himself rationally.

Except . . . Ford didn't believe in coincidences anymore, and there were too damn many of them anyway. Clay's daughter Sienna would be about twenty-three years old, and so was Taylor. Taylor's mother had died recently, as had Clay's ex-wife – of cancer, both of them. *And she had Clay's eyes.*

Except . . . Joseph had done her background check. A link to Clay would have surfaced. Joseph Carter did *not* make mistakes. Not when it came to Daphne's safety, and Taylor was someone who could get close enough to Daphne to touch her.

Shit. What if Taylor wasn't Clay's daughter? Why was she asking so many questions? What if she was up to something? Whatever it was, it wouldn't be good. That, he'd learned from personal experience. *Why is she here? Why was she pumping Dillon for information? What's her agenda?* The questions spiraled in his mind, growing faster and louder until one popped free that brought the runaway train in his brain to a screeching halt.

What if she came here to hurt someone?

Once – not even two years ago – he would have laughed at his own paranoia. He wouldn't even have thought to ask the question. But then he'd met Kimberly, who'd done exactly that. Had insinuated herself into his life for the sole purpose of betraying him. Kimberly had pretended to be good. Had pretended to be his. All while intending to use him as a pawn in a plan aimed at hurting his mother.

If Taylor hurts my mother, I'll gut her myself.

Whoa. Ford drew a deep breath and let it out, calming himself. Not everyone who asked questions intended to harm the people he loved. Logically he knew this. But emotionally? *Fuck.* Kimberly had fucked him up but good. Letting his fear drive his actions meant he was letting Kim win. *And that will not happen.*

He took another minute to let his fear subside to a point where he could at least think clearly. Taylor Dawson might be Clay's daughter, Sienna. It wasn't impossible. But even if she wasn't, she was asking questions that made Ford uncomfortable. She might still be up to something.

Except . . . He thought about how she'd sagged against the post when Dillon left. Whatever her reasons for her questions, she wasn't happy about asking them. Maybe she was being coerced.

Clay needed to know that there was someone on the farm asking about him. Someone who had his eyes, background checks be damned.

But if Taylor was Clay's kid, why didn't she just talk to him? That didn't make any sense.

Except that maybe it did. He'd heard understanding in her voice when she'd spoken about Jazzie knowing that her mother's murderer was still out there. As if she knew what it was like.

To be afraid, she'd said. *To always wonder if he's lurking, waiting to jump out from behind a tree to drag them away.*

Ford knew that Clay's ex-wife had hidden his daughter, but didn't know much more than Dillon did about why. He'd always wondered. Now he needed to know. He needed to understand exactly why Taylor Dawson was here. If she really was Taylor Dawson. Which sounded paranoid as hell.

Except that he'd learned to trust his paranoia. Kimberly had lied to him and he'd nearly died. His mother had nearly died. Ford couldn't afford to trust anyone anymore. Even a pretty intern who made him want to comfort and protect her – and that was just for starters.

He slipped out of the barn and into the yard, where his phone got a better signal. He stared at the screen for a long time before dialing

Clay's number. When he did, the phone rang so many times that Ford thought it would go to voicemail, but then Clay picked up, breathing hard.

'Yeah, Ford? What's wrong?'

Ford's mouth opened, closed, and opened again, but the right words simply wouldn't come. Everything he wanted to say sounded too crazy. 'Are you okay?'

'Yeah,' Clay said gruffly. 'Just had to run up the stairs for the phone.'

'Oh, okay. Um, can you come out here?' Maybe Taylor's reaction to meeting Clay would answer his questions without his having to ask them.

'Why?' The single word rang with impatience.

Because the new intern is asking questions about you and she has your eyes. And if Taylor was exactly who she said she was and was simply curious? He could be setting Clay up for a huge disappointment. He'd come straight to the campsite from the airport and it had been clear how devastated he was that his latest search had been fruitless. If Ford suggested to Clay that Taylor could be his Sienna and she turned out not to be? He didn't want to imagine Clay's pain.

So he lied. 'One of the cameras in the barn is acting wonky.'

A heartbeat of silence, followed by an equally impatient exhale. 'Look, Ford, I just got home after being gone for two weeks. I'm beat. And that's Alec's job, anyway. He knows how to fix shit like that better than I can. Call him. If the two of you can't fix it, call me back. We'll figure it out. All the kids are gone for the day, right?'

Of course Clay would say that the cameras were Alec's job, because they were. Clay's IT guy – who was also one of Ford's best friends – had installed nearly all the technology at the farm. The cameras were Alec's babies. He should have been Ford's first call.

'Right,' Ford mumbled, calling himself an idiot. He'd botched that one and now he couldn't come up with another reason without sounding like an even bigger idiot.

'Then put the alarm on when you close up for the night and I'll see that this gets fixed first thing tomorrow,' Clay said. 'Okay?'

'Okay. Thanks, Clay.' He ended the call and stared at the barn, then the farm house. He didn't live here, but he had a room here and tonight he'd make use of it. Just in case his paranoia was right for a change and Taylor wasn't what she seemed.

And if he got to spend some time getting to know her better, well, that was just a bonus.

Five

Clay Maynard tossed his phone to the nightstand and rolled to his side to study the woman in his bed. Their bed, their house. He'd married Stevie Mazzetti last Christmas Eve, and after New Year's he'd adopted Cordelia. He finally had a family of his own.

He'd loved Stevie Mazzetti from the first moment he'd laid eyes on her, but when he met her she hadn't yet finished mourning her husband. He'd waited for her to be ready, simply because his heart wouldn't allow him to do anything else. Now he had it all.

Immediately the bitterness came barreling through. *No, not all.* He still hadn't found Sienna, even though he'd started searching for his daughter the moment he'd learned of her existence, twenty years ago. He'd gotten close a few times over those years – he'd found his ex-wife, but Donna had hidden Sienna away and wouldn't even tell him *why*. Then a year and a half ago Donna had died and Clay had experienced a flare of hope.

If he'd only been able to get a few minutes with his daughter . . . just a few minutes . . . He wasn't sure what he could reasonably hope to achieve, but it didn't matter. He'd redoubled his search efforts since Donna's death, but had come up completely dry. Sienna was nowhere to be found.

He'd nearly given up a few times, but Stevie wouldn't let him, and it was one of the things he loved best about her. She knew what finding his daughter meant to him and she'd vowed that they'd

73

succeed, no matter how long it took. He hated having to tell her that he'd been unsuccessful yet again.

Stevie cuddled up against him, lightly running her fingers through the hair on his chest. 'What was that about?'

He put aside his disappointment at his most recent failure in California. 'It was Ford. A camera's gone "wonky" in the barn. I'll make sure Alec's fixed it before the kids start arriving in the morning.'

Clay had insisted on full camera coverage of the farm, for the safety of the kids as well as to legally protect Daphne and Healing Hearts. Kids who'd been abused and victimized often struck out, and sometimes they or their guardians even lied. He wanted the kids safe, but he also didn't want anyone accusing any staff members unjustly. It had already happened once, with one of the guardians making an accusation of inappropriate behavior by a staff member so that they could file a lawsuit. The suit had been quickly dropped when Clay had presented video proof to them and their attorneys. Daphne's lawyer had threatened a countersuit for defamation, but in the end they'd made it all go quietly away.

'Can't Ford fix it?' Stevie asked, her voice languid. Fully sated.

Which made Clay feel ten feet tall and bulletproof. He'd come straight home from Dillon's camping trip expecting nine-year-old Cordelia to meet him at the door with a huge hug, but what he'd found instead was Stevie in a little scrap of lace that had him losing his mind on the spot. Cordelia was having ice cream with her aunt Izzy, so he and Stevie had had the whole house to themselves and they'd taken full advantage of that fact. The first time had been up against the front door, and that little scrap of black lace was still on the foyer floor.

They needed to pick it up before Cordelia came home, but they had another hour or more. Izzy could make an ice-cream date last for hours, giving him and Stevie precious time alone, and for that Clay was profoundly grateful.

Their second time had been in their bed, and he'd taken his time. After a year and a half, he still wasn't sure which way he liked better, but he was pretty sure he wasn't going to be able to go for a third time to break the tie. Not in the next hour, anyway. The last few days had really wiped him out.

Ford was damn lucky he hadn't called a few minutes earlier or Clay wouldn't have been capable of intelligent thought, much less speech fit for public consumption. Especially to the son of his boss. Daphne was his friend first, but on matters of Healing Hearts, she was his boss and Clay never forgot that. They'd made a pact to keep the business separate from their friendship, and they'd been successful, even when they'd disagreed vehemently.

But Daphne was also a mama bear. Just like Stevie, who'd changed her whole life to protect Cordelia, leaving the Baltimore PD after years of service to become his partner in his private investigation business. Clay and Daphne had had only one major fight that had seriously threatened their friendship, and it had been about Ford. Clay wasn't going to let that happen again.

Unless the phone had rung when Clay had been deep inside Stevie, busy driving her to scream his name. He didn't think Daphne would fault him for impoliteness in that case.

'Don't know what Ford can or can't fix,' he said lazily. 'Don't particularly care.'

'Me either.' Stevie leaned up and kissed him on the mouth, so gently. 'Are you okay?'

He put on an aggrieved expression that was all show. 'Okay enough to make you scream twice in one afternoon.'

Her lips twitched, but her eyes were sober. 'You know what I mean, Clay. You haven't said a word about what happened in California. I need to know what's going on in here.' She tapped his chest. 'Don't shut me out.'

He closed his eyes on a sigh. 'I'm not. I promise.' He had to swallow hard against the emotion rising to clog his throat. 'It's just hard to say out loud, even to you. It's . . . Shit. Hell of a PI I am. I can't even find my own kid. It's like she vanished into thin air. I don't know where to look anymore.'

'Your dad called me when you got in from California,' Stevie said, in a serious tone that had him opening his eyes to stare up at her. 'He was worried about you.'

His father had hosted Dillon's bachelor party, taking the group out on his fishing boat to the campsite on one of the barrier islands along the Virginia coast and then loaning them his – thankfully air-conditioned – RV.

'Yeah, I know. I hate worrying him like that, but I was kind of low.'

'I got that.' Then she added quietly, 'You didn't call me.'

'I wanted to. But you were still with Cordy in Disney World and I didn't want to spoil your good time.' Clay had accompanied them the summer before and for a long weekend that spring, but this time he'd declined, his gut telling him that he needed to go to California. That something would have changed.

Something had changed, all right.

'Donna's aunt's house has been sold,' he murmured. 'She's dead and Sienna is . . . nowhere.' While she'd been alive, Donna had repeatedly ignored his pleas to see his daughter. Her aunt had been slightly kinder after Donna's death, but had continued to tell him that Sienna didn't want to see him. Now the aunt was dead, his last link to Sienna broken.

Hearing that his daughter didn't want to see him had broken his heart each time. Loving Stevie and Cordelia and them loving him in return had gotten him through.

'The college said Sienna never came back after Donna died. She's like . . . a ghost. No money trail, no credit card use. Nobody had seen her . . . There was nothing. I might have thought she'd died too, except that I couldn't find any death certificates or records of unclaimed bodies that met her description.'

Stevie laid her hand over his heart and rubbed gently, easing him. 'That's good at least.'

'Yeah.' He couldn't think about his daughter being dead. Not when he'd never known her. 'If I didn't know better, I'd think she never existed.' But he did know better, because he'd seen her. Once. She'd been six years old and playing in the schoolyard. Until she'd turned and seen his face. Then she'd run. Screaming in fear.

His baby had run from him. And that had been the last time he'd laid eyes on her. All because his ex-wife was a spiteful, evil, lying bitch, accusing him of a crime he'd never committed. And he couldn't even confront Donna about it, because she was dead. That he'd proven. He had the death certificate.

But there was no grave, no obituary. Nothing whatsoever he could use to lead him to his child. Who was now a woman. He'd lost her. Lost her entire childhood. The pain struck again, stabbing him so deep that nothing could heal it. He just had to ignore the pain and keep searching.

'I thought the same thing,' Stevie said. 'That it was like she'd never existed.' She drew a careful breath. 'So I did some digging while you were at the camping party.'

Clay sat up, bringing Stevie with him. 'Digging? What kind of digging?'

'The kind I would have gotten in trouble for when I worked for Baltimore PD,' she said dryly. 'I had an associate search the student records at the college Sienna attended.'

Clay's brows shot up. 'By "associate", you mean that Alec hacked into the college's files?'

She gave him a look. 'Do you want to know what he found or not?'

'Of course, but there was no reason to hack in. The college office gave me her transcripts. She attended for two semesters, then dropped out during her third to take care of Donna.'

'Which was odd in and of itself, right?' She tapped his chest thoughtfully. 'Do colleges normally just hand over transcripts without a pissing match?'

'Normally no,' he said warily, 'but the office secretary had some pity for my "client".' Which had been himself, of course, but he'd told the woman that he had a client who was searching for his child who'd been hidden by her mother. All perfectly true except for the name of the client.

'Which was kind of convenient,' Stevie said. 'Yes?'

'Yes,' he admitted. 'What did your "associate" find?'

'That there had been three Siennas who'd registered in the past fifteen years, but two are now in their thirties and the third is the right age but African-American. Not your daughter.'

Clay blinked at her, his heart pounding so hard that it was all he could hear. 'The college gave me a fake record.'

Stevie nodded, her eyes troubled. 'I believe so.'

Why? he wanted to scream. But he knew why. 'So I'd go away and stop asking questions. The college was a smokescreen.' He closed his eyes. 'Donna created a diversion. Sienna was never there.' He swallowed hard. 'Sienna doesn't want to be found, does she?'

'That was my take, yes. I'm sorry, Clay. I'm so damn sorry.'

'You think I should give up,' he whispered, his voice breaking.

'No, honey. I don't think that at all. You owe it to Sienna and to yourself to set the record straight. Donna poisoned her with lies about you for years. You deserve for her to hear your side. To know that you never forgot about her, that you sent her cards on her birthday and for Christmas every damn year, begging her for a few minutes of her time. Just so you could be sure she heard the truth at least once. You *deserve* those few minutes, Clay. I'm not going to stop until you've had them.'

'And – assuming we ever do find her – if she still hates me? What then?'

'I'll want to slap her face, but I won't. She's still your child and she's been victimized too. Lied to, manipulated . . . All because her mother told a lie that grew until she couldn't control it. But if you don't find her, you'll always wonder what might have been if she had listened. If she had believed you. Like I said, you deserve that chance, Clay.'

'I don't even know where to start anymore. Hell, I can't believe I didn't check out the transcript,' he added glumly. 'But why would the college give me a fake? Why would they lie for Donna?'

'I wondered that too. The woman you spoke with? The clerk in the office? She lives next door to Donna's aunt. I found photos on the clerk's FB page of the two women together. They were best friends for years.'

I was played. For all this time. He cleared his throat. 'That clerk got me good and I never suspected a fucking thing,' he said roughly. 'I've been chasing shadows.'

'You're too close to the case. You're a father searching for his child. I'm not as close, so I'm seeing things a little differently. Don't worry, we'll figure it out. Together.'

He swallowed hard again. 'I don't deserve you.'

She kissed his jaw. 'Too bad. You're stuck with me for the duration. I love you.'

His heart rattled hard in his chest, just like it did every time he heard her say the words. 'I love you too. Thank you for sticking with me through all this.'

She smiled at him and he could breathe again. 'We'll find her eventually. She can't hide forever.' She glanced pointedly at the clock on the nightstand. 'We have fifty minutes until Izzy brings Cordelia home.'

He shook his head ruefully. 'The spirit's willing, babe, but the flesh just ain't cooperating.'

She slid from their bed, grabbing her cane from where it leaned against the nightstand. The glitter covering the cane's surface, lovingly applied by Cordelia, sparkled in the sunlight streaming through the bedroom window. Stevie had needed the cane ever since being shot in the line of duty – a critical injury that had almost taken her away from him forever. Her dependence on the cane irritated her, but every time it sparkled he was almost painfully grateful. It was a shiny reminder that she'd lived.

She waggled her brows, giving his groin an exaggerated leer. 'Because I worked that flesh right down to the *bone*.'

He groaned at her pun. 'Really, Stevie? Really?'

She laughed. 'Couldn't resist it,' she said. 'Seriously, I was thinking of a bath. It's been a while since we've done that,' she said, tugging on his hand. 'Turn off your brain and let me take care of you. Finding Sienna can wait another hour.'

Baltimore, Maryland,
Saturday 22 August, 4.00 P.M.

JD dropped his duffel bag on the laundry-room floor, then unzipped it, wincing at the rank locker-room smell of his dirty clothes. Well, he had been on a camping trip for several days. In August. God, he wished that Holly and Dillon had picked a cooler time of year to get married. But Dillon was one of them, a friend, and when he'd asked for the camping trip in lieu of a raunchy bachelor night, they'd all agreed.

JD threw the clothes in the washer and added the extra-powerful odor-killing detergent that Lucy bought for the clothing he wore when investigating particularly grisly, smelly homicide scenes. He started the cycle, then went through the kitchen into the family room, where he stopped in the doorway and took a moment to simply look.

His wife of three years sat in her overstuffed chair, nursing their two-month-old daughter, while their eighteen-month-old son built a tower with soft blocks, his brow crunched in concentration as he positioned the top block with the utmost precision. Jeremiah was turning out to be a perfectionist. *Just like his mama*, JD thought, his chest tight.

He was just so damn happy to be home. He must have made a sound because Lucy looked up, her smile blooming bright. 'There you are.'

'Daddy!' Jeremiah popped to his feet and ran to greet him, arms outstretched. 'Up.'

JD obliged, scooping the boy up and planting a noisy kiss on his soft cheek, the sound of his son's giggles making him grin. He settled Jeremiah on his hip and crossed the room to Lucy, who turned her face up for a kiss. JD made it a good one, and her hum of pleasure made him ridiculously proud.

'We missed you,' she murmured against his lips.

'Not half as much as I missed you.'

Her mouth curved. 'You just missed the air conditioning.'

He chuckled. 'That too.' He leaned down further to brush a kiss on the baby's wispy-soft hair, the color of a sunrise. *Just like her mama*. 'How's my Wynnie?' he said softly, because Bronwynne had fallen asleep against Lucy's breast, her little belly full.

'Slept through the night last night,' Lucy said with a weary grin.

'Overachiever,' he teased. It had taken Jeremiah months more to sleep through the night. 'You want me to put her in her crib?'

'Please,' she said gratefully. 'I've been up and down those stairs fifty times today.'

JD blew a raspberry on Jeremiah's belly and gently lowered him to the floor. 'Build me a really tall tower, okay? I'm going to tuck Wynnie in.'

Lucy handed the baby up to him. 'Are you free for the rest of the night?'

He held his daughter close, rocking side to side where he stood. 'Unless something comes up. I have to make a phone call to Joseph, but after that I'm free. Why?'

Lucy lifted her brows. 'Because I have a babysitter for a few hours. Gwyn's picking up both kids and taking them to her place.'

Oh yeah, JD thought, instantly alert. Instantly horny. He'd only been gone a few days, but Lucy had only been cleared for sex by her doctor two weeks before that. JD had a lot of need stored up.

'Dog?' Jeremiah asked hopefully.

'Yes, you can play with Aunt Gwyn's dog,' Lucy told him, then met JD's eyes, hers growing dark with desire. 'I thought we could stay in. Should I call her to come over and pick them up?'

'Hel— heck, yes.' JD corrected himself at the last moment. 'Let me put Wynnie down for her nap and I'll make that call. Then I need a shower. I was in the morgue.'

'How is Neil?' Lucy asked affectionately. She'd become friends with Dr Quartermaine, who'd replaced her when she went on indefinite childcare leave.

JD remembered the weary look in the man's eyes. 'Tired. I think he needs a vacation. But he says hi. I'll be back in a bit.'

He took the stairs carefully and settled Wynnie in her crib. Making sure the baby monitor was turned on, he placed a careful kiss on her temple and backed out of the room, dialing Joseph.

'Hey, JD.' His boss sounded . . . rested. It made JD smirk. They'd both been away from home too many days. 'Is everything okay?'

JD switched mental gears from daddy to detective, focusing on the Jarvis case. 'It's fine. Maybe better than fine. Jazzie's aunt called me this afternoon. She said that Jazzie spoke during her session at the farm today. Seems to have taken a shine to the new intern.'

'Taylor Dawson?' Joseph asked, sounding mildly surprised. 'What did Jazzie say?'

'Just "thank you", but then she broke down in Taylor's arms and cried. They apparently bonded because Taylor recently lost her mother. The aunt is ecstatic, calling it a breakthrough.'

'She said two words,' Joseph said doubtfully. '"Thank you" isn't exactly baring her soul.'

'It's more than we had this morning. Jazzie's aunt – Lilah Cornell – was wondering if we could set up a safe place for Jazzie to meet with Taylor, away from all the adults, because she feels like they've been hovering. I was thinking Giuseppe's tomorrow afternoon. If we can get the private room, we can observe without Jazzie knowing we're there.' The restaurant had a room that was wired with cameras and mikes. 'Miss Cornell will be there as Jazzie's guardian. Maybe the girl will feel more comfortable talking with Taylor outside of the structured therapy. Taylor might be able to get Jazzie to tell her what she saw.'

Joseph sighed. 'That's a lot of pressure for an intern who's only been at the farm for a few weeks.'

JD heard a woman murmuring in the background, instantly recognizing Daphne's twang. Joseph said something back, his hand over the phone so that the words were muted, but his tone came through. Joseph Carter was a brooding, often intimidating man except when he was with his wife. Daphne softened his edges. *As Lucy does mine.*

'I'm putting you on speaker,' Joseph finally said.

'Hey, JD,' Daphne said, her voice carrying her smile. 'I think Taylor is truly gifted. She has an empathy and connection with the kids that few of our interns have shown. I just told Joseph that you should give it a try. As long as you can guarantee their safety.'

'At Giuseppe's we can,' Joseph said. 'And it won't scare the girl like coming into the police station would. I'll get it set up and text you the information, JD.'

'And I'll talk to Maggie about it,' Daphne added. 'She can ask Taylor if she's willing.'

'I already called Maggie,' JD said. He'd done so immediately after ending his call with Lilah Cornell. 'She's going to ask Taylor this afternoon.'

'Taylor will be happy to do it, if I'm any judge of character,' Daphne assured him.

'And you always are,' JD said with a smile of his own. Daphne Montgomery-Carter was one of his very favorite people. She had a knack for seeing what others tried to hide, a valuable skill for a prosecuting attorney. 'I do have one other thing to discuss with you, Joseph. It affects you too, Daphne. Denny Jarvis and his wife, Missy.'

'Our most probable leaks.' Joseph's voice held an edge.

At this point it was the only theory that made sense. Missy Jarvis worked in Daphne's office and had access to all the police reports – anything that went into the database, even if it was preliminary. That was where JD had noted that Gage was a suspect, after which an alibi was conveniently produced, and also where JD had noted that he'd had doubts about that alibi, after which Toby Romano was framed. It was more likely that Denny was involved than Missy, but the access would be hers.

Daphne sighed. 'I hope Missy is an unwitting participant in this mess. She's been our office clerk for two years now and she's really good at her job. We all like her.'

'I hope so too, for your sake and hers.' JD fidgeted, not sure if what he was about to propose was a good idea or not. 'If killing Toby Romano was intended to throw us off the scent, why don't we let his killer believe he's succeeded?'

'You mean plant a notation that the case is closed and Gage Jarvis is no longer a suspect?' Joseph asked.

'Exactly. We've kept everything important out of that database since we realized something was wrong.'

Joseph was quiet for a moment. 'If we do that, we need to make it worth our while from an evidentiary standpoint. Without Jazzie's statement, we have nothing more than circumstantial evidence against Denny and Missy.'

'Not nearly enough for a warrant, either to search their house or to tap their phones,' JD grumbled. 'Believe me, I've tried.' Because Denny was a defense attorney, it was really difficult to get any judge to agree to a wiretap.

'I know,' Joseph said. 'But we *can* put a tracer on the database itself because it's property of the state. We can track anyone who logs in and note if they're logging in from the office or remotely from home.'

'But . . .' Daphne paused, troubled. 'We won't know if it was Missy, Denny, or both.'

'I'll have plainclothes officers tail both of them,' Joseph said. 'If only Denny is involved, he's found some way to get Missy's password information. If it were me, I'd wait until my wife was out of the house before I took a chance in checking the database. Hopefully Denny is that careful. I'll make that happen, JD. Let me know what Taylor Dawson says about meeting Jazzie as soon as you hear from her.'

'Will do.' They hung up and JD started for the shower, but snuck one last look at Bronwynne in her crib. He loved her so much that sometimes he didn't think his chest could contain it. He'd never understood how parents could hurt their own children. Now that he was a father, he didn't even try to understand. He simply did his damnedest to make sure that the parents were punished and that the children were safe. The emotional debris he had to leave to the counselors and therapists.

He pulled the baby's door closed and sent up a prayer that Taylor Dawson was as good as Daphne thought she was. Jazzie Jarvis's life depended on it.

Six

Taylor got a bottle of water and sat in the chair on the other side of Maggie's desk. Maggie had swung her boots back to the floor and was scanning the contents of a manila file folder. 'Is everything okay?' Taylor asked cautiously, her worry over her scuffle with Ford shoved down to accommodate the bigger fear.

Does she know? No, she can't know. Joseph Carter couldn't find any holes in my background. Nobody knows.

Maggie looked up from the file, her eyes kind, and Taylor's gut relaxed a fraction. 'You're doing great. Actually, that's why I called you in here.' Maggie closed the file and slid it back into her drawer. 'You made a connection with Jazzie Jarvis today. I'd like you to spend some more time with her.'

Relief shuddered through her. Jazzie was a *much* better topic for discussion. 'I'd like to try again to get her to ride.'

Maggie shook her head. 'No. She's afraid of the horses. We won't force her to ride.'

'All right,' Taylor said slowly when Maggie said no more, simply watching her. *All right. How else can I spend more time with an eleven-year-old?* 'I suppose I could take her out for a soda or something. If that's okay.'

Maggie smiled. 'How do you feel about ice cream?'

Taylor's gut relaxed a little more. 'Very favorably. We can grab a cone near her house.'

'Good. Her aunt says that Jazzie's got a sweet tooth and ice

85

cream's the only thing she's really responded to since her mother's death.'

'Then that's a plan.' Taylor decided to take a chance. 'But if I'm going to spend more time with her, I need to know everything. Even stuff that's not in the file you just put away.'

Maggie's brows lifted. 'That wasn't Jazzie's file. That was yours.'

Taylor did a double-take, her mouth falling open. 'Mine? Why?'

'Because I figured you'd want to know more about Jazzie and I wanted to be very sure before I told you.'

Sure of what? Taylor had to shove her annoyance down. She'd passed the damn background check, for God's sake. What more did Maggie VanDorn want?

You mean the background check built on a mountain of lies? the little voice in her mind asked. *Really, Taylor?*

Dammit. She hated that voice. It was so smug. And irritatingly astute.

'You mean the fact that she's afraid of men?' Taylor asked out loud, proud that her voice remained calm. 'Ford told me. He suggested that Jazzie might have been molested.'

'Yes, Ford mentioned that he'd spilled that bucket of beans. But he doesn't know the whole story. What I'm about to tell you is not in Jazzie's official file. It was kept out on purpose – to keep her safe and alive.'

Taylor frowned. Safe and alive? *What the hell . . . ?* 'I don't understand.'

'The facts that Detective Fitzpatrick shared with us for Jazzie's official file were not entirely complete.'

'You mean he lied,' Taylor said flatly.

A shrug. 'Potato, po-tah-to.' Maggie watched her carefully. 'Should I trust you enough to continue?'

Taylor's temper bubbled up. 'You mean am I going to run out and publicize this situation for my own gain? No. If you have any doubts about me, don't tell me any secrets. If you honestly believe I could do that, then fire me. But I *can* keep a secret.'

Maggie's gaze locked onto hers. 'I'm sure that's very true,' she murmured.

A shiver of apprehension ran down Taylor's back. She struggled to think of something to say, but Maggie moved briskly forward. 'So, back to Jazzie. The official report says that Lilah Cornell found her sister, Valerie, and that the children were with Lilah when the police arrived, implying that the girls had also been with her when she discovered the body.'

Implying? Oh no. Horrified, Taylor's temper abruptly fizzled. 'But they weren't with her? The girls were alone when they found her?'

Maggie sighed. 'Specifically Jazzie. She's eleven and had come home from day camp by herself. Her grandmother was normally there to greet her, but got tied up in traffic doing errands. Jazzie let herself in and . . .'

'Oh my God,' Taylor whispered, able to visualize the scene – and Jazzie's horror.

Maggie sighed again. 'Lilah got a call from Janie's preschool a few hours later, when Valerie failed to pick her up. That had apparently happened a few times, when the girls' mother got delayed at work and lost track of time. Lilah was the emergency contact. She picked up Janie, brought her home, and discovered Valerie on the floor, beaten to death. Lilah fell to pieces when she found her sister's body, but quickly pulled herself together when she realized that Janie was standing there in shock, seeing everything. And then Lilah realized that Jazzie should have been home already. She said she heard a noise, a whimpering "like a wounded animal", coming from behind a chair. That was where she found Jazzie, rocking herself and keening. Also in shock.'

'That poor little girl,' Taylor murmured. 'Both of them.'

'I know. Nobody knows what Jazzie did or didn't see, because she won't talk. But based on the video taken by the lobby's security cameras, she arrived within minutes of the murder. The video shows the mother entering the lobby about an hour before her death, a man with a hoodie following her a minute or two later. Jazzie entered about thirty minutes after that, and then a man wearing a hoodie was filmed leaving.'

'So he may have still been in the apartment when Jazzie came home.'

'Yes. The police found that someone had washed up in the kitchen, but all the blood they found belongs to the mother. The man didn't leave anything that could identify him.'

'Unless Jazzie saw him while she was hiding behind the chair.'

'Exactly.'

Taylor suppressed a shudder. 'Did their mother come home that time of day regularly?'

'That's a good question. Apparently she did not, but had taken some time off to see Jazzie's work at the day camp's art fair. According to Fitzpatrick, she'd made no unusual calls that day, nor had she received any. Nobody saw her talking to anyone different.'

'Suspects?'

'I think the first in line is Valerie's ex-husband, Gage. He left her three years ago and hasn't been seen since. He's a known addict who'd been accused of assaulting Valerie. Apparently, however, he was in Texas at the time of the murder. He's got a decent alibi, according to Detective Fitzpatrick. Someone who saw him that afternoon.'

Alibis could be falsified, just like birth records, Taylor thought, but she wasn't about to say that out loud. 'Do the cops have any leads at all?'

'Not that they're sharing. But they want to find out what Jazzie saw, if anything. Lilah called Fitzpatrick today and told him that Jazzie had made an emotional connection with you. He wants you to have ice cream with her in a secure location. He wants to know if she can identify her mother's killer.'

Taylor grew cold as the importance of this ice-cream date hit her squarely. 'I'm not sure about this. I'm not a licensed anything yet. I'm a recent college graduate with a degree in psychology. The police must have counselors. What if I fu— I mean, mess this up?'

'BPD does have counselors, and both Jazzie and Janie will continue to see them. But Jazzie hasn't connected with them. In the meantime, Lilah's a nervous wreck, wondering if the killer's going to figure out that Jazzie was behind that chair.'

'How?' Taylor asked. 'How would anyone know if it's not in the police report?'

'Because Janie was there when Lilah found Jazzie hiding.'

'Oh God. That's why Jazzie sticks by her so closely. She can't let Janie tell.' That explained the misery in Jazzie's eyes as she watched her sister. 'She wants Janie to get better, but is afraid to let her speak freely.'

'That's my take.'

Shit. Taylor wanted to run away. She hadn't signed up for this. She'd come here to get the truth about Clay Maynard. 'But what if Jazzie didn't see anything? Lilah will be a nervous wreck forever because no one can definitely prove that Jazzie knows nothing.'

Maggie just looked at her, not saying a word.

Taylor sighed. 'You believe she did see something. Why?'

Maggie shrugged. 'My gut. I've been dealing with child victims for a long, long time. Jazzie knows something that she's not telling. Look, you don't have to do this if you don't want to. It's not part of your job description.'

Taylor thought of poor Jazzie and the nightmare the child had endured. A real nightmare, not the manufactured one Taylor had been put through. The effect was the same, though. A child with fear in her eyes.

And Lilah's in the same place Dad was all those years. Never taking her eyes off her child, never allowing Jazzie to go to a sleepover, fearing the day a predator would come and snatch her away. Changing her whole life around to protect Jazzie. Exactly as Frederick Dawson had done. *For me*.

Taylor owed her father so much. But the real tragedy was that neither Taylor nor Frederick Dawson had needed to endure any of it. The threat had been a total fabrication. *Thanks, Mom*.

Jazzie's trauma, though, was very real, the risk to her life a tangible one.

Taylor sucked in a deep breath. 'I'll do it. Just tell me where and when.'

Maggie smiled at her. 'Thank you. Fitzpatrick wants to do this at an Italian restaurant whose owner is a friend of Joseph's.'

Taylor frowned, confused. 'I thought we were going for ice cream.'

'The restaurant has ice cream on its menu. More importantly, it has a private room with only one door. Fitzpatrick can't protect you at the ice cream place, but at the restaurant you'll have protection at all times. He will be guarding the door, of course. And I'll have one of our people there too.' Maggie hesitated a single heartbeat. 'Clay Maynard, our security manager. I don't think you've met him yet.'

Taylor's heart sank. Maggie's hesitation shouted volumes. *She knows who I am. Why I'm here.* Taylor's gut was pretty good, too, and everything within her said that her jig was now up. But *how* did Maggie know?

Luckily Taylor knew how to maintain a poker face. 'No, I haven't, but I've heard nice things about him from Dillon.'

The tension in Maggie's body visibly eased, and Taylor understood. *Because I told the truth. She knew I talked to Dillon. She knew I asked about Clay.*

Taylor let out a long, quiet breath. *Busted.* 'Were you spying on me, Maggie?'

'Yes.' The answer was direct. Unapologetic. 'The barn is wired for both audio and video. I see and hear all.' She pointed to the monitor on her desk. 'My own eye in the sky.'

Dammit. Taylor had forgotten all about the fucking cameras. *Just . . . goddammit.* She lifted her chin. 'I never lied to you about anything. Taylor Dawson is my name.'

Maggie's head tilted slightly to one side, studying her. 'You have his eyes, Taylor. I saw it the first time I looked at the photo you attached to your application. I knew before I had Joseph interview you. I expected Joseph's background check to turn up something . . . inconsistent.'

Maggie had brought her here knowing? Or at least suspecting? That blew Taylor's mind. 'But it didn't turn up anything *inconsistent*. Because I *am* Taylor Dawson.'

Maggie swallowed hard. 'I don't understand.'

'I don't either,' Taylor admitted. 'Not fully.'

Maggie sighed quietly. 'Just . . . don't hurt him. I don't know why you're here, but please don't hurt him. He's been through enough.'

Taylor's simmering temper blew. 'Well, goddammit, so have I!' she snapped, and Maggie flinched. 'I'm sorry,' Taylor said quickly. 'I didn't mean to shout. I don't plan to hurt him. I don't plan to hurt anyone. I only wanted to meet him.'

'Why now?'

Taylor shook her head, unwilling to go there. Not until she'd seen him. 'I came here to meet him,' she repeated firmly. 'With no expectations. No risks. Can you respect that?'

Maggie said nothing for a long, long moment. 'For now. Please don't put this off, though. I can bring him over here tonight.'

'Jumping into a cold pool,' Taylor whispered.

'Usually the best way,' Maggie said wisely.

'All right.' Taylor nodded hard once. 'Fine. Bring him over. But please, don't tell him why. I don't want him to be disappointed.'

Maggie's brow bunched in bewilderment. 'I don't understand, Taylor. How could he possibly be disappointed? He's looked for you for your whole life.'

Taylor shook her head. 'I don't want to talk to anyone about this. Not until I've met him. I wanted to observe him. Safely. But I can't do that now.'

Comprehension dawned in Maggie's eyes. 'You wanted to be able to walk away. To disappear from his life with no trace. *Again.*'

Taylor ignored the pointed accusation in the older woman's voice. 'I still want that. And I will disappear if I feel I must.' But not without a trace. Not this time. *Dammit*. Her father had been right. Coming here had been foolish. *Unless Clay really is a good man.* 'However, I feel compelled to point out that your use of "again" is unfair. I didn't make myself disappear the first time. I was just a child. My mother "disappeared" me.'

A curt nod. 'True. I apologize for that.'

'Accepted.' Taylor drew a breath, let it out. 'I will talk to Jazzie before I disappear, if and when I decide to do so. I promise. And I don't break my promises.'

'Then I'll arrange for you to meet with her tomorrow afternoon, after all the therapy sessions are complete.'

Effectively dismissed, Taylor stood up. 'Are there cameras in my bedroom?'

Maggie's eyes flashed in annoyance. 'Certainly not.'

'Thank you. I'm going to call my father in California. I promised to check in with him, and I'm overdue. I'd like privacy.'

'Your room is private. Does that satisfy you, or should I bring in a sniffer to check for bugs to prove it to you?'

She let Maggie's sarcasm roll off her back, keeping a firm hold on her dignity. 'No, your word is sufficient. I'll see you at dinner.' Then, head high, she left the office without another word.

As soon as she was alone in the barn, her knees buckled. She grabbed a barn post and held on, willing her legs to hold her up. Her stomach was roiling, her head pounding.

This is what you came for. You came to meet him. But not like this. Not just . . . thrust together. She'd wanted to do it safely. *So you could tuck and run if you got scared.*

Yeah, that was pretty much it. But from everything she'd heard, Clay deserved better. *Maybe I do, too.* In the meantime, she needed to shore up her courage. And to update her dad.

Steeling her spine, she marched herself toward the farmhouse so that she could call the only father she'd ever known.

Hunt Valley, Maryland,
Saturday 22 August, 4.20 P.M.

Sitting at the kitchen table, Ford closed his laptop when Taylor came through the door, hiding the browser window with the barn's camera feeds. He'd watched her as she'd emerged from talking to Maggie, wanting to see her expression after their conversation.

He'd gone into the office earlier to confess to having told too much of Jazzie's story to Taylor, only to find that he'd misread the situation. The woman who'd been like a grandmother to him his whole life had quickly set his assumptions straight, telling him that JD believed Jazzie was afraid of men because she may have witnessed her mother's killer leaving their apartment, although she hadn't admitted to seeing a thing. *Poor kid.* That was a helluva burden for anyone to carry, much less an eleven-year-old.

Ford figured Maggie had wanted to see Taylor so that she could share the same information, but after hearing Taylor's conversation with Dillon, he wasn't sure she could be trusted with it. But there hadn't been time to tell Maggie about that, nor did he want to admit to having lurked in the shadows to eavesdrop. That made him sound like a creeper.

And maybe he was a creeper, because he'd watched Taylor again, this time with the camera that he'd told Clay was 'wonky'. He'd hoped her expression would be sad, even devastated, for what poor Jazzie had endured. He hoped he wouldn't see the gleam of a reporter who'd latched on to a choice story.

But he hadn't been prepared for the expression he'd actually seen on her face as she'd come through the office door. She'd looked stoic, her chin held high, until the door was closed, but then she'd crumpled, going glassy-eyed and pale. Holding on to one of the posts like it was the only thing keeping her vertical. Shaking like a leaf, she looked like she was about to throw up.

Christ, he hoped Maggie hadn't fired her. He couldn't think why, unless his slip of the tongue about Jazzie's fear of men had made Taylor a risk because she knew too much. He hadn't mentioned the punch Taylor had thrown in the lounge. Maggie might have seen it on one of the cameras, but she hadn't mentioned it.

Shit. He didn't want Taylor to be fired. For far too many reasons.

He didn't entirely trust her, but she intrigued him.

And then he'd watched her compose herself, her spine going straight, her expression smoothing to one of casual indifference. If he hadn't just seen her quaking with fear, he might have never suspected she was even capable of the emotion.

'Hi, Taylor,' he said as she carefully shut the door behind her.

She jumped, pressing her hand to her heart. 'I didn't know you were there.'

'Are you okay? You look a little green around the gills.' Hell, she looked whiter than bone china. 'Sometimes the heat can kick you in the ass if you're not used to it.' He got a bottle of cold water from the fridge and put it in her hand, curling her fingers around it when she didn't immediately take it. 'You need to sit down. You're scaring me.'

That was no lie.

She nodded numbly, not even protesting when he led her to a chair and gently pushed her into it. She sat staring at the bottle in her hand like it was some alien drink, so he wet a paper towel with cold water, wrung it out, and draped it over the back of her neck.

'Just sit for a minute,' he said. 'It'll pass.'

A slow, quiet sigh. 'No. It won't. But thank you.'

Ford said nothing for a long minute. 'Look, you don't know me from Adam, but I'm a good listener. I promise I won't judge like I did before.' When he'd assumed her reluctance to attend Dillon and Holly's wedding was because of their disability. 'I'm sorry for that.'

'It's okay,' she murmured. 'I might have thought the same thing under the circumstances. You were protecting the people you love. I get that.'

She said nothing more and, too full of nervous energy, Ford found he had to fill the silence. 'I heard you were from California,' he said sociably as he rummaged in the pantry for some saltine crackers.

'Who told you that?' she asked, her voice still too quiet. He wished she'd yell at him like she had that morning. He wanted to see the fire back in those dark eyes of hers.

He put a few crackers on a plate and slid them in front of her. 'My mom. You still look green. Putting something in your stomach might help. What part of California? LA?'

Taylor took a cracker and nibbled on the corner. 'No. The northern part. We're east of Eureka. Up towards Oregon.'

'You must know horses to have gotten the intern position. Do you ride at home?'

A glimmer of a smile. 'Yes. We have a ranch, a small one. About a thousand head of cattle. We all ride.'

'Even your sister Julie?'

'You remembered.' She held her cracker up in a mock salute. 'Points for that. Yes, Julie rides too, but with special equipment.'

Some of the color had returned to her cheeks and her breathing was less shallow, so Ford squashed his million questions and let her talk. 'I was interested in the Healing Hearts program for a lot of reasons, but one of them was to start a similar program at home. Julie learned to ride as part of her physical therapy, but I hadn't thought about the emotional therapeutic benefits of riding.'

Ford took a risk. 'I always loved to ride before . . . well, before I was . . .'

Her eyes lifted, meeting his for the first time since she'd come into the kitchen, and it was like a kick to the gut. There was understanding there. And compassion. And possibly something more. Maybe respect? He hoped so.

'Before your abduction,' she supplied without pity. 'I read about it. Pieces, anyway.'

'Yeah, well.' He forced himself to continue, because she was waiting patiently. 'Before my abduction I was a competitive rider. A jumper.'

The glimmer of a smile broadened, finally reaching her eyes. 'I do barrel racing. Never mastered jumping, though.'

Something within him stirred. The slim body with the subtle curves did barrel racing? *That* he'd like to see. He'd like to see a lot more, but he couldn't let himself think about that or he'd wind up with an embarrassing bulge in his jeans, and he didn't want her to get the wrong idea.

What, that you think she's hot? Well, she is. And she has to know it.

But Ford wasn't entirely sure that last part was true. Taylor had never been away from home without a family member. She'd been scared to come here. Yet she had.

Because she has questions about Clay. Ford needed to keep that front and center of his mind until he knew exactly why she was here. And because he hoped she'd 'quid pro quo' him with info about herself, he continued with the sharing.

'Well, after the abduction I stopped competing. My heart just wasn't in it. But I still ride. Just now . . . well, now, it's different. I always loved my horse before, but after the abduction he became . . .' He trailed off, losing his train of thought because her

95

eyes had grown soft and he couldn't look away if he'd wanted to. But he didn't want to.

'A haven,' she finished softly.

'Yes. You too?'

Her head dipped in a single nod. 'How did you know?'

'The way you talked about Jazzie being afraid that her mother's killer was lurking behind a tree, waiting to jump out. It sounded like you spoke from experience.'

'I did. But if it's okay, I really don't want to talk about it.'

He spread his palms on the table, fingers flexed wide. 'Up to you. Just remember that I am a good listener.'

Another smile, this one grateful. 'I'll bet you are. Maybe someday I'll take you—'

She was interrupted by the door opening. Maggie kicked off her boots, then gave the plate of saltine crackers an appraising look. 'You okay, honey?' she asked Taylor kindly.

Taylor nodded, her throat working hard. No words came out, even though she looked like she was trying to speak. Her skin had lost a little of the color she'd just gotten back, but she didn't look away, keeping her chin high.

'Good.' Maggie looked up at the clock on the wall. 'He'll be here in half an hour.'

Taylor's face went bone white once again. Carefully she pushed herself to her feet, trembling from head to toe. 'I'll be back down in thirty minutes, then.'

Ford wanted to rush to her side, to help her up the stairs, but she had a desperation about her, like an animal caught in a trap. He didn't think she'd welcome his help, so he stayed where he was and felt miserable about it.

He and Maggie waited silently until they heard a door close upstairs. Then Maggie leaned against the fridge, resting her forehead against the freezer door. 'God almighty.'

'Who's coming, Maggie?' Ford asked, even though he already knew.

She turned to look at him, studying his face. 'Clay.' She tilted her head. 'You knew.'

'I guessed. She's Sienna, isn't she?'

'I don't know, Ford. She insists her name is Taylor Dawson. What I do know is that she has been through some kind of hell. I don't know what, though.'

'She was afraid, as a kid.' He told her what she'd said about Jazzie. 'She just confirmed it with me, but said she didn't want to talk about it, which I get. I don't like to talk about what happened to me, either.'

Maggie sat in the chair beside him, concern lining her face. 'Are *you* okay, Ford? I don't ask you that often enough.'

He covered her hand and squeezed gently. 'You ask me that plenty. And I am fine. I'm not the same and probably never will be.' Not since he'd been kidnapped and held, not for ransom, but to lure his mother into a trap. His kidnapper had planned to kill her. Ford would be forever grateful to Joseph Carter for stopping that from happening. 'I wonder what Taylor's mother told her about Clay.'

Maggie's sigh was weary. 'I've been wondering the same thing. I hated putting that look in her eyes. But I also hate the look in Clay's eyes every time he thinks about her.'

'And every time he comes back from California without having found her,' Ford added. 'Did you tell him why he was coming out here?'

'No. I didn't know how.'

'Me either. I tried to get him here by making up a lie about the camera in the barn being broken.'

Maggie laughed unsteadily. 'I wondered about that. He asked if it was related to the broken camera. I didn't say yes, but I didn't say no. I just asked him to come out. He said he would, but that he'd have to bring Stevie and Cordelia. They promised Cordy pizza at her favorite place.'

'I'm glad they're coming with him. He might need them.'

Hunt Valley, Maryland,
Saturday 22 August, 4.35 P.M.

Taylor gripped her phone so tightly that it hurt her hand, waiting for her father to pick up. After a few rings, he did, and her pulse pounded harder.

'Hey, baby,' he said in that quiet way of his. Frederick Dawson was a level kind of man, but anyone who considered him weak was quickly re-educated. He was like a deep lake that hid an underwater river with a killer current. Strong and silent and . . . always there. Always vigilant. And always prepared to do whatever was necessary to keep her safe. 'Are you okay?'

A hysterical laugh bubbled up, but it came out a sob. 'Yeah, I'm okay.'

'No,' he said, tensing up. 'You're crying. What did they do to you?'

'Nothing. Nothing. They've been super-nice. It's just . . . I'm meeting him. Tonight.'

A long, long silence. 'You told them?' he asked carefully. 'I thought we agreed you'd at least wait until after you'd met him. After *I'd* come out there and met him.'

After Clay had proven himself trustworthy was left unspoken, but her father didn't need to say the words. He'd said them too many times as they argued about her accepting the internship.

'I didn't tell them. Maggie VanDorn knew.'

'How? That background check held up, didn't it?'

'Of course it did. I wouldn't have made it this far if it hadn't. Apparently I have his eyes. And . . . Maggie overheard me talking to one of the stable hands here. Dillon's a nice guy and he told me about Clay. I asked a few too many questions and I guess Maggie's initial suspicions were confirmed.'

'You need to come home, baby.' The fear in his voice was plain as day. 'Now. I don't care how much the plane ticket costs. Just come home.'

Taylor shook her head, forgetting for a moment that her father couldn't see her. 'You know I love you, Dad,' she said. And it was true. Frederick Dawson had been the only father she'd ever known. The sacrifices he'd made for her safety . . . The knowledge still choked her up. But Taylor also knew that he was afraid he'd lose her, that once she met Clay she'd forget her home. That she'd forget him. But nothing could be farther from the truth.

'I know. I love you too.' His voice cracked. 'Come home. Please. Just come home.'

'Daddy, listen. Please listen. I am so grateful for everything you've done for me. Every hug and every time you treated me like one of your own daughters.'

'You *are* my own daughter,' he insisted.

'Of course I am. And I always will be. You'll always be my dad. But Daddy, *Mom lied*. She lied about Clay. He's been looking for me for years. *Years*, Dad.'

Silence.

'Daddy? Are you still there?'

'Yeah. I'm . . . I still can't process any of this.'

Meaning the fact that her mother – his wife – had lied for their entire marriage about her 'dangerous ex-husband' who'd abused her and whom she'd fled out of desperation. Who'd stop at nothing to kill her and take her daughter away.

His wife, who'd let the lie go on, spiraling out of control. Allowing him to completely sacrifice his old life, giving up his successful law career in Oakland for that of a rancher in the middle of nowhere in Northern California. Allowing him to sacrifice his own daughters.

'I know, Dad. I'm so sorry.'

'It's not your fault,' he said fiercely. 'You didn't do anything wrong.'

'I don't think Clay did either,' she said as gently as she could. 'He was out there looking for me just last week.' She sighed, trying to find the words to reassure him. 'According to Dillon, he's got a family now, complete with a little girl.'

'He got married again? I thought you checked for that.'

'I did, although I only searched the local courthouse records. Maybe they got married somewhere else. But the important thing is that his new wife has a child from a previous marriage, a little girl whose dad died. The girl is part of the program here, but I haven't met her yet. Apparently she was threatened by a man with a gun and she still has nightmares about him.'

'God. Poor thing.'

'I know. Dad, Dillon told me that Cordelia doesn't tell her mom about the nightmares because she doesn't want to upset her, but she trusts Clay with them. Just like I trusted you with mine.'

Another long silence was followed by a huge sigh. 'I wish I could be there when you confront him.'

'I wish you could, too. But I'm trying not to think about it being a confrontation.' She was trying, but it really wasn't working. She wished she'd grabbed the saltine crackers before coming upstairs. That had been so thoughtful of Ford.

Whose experiences also sounded sadly familiar to her own. *And now you're stalling.*

She forced her thoughts back to meeting Clay, trying to picture herself as a rational adult, not a terrified child. 'I'd like to think of it as getting rid of my nightmares.'

'And then you'll come home?'

'Then I'll finish out this internship.' She understood now why Maggie had hooked her into helping Jazzie – so that she'd feel obligated to stay whichever way things went between her and Clay Maynard. Maggie was a clever woman. Taylor would do well to remember that.

'And *then* you'll come home?' he pressed.

Taylor smiled into the phone. 'And then I'll come home. For at least a while. Daddy, I want to see stuff. See the world. I've been so afraid for so long, but I don't want to be. I don't want you to be afraid for me. I want you to have a life too, especially now that Mom's gone. I don't want you to be lonely.'

More silence, then a shuddered sigh. He'd been crying. Her strong, quiet, loyal father had been crying and Taylor had to blink back her own tears.

'I know you need to spread your wings.' A sad little chuff. 'I just hoped you'd spread them closer to home. Like, say, McKinleyville.'

She snorted a laugh. 'Two whole hours away? Are you sure you could handle that?'

He laughed along with her and she knew they'd be okay. 'Hell, baby, I let you go all the way to Baltimore. Not that I could have stopped you.'

'Yeah, you could have. If you'd point-blank told me not to go, I'd have obeyed you. But you didn't and I'll love you forever for that alone. You're my dad. Don't ever worry that I'll forget that. You are my father and I love you.'

He sniffled. 'I guess I can't ask for more than that, because that's all that's important. Go meet Clay. And then tell him that the next time he comes to California, he should come to the ranch. We'll have a chat. Maybe a beer.'

'What about the good whiskey that you hide from everybody?'

'Now you're pushing it, baby. Go. Call me later. I'll be waiting.'

Baltimore, Maryland,
Saturday 22 August, 5.00 P.M.

'Jazzie! Dinner!'

Jasmine snuggled a little harder under the covers and closed her eyes, focusing on the deep rhythmic breathing that seemed to fool Aunt Lilah and Grandma into believing she was asleep. They always left her alone when she was asleep.

She pretended to sleep a lot.

The door opened and she could smell dinner and lemons. Aunt Lilah always smelled like lemons. *Just like Mama.* Or like her mama used to. Jasmine clenched her jaw, holding back the tears. *Breathe in, two, three, four. Breathe out, two, three, four.*

'Jazzie— Oh,' Aunt Lilah said, all hushed. 'Jazzie?' she whispered.

Jasmine. I'm Jasmine. She wasn't Jazzie anymore. She'd lost Jazzie a month ago.

Aunt Lilah sighed and pulled the door closed quietly. Jasmine waited for the smell of lemons to fade away before she chanced peeking out from under the covers.

101

She's gone. Jasmine knew she should feel guilty about pretending to sleep, because it was kind of lying, but . . .

Aunt Lilah meant well. Jasmine knew this, but . . . *I just want to be left alone.*

Because she *hurt*. Deep inside, she hurt. Everyone wanted her to smile. To be happy again. To get over it. But Miss Taylor had understood.

I'm allowed to hurt. Jasmine wanted to shout it out at the top of her voice, but that was never going to happen. She'd stutter and ruin it. Just once she'd love to stand in the middle of a field and scream all the words in her head so that the world would pay attention. But dramatic speeches only worked if you could speak. When people tried to finish your sentences to 'help' you? Not so much.

So she kept the speeches in her head. Along with the whispering voice that made her want to throw up. It was always there. Always whispering.

He's coming back. He'll find out you were there and he'll come back. For you. And then she'd end up just like her mama.

Jasmine curled up in a ball, trying to stop shaking. She was so *scared*. And tired. Watching every word that came out of Janie's mouth was hard. Janie didn't understand what she shouldn't say. And *she* didn't stutter. People listened to her. *If Janie tells that I was there, that I was hiding . . .*

Someone would tell someone else and it might end up on the news. And then people would wonder *why* she'd been hiding. They'd wonder if she'd seen anything and then they'd speculate. That was the word Aunt Lilah used. They'd speculate and rumors would start.

He might hear them. And come back. Part of her wished he would, because she wanted to ask him *why?* Why had he done it? He was supposed to love Mama. *He was supposed to love me too.* But he'd killed her mama and she had no doubt that he'd kill her too.

She could hear Aunt Lilah in her head along with the whispering voice. *Talk to the nice policeman, Jazzie. Tell him what you saw. He'll protect you.*

Jasmine wanted to believe that. She really did. But she wasn't stupid. She watched TV. Cops made promises just to get people to talk. To make their job easier. Detective Fitzpatrick might even mean what he promised, but it didn't mean it would happen. The detective would have to go home sometime, and *he* would be waiting. *And then I'll be dead.*

Somebody needed to know. *Just in case he finds me. And kills me.* Somebody needed to know who'd killed her mama. Janie needed to know so she could hide. So she wouldn't trust him.

Because Janie wouldn't know not to trust her own daddy unless somebody warned her.

Jasmine reached under her pillow and pulled out Miss Taylor's business card. She was so nice. Jasmine really liked her. And she hadn't told Jasmine to call. She'd made sure to tell Jasmine that it was okay to text or email because she knew how hard it was for Jasmine to say words. Jasmine didn't have a phone yet, but she did know Grandma's computer passwords. She could send an email and then delete the record so that Grandma would never know.

And Miss Taylor wasn't allowed to tell anyone what Jasmine said, because Healing Hearts was therapy, right? *She has to keep my secrets. It's a law.* It was something to think about.

Because *somebody* needed to know, in case her father came back.

Seven

Ford was pacing in front of the living room window, watching for Clay's truck, when he heard Taylor come downstairs. He found her in the kitchen, searching the cupboards. 'What do you need, Taylor?'

'I'm thinking it would be good to eat those crackers now.'

'Sit,' he said gently. 'It's going to be okay.'

Taylor sat and blew out a breath. 'Easy for you to say.'

Ford said nothing, just got her the box of crackers and another bottle of water, then sat next to her. 'Your mom made you afraid of him.'

It was a statement, not a question, but still she nodded. 'Yeah.'

'It was him who was lurking, waiting to jump out and grab you in the dark?'

'Yeah.' It came out a choked whisper, and Ford *had* to reassure her somehow.

'Clay Maynard is a good man, Taylor. One of the best I've ever known.'

Taylor moistened her lips. 'Maggie told you?'

'No. I'd already figured it out. I, uh, was in the barn when you were talking to Dillon.'

Her temper flashed, the cracker in her hand crumbling into dust. 'Spying again?'

'Not at first. I didn't come out because I was afraid you'd think I *was* spying again and be angry with me.'

She frowned, then laughed reluctantly. 'You're crazy, you know that?'

He grinned at her. 'So I've been told.' He shrugged then, his grin fading. 'I didn't mean to spy at first, but then all the questions you asked about Clay worried me, so I listened. He's important to me and he's been hurt. I know you have too. Your eyes seemed familiar to me, so I put it together and had to wonder what you were doing here, working under an assumed name.'

'It's not an assumed name. I *am* Taylor Dawson. My father is Frederick Dawson. He adopted me when I was eleven.' Dropping her gaze, she started picking at the label on the water bottle. She flinched when Ford's hand lightly settled on her back and began to rub lazy circles between her shoulder blades.

'You want me to stop?' he asked quietly.

'No. I'm . . . God, I'm so scared. I'm about to jump out of my skin. I'll take all the help I can get. So don't stop. Please.'

'Whatever you need, Taylor. I mean that.'

Her nod was shaky. 'You need to understand. Frederick Dawson is my father and he's a good man too. The best *I've* ever known. He and I were under the mistaken impression that Clay Maynard was a cross between Ted Bundy and Adolf Hitler. My mother told us that Clay had raped her and slapped her around and threatened to kill her if she told anyone.'

'Why?' Ford asked, keeping his voice as gentle as his touch, thrilled when she leaned into him, seeking more comfort. 'Why would she say that, Taylor?'

'I didn't know then. Neither did my dad. I didn't find out the truth until my mother was literally on her deathbed in the hospice center. She asked to speak to me alone, so everyone left the room. She whispered that she was sorry, that she'd lied. That my father was not a cruel man. At first I thought she was talking about Frederick and I was confused, but then she said she'd lied about Clay. She told me that he'd never laid a hand on her, that he'd never raped her. That she'd slept with him when they were in high school to make her ex-boyfriend jealous, but then she got pregnant with me and her parents forced her to marry him. Her

105

boyfriend wanted her back later, but her parents were very religious. She knew they wouldn't let her get a divorce, especially since she was pregnant. Not unless there was abuse involved.'

Ford could feel her trembling under his hand and felt so damn helpless. Her mother had lied to her. Betrayed her. Made her afraid of her own father, who was a damn good man.

'So she lied.'

Taylor nodded miserably, her eyes glued to the label she was systematically peeling from the bottle. 'She told my grandparents that Clay had beaten her and raped her. That he'd never let her or his baby go. So they decided to tell him that she'd had a miscarriage and she filed for divorce when he was away in the Marines and couldn't fight it.' She shrugged. 'He'd only married her because of me. Or what was to become me. I guess he figured letting her go would be easiest for both of them.'

Ford wanted to scream with rage at her mother – ruining so many lives for the sake of her own convenience. But he didn't scream. He didn't raise his voice. He didn't want to upset Taylor any more than she already was. 'How did Clay find out that you were alive?'

'I don't know.' Anxiously she glanced at the clock. 'I guess I'll find out soon enough.'

She peeled off the corner of the label and put it carefully on the table before starting on the next corner.

'Clay does that,' he murmured. 'Peels the label and puts the pieces on the table. Are you planning to put it back together like a puzzle?'

She turned to look at him, her dark eyes devastated, glassy with tears. 'Yes. I was.'

Ford dabbed at her eyes with a paper napkin. 'He does that too. The puzzle thing. Go on talking if you want to. If you don't, we can just sit here until he arrives. No pressure.'

'Thank you. But please understand, I meant no harm in coming here. To anyone. I just wanted to meet him. If it didn't work out, I could go home and he'd never know I was here.'

Ford thought of the sadness in Clay's eyes when he finally got to the campsite last week. 'Except that he'd keep searching for you. Maybe for the rest of his life.'

'I didn't know he was doing that. Honest.' Her voice rose, slightly panicked. 'Not till Dillon told me.' The tears spilled out of her eyes and down her cheeks, and that seemed to open the floodgates. A sob rushed out and all of a sudden she was in his arms, crying like her heart was going to break. 'I didn't know. I swear it.'

He wrapped his arms around her, scooting his chair closer to hers so that he could rock her. 'I believe you. Sshh, don't cry. He'll believe you too.'

Maggie came into the room then, a box of tissues in her hand. She slid them across the table to where they sat, and Ford tucked a few into the fist Taylor had clenched against his chest.

He rocked her until her sobs stilled, but she didn't pull away and he liked that. Liked the way she felt in his arms. Liked that she'd had the courage to come three thousand miles to meet the man who'd sired her. And that she maintained a fierce loyalty to the man who'd raised her.

He just plain liked her. And for now he wasn't going to analyze it any further than that.

Maggie walked to the back door and peered through the curtain. 'He's parking his truck now. His wife and daughter are with him. Dry your eyes, Taylor. It will be okay. We'll stay if you want us to, or we'll go. Your call.'

Taylor drew a breath and let it out, pressing her forehead to Ford's chest so that she could hide her face while she cleaned up.

Ford tipped up her chin, unsurprised to find she was just as pretty with a red nose and puffy eyes as she'd been earlier. 'Try to relax. Do you want us to go? Either of us?'

'No. Stay. Please.' She tried for a smile. 'And thank you. You are a good listener.'

She pulled away as the door opened. Straightened her spine and squared her shoulders as Ford had seen her do in the barn. He took her hand and gave it a little squeeze, and when he tried to pull his hand away, she wouldn't let him.

Clay came through the door like he always did – big, strong and confident. Because he was all those things. Stevie was right behind him, leaning heavily on her cane. Cordelia followed her in, giving Ford a sunny smile of greeting.

'What's this all about?' Clay asked when he saw Ford. 'The camera?'

'No,' Maggie said. 'I think that was a ruse. Ford's way of getting you over here.'

'Why?' Stevie asked.

'Because of me,' Taylor said quietly, and all eyes swung her way.

Maggie cleared her throat. 'Clay, I wanted to introduce you to our new intern. Her name is Taylor Dawson.'

'It's nice to meet you, Tay—' Clay had taken a step forward, his hand extended in greeting, but now he stumbled, going statue-still. His expression went from polite confusion to wary recognition to all-out shocked disbelief in a matter of seconds.

For a long, long moment, no one said a word. It was like everyone was holding their collective breath. Clay's gaze locked on Taylor's face. His mouth was open, his throat working to speak.

'Oh my God,' he finally whispered weakly. 'Oh my God.'

Stevie moved behind him, resting her hand on his back, just like Ford had done to Taylor minutes before.

Taylor let go of Ford's hand and rose from her chair, gripping the edge of the table for support, her gaze locked on Clay's.

He came closer, lifting his hand slowly, almost fearfully, then touched her cheek with one finger as if he'd needed to prove she was real and not a dream. 'Sienna,' he whispered, hope flaring to life in his eyes, so like hers. 'It's you. Isn't it? Is it really you?'

Taylor nodded once, then blinked, sending new tears streaming down her cheeks. 'I'm sorry,' she said, her voice tortured. 'I'm so damned sorry.'

In a rush, Clay pulled her into his arms, his big shoulders shaking, and for the first time Ford saw his friend cry. Not just a tear or two, but deep wrenching sobs that tore Ford's heart out. He couldn't have held his own tears back no matter how hard he tried.

Happy tears for the reunion Clay had sought for so many

years. Sad tears for the years they'd lost because of a lie. Anguished tears for the apologies that Taylor was repeating over and over.

'I'm so sorry,' she kept saying. 'I never meant to hurt you.'

Stevie stood, her hand over her mouth, tears rolling down her face too. Maggie was holding it together, but only barely. Ford wiped his eyes without apology.

Cordelia was clearly concerned and confused. But she stayed where she was, never disrupting the scene playing out before her. Ford gave her an encouraging smile and got a tentative smile back. 'It's okay,' he mouthed, and the little girl visibly relaxed.

'Sshh.' Clay's voice was harsh, breaking. 'It's all right, baby. You're here now. It's going to be all right. You're here and that's all that matters.'

'Don't hate me,' Taylor pleaded, sounding like the scared little girl she must have been, and Ford wished her mother weren't dead so that the woman could see the devastation she'd caused her own child. 'Please don't hate me.'

Clay cried so hard that his whole body shook. 'I could never hate you. *Never*. I've searched for you for so long. Lost hope so many times, but now you're here.' Lifting his head, he cradled Taylor's face tenderly, staring down at her as if she were a miracle. 'I could never hate you. You're my daughter.'

Hunt Valley, Maryland,
Saturday 22 August, 5.15 P.M.

Clay sat at the head of Maggie's kitchen table clutching Stevie's hand, the first wave of shock and tears past. He couldn't take his eyes off the young woman sitting to his right, her face as tear-streaked as his own.

She was simply beautiful. And he wasn't being biased because she was his daughter. Based on the way Ford hovered at her other side, the kid thought so too. She'd been clutching Ford's hand when they'd come in, and now that things had quieted down, she clutched it again.

He wondered what was going on between them, then let it go.

This was a moment. Their moment. *I've waited so damn long . . . and here she is. Right under my nose.*

She'd come to find him, and that made his heart swell. But she'd come under an assumed name, and that made his heart want to break in two. Why? Why had she come here using a fake name? How had she passed the background check? Because Joseph didn't make mistakes.

She said her name was Taylor, but in his mind she was Sienna. The child he'd been cheated of. But he couldn't let bitterness eat at him. Not tonight, with her sitting next to him.

Finally. Thank you, God.

Maggie was at the other end of the table, Cordelia sitting in her lap. Cordelia's face was carefully blank, the way it got when she became upset and didn't want anyone to know because they'd worry. This had come as a shock to all of them, but Cordy was only nine years old and didn't trust easily. *But she trusts me.* Clay wasn't going to sacrifice that miracle for anything.

'Just a minute,' he said to Sienna. He walked to Cordelia's end of the table and went down on one knee. 'You know this changes nothing between us, right?' he murmured, and watched his littlest girl's shoulders relax ever so slightly. 'You're still my daughter and will always be. You're stuck with me. Forever.'

'I know,' Cordelia said softly. But he could tell she wasn't yet convinced, so he pulled her into a hard hug.

'You're mine,' he whispered in her ear fiercely. 'I would have searched for you to the ends of the earth if you'd disappeared away from me. You know that, right?'

She hugged him back hard, her little body trembling. 'I know. It's okay, Daddy. You can love her too.'

Clay swallowed hard. It had taken Cordelia several months, plus the sight of an engagement ring on her mother's finger, before she had called him 'Daddy' for the first time. She did it all the time now, but it still took his breath away.

'I will, but I could never love you any less. Like I said, you're stuck with me.' He kissed her forehead and returned to his seat, aware that Sienna had watched the interchange closely.

110

'I didn't come here to make trouble for you and your family,' she said. 'I'm sorry.'

Clay reached for her hand that wasn't clutching onto Ford Elkhart's and held it tightly. 'You aren't making trouble. I . . . still can't believe you're here. Just this afternoon I was wondering if you were dead.'

'I'm not,' she said quietly.

'You hid, though,' Stevie said, just as quietly, which did not bode well. But Stevie had ridden this roller coaster with him for the year and a half they'd been together, and he figured he owed her the opportunity to get her questions answered, too. 'You pretended to be a student at the community college near your house to throw us off the scent,' she accused.

Sienna's nod was shaky, but she met Stevie's gaze squarely and said, 'I did. That was before I knew the truth.'

Clay closed his eyes. He could only imagine what Donna had told her. 'What do you know to be the truth?'

Sienna glanced around the table tentatively, pausing a long moment on Cordelia before returning her gaze to Clay. 'I know you didn't do any of the things my mother accused you of. She told me, hours before she died. I know she lied to you and about you and manipulated everyone around her. Including me. And my dad.'

Clay flinched. He couldn't help it. 'Your . . . your dad?'

'Yes,' she said calmly, but her lips trembled. 'His name is Frederick Dawson.'

Clay knew the name. 'He married your mother when you were nine years old. But they divorced when you were eleven and your mother moved back in with her aunt outside of Oakland. You lived there until your mother died. That's when I lost the trail.'

Sienna shook her head. 'No, that's not what happened. That's just what they let everyone think. Dad wanted Mom to marry him for years before they actually did, but she was afraid of you finding her if she left a paper trail – a marriage license. Dad convinced her that it would be okay, but then realized that she was right. At least he thought she was. They did get a divorce when I was eleven, so that they'd leave a fake paper trail you could follow. Then my father took all of us – my mother included – to Northern California. He was a partner in a big law firm, but he gave it up to live in the country and raise cattle. My mother's aunt continued to live in her house outside of Oakland and they pretended that my mother and I lived there too. Mom had her mail forwarded from a PO box in Oakland to a UPS box near the ranch. Anything that made it through to her aunt's house, her aunt would forward.'

Clay frowned. That didn't mesh at all with what he'd discovered over the years. 'I checked Dawson out. I never found a ranch.'

'My father made sure of it. He bought it in the name of a corporation. His name is never tied to anything. We kept a low profile for years. Hardly ever went into town. I never went to a real school. We never even went to church.' Her shoulders sagged. 'Because we didn't want to draw your attention.'

Clay's jaw clenched, fury swirling inside him, expanding to push at his chest from the inside out. *That man took my child. Hid my child. Stole her from me.*

'He thought he was doing the right thing,' Sienna whispered. 'He's a good man, too.'

Too. Clay forced his jaw to relax and tried to see it from Dawson's standpoint, for Sienna's sake. What the man had done had kept Clay separated from his child, but he had to admit that Dawson had done a damn fine job hiding her. *I would have done the same, given the same lie.*

It was a hard truth to swallow.

'I never caught a whiff of the corporation. I figured he'd had enough of Donna and walked away. Which was exactly what he wanted me to think.' He shook his head, unable to comprehend it all. 'I got played by a *lawyer*.' He couldn't hide his disgust at that.

Her swallow was audible, her voice grown small. 'I'm so sorry.'

Clay gave her the best smile that he could. 'You were just a child.' *My child.* Grief rose from the fury, closing his throat until he could barely breathe. *My child that I never got to know. I never got to hug. Never got to read a bedtime story to or tell her I loved her. Never got to hear her say she loved me.*

Goddamn you, Donna. I hope you're burning in hell for what you did. To all of us.

Stevie squeezed his hand and he found his strength when he looked in her eyes. But he still couldn't speak. Couldn't get past the pain that was shredding his heart.

'I know,' Stevie murmured. 'But she's here. You need to put all that away, for now.'

He nodded. 'I'm trying,' he whispered. 'But this is hard.'

Stevie brought their joined hands to her lips and kissed his knuckles. 'I know. You can work through the anger later. For now, I want answers.' She turned to Sienna. 'Why did Mr Dawson do something that drastic?'

Mr Dawson. Clay preferred that to *your father*. Every time he heard Sienna say *my father*, it was like a kick in the nuts.

Stevie had asked the question, but Sienna responded to Clay. 'Because of the PI you hired to watch me. My mother was so scared that she had the man arrested, had him charged as a pedophile. That's when my father decided we needed to disappear. He knew you'd never give up trying to find me.'

Clay's lungs emptied on a weary sigh. 'Dammit.'

'Was the PI a pedo?' Ford asked.

'No,' Clay said firmly. 'I hired him to make sure that Sienna had a good home. That Donna was a good mother. Once we'd proved that I'd hired him, the charges were dropped against him. I knew your mother lied about me.' He held Sienna's gaze. 'I had to be sure she wasn't mistreating you.'

Sienna's eyes had grown wide. 'You knew about the lie she'd told?'

'Yes. Her aunt finally told me.'

A rapid blink. 'She did? When?'

'You would have been about thirteen by then. I'd gone out to her house to try to talk to you, and I was simply devastated when your mother told me that you didn't want to see me. Her aunt followed me out to the car and told me what your mother had told her parents. Apparently your mother had confided in her when the two of you first came to live with her. Your aunt told me about how Donna had

113

lied to get their blessing for her divorce and how she couldn't tell the truth because her father would have a heart attack. But your aunt also said that she'd never admit she'd told me any such thing, and if I tried to take legal action against Donna or to get you back, the two of them would make sure that everyone believed that I'd . . .' He glanced at Cordelia. 'That I'd done the things Donna accused me of. They'd ruin my career and make sure that you were hidden somewhere I could never find you. Donna's aunt also said that she was the only one who knew. So no one could corroborate the true story.'

Sienna looked as exhausted as he felt. 'What my aunt told you was true, I think. But not complete. My mother really didn't want my dad to know. Maybe she thought he wouldn't love her anymore. Maybe she'd have been right. All these years I've thought that PI was spying on me.'

'Well, he was,' Clay said, 'but only because I was afraid to approach you myself. You'd run screaming from me the only other time I'd seen you.'

'That day on the playground,' she said, so softly he almost didn't hear her.

His eyes stung with new tears. 'Yeah.' He had to give himself a minute. 'That was a bad day.' Which was the understatement of the century. He'd been crushed, the memory of her running away screaming revisiting his nightmares ever since. 'I did find your mother because of her marriage to Dawson, but I didn't want to scare you and I didn't think I could handle it if you ran from me again like I was a monster. So I hired the PI to make sure you were okay. And to gather any evidence I could have used in a custody battle. You were only six that day on the playground. The PI watched you for months when you were eleven. But I didn't get the full truth from your aunt until two years after that.'

Sienna's eyes grew wide. 'You were going to sue for custody? Legally?'

Clay's jaw tightened as he imagined the things she'd heard about him. 'I wasn't going to grab you and run, for damn sure,' he said roughly. 'But my PI said you seemed healthy and happy, that you had a home with a picket fence and a dog.'

'Rufus,' she said with a fond little smile that tugged at Clay's heart. 'He was a good dog. My first pet. I never knew you wanted to keep me,' she added wistfully.

'Then why the hell did you think I was looking for you?' Clay demanded, then sighed when she flinched. 'I'm sorry. I didn't mean to shout. What did your mother tell you? Although I'm afraid to know.'

Sienna glanced at Cordelia again, hesitation written all over her face. 'She said you were furious that she'd gotten away and that you'd promised you'd kill her before you let her live with anyone else. She told me that you were looking for me to get to her, and that when you found me, you might kill me too.'

'That's a lie!' Cordelia shouted. 'My dad would never hurt you. *Never.*'

Sienna turned in her chair and met Cordelia's angry gaze head-on. 'You're right. It *was* a lie. And because of her lies, I was scared every day of my life. My father was afraid to let me out of his sight. Until this trip, the farthest away from home I'd ever been was the college I attended, and that was only because my middle sister, Daisy, went there too, and because it was close enough that we didn't have to live on campus. We were college-aged, but he dropped us off in the morning and picked us up in the afternoon like we were little kids. We carried Mace and knives in case we were ever attacked and tracking devices in case we were abducted. We even had a bodyguard who signed up for the same classes we did – the ranch foreman's son. I've never been on a vacation. I've never had a sleepover. I've never had a school picture taken. I was homeschooled all the way through high school. My first day of college was the first time I set foot in a classroom and I just knew Clay was going to pop up and steal me away. Or worse. So you're right. It was a lie. But I can't confront my mother about it because she died.'

'But why?' Cordelia asked plaintively. 'Why'd she lie about my dad that way?'

Damn good question, Clay thought bitterly. To his knowledge, he'd never been anything but kind when they were married. He'd only been eighteen when Donna got pregnant, but he'd wanted to do the right thing. And for that, his ex-wife had made his life hell.

Sienna sighed. 'She told the first lie so that her parents wouldn't stop her from getting a divorce, because she wanted to marry someone else, and—'

'The lawyer?' Stevie interrupted. 'Mr Dawson?'

Sienna shook her head. 'No. This was long before she met my dad. This would have been her ex-boyfriend in high school.'

'The one she was using me to get back at,' Clay said, 'back when we were only eighteen. That's what Donna's aunt told me.'

Sienna nodded gravely. 'Yes. So my mother lied the first time to get a divorce, but the lie grew and grew. Sometimes I wonder if she believed it herself, she told it so many times.'

'But she told you the truth on her deathbed,' Stevie said, her flat expression that of an interrogating cop.

Sienna's chin lifted ever so slightly. 'Yes, ma'am,' she said stiffly.

'That was over a year and a half ago.' Stevie's voice bordered on harsh. 'Why did it take you so damn long to come here?'

'Stevie,' Clay murmured.

'No, she's right,' Sienna said, locking gazes with Stevie even though she continued to speak to him. 'I didn't come right away because I didn't believe her at first. She was on heavy pain medication and nearly out of her mind at the very end. She'd also said that I shouldn't forget to feed Rufus, and he'd died years before. I took her confession as a hallucination.'

Stevie nodded. 'All right. I can accept that. But eventually you believed her?'

'Yeah,' Sienna said flatly. 'After the funeral, after things started to get back to normal, I couldn't get what she'd said out of my mind.' She glanced at Clay. 'I Googled you. I hadn't done that before.'

Stevie's brows shot up. 'Not even once? You weren't even curious about what he looked like?'

A huff of laughter that held no mirth. 'I knew what he looked like. My mother used to show me his photo and said if I ever saw him to run and scream.'

Clay felt the words stab his heart just as surely as if she'd used a knife. But she wasn't finished.

116

She dropped her gaze to the tabletop, her hair sliding forward to hide her features from view. 'I saw your face in my dreams,' she whispered hoarsely. 'In my nightmares. I'm so sorry.'

New sorrow welled up within him. Pain that she'd feared him, but greater pain that she carried the burden of guilt when she never should have had either emotion. Only love.

'I would have loved you,' he whispered back, his voice breaking. 'I would have loved you so much.'

She nodded, her face still hidden, new tears falling to the tabletop. 'I believe you.'

'Did you tell Mr Dawson what your mother had told you?' Stevie asked, more kindly now.

Sienna was shaking her head. 'Not at first. I couldn't. Not even when I started to wonder if it could have been true. Because if it *was* true, it meant she'd lied to him too. Even when I was a kid, I knew what he'd given up for me. I'd always felt guilty for that, although I know he did it because he loves me. But our entire family was uprooted. We went from living in a nice house on a quiet street to living in the middle of nowhere and being homeschooled.'

She looked up, her hair parting to reveal the intense pain flickering across her face. 'I have three stepsisters, Dad's daughters with his first wife, who also died. My youngest sister, Julie, has always needed physical therapy that she could have gotten in a bigger city, but we lived so far out that Dad had to hire a live-in therapist. My oldest sister, Carrie, ran away a few years into her "sentence in the East Bumfuck Pen", as she called it, because she felt like she was in prison. She hated the ranch and ran away to LA. Fell in with a bad crowd and OD'd. She never made it to twenty years old.'

Ford rested his hand on the middle of her back, and she gave him a grateful glance. 'And your middle stepsister?' Ford asked quietly.

'Daisy's my age. We did everything together because we were the only kids we knew. She's also been terrified to let me out of her sight. All the cloak-and-dagger shit had her so anxious that she began to drink. A lot. Dad finally broke down and sent her to rehab because she was going down the same path that Carrie did. Now

117

Daisy's a recovering alcoholic at twenty-three years old. I was afraid to leave her alone to come here, but I had to get away. I had to know.' She swallowed hard, met Clay's eyes again, her devastation breaking his heart. 'I had to see you. I had to know if you were good. And now all I can say is that I'm sorry.'

'Sienna, stop,' he whispered. 'No more sorry, okay?'

'But I am,' she whispered back. 'How can I not be?'

Stevie sighed. 'Look, I'm sorry too. I'm sorry to hear about your sisters and the sacrifices Mr Dawson made. But I've had to watch this tear Clay to pieces and I need to understand why you took so long to find him. You said you Googled him. When?'

Clay squeezed Stevie's hand. 'She's not on trial here, babe. I know you're doing the thinking for me now, and I appreciate it, but can you think a little less hostilely?'

Stevie's lips twitched. 'Okay. I don't mean to be hostile, Sienna.'

Sienna's jaw tightened. 'Please call me Taylor. That's my name.'

Stevie blinked, her gaze cutting over to meet Clay's. Clay shrugged. She hadn't asked him to call her Taylor, had allowed him to call her Sienna without reproach. But it seemed he was going to be the only one allowed to do that.

'All right,' Stevie said quietly. 'Taylor, when did you finally Google your father?'

A muscle twitched under Sienna's left eye. *Just like me when I'm really pissed,* Clay thought. It made him happy and sad all at once.

'March, a year ago. There was a news story about you, Detective Mazzetti. Clay had been injured saving your life.'

The whole mess came back to Clay in a rush – searching for the man who'd had Stevie's first husband and son murdered ten years before, because that same man had resurfaced, targeting Stevie and Cordelia. They'd been lucky that everything had turned out all right. Stevie was safe. Cordy was safe. They loved him. The only thing missing had been Sienna.

'I'm no longer a detective,' Stevie told her. 'I'm a PI now. I work with your dad.'

'That's good.' Sienna sounded stiff but sincere. 'I'm glad he has you to watch his back. Anyway, the article said he'd be okay, that he

118

acted heroically and helped bring a murderer to justice. That didn't sound like the man who'd been the monster in my closet for as long as I could remember. I dug a little more, but there wasn't much media coverage.' She glanced at Clay. 'You keep yourself under the radar.'

'Old habits,' he said with a shrug.

She nodded. 'I get that. I did find pictures of you at a fundraiser with Daphne taken the year before. I thought you were her boyfriend. I figured you'd gotten over trying to find me and my mother since she was gone. That you'd gone on and found someone else. I was . . . relieved.'

'Because you were still afraid,' Ford murmured behind her, and Sienna turned in her chair to look up at him.

'Yes.' She drew a breath and spoke to Ford, although Clay knew the words were meant for him. 'I still am. It takes a while to get past the pictures in your mind. Even when you know they're not true.'

Ford nodded once. 'I understand.'

'I don't,' Stevie said bluntly, and Sienna pivoted in her chair to glare at her. 'You Googled your father a year and five months ago. Why did you wait so long to find him?'

Sienna flashed Stevie a look of muted anger that Clay understood too well. He was madder than hell about all this, but he couldn't lash out. Donna wasn't around and everyone else was a victim too. But that didn't mean the rage disappeared, for him or for his daughter. Frankly, he was proud of her for her restraint. At her age, he'd have been punching holes in the walls.

Maggie cleared her throat, speaking for the first time. 'Or perhaps we should be asking what made you decide to find him *now*?'

Eight

Taylor pressed her fingertips to her left temple, a headache beginning to make her queasy again. This wasn't going well. She understood Clay's wife's anger, but dammit, this wasn't easy for any of them. The woman didn't have to be such a bitch.

Suddenly she wished she'd waited until her dad could have been there with her. But Ford had stuck like glue and for that she was grateful. She only hoped she could make Clay understand what had taken her so long. She didn't care if Stevie Mazzetti understood or not.

She turned to Clay wearily. 'Six months ago, my mother's account at the UPS store became overdue.'

'You're going to need to be more specific,' Stevie snapped, back in interrogation mode.

Taylor's fuse popped. 'And *you're* going to need to *back off*, lady,' she snarled, then felt instantly guilty at her outburst. Stevie's expression darkened further, but Clay closed his eyes, looking like a man who was being cleaved in half. Which was exactly what Taylor had wanted to avoid like the goddamn plague. 'I'm . . . I apologize. *God.*'

'Let's take a time-out, folks.' Ford got up, fetched a bottle of pain reliever from the cupboard and shook out a few pills. 'Take these,' he said, handing them to Taylor, 'and eat a cracker or two, or your stomach will make you pay.'

'It's already making me pay,' she muttered but swallowed the pills, chasing them with a couple of saltines while everyone waited patiently – even the nine-year-old at the end of the table.

Cordelia still had nightmares about her own brush with violence, Dillon had confided. A man with a gun. That hadn't been in any of the articles Taylor had found when she'd researched Clay. She promised herself that she'd get the child help before she left.

She polished off the crackers and some cheese Ford had insisted she eat. She whispered a thank you, calming further when he took her hand once again. He was a good guy, making this whole scene so much easier than it might otherwise have been, simply by being there.

'Better?' Ford asked. 'Good,' he said when she nodded. 'Then maybe we can go back to "What made you decide to find him now?"'

With a 'back off, bitch' glare at Stevie, Taylor turned to Clay to tell him the rest of the story. She owed him that much, at the very least.

'As I was saying, six months ago, my mother's account at the UPS mailbox store became overdue. This was over a year after her death. Since she'd had a box with them for so long, they gave her a three-month grace period. Finally, they called the house and I answered. This was in May. I told them she'd died two Decembers ago and they were stunned. They hadn't even known she was sick.'

Stevie frowned. 'You can only pay mailboxes out twelve months ahead. It doesn't matter if they're UPS boxes or post office boxes – there's a twelve-month limit. If she died in December, how did she pay her box ahead to the following February?'

Of course the woman had hit the nail on the head. Taylor was annoyed, but underneath it she was grateful that Clay had someone so sharp in his corner.

'She'd given the renewal checks to her aunt Laura in Oakland, who mailed them the month after my mother died. That's when the yearly bill came due the first time. My mother had taken care of paying the bills and managing the ranch's ledgers for years. She'd handed most of her responsibilities over to Aunt Laura a few months

121

before she died so that my dad could continue to focus on running the ranch and taking care of us.'

'Why did your aunt mail the check?' Stevie pushed. 'She could have simply canceled the box and anything addressed to your mother would have been returned to sender.'

'I don't know for certain,' Taylor said, 'but I can guess. My mother was very organized. She wrote checks for recurring expenses and put them in one of those accordion folders by the month they were due. I think Laura was still grieving a month after my mother died and maybe not thinking straight. Most of us weren't thinking straight for a while.'

'You just operated on autopilot,' Ford said softly, giving her arm a quick stroke.

'Exactly. Laura must have grabbed the letters in the January folder and mailed them. I didn't know that she'd paid the bill. I didn't know about the box period until the local store called me the following year. By then Aunt Laura had died too. She'd never canceled the box, and so, when nobody was left to pay the bill, the account came due. When I saw what was in the box, I knew that my mother really *had* lied and that she'd never intended to tell me the truth. For some reason, she changed her mind at the last minute.' Taylor rubbed at her forehead. 'That she did tell the truth at the end doesn't clean her slate by any stretch, because you're absolutely right. Her behavior was unforgivable. I'm not sure what more I can give you than that, Miss Mazzetti. Unless you want me to dig her up and spit on her corpse,' she finished bitterly.

Stevie flinched. 'Sienna.' She gave her head a shake. 'Taylor. I'm sorry. I know she was your mother and I know you're struggling with all this. I'm not being helpful, but I do need to understand how it happened. Clay deserves no less.'

The change in the woman's tone made Taylor's eyes sting, but she didn't want to cry anymore. Her head hurt enough already. 'I know. That's why I'm here.'

'Sienna,' Clay said quietly. 'What was in the UPS box?'

Taylor swallowed hard. 'Cards and letters addressed to me. From you. Nine of them. The oldest was from the October before my mother died. I guess she got too sick to check the box out.' She rubbed the tears from her eyes with the back of her hand. 'One birthday card, two Christmas cards, plus two from Valentine's Day, Easter and Halloween.' Taylor assumed there would have been a tenth card for her birthday at the end of August.

She was so glad she hadn't waited any longer to find out.

Clay's throat worked as he tried to swallow. 'Did you read them?'

'Yes.' She'd meant to say it firmly, but the word came out hoarse with the same emotion she'd felt the first time she'd read them. Because in every single one he'd told her how much he loved her and how much he would love to meet her. Just once. It had broken her. She met his eyes squarely. 'Thank you.'

'I sent a lot more. Plus wrapped gifts every year on your birthday and Christmas. Your mother always returned them, unopened. Cards, letters, gifts. All of it.'

'For how long?' she managed to ask.

'Since I found out you existed. Well, since I found out where your mother had run to, anyway,' he amended. She wondered how he'd discovered her existence, but he was going on before she could ask. 'I've kept everything your mother sent back. I kept hoping I'd get to give them to you in person.'

Taylor had thought her heart couldn't break any more, but she was wrong. God, thinking about him writing all those cards for all those years . . . Her heart physically ached.

'I never knew. I'm sorry.' She shuddered. 'I know I didn't do anything, but I'm still sorry. Not just apologetic. I'm *sorrowful*. For both of us. I wish I'd known. There are times I *am* tempted to dig her up and spit on her corpse. The thing is . . . she wasn't a bad person when it came to everything else. She took care of me. Played with me. Taught me to sew and knit and bandaged me up when I skinned my knees. I don't understand where all that . . . meanness came from. I never saw it coming.'

Clay smiled sadly. 'You were a tomboy?' he asked, ignoring the rest.

'Yeah. Still am. It helped growing up on a ranch. Did you say you have all the letters?'

He nodded. 'In my attic. Would you like to see them?'

She managed a nod.

'Then I'll bring them to you. Tomorrow.'

Taylor opened her mouth to reply, but Stevie held up her hand.

'Hold on,' Stevie said. 'You saw the letters in May. This is August.'

Taylor really wanted to roll her eyes, but she fought the urge. 'I'm cautious, okay?' she snapped. 'I still didn't know anything about him and I especially didn't know if he was a nice person. And I didn't know how to approach him. It wasn't like I could walk up to him with my hand out and say, "Hey, Pop, you're my long-lost daddy. Let's be friends."'

Stevie drew a breath, hissed it out through her teeth. '*Yes, you could have!* And you *should* have! Do you know what your being *cautious* has cost him? Every damn day you waited because you were too cautious has *killed* him. Don't you understand that?'

Taylor's mouth fell open, unable to conjure a response to the woman's unleashed fury. But it turned out that she didn't have to respond, because Cordelia did it for her.

'*Leave her alone, Mama.*'

Everyone's gaze swung to the end of the table where Cordelia sat, still in Maggie's lap. Maggie looked as surprised as any of them.

'Not everyone can make their nightmares go away like *that*.' Cordelia snapped her small fingers, looking like a queen on a throne. But then she seemed to realize that she'd actually said the words aloud and curled into herself. 'You don't know how it is, Mama,' she said softly. 'You're never afraid. You're *brave*. But the rest of us . . . We're afraid.' She lifted her little chin, all the more heartbreaking because it quivered. 'I think Taylor or Sienna or whatever her name is . . . *I* think she's brave. She came all this way by herself even though she was scared. Clay's not yelling and he was hurt the most, so don't yell at her anymore.' A beat of silence. 'Please,' she whispered, then looked at the faces around the table uneasily. 'I'm done now.'

Maggie huffed a surprised laugh. 'Out of the mouths of

124

babes, Stevie. You've raised this girl well. I think you should listen to her.'

But Stevie was staring at Cordelia, her eyes filled with horror. 'You still have nightmares?'

Cordelia's unease became more intense. 'I wasn't talking about me.'

Stevie looked around the table, much as Cordelia had done, seeing no surprise on any of their faces. 'You all knew? You knew and didn't tell me?'

'Stevie,' Clay murmured once again. 'Cordelia didn't want you to worry. Let this go for now. We'll deal with it later. At home.'

'You're damn straight we will,' Stevie shot back acidly, and Clay winced.

Taylor pressed her fingers to both temples this time. The headache had spread, despite the painkillers Ford had given her. She glanced up at Stevie, sighing when she saw the woman's lips trembling. 'This right here, *this* is why I didn't want to just walk up and say, "Hey, Pop." I worried that I'd still be afraid and that would hurt him. I didn't know until I saw him that I wouldn't run screaming again. But I also wanted to avoid *this*. I've disrupted his life enough already. I didn't want to spoil anything more for him.'

'You haven't,' Clay said fiercely. 'You are welcome here.'

'Absolutely.' Stevie said, the malice gone from her voice. 'This part isn't about you.'

Taylor shook her head. 'Of course it is. I've whipped everyone into a lather.' She met Stevie's eyes, now carefully blank. 'There was another reason I didn't rush out here after I read the letters in the box. My dad, Frederick Dawson, had had a few TIAs around that time. You know what TIAs are, right?'

Stevie nodded woodenly. 'Little strokes.'

'Yes. In his case they didn't cause any permanent damage, but I wasn't going to leave him until he'd had a full workup and his doctor said he was okay. I'm still worrying about the effect all this is having on him. The TIAs are one of the reasons he didn't come to Baltimore with me. He's supposed to be taking it easy. But then this

125

internship opportunity came up and . . .' Taylor looked at Clay. 'I
had to know. So I left him home with my sister, Daisy. She's taking
care of him and Julie right now.'

'I understand,' Stevie said quietly.

'Thank you.' Taylor turned to give Cordelia an encouraging
smile, grateful when the little girl gave her a small smile back. 'And
thank *you*, Cordelia, for sticking up for me. It's nice when someone
knows how you feel. Makes it not so lonely or scary. But I have to
tell you, kid, you're wrong about one thing. Your mama may be a
badass, but you are every bit as brave as she is. To stick up for
someone's feelings when it puts your own at risk . . . that's courage.
I hope we get a chance to talk some more.'

Maggie gave the girl in her lap a hard hug. 'I think we can arrange
that, eh, Cordy?'

Cordelia nodded, the small smile fading as she looked at her
mother. 'I'm sorry, Mama. Not for what I said, but for surprising
you. I know you don't like that.'

Grabbing her cane, Stevie moved from the chair next to Clay
down to Maggie's end of the table and pulled her daughter to her
own lap. 'I love you. I'm not upset with you.'

'Of course you are,' the girl said, sounding way too grown-
up. 'But don't be. And don't be mad at Clay. He has nightmares
too.'

'So do I,' Stevie confessed.

Cordelia's eyes grew wide. 'You do?'

'Of course I do.' Stevie imitated her daughter's tone, making
Cordelia laugh. 'We'll talk about this later, okay?'

'Over ice cream?'

Stevie's dark brows went up. 'You just had ice cream with Aunt
Izzy.'

'I don't think you can ever have too much ice cream, Stevie,' Ford
said, giving Cordelia a wink, making her giggle. And just that fast,
the mood in the room lifted.

Taylor turned to Clay. 'I hear we have an ice-cream date with
Jazzie tomorrow after I finish my therapy sessions.'

Clay's eyes widened. 'We do?'

Maggie coughed. 'Well, I might have volunteered you to escort Jazzie and Taylor for an off-site therapy session. JD's coordinating it. I'll fill you in later.'

Clay's eyes met Taylor's, and for the first time since he'd entered the room, joy outweighed his sadness. 'That's fine with me,' he said. 'Any way I can spend time with you. There's so much I want to know.'

She smiled at him. 'I guess we have a lot of catching up to do.'

'I will be asking about the new name,' he warned lightly. 'Mostly because I need to know how Dawson got it past me. It's a professional embarrassment.'

Dawson. Not *your father*. Taylor couldn't blame him, though, and she wouldn't correct him for it. 'I'll tell you all, I promise. I have a lot of questions too.'

'Come by tomorrow morning, Clay,' Ford said. 'I'll make you guys breakfast and leave you alone to talk. Therapy sessions don't start till ten.'

Taylor looked over her shoulder at the young man who'd been a quiet rock. 'I have stalls to clean, too.'

Ford shook his head. 'I'll do it for you. This is a special occasion. Like a birthday.' He smiled at her and she caught her breath. He'd been handsome before, but now . . . He was a white knight with the shiniest armor.

'Thank you.' She turned back to Clay and her cheeks heated at the eyebrow he quirked up. 'Tomorrow, then. I'll be waiting for you.'

Baltimore, Maryland,
Saturday 22 August, 6.10 P.M.

Gage blinked awake, glaring at the cheap digital clock on his night-stand. It wasn't set to go off for another forty minutes, but somehow it was ringing already. He'd been up all night dealing with Toby Romano and all that mess. The few lines of Cleon Perry's coke that he'd snorted had kept him going until mid-afternoon, but once Denny had left, Gage had crashed.

He had a dinner meeting with his new boss tonight and wanted to be sharp. He needed that extra sleep. He smacked the clock, but the alarm kept ringing.

Oh. It was his cell phone. He squinted at the caller ID. Denny. Probably calling to apologize. *Asshole. Let him try. Let him grovel. Let him beg.* Gage hoped his brother begged. Denny needed to know his place.

'What?' he snapped, cursing the headache behind his eyes and wondering what Cleon had used to cut the coke he'd been selling. Rolling up to sit on the side of the bed, he washed a few ibuprofen down with the bottle of water on his nightstand.

'It's Denny.' And he didn't sound apologetic. He sounded panicked. 'Ma called, so happy she was almost crying. Jazzie made some kind of breakthrough.'

Gage pinched the bridge of his nose as his brain slogged through the headache, slowly rebuilding the wall of information that got smashed while he slept off a buzz. *Jazzie.* His lip curled in a sneer. *Valerie's little bastard.* 'What kind of a breakthrough? What are you blathering about?'

A beat of tense silence. 'I'm blathering about you, asshole. You and the kid you left motherless. She hasn't spoken to anyone since Valerie . . .' He hesitated. 'Died.'

'So? So what? I don't have all night to dick around with this.'

Denny huffed angrily. 'I don't know why I even bother.'

'I don't know why you bother me either,' Gage replied, bored. 'I need to—'

'I don't know,' Denny pushed on as if he hadn't spoken, 'except that it would kill Ma if you got your ass arrested for murder. So you'd better listen to what I'm telling you. Your kid, who hasn't talked to a damn soul since you killed her mama, started talking to some damn therapist today.'

'So what?' But Gage's heart skipped a beat. This felt important and he didn't know why. 'Well, what did she say?'

'I don't know exactly, but Ma said it was significant.'

Gage waited for more, then frowned when it was clear no more was coming. 'That's it? You called to tell me this?'

'That's it for now. Jazzie also cried for the first time since she found her mother's body. Ma said that Lilah is praising it as some kind of breakthrough. Jazzie's gonna meet her therapist tomorrow afternoon for ice cream and a little heart-to-heart.'

'So why's Ma happy about that?' Gage demanded.

'Because she really believes you were in Texas and thinks that if the therapist can get Jazzie to talk, she'll tell everyone who the "real killer" was.'

Oh for God's sake. What bullshit. Denny was just yanking Gage's chain. 'She doesn't know anything,' he said dismissively. 'Didn't see anything. Nobody did. Nobody was there when I left Valerie's apartment.'

Another long pause. 'Are you sure? Ma seems to think Jazzie knows something.'

Gage's heart began to pound harder. *No, it's not possible. Was it?* 'Well, fucking find out!' he snarled at his brother.

'I did my part. I got you an alibi. You could have left town. You could have been in Mexico by now.'

'I told you. I have a new job.'

'Yeah,' Denny said with disgust. 'With a drug lord. Dammit, Gage, just leave. Run while you still can.'

Gage frowned. 'What do you know? Have they named me as a suspect again?'

'Not yet.' But Denny had hesitated. Just enough to let Gage know he was lying about something.

'I'll find out for myself,' Gage said quietly. 'And if I find out you've been lying? Your sons have softball games tomorrow. Back to back, starting at two o'clock. Missy never misses their games, which is so nice for the boys. It would be so sad if she never made it to the game tomorrow.'

Denny's gasp was audible. 'You motherfucker,' he whispered, his voice shaking. 'You will not touch her.'

'Or you'll tell?' Gage mocked. 'Go ahead, Denny. We both know you won't. So why don't you spare both of us your hysterics and tell me what I need to know.'

A swallow was followed by a frustrated growl. 'They've cleared you. The case is closed. It's not official yet. The paperwork has to be signed off.'

Gage smiled. *Excellent.* 'As of when?'

Another hesitation, but this one had the feel of defeat. 'I checked Missy's email right after Ma called to tell me about Jazzie. But if Jazzie saw something, they'll reopen the case. That's why you need to leave while you still can.'

'She did not see anything,' Gage repeated.

'Are you sure?' Denny asked again.

'I'll find out from Ma. I was going to call her tonight or tomorrow anyway. You know, to tell her that I've been in rehab for the past month. In Texas. Thanks for the alibi, by the way. I really am grateful.'

Denny drew an angry breath. 'Yeah, right. Fine. Call Ma. She's always bought your bullshit – hook, line and sinker.'

'It's true,' Gage agreed. His mama wanted to believe he was perfect, so she did.

'Ask her about Jazzie,' Denny added bitterly. 'Just know that if you get yourself arrested, I'm washing my hands of you. As you pointed out, this could ruin my career.'

Sanctimonious prick, Gage thought, but didn't say it out loud. 'So noted. Thanks for the call.' He hung up and tossed the phone onto the nightstand.

Valerie's daughter could not have seen anything that day. The apartment wasn't that big and he'd kept Valerie with him, dragging her to the bedroom to force her to show him where she'd hidden her cash. It was in her jewelry box, a wad of large bills along with the platinum wedding ring that Gage had put on her finger. The ring was in an envelope with an appraisal ticket and a receipt for the sale of the diamond engagement ring. She'd already sold the five-carat ring – that *he'd paid for.*

That was when he'd snapped. That was when he'd dragged her back to the living room and beaten her until she was dead.

He didn't realize he'd clenched his fists until they spasmed. Someone could have come in when he'd dragged her to the bedroom. Or when he'd searched the coat closet for her bank records, still convinced she was lying to him about having no money from the sale of his house. Val had been limp by then. He'd thrown her into the coffee table and she hadn't moved after that. So he'd left her lying on the floor while he'd searched the closet. And then he'd discovered she was dead . . .

And I went into the kitchen to wash her blood off my hands.

Still, he would have heard if anyone had come in. He would have.

Except that he'd been out of his mind, so damned angry. Valerie's older daughter had always been a scrawny kid. Timid. Like a squirrel. She'd stuttered and it had irked him to no end – and that was when he'd still thought she was his.

She'd been very good at hiding back then.

She could have been hiding in the apartment. His stomach did a slow, sick roll. What if Jazzie had seen something? Right now, nobody knew what the kid had seen because she hadn't said a word. He needed to get close enough to her to find out exactly how bad this was before she did say something. Lilah wouldn't let him see Jazzie, but his mother would. And if she asked where he'd been, he'd distract her with the rehab story.

She'd believe it because she'd want to. He'd tell his mother that he'd seen coverage of Val's murder on the news. That knowing his little girls needed him was the boot he'd needed to kick him into rehab and make it stick.

'I've been clean and sober for thirty-three days, Ma,' he practiced saying aloud, and smiled. He sounded perfectly sincere. Believable, even. He reached for the phone to call her, but his alarm clock started to beep for real, reminding him that he had an appointment to keep. He needed to shower, trim his stubble, and dress in his new suit. He didn't want to be late.

He was getting his life back.

And if the kid did see something . . . like, maybe me? What then?

He didn't want to hurt her. It wasn't her fault that she was an illegitimate little bastard or that her mother was a calculating, lying, adulterous bitch.

But it's not my fault either.

131

He wasn't going to borrow trouble until he'd checked the kid out himself. He had a little time. Denny said she was meeting with the therapist tomorrow afternoon. If she hadn't said anything yet, she was unlikely to spill her guts in the next few hours.

And if she had seen something, he'd deal with it. Somehow. Because the only thing he knew was that he wasn't going to let anyone put him in a cage. He'd do what needed to be done to stay free.

Nine

Hunt Valley, Maryland,
Saturday 22 August, 6.15 P.M.

Ford and Maggie walked Clay, Stevie and Cordelia out to their truck, giving Taylor a few minutes to herself. Ford hoped she'd still be in the kitchen when he got back. He wanted to make sure she was truly all right.

There was a fragility to her that made him protective.

But he saw in her an even greater strength, which made him the tiniest bit horny. *Okay, fine. There's nothing tiny about it.* He headed for the driver's side of Clay's truck, out of vision of the others so that no one would see him adjust himself. He'd been hard as a rock from the first moment he'd touched her.

From the moment he'd first seen her in the training ring, if he was being honest.

'So there really wasn't a problem with the camera?' Clay asked, coming around the truck.

'No. I wasn't sure then and I didn't want to get your hopes up. I was hoping you'd recognize her.' He smiled at his friend, just so damn happy for him. 'Just like you did.'

'She just showed up here? Out of the blue?'

'She applied to the program first and got accepted. I'm still floored that Joseph's background check didn't raise any flags. If you think you were "professionally embarrassed", then think about the ring Joseph's gonna shit when he finds out.'

Clay's grin was quick and wicked. 'I'm going to have fun with that.'

Ford laughed. 'I'll bet you will.' He knew that Clay and Joseph were fast friends, but they had a long history of one-upmanship.

Clay's smile faded as Maggie helped Cordelia climb into the back seat and fastened her seat belt. 'Dammit, Ford, Cordy looks so lost. Just when I think we've cleared a hurdle . . .'

'I know. I didn't know about the nightmares either, if it will make Stevie feel better. I overheard Dillon talking to Taylor this afternoon in the barn and he accidentally spilled the beans. He made her promise not to tell.'

Clay looked surprised. 'You were eavesdropping on their conversation?'

'Hell yeah. I thought she might have been a reporter. I didn't want her getting close to you or anyone else in the family.'

Clay's eyes warmed at being called family, then his jaw went taut at the look Stevie gave him as she grabbed the rollbar and swung herself up to sit in the passenger seat. 'Yeah, well, I don't think any of that's gonna make Stevie any less mad.'

Ford winced. 'Sorry, man.'

Clay shrugged as he pulled his door open. 'Part of a relationship, I guess.' He looked at the door to Maggie's kitchen, behind which his daughter sat. 'I don't want to let her out of my sight again, you know?'

'I know. You're worried she'll take off.'

A sober nod. 'She's good at hiding.' A hard swallow. 'I hate that she's had to be,' he whispered. 'Dammit. I hate being the man she was so afraid of for her whole fucking life.'

Ford clapped him on the shoulder and gave it a fast squeeze. 'Not your fault, Clay. You did everything humanly possible to find her. You loved her even when it seemed hopeless. I think she got that tonight. I'll make sure she's here in the morning.' If he had to stay up all night and guard the doors.

'Thanks, kid. See you tomorrow.' Clay took his place behind the wheel and backed out of the driveway.

Ford and Maggie stood there watching until the truck's taillights disappeared.

'Stevie's pissed,' Maggie said.

'Yeah, I kinda got that. I think everyone in Hunt Valley felt the chill.' Ford exaggerated a shiver. 'I hope she understands that Clay was just keeping Cordelia's confidence.'

Maggie's expression was troubled. 'I was your mother's confidante when she was Cordelia's age. I never told your grandmother, and when she found out, it nearly ended our friendship.'

Ford frowned. He knew the details of his mother's traumatic childhood, but he hadn't known that Maggie had been privy to those secrets at the time. 'You and Gran are still friends, right? So you must have worked it all out.'

'We did, but it was dicey for a while. Your mom had her reasons for keeping secrets from your grandmother, just like Cordelia does. It's hard to stay impartial when you're personally invested with all the participants in an emotional situation.' She tilted her head, brows lifted in question. 'Wouldn't you agree?'

Ford's cheeks heated. 'I'm not personally invested.' *Not yet.* But he wanted to be.

Maggie snorted. 'Yeah, right. I'm surprised you still can move your fingers considering how hard she was squeezing your hand. She is awfully pretty, though, isn't she?'

Yes. She is. Ford huffed out a breath in warning. 'Maggie.'

'Fo-ord,' she teased back. 'Well, tell your mom I said hi when you get home.'

'Tell her yourself. You know you're gonna be on the phone to her as soon as you get back in the house, telling her about the reunion.'

'You know me too well, son. And I know you, too. You're not planning on going home tonight. You're staying here so Taylor can hold your hand some more.'

Ford stiffened, because that was far too close to the truth. Hell, it *was* the truth. 'I promised Clay that she'd be here tomorrow morning.'

Maggie smiled affectionately. 'You always were the multitasker.' She took his arm and started back for the house. 'I'll make myself scarce if you make dinner. I have a chicken in the fridge. Hopefully with all that over with, the child will be able to eat more than crackers.'

135

They found Taylor still sitting at the kitchen table, staring at her phone and looking generally shell-shocked. Ford watched the relief flash in her eyes when he walked through the door, and it made him feel . . . good. About himself. About her. About the whole damn world.

It hit him just how long it had been since he'd felt this way. Twenty months. *Twenty.* That was how long it had been since Kimberly had pulled the rug right out from under him. For the first time in twenty months it didn't hurt to think Kim's name. Because he felt good.

Maggie gave Taylor an encouraging hug before excusing herself and going into the living room. Seconds later, just as Ford had predicted, she was dialing the phone.

Ford took the seat next to Taylor, inhaling as discreetly as he could. She smelled good and he wanted to fill his head with her scent. He gestured to the phone in her hand. 'Did you call your . . .' He stumbled over the word, not wanting to betray Clay. But even more, he found he didn't want to hurt Taylor. She loved her stepfather. The man had loved her, protected her, even when he hadn't needed to, and all because of a damn lie. 'Did you call your stepdad?'

Taylor gave him a look of desperate appreciation. 'Not yet. I don't know how to tell him about all this. I don't want to hurt him.'

'You can love both your dads, Taylor,' he said gently. 'The man you've described will surely understand that.'

She smiled sadly. 'He will, but that's not what's gonna hurt him most.' She dropped her gaze to her phone again. 'He didn't want me to come here. Didn't want me meeting Clay, not in any capacity. At first I thought he was afraid that I'd love him less, but that wasn't it. He didn't want me to find out that Clay was legitimately good, because that would mean that my mother really did lie to him all those years. That she kept lying, kept him thinking we had to hide, even when Carrie ran away.' Her lips twisted bitterly. 'Even after Carrie died and Julie needed intense physical therapy. My mother was so damn selfish and he gave up everything. For a lie.'

Ford let out a slow breath. 'It's the ultimate betrayal. I get that.' *Oh, how I get that.*

She looked up then, her eyes filled with grave understanding. 'I know you do.'

He couldn't control his wince. She knew. She knew what Kimberly had done. *How stupid I was.* How much Kim's lie had cost the people he loved.

Of course she knew. Taylor had researched each and every one of them. One only had to Google 'Ford Elkhart' to get hundreds of hits about Kimberly and the trial.

Ford didn't want Taylor to know. He didn't want anyone to know. But it was too late for that. *Everybody knows.* And now people would know that Taylor's stepfather had been hoodwinked as well. It wouldn't be in the papers – Ford hoped – so the number of people aware of Frederick Dawson's humiliation would be a lot smaller than the number aware of Ford's, but still . . . It was going to humiliate Taylor's stepfather for a long, long time.

Because it still humiliates me, and Kimberly wasn't even my wife. Although he'd wanted her to be. He'd all but popped the goddamn question. *Thank God I didn't go that far.*

But as much as Ford sympathized with Taylor's stepfather, he did not want her sympathy or her pity for himself. And right now? That was exactly what he was seeing in her eyes.

Darting a glance into the living room, he could just see Maggie sitting in her big easy chair, one foot bobbing as she talked on the phone. He couldn't hear Maggie's end of the conversation any more than she could hear theirs, but she met his eyes from across the room, brows arched.

Immensely grateful for the diversion, Ford gave Maggie a brief nod before turning back to Taylor. 'Maggie's talking to my mom. Your secret's out, I'm afraid.'

Taylor looked resigned. 'I expected this to happen. You guys are a tight-knit group.'

'We are. They'll want to meet you – the whole lot of them. Are you ready for that?'

'Will they be like Stevie?' she asked uncertainly. 'I don't want to go through that inquisition again.'

'They'll want answers to the same questions, only because most

137

of us have seen how devastated Clay was every time he came back from California without finding you. I'll talk to them first. Don't worry. They'll accept you because you're Clay's daughter. Even Stevie will come around.' He shrugged, hoping he wasn't telling a lie. 'Eventually.'

'Eventually.' She looked away. 'I guess I expected that too. It's what I deserve.'

Ford frowned at her. 'No, you don't. You've been through hell too, and you took the initiative to meet him. That you did it on your own terms is your own business.'

Her smile was small but real, and it lit him up inside like a Christmas tree. 'Thank you, Ford. You've been very nice to me when you didn't have to be.'

'I'm . . . It's okay.' *Mission accomplished.* The sympathy in her eyes had been eradicated. *Now, back to our regularly scheduled program.* 'Are you going to call him? Your stepfather?'

Her smile disappeared, but she squared her shoulders and nodded. 'I have to. I know he's waiting by the phone. I can see him pacing right now.'

'Then call him,' Ford murmured. 'You want me to stay or go?'

She suddenly looked years younger than she had seconds before. Younger and a million times more vulnerable. 'Will you stay?'

'Of course.' He held out his hand, blinking when she gripped it even harder than she had earlier, which he hadn't thought possible.

'I don't know what to say to him,' she whispered. 'I've never dreaded calling him, not in my whole life. Not until I came here.'

'Your mother's lies weren't your fault, Taylor. You're the victim, just like your father. Just like *both* of your fathers.'

She nodded, her swallow audible, her hand trembling as she swiped to the favorites screen and tapped the name at the very top. *Dad.*

Ford's heart hurt. For Clay, for her. But also for Frederick Dawson, the man who'd protected her all these years.

'Hi, Daddy.' She listened a moment, her lip quivering. 'Yeah, I met him. He's . . .' Her voice broke. '*Nice*, Dad. He's so damn *nice*.

138

He knew me, right away. He cried, Daddy,' she ended in a little whisper. 'When he saw me . . . he cried.'

She shook her head, back and forth. 'No, no, no. Not your fault. None of this is your fault. Please don't . . . Dammit, Daddy, please.' Still clutching Ford's hand, she met his eyes miserably.

'He's crying too,' she mouthed silently, then started to cry as well, deep body-racking sobs. Ford's chest grew tight. He needed to do something, so he put his free arm around her shoulders, pulling her close and rocking her gently.

'I'm so sorry,' she said to her stepfather, and Ford realized he'd lost count of how many times she'd said those words since she'd come face-to-face with the truth. 'Say something,' she pleaded. 'Please, Dad. You're scaring me.'

She listened again, a fraction of her tension fading even as her tears continued to fall. 'I'd say it's pretty conclusive. She lied, Dad. And he knew. All these years. Clay knew about it too. Aunt Laura told him. Years ago.'

Ford grabbed a napkin from the holder and pressed it into her hand, not letting her go as she dried her face. She glanced at him with a grateful grimace before dropping her eyes back to the table, her face hidden behind the curtain of her hair. Ford's fingers itched to pull it back so that he could see her expression, but he contented himself with a gentle stroking of the back of her head, his heart beating faster when she leaned into him.

Another pause was followed by her giant sigh. 'Yes, he did hire the PI, but not to kidnap me. He said he wanted to make sure Mom was a good mother. He said he wanted joint custody, but by then we'd disappeared.'

Her chin jerked up. Her hair slid back, revealing her face once again. 'I told you,' she said carefully, 'that I'll finish out this internship before I come home.' She flinched, pain flitting across her expressive face. 'You gotta trust me, Dad. I need to be here.' Her eyes welled up with new tears. 'That's not fair. I love you. *You're my dad.*' The last words were whispered fiercely. 'I'll call you tomorrow, I promise.' She closed her eyes, and the tears spilled down her cheeks. 'I will. I promise that too. Bye, Dad. I love you too.'

139

She pressed END, then put the phone on the table, lining it up precisely with the table's edge. She tugged her hand from Ford's and stood, but her head hung and her shoulders sagged as if she carried a huge weight. Because she did. Through no fault of her own.

Furious with her mother and feeling helpless, Ford stood as well. He brushed his fingertips over her shoulder. 'You okay?' he murmured.

She shook her head. 'No. That was . . . much harder than I thought it was going to be.'

She looked so alone, standing there with her head down. Before he could tell himself this was a bad idea, he turned her so that she faced him, then, as gently as he could, pulled her into his arms. She came to him carefully but willingly. More doll than woman. At first at least.

He wrapped himself around her, bending his body so that her head came to rest on his shoulder. For three long heartbeats she simply stood there, her hands at her sides. Then she was hugging him back, her arms like a vise around his waist. She clung, burying her face in the front of his shirt, while her fingers clutched at the fabric in the back. He stroked her hair, patted her back, rested his cheek on the top of her head, simply breathing her in.

And trying to ignore the soft pressure of her breasts against his chest and the way her body began to relax, becoming as pliable as melted wax, molding itself against him as the seconds ticked by. He tried to ignore all of those things, but his own body was totally not on board. He was so hard that he ached, and his hips wanted to thrust into all that softness so badly that he trembled with the effort of holding back.

Gritting his teeth, he shifted so that she touched him only from the waist up, regretting that he'd started something he had no hope of finishing. Well, maybe not *no* hope. He was a guy after all. All guys *hoped*. But he certainly had no business finishing anything with her.

She was temporary. She'd be going home in a month. This could only be a fling.

So? And anyway, planes fly between Baltimore and California every day.

No. She was hurting. He couldn't take advantage. But . . . *I hurt, too.* His heart and his pride and his sense of being a man had taken a huge hit when Kimberly had betrayed him. He was man enough to admit that, if only to himself. He'd been so lonely for so long. Taylor was the first woman to motivate him into trying to change that. So maybe giving each other some respite wasn't too wrong. Was it?

Respite? the voice in his head asked mockingly. *Is that what we're calling it now?*

Well, respite would certainly be part of it. They were two lonely people, both old enough to know what they wanted. What was the harm?

She's Clay's daughter, the voice reminded him sharply, *and he can murder you in ways no one will ever suspect and then hide your body where no one will ever find it.*

Okay, *that* argument was enough to knock the wind from his sails. Or it should have been. His body had other thoughts. Way too many other thoughts. *Hell, Elkhart, you need to find yourself a date. One that won't get you murdered. Stat.*

He eased out the breath that was backing up in his lungs. Taylor had stopped crying at least, and for that he was grateful. Her hands slowly released his shirt and she lifted her chin, her eyes meeting his. He forced his arms to open so that she could back away.

But she didn't back away. She stood there in the quiet of the kitchen, staring up at his face, her gaze . . . aware. Interested. Defiant. And just a little bit reckless.

No, no, no. Bad idea. Very bad idea, for too many reasons. But the sight of the tip of her tongue venturing out to lick her lower lip made him forget every single one of those reasons. He lifted his hand to her face slowly, giving her time to back away if this wasn't what she wanted. But she stayed put. Staring at him like she was trying to see under his skin. He brushed the back of his fingers over her cheek, his chest expanding painfully when she turned her face into the small caress. Her eyes closed and her expression was one of . . . wonder.

Shit. She'd never been touched like this. Until coming here, she'd

141

never been away from home without an escort. That her over-protective stepfather would allow her to date? Ford simply couldn't see that happening.

I'd be her first. The realization was the splash of cold water he'd needed. He wasn't going to do this. Not right now. Not when she'd had one shock after another.

Gently, he gripped her chin. 'Taylor,' he whispered. 'We can't.'

She opened her eyes and Ford saw the flash of embarrassed understanding. 'Shit,' she whispered back, jerking away from his hand, her cheeks red with shame. 'I'm . . . Never mind. I'm going to my room.'

He grabbed her arm, holding it only long enough to keep her from walking away. 'Wait.' Slowly he dropped his hands to his sides. 'It's not what you think.'

Her jaw jutted out. 'And exactly what *do* I think?'

He opened his mouth. Closed it again. Chose his words carefully. 'Truthfully, I don't exactly know. But I . . .' He blew out a breath. 'I'm feeling about fifteen years old all over again,' he confessed. 'And fifteen sucked.'

'That it did,' she said evenly.

'The truth is that I'm terrified I'm going to say the wrong thing.' Ford made a face. 'You have a scary right hook.'

Her lips twitched. 'I promise not to hit you again.'

He grinned down at her, at ease once more. 'Thank you.' He sobered, his grin quickly fading. 'I don't know what you thought just now, but I really did want to kiss you.'

Her throat worked as she fought to swallow. 'Why didn't you?'

'Because I'm not a dick,' he said ruefully. 'You had a shock today. I had a shock today.' He rubbed his jaw. 'More than one, actually. I'm not going to take advantage of you.'

Her chin lifted and he got the feeling he'd stepped in it once again. 'You're saying that I'm too fragile to know what I want.'

'"Fragile" was not the word I had in mind,' he said wryly, making her lips twitch again. '"Conflicted" might be a better one. "Shaken".' He decided that touching her again was worth the risk, so he cupped her face in his palm. 'I'm selfish enough to want a kiss to mean

142

something. I want it to be because you want *me*. Not because you're shaken up and I'm available.'

She was quiet for nearly a minute before squarely meeting his eyes. 'And once I'm not conflicted or shaken up?'

'Then if you still mean it, I'll want it,' he said simply. 'Until then, I'm here for whatever else you need.'

She frowned. 'Why?'

He was taken aback by the question. 'Because I like to think I'm a nice guy. And because you've been dealt a really shitty hand, but you still seem to care about other people. Like your dad and Clay. And little Jazzie.' He leaned into her space to whisper in her ear. 'And because when you're no longer shaken up, I want you to care about me. I want you to want me.'

Her breasts rose and fell as she drew a deep breath, her cheeks darkening again, but this time it wasn't shame. It was need. He started to reach for her once more, but shoved his hands in his pockets instead. He needed to change the subject, and his stomach cooperated by growling loudly. Food. He'd promised Maggie that he'd make dinner.

He took a giant step back, rounding the table to gather the ingredients from the refrigerator. Holding the package of chicken in one hand, he turned to find Taylor escaping up the stairs. He wanted to beg her to stay, but knew she needed space just as he did. So he kept his tone light. 'You're not a vegetarian, are you?'

Her smile was wry. 'No. Growing up on a cattle ranch, that would have been a little hypocritical, don't you think? I'm going to my room to lie down for a while. Like you said, I had a shock today. I think it just caught up with me. I'll be down for dinner.'

Baltimore, Maryland,
Saturday 22 August, 7.15 P.M.

Gage took a moment to check his reflection in the glass door of the very expensive restaurant that Cesar Tavilla had picked for their first meeting. He looked good. Really, really good. Good enough to draw admiring glances from many of the women sitting at Tavilla's

143

table. That was just one of the many things Gage admired about Tavilla. He surrounded himself with stunningly beautiful women.

It had been a while since Gage had had a stunningly beautiful woman. They'd been in ample supply when he'd first left Baltimore for the condo he'd kept in Miami, set up under layers of corporations so that it could never be traced to him. He'd rewarded himself with the condo after his first big bonus check, shortly after making junior partner at his old law firm. He'd used it to get away whenever he needed a break – his secret retreat.

Valerie had never even been suspicious. She'd been too busy banging lovers while he'd been gone. That he'd also banged lovers was immaterial. He'd worked hard, so he'd played hard. He'd earned the money and it was nobody else's business how he spent it. Valerie's only job had been to keep his household running smoothly and to raise his children.

Which had ended so well, he thought bitterly.

But he wasn't going to think about that now, because his new boss was waiting for him at his table, a woman on either side of him and one in his lap. Tavilla nudged them all away, motioning Gage to sit in one of the vacated seats.

'Mr Jarvis,' he said, flashing a very white smile. 'It's good to see you again.'

'Likewise, Señor.' Gage took the seat and lifted the glass of wine that a waiter immediately set at his elbow. 'I look forward to getting back to work.'

One side of Tavilla's mouth curved. 'I imagine you do. How is your family, Mr Jarvis?'

Gage blinked. 'My family?'

'I read the newspaper story about your wife. That she was murdered in her home. It is a senseless tragedy.'

'It is.' For some reason Gage hadn't expected Tavilla to know his business. *I should have.* The man wouldn't have become so successful if he hadn't been thorough and very careful. Gage wouldn't be making that mistake again. Dropping his gaze to the white tablecloth, he made himself the picture of despair. 'Our children have been devastated, as you can only imagine.'

'They are quite young?'

'Yes. Eleven and five. They're in counseling, but . . .' He looked up and met his employer's eyes squarely. 'I'm doing my best to be there for them.'

'As a father should,' Tavilla agreed with a sage nod. A server approached, his tray laden with food, and Gage's stomach growled, making Tavilla chuckle. 'I took the liberty of ordering for you, Mr Jarvis. The house specialty.'

'Thank you,' Gage said, a little annoyed and trying to decide if he wanted to show it. He decided he did, and smiled at Tavilla. 'I'm sure it's wonderful. But in the future, I'd really like to choose my own meal.' It was all about setting expectations up front. He was not one of Tavilla's fawning lackeys. He was the man's attorney and needed to be free to speak his mind.

Tavilla looked amused. 'Of course. My apologies.'

'Thank you.' Gage took a few bites of the large steak that had been set in front of him, then dabbed at the corner of his mouth. It really was delicious. 'I'd like to know a bit about the cases I'll be taking on when I start on Monday.'

'The briefs will be waiting on your desk,' Tavilla said smoothly, and motioned to the server to refill their wine glasses. 'So, the man suspected of killing your wife was found dead this morning.'

Gage had just swallowed a mouthful of wine and had to breathe through his nose to keep from choking. Tavilla had timed that perfectly. Gage cleared his throat. 'Yes, he was. The police informed me.'

'The word is that the young hoodlum overdosed and that the dealer who sold him the poison was killed by a policeman.'

Sonofafuckingbitch. Gage lifted his shoulders in a very slight shrug. 'I was told that an officer and a dealer were also killed.' Because as the grieving widower, he'd be informed by the police. 'But I didn't realize who'd killed whom. The police keep some of the facts close to the vest.'

'That they do,' Tavilla said levelly. 'It is a nice tidy resolution to your wife's murder.'

Gage fought the urge to swallow nervously, drawing on his

growing irritation. He'd faced down scarier assholes in court. *Bring it on.* He didn't blink. 'It is.'

'Just in time for your first day with me.'

Gage shrugged again. 'I'm not going to look a gift horse in the mouth.'

Tavilla smiled tightly, his amusement completely vanished. 'Yes, well, I hope your gift horse is not a Trojan trap. I'd hate for there to be any . . . repercussions once you've officially entered my employ.'

'There won't be,' Gage said, quietly but firmly.

'Good.' Tavilla nodded. 'See that there are not. Now please eat, Mr Jarvis.'

Gage complied, even though his gut was churning anew.

What if the girl actually saw something? What if she tells? He'd have no choice but to run, just as Denny had recommended. It was clear Tavilla wouldn't tolerate any . . . complications. And he was pretty certain his new boss favored quick and decisive solutions when they arose.

I'm not going to run. Because once he did, he'd never be able to rest. He'd always be looking over his shoulder. If the girl had seen anything, she'd have to go.

That Denny would die had been a given from the moment he'd threatened to tell. Gage had planned to make it happen in a few months, when it could appear to be an unfortunate accident. If Jazzie had witnessed anything . . . well, accidents happened every day.

Hunt Valley, Maryland,
Saturday 22 August, 7.35 P.M.

Clay couldn't remember eating a meal as tense as this one had been. The drive from Maggie's farmhouse to the pizzeria had been glacially silent, his gut clenching every time Stevie worried her lower lip – something she did when she wanted to cry but refused to allow herself to do so.

He wanted to apologize, but he wasn't sure exactly what he'd be apologizing for. He'd known Stevie would be hurt when she found

146

out that Cordy still had nightmares, but he thought he'd have a little more time to grease the skids between Cordy and her mom, so that his little girl could tell her mama all by herself. That would have been best.

Still, Stevie wouldn't have taken it so personally had it not been accompanied by Cordelia's reproof. The atmosphere in Maggie's kitchen had been so incredibly strained already.

Because of Sienna. *Sienna. My baby.* Clay's throat closed. He'd found his daughter. *Finally.* He'd held her in his arms and touched her face and she hadn't run away screaming. She'd come on her own. *To meet me.* And she'd done it so stealthily that neither he nor Joseph Carter had suspected she was right under their noses. Pride tingled in his chest.

But it was a short-lived tingle, because so much remained unsettled. She'd changed her name. She lived three thousand miles away. She already had a man she called Dad.

Who isn't me. Pain gripped his heart, squeezing brutally. *She loves him. Not me.* Because they'd never been given a chance. They had a chance now – if she didn't disappear again.

I should be camped out at Maggie's making sure Sienna doesn't bolt. He'd found his daughter after all these years, only to walk away and leave her alone with Ford Elkhart. *Just for the evening, to allow her to regroup.* And Ford was an honorable young man. If he said he'd make sure Sienna remained until morning, she'd be there.

Clay hoped Sienna's dinner with Ford and Maggie was less stressful than this one had been. He and Stevie had basically chewed and swallowed, while Cordelia pushed her food around on her plate, her expression sullen.

Sitting in Maggie's kitchen, he'd really thought that the lightening of the mood between Stevie and Cordelia there at the end had meant they were all okay, but he guessed he had a lot to learn about women. Apparently both mother and daughter had been pretending.

Nobody was pretending anymore. They were all legitimately miserable.

'You need to eat, baby,' Stevie murmured to Cordelia, the first words any of them had spoken since giving the server their orders forty minutes before.

Cordelia's fingers tightened on her fork. Her chin jerked up and her eyes flashed. 'I'm not a baby and I'm not hungry.' She paused for a heartbeat. 'Ma'am,' she added crisply.

Stevie winced and Clay felt like shit. 'Got it,' Stevie said softly.

Clay opened his mouth to say something, but both Stevie and Cordelia gave him the stink eye. He closed his mouth, pushed his half-eaten dinner away, and waved the server over. 'We'll need boxes to take this home,' he said when the young woman approached with understandable caution. As a family unit, they were a simmering pot, ready to boil over.

He rubbed his palms over his face. 'I'm sorry,' he murmured to Stevie.

'I know,' she said quietly.

'I never thought . . .' He let the words trail away. Sienna had been the spark that ignited this situation, but the kindling had been set up long ago. As soon as he'd agreed to keep Cordelia's secret. 'Forgive me,' he said in a whisper barely audible. 'I'm new at this parent stuff.'

Stevie's sad smile cracked his heart in two. 'I'm not, so let me warn you that it doesn't get any easier.'

He squeezed her thigh under the table. 'Let's go home.'

Baltimore, Maryland,
Saturday 22 August, 7.40 P.M.

Mmmm. Mama's making cookies. I hope they're chocolate chip. Jasmine's eyelids fluttered open as the familiar aroma tickled her nose. *Mama's making—*

No. Mama wasn't making cookies, because Mama wasn't here anymore. *Because she's dead. Say it, Jasmine. Say. It.*

Fine, she snarled to herself. *She's dead, all right? She. Is. Dead.* She ripped off the blanket and sat on the edge of her bed, *so damn mad.* But there wasn't anybody to blame.

Nobody but the man who'd actually killed her mama, and

Jasmine couldn't blame him. Not out loud, anyway. *Grandma won't believe me. She'll tell the police I was lying.*

Because Grandma had done it before, swearing to the police that her son wasn't capable of hitting anyone. But Jasmine knew the truth even though she'd been only eight then. Mama had gone to bed early that night with an icepack on her face, because it had turned all black and blue. And Mama had been crying so hard that Jasmine had gotten scared and called Aunt Lilah.

Aunt Lilah had come right over and she'd called the police, who took pictures of Mama's poor face. Mama told the police that her husband had hit her and that she'd made him leave.

Jasmine had hoped it would be okay then. Her daddy had become really scary and she was glad he wasn't coming back. But Aunt Lilah had to go to work the next day and that was when Grandma had come to their house, screaming so loud that Janie had started crying and Jasmine had hidden behind her wingback chair. The same one she'd hidden behind a month ago, though it was in their old house back then.

Grandma called Mama a liar and said that she'd told the police that, too. She said that Mama had ruined Daddy's life by accusing him of hitting her – that he'd get disbarred and lose his job. Then Grandma had gotten so quiet that Jasmine almost didn't hear her call Mama a dirty whore. She said she knew that Mama had a boyfriend who came over when Jasmine was at school and Janie was napping. Grandma swore that if Mama didn't call the police back and say that she'd lied about who hit her, she'd tell Jasmine's father and there would be no alimony.

That was the first that Jasmine had heard about her parents getting divorced, and she'd been so *glad*. She'd wanted to jump out from behind the chair and yell at her grandma for accusing her mama of cheating, because even though Jasmine was only eight, she knew what cheating was. She kept thinking that her mama would tell Grandma to *shut up*, that it *wasn't true*. But Mama never denied it. Not even when Aunt Lilah came back later that night, as mad as Grandma had been, because Mama *had* called the police and taken it all back.

149

In bed by then, Jasmine had snuck downstairs and listened while Mama calmly told Aunt Lilah that she'd realized there would be no alimony if her father was convicted of assault, because he'd have no money to give her if he lost his job. She didn't mention Grandma's visit or her threat. She didn't mention the secret boyfriend. Not once.

And that was when Jasmine knew it was true, that her mama *had* cheated. She also knew she couldn't let on that she knew. They needed that alimony because Mama didn't have a good education like Aunt Lilah did. Mama wouldn't get a good job and they'd be poor.

Aunt Lilah had just sighed and told Mama that everything would be all right. That she'd keep quiet too, because paying alimony would probably hurt her father more in the long run.

The divorce never ended up happening, because her father quit his job and ran away. There was no money at all. Mama worked so hard to keep the house, but in the end they'd had to give it back to the bank, and they'd moved to the apartment.

The apartment where her mama had ended up dead.

Mama and Grandma didn't talk for a long time after that day Jasmine had hidden behind the chair. Not until Mama moved them to the apartment. Jasmine remembered being asleep in her bed, waking up to hear Grandma's voice. Wondering why, she'd snuck out of bed to listen.

Grandma had lost her house too, to pay for her father's rehab. He was getting better, Grandma had been sure of it, and he deserved another chance to rebuild his life after Jasmine's mama had ruined it by cheating. But now Grandma had no place to live. Mama had said no – until Grandma reminded her that she could still tell about Mama's secret boyfriend. And that Mama had been drinking.

Grandma said she was worried that their mama wasn't taking care of them right, that Grandma could take care of them better. That had made Jasmine so mad that she'd almost burst into the room yelling, because Mama *was* taking care of them – with Jasmine's help. They didn't need Grandma butting in where she wasn't wanted. But Grandma's next threat had Jasmine stunned and silenced.

Grandma had threatened to report Mama to the child protection people. She threatened to sue for custody – to take them away from their mother forever.

Mama had been stunned too – and frightened. The next thing Jasmine knew, Grandma had moved in, taking Mama's room and making Mama sleep on the sofa. Jasmine hadn't said a word, because she hadn't wanted her mama to be even sadder. She'd obeyed her grandma, even though she hated the old woman *so much*.

She'd been 'Mama's good girl', but now Mama was dead. The police had come and asked all of them – Grandma, Lilah and Jasmine herself – about her father, could he have done it? Lilah had said *yes*, and Jasmine had been so relieved – she hadn't had to say what she'd seen!

But she'd been shocked once again when Grandma told her that her father couldn't have done it, because he was in Texas. Detective Fitzpatrick had told Grandma so. Still, Jasmine had hoped he'd come back and say it wasn't true. But he hadn't. He'd believed the alibi, which meant he was either stupid or lazy, only wanting to make his job easier. It couldn't be because the alibi was true, because Jasmine knew that it wasn't.

The scary thing was, Jasmine knew that her grandma really did believe her son was in Texas. She believed he hadn't beaten his wife to death, just like she'd believed he hadn't hit Mama when Jasmine was eight. Or that he wasn't really an addict, even though he'd flunked out of rehab three times and made her lose her house. That somehow he'd change.

Grandma wasn't going to believe her. Ever. But it didn't matter, because once Jasmine told anyone, *he'd* find out. And unless the police caught him super-fast, *he'd come back*.

Jasmine wasn't willing to trust the police to catch him at all, much less super-fast.

But I can't go on like this, watching Janie's every move, watching every word that comes out of her mouth. It was exhausting, for one. But more importantly, school was starting soon and she and Janie didn't even go to the same school. *If I'm not there to watch her, Janie could tell anyone that Aunt Lilah found me behind the chair.*

151

Reaching under her pillow, Jasmine pulled out Miss Taylor's card. Maybe she'd send her an email later tonight when Grandma had gone to sleep. *There has to be a way out of this.*

Her stomach picked that moment to growl, and Jasmine remembered that she'd missed dinner. And the cookies smelled really good.

She made her way to the kitchen, where Grandma stood at the sink washing dishes while Janie and Aunt Lilah spooned cookie dough onto a baking sheet.

'Jazzie. I'm glad you're awake.' Aunt Lilah was smiling, and that was good to see. Lilah hadn't had much to smile about lately either. *We're a lot of work, Janie and me.* Plus Lilah didn't really like Grandma either, but she hadn't been willing to throw an old woman out with no home to go to. The old bat could have moved in with Uncle Denny and Aunt Missy, but Missy didn't like Grandma either.

And Grandma didn't like Denny. *So we're stuck with the old bitch.*

'Do you want some dinner?' Grandma asked, and Jasmine nodded. 'Well then, sit down and I'll warm up your plate as soon as I'm done with the dishes.'

Sometimes Jasmine didn't completely hate her stutter. It gave her an excuse not to talk to people she didn't like.

'Jazzie!' Janie had flour on her nose and a sunny smile on her face, and Jasmine's dark mood lightened just a smidge, as Mama used to say. 'Me and Aunt Lilah are making cookies, Jazzie! Want some dough?'

Grandma threw an exasperated look over her shoulder. 'Janie, I told you not to eat the dough. You'll get worms or something.'

'I don't see no worms,' Janie said, squinting at the lump of dough on her spoon.

Aunt Lilah bit back a smile. 'You won't *see* the worms, baby. They're microscopic.'

Janie made a horrified face. 'You mean cookies are full of cooked worms?'

Aunt Lilah chuckled, sounding so much like their mama that Jasmine's eyes burned. 'No, baby. But grownups have to tell you not to eat the dough, just in case.'

152

Janie inspected the spoon again. 'So I probably won't get sick?'

'Probably not,' Aunt Lilah agreed. 'Keep it to one spoonful, okay?'

'Lilah!' Grandma snapped, upset. 'Don't be telling her things like that.'

'Eunice,' Lilah responded patiently. 'I've eaten cookie dough my whole life and I've never been sick. The girls don't need to be afraid of everything. Okay?'

Grandma turned back to the sink with a sniff.

Aunt Lilah rolled her eyes, then smiled at Jasmine. 'We're indulging tonight. A little celebration. Come sit with us.'

Jasmine dragged herself to the table and sat next to Aunt Lilah, cocking her head in question.

'Why are we celebrating?' Aunt Lilah asked. 'I think just because it was a good day.'

Janie's lip poked out in a pout. 'You get to cel'brate tomorrow too, and it's not fair. Why can't I have ice cream too, Aunt Lilah?'

'If you stop whining, I might get you some,' Aunt Lilah said, then turned back to Jasmine. 'You've hit it off pretty well with Miss Taylor at the farm, haven't you?'

Jasmine nodded warily, wondering if they could have seen her looking at the business card.

'Good,' Aunt Lilah said. 'Would you enjoy some time with her away from the horses?'

Jasmine nodded hard. Because the horses were freaking terrifying.

Aunt Lilah smiled. 'Excellent. I set up some time for the two of you to have ice cream tomorrow afternoon. You seemed to like talking to her, so I thought maybe . . .'

Jasmine's eyes widened. *I didn't talk to her. I said thank you. That's it.* But Aunt Lilah looked so hopeful that Jasmine nodded a final time. Maybe this was a sign that she should tell Miss Taylor the truth. Just so somebody would know. In case he came back.

Ten

Hunt Valley, Maryland,
Saturday 22 August, 7.45 P.M.

The knocking on her bedroom door had Taylor jerking out of a
light sleep. Her chin snapped up, causing the back of her head to
smack the headboard. She rubbed her head with a wince. *Exactly
what my headache needed.* 'Yes?'

'Dinner will be ready in five minutes,' Maggie said through the
door. 'Ford wanted me to tell you that if you want, he can make you
a plate. I can bring it up.'

Taylor almost said yes to that, the idea of hiding from Ford a
little too appealing. She'd all but thrown herself at him – but he
hadn't caught her. Instead he had to be a nice guy. At the moment
Taylor wasn't feeling very nice. She was itchy. Needy. *Horny*, she
admitted.

But Ford was right. Today wouldn't have been a good time to
start anything – for either of them. He was vulnerable too. She didn't
want to hurt him. She didn't want to hurt any of them. But she
would. She already had hurt Clay.

Goddamn you, Mom.

'Do you want me to bring your dinner up?' Maggie prompted.

'Is . . . is it just the three of us?'

'Not exactly,' Maggie hedged. 'Can I open the door?'

No. 'Yes, ma'am.'

The door opened a crack and Maggie stuck her head in, wincing
when she saw Taylor's eyes, red and swollen. 'Oh, Taylor,' she
murmured.

154

'I'll be all right. Who's here?'

'Right now, just the three of us. But Daphne is on her way over.'

It was Taylor's turn to wince. 'Is she angry?'

'No. Joseph was fit to be tied when he heard the news.' A little smile curled at the corners of Maggie's mouth. 'He wants to know how you bamboozled his background check.'

Taylor's lips twitched. 'Bamboozled?'

Maggie's eyes twinkled. 'He used a different, less polite word. Luckily he's off on a case. He won't be able to interrogate you until at least tomorrow. I think Daphne's mad at herself for not seeing the resemblance between you and your father. She was plumb flattened.'

Maggie's West Virginia twang was out in full force and Taylor understood it was to disarm and charm. She'd heard Maggie fall back into the accent with some of the program's participants. She would get all folksy, putting kids and their parents at ease. It was putting Taylor at ease right now.

She smiled at the older woman. 'So four of us for dinner?'

'Unless someone else shows up, but they shouldn't. We'll ask everyone to wait until you and Clay have had more of a chance to talk.'

Taylor's smile faded. 'I hate to think I made problems for him with his new family. That's not why I came.'

Maggie sat on the edge of the bed and patted Taylor's knee. 'I know that. So do Daphne and Clay. Stevie will come around because she loves him. This thing with Cordelia has been brewing for a long time, so don't you worry your head about it. Daphne will also understand if you want to eat in your room tonight. She's coming to check in with Ford as much as to see you.'

Taylor frowned. 'Why? Why does she need to check on Ford?'

Maggie hesitated, then sighed, apology in her eyes. 'Because I'm a busybody. I guess I was feeling guilty for keeping Cordy's secret from Stevie, so I went a little overboard in telling Daphne about Ford.' Gray brows lifted. 'And you.'

Taylor stared, stunned. 'We didn't do anything.'

'You would have if Ford hadn't stopped. And before you get

155

your panties in a twist, nobody's mad about that. It's just that Ford's our boy. Daphne, her mama and I watched him grow up, taught him how a man should treat a woman. God knows he never had a decent role model in his own sperm donor,' she added in a mutter.

'Did Ford's dad . . . did he abuse Daphne?'

'He didn't hit her, but he and that family of his did everything they could to manipulate and destroy her.' Maggie hesitated. 'Daphne was only fifteen when Ford was conceived. Travis Elkhart got her tipsy and she was . . . well, let's just say she knew the birds and the bees, but nobody had prepared her for the alley cats with their smooth lines and expensive champagne.'

'Ford's father was her first,' Taylor said quietly, understanding. Daphne had only been fifteen. 'He took advantage of her innocence.' And so Ford would not take advantage of Taylor after she'd had a shock. That made sense. It was sweet, actually.

But I'm still horny, she thought irritably. *I should have been the one to decide what we did. Because I knew what I wanted.*

Maggie hesitated again. 'Look, you lost your mom, Taylor, so I'm going to be presumptive and give you a motherly talking-to. You are, pretty literally, just off the farm, finally free of your daddy's leash. It's normal to explore. Totally normal. But you need to take care with whom you explore. Once that door's been opened, it can't be closed again. Ford would treat you right, but . . .' She tilted her head forward, her smile gentle. 'Maybe you both deserve better than a quick tumble in my kitchen.'

Oh. Oh God. 'I wouldn't have . . . would never have . . . Wait. How do *you* know?' Taylor's cheeks burned. 'You spied on us? Cameras in the kitchen? Really?'

Maggie had the good grace to look embarrassed. 'No, no cameras in the kitchen, but I was sitting in the next room. It wasn't that hard to know what was happening. But I didn't see you. Ford told me. He wanted to come up here and try to explain, but I convinced him to give you an hour or so and let you keep your pride. Ford understands pride.'

'Because he lost his to Kimberly,' Taylor murmured.

Maggie looked impressed. 'So you're not as fresh off the farm as you appear.'

'I read Ford's court transcripts. I read about you all, hoping to find some information about Clay.' There really hadn't been any, though, and all Taylor had learned was that Ford's ex was a horrible person. 'I know that Ford's ex-girlfriend set him up to be kidnapped. I know that she was only pretending to love him. I'm not stupid, Maggie.'

'No, you're not.' She patted Taylor's shoulder. 'You've got brains and guts. And I think you have a good heart. Just remember that Ford looks big and tough and brawny, but down deep he may be as scared as you are.' Maggie stood up and walked to the door, her step slower than it had been earlier in the day. It was hard to believe the woman was in her seventies until you saw her move at the end of a long day. 'Should we bring your dinner up here?'

Pull up your big-girl pants, Taylor. Look Ford in the eye and don't be embarrassed. 'No, ma'am. I'll be down in a few minutes.'

'Good girl,' Maggie said approvingly. 'Wash your face, child, and lay a cold rag on your eyes. They're only one step up from ground hamburger.'

Taylor's laugh surprised her. 'Yes, ma'am.'

By the time Taylor made it to the dinner table, Maggie was gone, as was her plate. Ford was waiting in a chair quietly, his plate still empty. He'd set Taylor's place right next to his.

'Maggie took her dinner to the front porch,' he said. 'She said she'd waylay my mother for a little while. Just to let you finish eating before Mom comes to talk to you.'

Taylor forced back a shudder. 'Maggie said that your mom's not mad.'

Ford gave her a sympathetic smile as he dished up chicken and vegetables for them both. 'She won't be. She *will* be nosy. She might be a bit worried.'

'Worried?'

'Well, about the program. You slid through Joseph's background check like a hot knife through butter. That could jeopardize Healing Hearts – especially if you also falsified any other important items.'

157

Taylor felt the blood drain from her head. 'Jeopardize Healing Hearts? What items?'

'You could have a criminal record.'

'I don't!'

He lifted a shoulder. 'I believe you, but . . . you came here under false pretenses. I don't know if there will be any repercussions from that.' He met her eyes squarely. 'You didn't lie about your qualifications, did you?'

'No. I really do have a degree in psychology and I really did grow up around horses. The only thing I hid was my birth name.'

'And your reason for being here,' he said mildly.

'Oh God.' Taylor hadn't really considered what would happen after telling Clay who she really was. She hadn't expected to like everyone on the farm so damn much. She hadn't expected the program to be so important.

She hadn't, but she should have. 'What could happen?' she asked hoarsely.

'The state licensing board could put the program on probation. Worst case, they yank Mom's license and she'd have to shut down.'

Taylor's stomach heaved. 'I'd throw me out,' she whispered. 'If I were your mother, I'd call the cops on me.'

'That's the worst case. Best case, nothing happens because nobody finds out. Try to relax. Mom might be worried, but she isn't going to yell or scream at you.' But Ford's hand wasn't exactly steady when he picked up the bottle of wine on the table and poured himself a half-glass. 'Would you like some?'

She eyed the bottle wistfully, then shook her head. 'At this moment, I almost wish I drank.' But it was at this moment that she needed to be stone-cold sober.

She thought of Jazzie and Janie and the other children who'd come to therapy during the past two weeks. This program was important – critical – to their recovery. *Please don't let me have hurt the program. Please.*

Baltimore, Maryland,
Saturday 22 August, 8.00 P.M.

The buzzing of his cell phone roused JD from his pleasantly sated drowse. He checked the number, saw it was Lilah Cornell. This was a call he had to take. He glanced down at the woman in his arms. Lucy was still sleeping, her head on his shoulder as he sat propped against the pillows of their bed. He'd exhausted her, but he couldn't be sorry. Dropping a kiss on her strawberry-blond hair, he answered quietly. 'Detective Fitzpatrick.'

'Detective, this is Lilah Cornell. Jazzie's aunt. Is this a bad time?'

'No, of course not, Miss Cornell,' he murmured. 'I'm just not in a place where I can talk loudly at the moment. Did you speak to Jazzie about meeting with Taylor Dawson?'

'I did. She seems to like the idea. Especially since they wouldn't be around the horses. Jazzie is afraid of them, I think.'

Poor kid's afraid of too many things, he thought. 'Good. I'll follow up with Miss VanDorn. She was going to check Miss Dawson's availability. I'll call you with the time.'

'Perfect. Thank you so very much.' The gratitude in her voice was nearly as heartbreaking as her next words. 'We need this to be over. I'm about to break from the strain and I'm . . . well, old enough to have coping skills. Jazzie's too young to carry this burden, this fear. She's withdrawn so deep that I'm afraid we won't be able to pull her out.'

He wanted to reassure her, to make promises, but he'd been a cop too long. He knew never to promise. But he could hopefully give her a little comfort. 'You're not alone in this, Miss Cornell. Our department is working the case as its highest priority, and Healing Hearts will support you as well, however you need them.'

'I know,' she whispered. 'I'll keep hoping.'

He hesitated. But she needed to be aware of the potential danger. 'Have you heard from the girls' father?'

A long pause. 'No. Can you hold on for a moment?' From the other end there was quiet conversation, then the sound of a closing door. 'Sorry. I didn't want to have this conversation around

Eunice, the girls' grandmother. She's . . . well, she still trusts her son.'

'You don't?' He'd asked Lilah this question before and her response had always been consistent. JD liked consistency, and Lilah's had made him less nervous about the children living with her while they searched for Valerie's killer. Once again, she gave the same answer.

'No,' Lilah said curtly with not a beat of hesitation. 'He's a liar and abusive. Why? Have you found him?' Her voice grew shaky. 'Is he here? In the city?'

'We don't know. We haven't had any reports that he is. I'm just trying to cover all the bases.'

Her swallow was audible. 'Is Jazzie in danger, Detective?'

'I don't know,' he answered honestly. 'Just keep her close to you for the next few days.' He'd told Joseph to expect Gage Jarvis to surface. His gut told him that it would be sooner rather than later. 'I know that's vague, and I don't have any more information for you at the moment, but as soon as I do, I'll let you know. Either way, I'll call you back with the time for the meeting tomorrow. The place is a restaurant called Giuseppe's.'

'I know it. Can you keep my niece safe there?'

'Absolutely. We have a secure room with a private entrance at the back. Text me when you're five minutes out, then park in the lot behind the restaurant. I will be waiting for you there, and I'll escort you both inside. We can guard Jazzie's safety in the private room and listen to her conversation with Miss Dawson without her knowing we're there.'

'It feels wrong, listening to her conversation when she thinks it's private,' Lilah admitted. 'But I'll make sure she's there. I'm at my wits' end with worry. Something has to change or we'll all implode from the stress.'

If Jazzie wasn't taken out by her mother's killer first. 'If you hear anything suspicious, call 911, then me. Don't hesitate, even if you think it's silly.'

'Don't worry,' she assured him with a shaky laugh. 'I won't. Thank you.'

He hung up, then glanced down again to find Lucy's eyes still closed, her breathing even. He had to make a few more calls but didn't want to wake her. He considered moving, but knew that would wake her up, and she needed her sleep.

He called Maggie next. 'It's JD,' he said when she answered. 'I can't talk loud because Lucy's asleep. Can you hear me?'

'I can. Poor girl needs her sleep. Chasing after that hellraiser of yours is hard work, JD,' Maggie said fondly. But she sounded off. Subdued.

'Jeremiah is a handful,' he agreed. 'What's wrong?'

'Nothing. Really. I assume you're calling about Taylor meeting with Jazzie? Taylor has agreed. She's on duty tomorrow, but lessons should be finished by two. She'll need time to brush down the horses and clean up after lessons. She could be there by four.'

'Sounds like a plan. Are you sure you're okay, Maggie? You don't sound like yourself.'

'I'm fine,' she said warmly, all traces of her off-ness disappeared. 'Though I appreciate you asking. '

He suspected she was blowing smoke his way, but he knew better than to push. Maggie carried as many secrets on her shoulders as he did. 'Thanks. I'll call with final details tomorrow.'

He hung up and dialed Hector. 'How you doin', man?' he asked when Hector answered with a grunt. The loss of any cop hurt, but Mancuso had been Hector's friend.

'Fine.' The single word was curt and filled with contained rage. 'I tracked down a description of Cleon Perry's car. He drives a piece-of-shit Chevy that no one's seen since yesterday. Too old for GPS, so we can't track it. I put out a BOLO on it. Figured that's how the bastard got away so fast this morning.'

'Plus it's probably how he hauled Romano's body around,' JD agreed. 'And probably Perry, too, before he killed him in the alley. Good work, Hector. We have the green light on the meet with Jazzie Jarvis and her therapist at four tomorrow. Can you meet me at Giuseppe's by three to set up?'

'Yeah. Listen, I'm at Mancuso's house with his wife and kid. I need to go. She's . . .' Hector drew a harsh breath and let it out. 'She's not doing well at all.'

Dammit. 'I'm sorry,' JD said, hating the words because they were so inadequate. 'Let us know what she needs, okay? Besides her husband's killer roasting over a spit.'

Hector's laugh was a grating bark. 'Yeah. Thanks, JD. Later, man.'

With a silent sigh, JD called Lilah Cornell, told her what time to be there tomorrow, then hung up and placed his phone on the nightstand, careful not to make any sound. He slid down the pillows a little and closed his eyes when they stung.

He thought of Jazzie and her sister, motherless, and Mancuso's kid, fatherless, all because a piece of shit was snipping loose ends. His indrawn breath was shaky and he shuddered out the exhale as he tried to stave off tears. Dammit, he never used to be so emotional. Fatherhood had changed him in ways he'd never imagined.

'It's okay, you know,' Lucy said softly against his chest. 'To get a little weepy.'

He stiffened. 'I thought you were asleep.'

'Nope. You've been too restless.' She kissed his pec, pressing her hand to his heart. 'You're wound tighter than a drum. You want to talk about it?'

'You don't want to hear this,' he said, but even he could hear how needy he sounded.

'Maybe not, but just talking about it might clear your mind. Talk to me, JD. Then we can both sleep.'

He'd used her as a sounding board back when she'd been the ME, and she never failed to help him sort things out, even when she didn't say a word. So he told her everything, stroking her hair as he talked.

'So you like the ex-husband for the murders?' she asked when he was finished.

'Not ex. Just estranged. Valerie never divorced him. But yeah, he looks good for it.'

'Why did he come back?' she asked. 'I mean, he's gone for almost three years. Why choose *now* to come back?'

As usual, she'd hit the nail on the head. 'I've wondered that myself. I asked his former boss and co-workers, his brother, his mother. Nobody will admit to having seen him, much less offer up a reason for his return. Of course I could be barking up the wrong damn tree. Maybe he hasn't come back at all.'

'For now, assume you're right and that he has. What about his friends? If I were coming back after three years, I might hit up friends before family and former co-workers.'

'I couldn't find anyone who'd claim Gage Jarvis as an acquaintance, much less a friend. He didn't seem to have friends outside of work. No clubs, leagues, teams. He worked all the time and his co-workers gave me the bullshit line. Claimed that he was a great guy, that everyone loved him. But no one could give me one example of *why* he was such a great guy, and no one's had any contact with him since he left the firm. It was like talking to the Stepford lawyers.'

'Maybe you've been asking the wrong people,' she said, stifling a yawn. 'He was a high-profile defense attorney, right? Ask other lawyers. Maybe they knew him, or at least knew where he'd hang out when he lived here.' She patted his chest. 'Ask Thorne. He knows everyone in the city, I think. Especially the lawyers. If there's any dirt to find, Thorne will dig it up.'

That was a slight overexaggeration, but Lucy had a point. She, Thomas Thorne and Gwyn Weaver had been best friends for years. The three of them co-owned Sheidalin, a nightclub that featured live music and performance art. Gwyn managed the club with Thorne's assistance as needed. Lucy was a club favorite when she performed with her electric violin, although she hadn't been on stage in several months. Her babies were definitely her first priority. Thorne managed the front, mingling and chatting with guests. He was the trio's people person.

He was also a successful defense attorney, but unlike Gage Jarvis, Thomas Thorne was a good guy. Honest. Loyal to a fault. While Thorne helped Gwyn with the running of the club, Gwyn assisted Thorne in his law firm, and somehow the two of them made it work. JD trusted both of them with his life, and – more importantly – with the lives of his family. Gwyn was Bronwynne's godmother and Thorne was Jeremiah's godfather.

163

Still, JD was tentative as he dialed Thorne's cell. Blaring music met his ears.

'Hold on,' Thorne said, and a half-minute later, the music was abruptly silenced. 'Had to go to my office for peace and quiet. What's up?'

'Not sure, but I could use any info you have on a guy who was a defense attorney in the city three years ago. His name is Gage Jarvis.'

'What do you want to know?' Thorne asked, suddenly wary.

'Anything you can tell me. Who his friends were, where he hung out, where he went when he left here three years ago. If anyone's seen him here in town in the last four weeks.'

JD could hear the tapping of computer keys and Thorne's voice quietly swearing a blue streak. 'You suspect he killed his wife?'

JD hesitated, then went for broke. 'Yes.'

It was Thorne's turn to hesitate. 'Let me see what I can find,' he finally said. 'I'll get back to you if I turn up anything useful.'

'Thanks, Thorne. Lucy says hi,' he added when his wife waved at the phone.

'Hi back. Tell her we miss her around here.'

'Come over and tell her yourself. We always need babysitters.'

Thorne snorted a laugh. 'Gwyn's got your little monsters right now.'

'So it's your turn next,' JD said lightly, then sobered. 'Thorne? Nobody can know I'm asking about Jarvis.'

'You have my word.'

That would have to be good enough. 'Thank you.'

Lucy snuggled closer when he'd hung up. 'Now rest, JD.'

'What do I get if I obey?' he asked cagily.

'Private performance,' she said with a yawn. 'Me and my violin. Nothing else.'

His mouth watered, imagining it. 'Naked? Really?'

'If you're *quiet* and let me *sleep*.'

JD pursed his lips tight. He wasn't going to make another sound.

Hunt Valley, Maryland,
Saturday 22 August, 8.05 P.M.

Sitting at the farmhouse's kitchen table, Ford watched Taylor's lips move soundlessly. *Please don't let me have hurt the program. Please.*

He didn't think she had, despite her coming here with an assumed name and a secret agenda, but he wouldn't promise her that it would be okay. He wouldn't lie to her.

Not like her mother had. Goddammit all. Instead he addressed her almost mournful refusal of wine. 'You don't drink?' he asked, and she shook her head.

'Not after what happened to my oldest sister. Carrie started drinking when we moved out to the ranch. The drugs followed later. When they found her body, she'd OD'd on heroin and her blood alcohol was over 0.45.'

His eyes widened. 'Holy hell.' That was five and a half times the legal limit. Shooting heroin was one thing. One pop of a needle and it was done. But how did a person physically manage to drink that much? Ford pushed his wine away, no longer wanting it.

She nodded at his rejected glass. 'Yeah. That's the way I feel about it. When Carrie started drinking, my folks didn't know what to do to stop her, and when LAPD found her body . . . my dad was devastated, as I'm sure you can imagine.'

'I don't know how to imagine that,' Ford said quietly. 'Losing your child that way.'

'I can't either. When my middle sister, Daisy, started drinking, it nearly pushed Dad over the edge. She's sober now, but he worries. So I won't put him through that again.' Another look, this one a half-wince. 'Plus, my mother told me that my . . . well, that Clay was a mean drunk. An alcoholic. I figured if it ran in the family, I'd just be smart and avoid the temptation entirely.'

Ford frowned. 'Clay's not,' he insisted harshly. 'I've seen him drink a few beers. I've never seen him drunk and I've never seen him mean. Of course, anybody messing with his family will pay the price, but that's not being mean. That's justice.'

'Well, as it happens, my mother's rep for the truth isn't sterling, so I'll take your word for it.' She picked up her fork, but set it down again abruptly, staring at her plate.

Ford frowned again. 'What's wrong with the chicken?'

'Nothing. I'm sure it's fine. It's just . . .' She glanced through the kitchen doorway to the front door. Then closed her eyes. 'Ever since I found out that my mother lied, I've been so angry. But now . . . I lied too.' Her lips trembled. 'The apple didn't fall too far from that tree.'

Ford wanted to comfort her, but held himself back. She *had* lied. She'd used their program for her own agenda. 'Did you come here planning to ditch the internship when you met Clay?'

'If I had to,' she said, but her lips trembled. 'If I met him and he wasn't nice or if I couldn't look at him without screaming . . . yeah, I planned to run home and have you all be none the wiser.'

'But now?'

'I'm staying,' she said firmly. 'I owe Maggie and Jazzie. And Clay.'

'And yourself,' he said quietly. 'You owe it to yourself to get to know your father.' She might not be able to accept that Clay *was* her father, at least not out loud, but Ford wasn't going to go along with that. 'Clay *is* your father, Taylor.'

She opened her mouth, denial in her eyes, but she sighed instead of voicing it. 'I never expected Clay to know me on sight. I never expected you or Maggie to suspect. I saw photos of him, of course, but I never realized how much I resemble him until I saw him in person.'

'It's your eyes. Not just the color and the shape, but also the intensity.'

She bit her lip. 'In the photos I found online, he looks cold and scary. Like he'd just as soon break your neck as not. Seeing his photo made every word my mother said about him ring true. I wouldn't have come had I not read his letters.' She swallowed. 'They weren't cold at all.'

It was true. Clay did look like a scary badass in his public photos. 'Most of his pictures online were when he was working a case. Even the ones of him in a tux, where he and Mom were at some charity function, Clay was working. This was all pre-Joseph, of course. Now, Joseph is mom's guard dog in a tux. But back then Clay considered himself Mom's bodyguard, even though she hadn't hired him at that point. Whenever he was interviewed by the media, it was because one of his cases got publicized by someone else, not because he sought attention.'

'So cold-and-scary is only a persona? Not the real him?'

Ford grinned. 'Hell, no, it's him all over. When he's working. When he's off the clock, he's a marshmallow. Cordy has him wrapped around her little finger.'

Taylor smiled back, wistfully. 'I could tell.'

Ford pulled his phone from his pocket and searched through the photos. 'Here. Look at this one.' It was Clay and Cordelia holding the handle of a heavy bucket as they crept on tiptoe, hunched over like they were sneaking up on someone, both wearing conspiratorial grins. 'I took this at Cordy's birthday party a few months ago.' He angled the phone Taylor's way, gratified when she leaned closer to see. She smelled really good. Like sweet flowers. He had to will himself not to sniff at her like he was a puppy.

A puppy. The anticipation tightening his chest abruptly wilted. Because he'd been called a puppy before. He closed his eyes, Kimberly's voice encroaching where it wasn't welcome. *You were a puppy, Ford. I felt sorry for you. That's all.*

A puppy. Kimberly had been his first. He'd loved her, but he'd only been her puppy. At least she hadn't said that on the witness stand, waiting instead to wound him with that final arrow in the privacy of the visiting booth at the prison. It didn't make it any less humiliating.

Oblivious to his mental tangent, Taylor had sucked in a surprised breath, her gaze on the photo. 'Wow,' she murmured. 'I really can see the resemblance between us now.' Tentatively she flicked her thumb and forefinger across the photo, enlarging Clay and Cordelia's faces. 'They look like they're about to get into trouble.'

Ford forced a chuckle past the lump in his throat and swiped a finger across his phone's screen, showing her the next photo. The bucket lay empty on the ground and a soaking-wet Stevie sputtered

167

in shock. 'Cordelia and Clay were laughing like loons,' he said, sounding subdued to his own ears.

Taylor twisted back to study his face, her eyes slightly narrowed. 'Was Stevie mad?'

He told his lips to curve and prayed that they obeyed. 'Nah. How could she be? Cordy was laughing and that doesn't happen too often. Clay lets his guard down around Stevie and Cordy.'

'But not with his other friends? It seems like he has so many friends.'

Again Ford sensed her wistfulness and thought about how lonely she must have been on that ranch in the middle of nowhere. He knew lonely, even though he'd been surrounded by a city full of people. 'He does have a lot of friends, and they see him laugh and smile, but it's more controlled somehow. With Cordy and Stevie he's . . .'

'Free,' she whispered.

Ford's heart stuttered at the raw longing on her face. 'I was going to say younger, but free works, too.'

She tilted her head, her attention suddenly shifting to him. 'Are you okay?'

Hell, no. But he would be. He shoved Kimberly out of his head, picturing her falling on her ass in the dirt, then visualized himself turning his back and leaving her there.

Instead he focused on Taylor. Who needed him. At least for now. 'I'm fine. Just old tapes.' *Shut up, Ford.* 'Nothing to do with this. With Clay or Cordelia or you.' She was silent, her gaze remaining watchful. 'Stray thoughts, y'know,' he went on, his mouth determined to fill the silence even though his brain was yelling for him to *shut up*. 'They hit you when you least expect them.' He closed his eyes. *For the love of God, shut up.*

She squeezed his hand briefly, sending a shiver down his spine. 'If you want to talk, I'm safe,' she murmured. 'I won't breathe a word. And I obviously know how to keep secrets.'

'Thanks.' It was all he could manage. Opening his eyes, he fixed his gaze on the plate she hadn't yet touched, pointing at it. 'Eat.'

She huffed a small laugh. 'Yes, sir.'

They were both quiet as they ate, Ford keeping his eyes on his plate until he heard her pushing her chair back from the table. He glanced at her empty plate, then up at her face. She looked nervous, but her mouth was set in determination.

'I'm going out to the porch to talk to your mother and face the music,' she said. 'I never considered that I'd want to stay after I met Clay.' Her lips quirked self-consciously. 'But now I find myself hoping Daphne doesn't throw me out on my ass. Wish me luck.'

That she and her ass could stay with him if his mother threw her out of the Healing Hearts program hovered on the tip of his tongue, but he bit it back. 'She won't throw you out,' he said instead. 'Up until today she thought you walked on water. Clay being your father won't change that. It'll probably make her like you even more.'

Hope flashed brightly in her eyes. 'You think?'

'You came to him of your own free will, so yeah, I do think.' He tried to smile for her sake. 'But good luck, just in case.'

'Thanks for dinner and . . .' She hesitated, then leaned forward and quickly kissed his cheek. 'And for being so nice. I want to think I could have made it through today without you, but I'm really glad I didn't have to find out.'

His breath backing up in his lungs, Ford waited until she was out of the kitchen before exhaling in a rush. Her chaste kiss had rocked him, wiping his brain's slate clean and leaving him wanting so much more.

Hunt Valley, Maryland,
Saturday 22 August, 8.30 P.M.

Clay found Stevie exactly where he'd figured she'd be – leaning against their bedroom window watching the sky grow dark. The window faced west, and she loved to watch the sun set over the trees that bordered their backyard. The trees stretched as far as the eye could see. *All ours.* They gave them a measure of privacy. Of security. Of safety.

All so important to the little girl who'd stolen his heart when she'd opened up her own.

169

'Cordy wants you to tuck her in,' he said, covering Stevie's stiff shoulders with his hands. She was still hurt. Clay knew she had a right to be, but damned if he knew what to do about it. 'Stevie.' He kissed her neck below her ear and drew in her scent. 'I'm sorry.'

He heard her swallow in the quiet of the room. 'For what? For being what my baby needs? I'm . . . happy she has you to talk to. To confide in.' Her voice broke. 'I really am.'

She was. He knew that. 'But you don't understand why she doesn't confide in you.'

A shaky nod. 'I've tried so hard, Clay. I messed it up before by being too busy, too remote. I know that and I thought I'd fixed it. What more can I do?'

Her job as a homicide detective had kept her away from home far too many nights, leaving Cordelia's care to Stevie's sister Izzy. Quitting the force allowed her to spend real time with her daughter now – quality and quantity.

The remoteness had stemmed from Stevie's mourning of her first husband and their son, and the unconscious hardening of her heart to avoid ever feeling that depth of pain again. It had all but destroyed Cordelia until Stevie realized what she was doing to her child. Since then she had done everything humanly possible to make Cordelia know how much she loved her.

'I'm not sure you completely understand why Cordelia isn't telling you about the nightmares,' he said softly.

He wrapped his arms around her, relieved when she let herself melt back into him, folding her arms over his. She settled her weight against him, allowing him to support her, physically and emotionally. 'Then help me understand,' she whispered.

'You've given up everything for her – your job, your house, even your identity, in a way. She's just a little girl, but she under-stands that being a cop was a huge part of who you were.' Stevie had been offered a promotion after she'd recovered from her injury. The job had been an important new role, created just for her, taking into account her disability. She'd never be a detective again, but she could have continued contributing in a meaningful way to the BPD. She'd turned it down, choosing instead to join Clay's

PI team, mostly because of what her police career had cost her child.

'None of that mattered,' Stevie insisted. '*She* mattered.'

'But you miss it sometimes, being a cop.'

'Sometimes, sure,' she admitted. 'When JD comes over to talk about his newest case, I occasionally feel wistful. I thought I'd hidden it, but Cordy knows, doesn't she?'

'Of course she does, because she's just as smart as her mama. She knows you miss it. She understands that she's the reason you walked away from your career, and part of her is okay with that. Most of her is okay with that, actually. But she wants to be worth your sacrifice.'

Stevie twisted abruptly so that she was looking up into his face. 'Worth my sacrifice? What does that even mean?'

'You sold the house that you lived in with her father, Stevie. The man you loved long after he was gone – that you still love.'

Her eyes widened in alarm. 'I love you, Clay. You know that I've put Paul to rest, right?'

'Sshh,' he soothed. 'Of course I know that. So does Cordy. But you sold the house because she was afraid to live there.' After a suspect on one of Stevie's old cases had broken in and held Cordelia at gunpoint to force Stevie's cooperation, the house itself had become part of the little girl's nightmare. 'She doesn't want you to know she's still having the nightmares because she—'

'She doesn't want me to think I sold the house for nothing,' Stevie whispered. 'Oh God, Clay. She doesn't want me to think I made all the changes for nothing.'

Clay kissed her temple. 'Tell me this: if you had known about the nightmares, what would you have been doing differently?'

'I . . .' Stevie faltered. 'I don't know. I take her to therapy. I'm here when she wakes up and when she goes to sleep and when she gets home from school.'

'That's exactly it. You're *here*. That's what she needs.' And what he hadn't been allowed to be for his own child, he thought bitterly.

Focus. This is not about Sienna. This is about Cordelia and Stevie.

Stevie was nodding thoughtfully. 'She also needs to understand that I made all those changes for myself as much as I did for her. I like what I'm doing. I like where I'm living.' She leaned up on her toes and kissed him. 'I get to wake up next to you. And when I finish each day, I know that I've built our business a little more. I'm helping build our lives. Here, together.' She kissed him again, longer this time. 'And after the day is done, I get to go to bed with you, and you make me so very happy. Inside and out,' she added in a sultry purr.

He smiled against her lips. 'So tell her that. Just not the part about going to bed.'

She laughed. 'I figured that out by myself.' She rocked back on her heels, standing in the circle of his arms, her expression sobering. 'I'm the one who should be sorry, Clay. You got the most awesome surprise imaginable tonight with Sienna popping up, but I spoiled it for you, making it all about me.'

'It's okay, Stevie.'

'No, it's not. I'll apologize to Sienna first thing tomorrow. I'll call her "Taylor" and I'll be really nice. I promise.'

'You're going with me to breakfast?'

'Unless you don't want us to. Cordelia and I haven't gone riding in two weeks and we're overdue. We can go over to Maggie's with you in the truck, I can apologize, then Cordy and I can make ourselves scarce.'

He smiled down at her. His wife was nothing if not transparent. 'And then later you can watch Sienna giving lessons to the kids in the program, just to be sure she's on the level?'

Stevie wrinkled her nose at him. 'Smartass.'

He tapped her nose. 'But right?'

'Yeah,' she said grudgingly. 'Daphne says Sienna is legit, so I *think* that's true. But I don't just want to *think* it. I need to *know*. I need to be doubly, triply sure that she is on the level, because I take care of what's mine. And you're mine.'

His shoulders relaxed. At least this part of his life seemed to be back under control. 'And glad to be. Go tuck Cordy in, and then come back and take care of me some more.'

Eleven

Hunt Valley, Maryland,
Saturday 22 August, 8.30 P.M.

Taylor psyched herself up for the worst and opened the front door, then stepped out onto the porch. Daphne and Maggie sat on the swing, sipping glasses of wine. Daphne was pushing the swing idly, but brought it to a halt when she saw Taylor standing there.

'Hi,' Taylor said quietly.

Daphne's smile was warm. 'Hi yourself, sugar. Come, sit with us.' She pointed to a wicker rocker next to the swing, then leaned in to peer at Taylor's face once she'd sat down. 'Damn,' she whispered, her twang lengthening the single syllable to four. 'You're right, Maggie. I cannot *believe* I missed it.'

Taylor had no idea what to say, so she twisted her hands together in her lap.

'You were looking at her résumé,' Maggie remarked. 'Not her face.'

Daphne's eyes – so like Ford's – narrowed slightly. 'Is your résumé real, Taylor?'

'Yes, ma'am. I really did graduate from college this past June and my degree really is in psychology.'

'And your desire to do equine therapy with kids who've suffered emotional trauma?'

Taylor flinched, realizing she'd tightened her grip on her hands to the point of pain. 'Well, that wasn't my first plan,' she said nervously. 'But now that I'm here . . . It's a good place. Healing Hearts with Horses, I mean. Now that I've seen it in action, I can see myself working with kids. More so than my first plan, actually.'

One side of Daphne's mouth lifted. 'What was your first plan?'

'To go to law school and become a family lawyer,' Taylor admitted. 'Because of my mother. She always told me that before she met my dad, she'd tried to get restraining orders to force Clay to stay away, but that she couldn't get anyone to listen to her. Nobody would help her because she had no money and the Legal Aid office was too swamped to give her any attention. My dad offered to help her get a restraining order before we went into hiding, but then she said that she didn't want Clay to know where we were living, and Dad agreed to protect us. I know now that none of that is true,' she said in a rush because Daphne's mouth had opened indignantly.

Daphne's expression settled, becoming sympathetic. 'But back then you believed her. And why wouldn't you? Nobody expects to be lied to by the people who are supposed to love them.'

'It's still hard not to feel stupid,' Taylor murmured. 'Especially now that I have to face you all. And explain. Again.'

'Maggie's already relayed your explanation,' Daphne said. 'I guess the big question is how you slipped through our background check. We can't have that happening. These kids depend on the security and safety we promise them.'

'Is Agent Carter very upset with me?' Taylor asked tentatively, then blinked when Daphne abruptly grinned.

'He's bracing himself for the ribbing of a *lifetime* at Holly's wedding on Monday, because *everyone* will be there and will know he messed up. But mostly he wants to know how you did it.'

Taylor hesitated. 'My dad can't get into trouble. He was trying to protect me.'

Maggie and Daphne shared a long glance, Maggie giving Daphne a hard nod before they both looked back at Taylor. 'This will be off the record,' Daphne said softly.

It was Taylor's turn to narrow her eyes. 'Why? You're a prosecutor. You're married to a federal agent. Why would you allow me to speak off the record?'

Daphne's gaze didn't falter. 'Because I was once a terrified little girl who looked over her shoulder all the time, expecting the monster

174

to appear. I was abducted when I was a little younger than Cordelia is now. It was . . . horrific. All these years later, I still have trouble speaking about it. But I survived, physically and emotionally, mostly because I had my mom and Maggie in my corner. They loved me and made me feel as safe as they possibly could. Your mother lied to you. Made you fear your biological father when she should have made you feel *safe*. That was her job, and she failed you. But at least you had your stepfather in your corner. Whatever he did, he made you feel safe, and somehow you grew into an adult with enough courage and compassion to search for the truth. To try to right your mother's wrong.' She shrugged. 'So whatever he did is off the record.'

God, Taylor wanted to believe her. 'But what happens when Agent Carter finds out?'

Daphne's smile returned. 'I'll tell him just what he needs to know to make the program's vetting system safer. He and I have already discussed this. We're not out to punish your stepfather, Taylor. It seems like he was as much a victim as you and Clay.'

Holding her breath, Taylor stared hard at the two women, then decided to trust them. And prayed she wouldn't come to regret it. 'When my dad relocated us from Oakland to Reedsville – this was after Clay hired the PI to find me – he got new identities for me and my mother. Dad was a defense attorney in Oakland. He had . . . contacts.'

'He bought your identities off the black market,' Daphne said in a no-nonsense way.

'Basically, yes. My mother's wasn't as ironclad as mine because she wasn't going to work outside the home, and because she and Dad had legally divorced, she wasn't listed on his taxes. But he wanted my identity to be rock-solid so that I could do anything I chose with my life. He didn't want me to be cut off from applying to college or for a job once I grew up.' She sighed. 'I didn't know about any of this until I was eighteen and had to use my social security number for the first time. I knew my mother had always worried hers would pop up fake, and I nagged my dad until he told me why he was so sure mine wouldn't. I didn't steal anyone else's identity, although back then I was so scared, I might have. If it had come down to it.'

'We're not judging,' Daphne said. 'I have to admit to being intrigued, though.'

'My dad had a housekeeper named Clara who had a daughter my age. Has, I mean. Both Clara and her daughter are alive and well back in Oakland. Anyway, Clara had known Dad since they were kids – her mother was his mother's housekeeper. They were family. No one wanted to see me taken away by Clay, so the family had a brainstorming meeting. What they did was actually Clara's idea. My mother and I had lived with my dad for a while by this point and Clara loved me like she loved all the girls in the house – Julie and Carrie and Daisy, Dad's biological daughters, as well as her own daughter, Nicole.

'Up until then I went by Sienna Smith.'

Daphne's lips turned up. 'Original.'

Her boss's smile helped ease a little more of Taylor's strain. 'Smith was my Aunt Laura's last name by marriage. My mother legally changed our last names when Aunt Laura took her in. Anyway, Dad had my name changed to Taylor Williamson, the "abandoned child" of one of his former clients, an addict who'd all but dropped "Taylor" on his doorstep. The addict client was fabricated, of course. Because I'd been supposedly abandoned without any documents, the state had to issue me a new social security number. Dad petitioned to adopt Taylor Williamson and he had friends in the courts, so it happened quickly – no fuss, no muss. My mother wasn't on the adoption app because they'd legally divorced by then, so even if Clay had found her, there would be no tie to me. Dad wanted all my paperwork to be completely legal, with no loopholes anywhere. That meant complying with home visits from social workers and jumping through all the hoops adoptive parents are required to jump through. Whenever the social workers visited, Clara's daughter Nicole pretended to be Taylor. That way any photographs or physical descriptions in my file weren't of me.'

'They were of Nicole,' Daphne said with a nod. 'So if Clay ever investigated Frederick Dawson and saw that an adoption had happened, your face wouldn't be in any of the records.'

'Exactly. When the adoption was finalized, Clara and Nicole moved into a nice apartment and we moved to the ranch.'

'And neither of them spilled the secret?' Maggie asked, incredulous.

'No. They're family. Plus my father made sure they were well cared for. Clara works in a fashion boutique and Nicole's in med school, on a scholarship from Dad's old law firm.'

'So Mr Dawson paid for her education,' Daphne murmured.

'Essentially, but it wasn't as payment for helping with the adoption. He'd set up Nicole's college fund long before he ever met my mother and me. Nicole and I were best friends.' Taylor drew a deep breath. 'I hated leaving her behind. We all hated leaving our lives behind, but we thought that if Clay found me, he'd snatch me off the street and they'd never see me again. So one night we piled into the car and drove away. None of us kids got to say goodbye to our friends. It was especially hard on my oldest stepsister.'

'The one who OD'd,' Daphne said wearily. 'Maggie told me about her.'

Maggie's brows were still furrowed in a slight frown. 'I don't understand why your stepfather didn't just buy you a fake ID and tell people you were his daughter, without going through the whole adoption process.'

'Because of my youngest stepsister, Julie. She's cognitively challenged and sometimes blurts out things we'd prefer she kept to herself. She might have told someone that I hadn't always lived with them, or that I had a different mom. The adoption took care of that. And then I had an airtight, background-check-proof identity.'

Daphne glanced at Maggie. 'It's not a bad MO,' she said thoughtfully.

Maggie gave her a stern look. 'Please tell me you're not planning to go into the fake ID business. Promise me. Hand on the Bible, girl.'

Daphne grinned at her. 'Never say never.'

Suddenly Maggie looked worried. 'No. Just . . . no. We're not

177

going to risk the therapy program doing illegal stuff like that. *Please*, Daphne.'

Daphne chuckled. 'Relax. I'm kidding. Mostly.' Before Maggie could say another word, Daphne turned back to Taylor. 'So you became Taylor, but your mother kept Sienna Smith's identity alive. When Clay visited your mother's aunt's house, the neighbors confirmed they'd seen you from time to time. He was able to find the record of your GED diploma. How? And why? Was it just to torment him?'

'*How* is easier than *why*. "Sienna" is on record as being home-schooled in Oakland, where she and her mother lived with her mother's aunt. I was actually homeschooled on our ranch. My mother kept two sets of records to prove I'd completed the work, because she didn't want it to look like Sienna just disappeared. If that happened, someone might come looking, or if Clay checked, he'd dig deeper to find out what had happened to me. Mom took me back to Aunt Laura's house every so often so that the neighbors would see me. I took the GED test as both Sienna and Taylor so that I could actually attend college as Taylor. As for the why, it was to keep Clay looking for Sienna, because as long as he believed that she existed, he wouldn't dig any deeper.'

'And Taylor would slide under the radar,' Daphne finished. 'As much as I've hated watching Clay chase his tail all these years, I have to admit it was a smart move. But I still don't understand why your mother held on to such a vendetta for so long. She couldn't have hated Clay that much, could she?'

Taylor shrugged. 'To tell you the truth, I don't understand my mother at all after what I've learned. I guess that she'd dug herself in too deep with my grandparents to come clean. She told me on her deathbed that she didn't want to upset them because both of them had heart conditions. By the time they died, she'd already met my dad and she didn't want him to know she was a liar. It kept getting worse and worse. Looking back, I think she may have actually thrived on the drama.'

Taylor could hear the venom in her own voice and clenched her teeth to keep herself from saying any more about her mother. 'But I suppose that's all water under the bridge now. I can only move forward and fix what I can. What will you tell Agent Carter?'

'That he doesn't need to worry about his background check process,' Daphne said. 'There was no way he would have picked up on your double identity and I don't think we'll have many interns come through the program who're in your situation.'

Taylor hesitated. 'Did I damage the program in any way? I didn't mean to. I didn't think about there being any consequences to the program if I snuck in. I was so focused on minimizing the risk to myself that I didn't even consider the kids. I was selfish and I'm sorry.'

'It's all right, Taylor,' Daphne said comfortingly. 'The instinct for self-protection in traumatized children is a strong one. You sometimes make decisions that seem right at the time, but that you regret later.'

'But I'm not a child. Not anymore.'

'Neither am I. But we both were children who grew up looking over our shoulders and fearing the monster in the closet.'

Taylor swallowed hard. 'Does it ever go away? The fear? And the panic attacks?'

Daphne's smile was a little sad. 'Not really. You learn to cope, and eventually the reflex to protect yourself weakens, but it never really goes away. I still have panic attacks from time to time. The most unexpected things can trigger them, so I have to always be prepared, and that in itself can be exhausting. Have you had any counseling?'

'No. We lived in a pretty isolated area, and when I did go to college, I was never alone. I majored in psychology. Maybe I thought some of it would rub off and I could . . . fix myself. But . . . yeah.' It sounded utterly silly when she said the words out loud. 'I probably should talk to an actual professional, huh?'

Daphne's lips quirked up. 'Y'think? At any rate, there's been no harm done to Healing Hearts. Do you plan to continue with us through the summer?'

'Yes, ma'am, if you'll have me. Especially now that I may be able to help Jazzie.'

179

Daphne's nod was approving. 'And after this summer is over? What then?'

'I don't know. I'd like to get to know Clay better.' *And Ford, too,* she thought. The memory of that almost-kiss blazed through her mind and she dropped her gaze to her fingers, hoping to high heaven that she wasn't blushing. 'But I have my dad back in California and he needs me too. He sacrificed so much to protect me. I can't abandon him.' Tears stung her eyes and she looked up to find both Daphne and Maggie wearing sympathetic gazes. 'I'm torn.'

'Well, you don't have to decide tonight,' Daphne said. 'It'll all still be here tomorrow.'

'And you'll think more clearly after a good night's sleep,' Maggie added kindly.

'I sure hope so,' Taylor said. 'On both thinking more clearly and being able to sleep.' She had to be alert tomorrow. She'd face Clay again over breakfast, then Jazzie after lunch. And of course there was Ford, who seemed to be staying the night at least.

She held her breath, hoping he'd be waiting for her when she returned, but the kitchen was empty, the only sound that of the dishwasher's rinse cycle.

But he'd left her a note that made her smile. *Sleep well. Everything will be okay.*

Baltimore, Maryland
Saturday 22 August, 9.45 P.M.

'Beautiful,' JD murmured, coming up behind Lucy where she stood in front of the mirror, brushing her hair. He slid his arms around her waist, tugging her against his chest, hunkering down to rest his chin on her shoulder so that their faces were reflected side by side. 'You take my breath away.'

Her smile was a little bit shy. 'We don't have time for another round.'

'Maybe Gwyn tired the kids out for us. Maybe they'll go to sleep right away and we'll have a quiet night.' JD kissed her neck where he knew it would make her shiver, grinning when it did.

'Dream on,' Lucy said with an eye roll, then gave their reflections a critical look. 'You're all grins and I look relaxed for the first time in days. Gwyn's gonna know what we've been up to.'

JD laughed again. 'Like she didn't when she agreed to babysit?'

'True,' Lucy conceded, then sighed when the doorbell chimed. 'That'll be her now. Our little break is officially over.'

'I'll let her in.' JD stole a quick kiss. 'You think really stressful thoughts so you don't look relaxed and I'll scowl so she won't think we've been up to anything,' he said, and the sound of Lucy's laughter followed him down the stairs. There was no way he could scowl. Not when he had everything he'd ever wanted.

He opened the door to find Gwyn in full stage makeup, holding Bronwynne crooked in one arm and Jeremiah by the hand. She took one look at JD's grin and rolled her eyes. '*Tell* me you didn't make any *more* of these?' she said dramatically, indicating the children. He knew her snarky attitude was all for effect. She loved his and Lucy's two kids like they were her own.

He also knew the snark had become her normal face to the world, a shield behind which she hid because she was afraid to let anyone get too close.

'Not yet,' he said. 'Two's enough. For now, anyway.' He reached for Jeremiah, laughing when he saw his son's face made up like a member of KISS. 'Recruiting them early for the band, aren't you?' He settled Jeremiah on his hip and stepped back to let Gwyn inside.

She curled her lip at JD, once again her bluster all for show. 'We're taking whatever talent we can find. We've had to scramble to fill the hole Lucy's left in the schedule for months because of you. All because you knocked her up a second time.'

Lucy's electric violin sets were wildly popular, but they'd had a number of guest performers since she'd been on maternity leave. JD knew that Lucy had been itching to be on stage again, making that violin of hers sing. He'd certainly enjoyed the private performance she'd gifted to him upstairs.

His grin widened. 'What can I say? I couldn't keep my hands off her.'

Gwyn narrowed her eyes. 'Wait till you see the D-R-U-M-S that

181

I'm getting Jeremiah for Christmas. You won't be smiling so much then.'

JD just shrugged. 'I'm feeling too good right now to worry about it.' He leaned down to kiss Gwyn's cheek, careful not to smudge her makeup. 'Thank you,' he whispered. 'We needed the time together.'

A temporary fissure in her shield of sarcasm allowed her true smile to peek through. 'Any time,' she whispered back.

'Holy cow!' Lucy exclaimed, coming down the stairs. 'Jeremiah, you look awesome!' She ruffled his hair. 'I think we've got ourselves a budding rock star.'

'Wanna *rock*,' Jeremiah said with a hard nod.

Lucy snorted. 'Did Uncle Thorne teach you that?'

Gwyn rolled her eyes again. 'Thorne came by to take me to the club, but I think he just wanted time with the kids.' She shifted the baby into Lucy's arms. 'Jeremiah's makeup will wash off with water.'

'I figured as much,' Lucy assured her. 'So, you're on tonight?'

Gwyn nodded. 'The scheduled act bailed on us at the last minute. I'm pinch-hitting.' Her skill on the piano was nowhere near Lucy's on the violin, but it didn't matter. Gwyn's real talent was her voice. She could croon oldies, twang country, sing the blues, and belt out classic rock or opera like no one else JD had ever heard. It just depended on her mood. Tonight's makeup and costume suggested she was going with heavy metal. Always an interesting choice.

Gwyn looked over her shoulder with a frown. 'Thorne was right behind me with all the baby crap. Where'd he go? He had one job, to carry the baby crap.'

'I'm coming,' Thorne snapped as he came up the walk and through the front door, laden with car seats and diaper bags. He met JD's eyes and gave him a quick nod before resuming his rant. 'Kids need to be trained to carry their own crap.'

JD felt some of his tension ease. Thorne had found something on Jarvis, something he'd needed to share in person. It would either be incredibly useful or royally disastrous. JD hoped for the former.

182

'When they get big enough to carry all that crap, they don't need it anymore,' Gwyn snapped back at Thorne. The two bickered with each other all the time. 'What took you so long?'

'I'm afraid we waylaid him, sugar,' came the twanged answer, as Daphne and Joseph followed Thorne through the front door. Both of them carried zippered clothing bags. 'We were assigned by the bride to deliver the wedding attire.'

Because Holly and Dillon's wedding was the day after tomorrow.

'Your tux,' Joseph said dryly, handing JD one of the bags. JD could tell from Joseph's expression that the delivery had been an excuse and that something else had come up.

'And your dresses,' Daphne added, handing bags to Lucy and Gwyn. 'I'm so glad you're here, Gwyn! You saved us a trip.'

Lucy and Gwyn had been asked to provide the music for the prelude and processional. Some would be simple instrumental duets, Gwyn on the piano and Lucy on the acoustic violin, which still stirred JD's emotions every time she drew her bow over the strings. A few of the selections Gwyn would sing, Lucy providing the accompaniment. The couple had made other arrangements for music during the ceremony itself.

Gwyn feigned surprise. 'We have dresses?'

Lucy caught on, mirroring Gwyn's expression. 'We thought we'd just wear our club clothes.'

JD chuckled, passing Jeremiah to Joseph so that he could hang all the bags in the closet. Gwyn and Lucy wore leather micro-miniskirts when they performed at the club. 'I personally like that idea a lot,' he said, waggling his brows.

Daphne skewered Lucy and Gwyn with a look. 'If I can't wear a miniskirt to the wedding, you can't either.'

'I couldn't wear mine anyway,' Lucy said with a sigh. 'I haven't lost enough of the baby weight to get into it.'

'Because Romeo there keeps knocking her up,' Gwyn added, then tilted her head at the Carters. 'We were supposed to pick these up tomorrow at the rehearsal dinner. And you look . . . weird, Daphne. Joseph looks annoyed as hell. What gives?'

Daphne frowned again. 'I have a poker face.'

Lucy shook her head. 'No, honey, you really don't. What's wrong?'

Daphne briefly glanced at Joseph, who was now scowling openly. 'Do you guys have a few minutes?' she asked. 'We have some news and wanted to make sure people knew before the wedding so all the surprise and shock can be gotten over with.'

Joseph exhaled harshly. 'God,' he muttered. 'I still can't believe it.'

'What's wrong?' Thorne repeated Lucy's question before JD could.

'Well, nothing really,' Daphne said. 'But we should sit down.'

Unconvinced, JD led them into the living room, where everyone found seats. Joseph put Jeremiah on the floor near his blocks and took his place next to Daphne on the sofa.

Daphne sighed. 'Clay's daughter showed up today.'

There was a shocked silence. JD recovered first. 'Sienna? The daughter he's been searching for for twenty fu-reaking years?' He caught the curse just in time, because Jeremiah had developed a recent talent for repeating swear words. 'She just showed up?'

'What did she want?' Thorne asked, sounding suspicious as well.

'She didn't "just show up",' Joseph corrected. 'She's been at the farm for two fu—'

'Freaking!' JD interrupted.

'Weeks,' Joseph continued. '*Two weeks.* Right under my fu-*reak*ing nose.'

'Wait,' JD said, shaking his head. 'Did you say she was at the *farm*? Healing Hearts?'

'That's the only farm we've got,' Joseph said darkly.

Well, that explains Maggie's subdued tone on the phone, JD thought, stunned.

'But how?' Gwyn demanded. 'I volunteer there and I had to practically donate a kidney to pass the background check. How did you not know she was there?'

Joseph glared at no one in particular. 'She had help.'

'Joseph,' Daphne admonished. 'You make it sound like she's part of the Mafia.'

'Is she?' Lucy asked very seriously. Clay and Stevie were part of their family and Lucy did not take kindly to people upsetting their family. 'Does she intend to hurt Clay? More than she already has anyway, by hiding from him for so long.'

Daphne sighed again. 'It's a long story and you'll all hear it, but just know that she didn't mean to hurt anyone. She was lied to by her mother, Clay's ex-wife. Led to believe that Clay was a horrible person and he'd hurt her if he ever found her. Taylor knows that's not true now, but it was something she believed her whole life.'

Lucy frowned. 'Taylor? His daughter's name is Sienna.'

Daphne gave JD a meaningful glance. 'Sienna's name was changed to Taylor Dawson when she was a child.'

JD blinked. 'Taylor Dawson? As in the intern who connected with Jazzie Jarvis?'

Daphne's nod was sober. 'The very same.'

JD's mind was already charging ahead at light speed. *Clay's daughter just shows up and connects with the only witness to a brutal murder?* On the same day that three people were killed to make it look like the murderer of Valerie Jarvis had met his own end?

'Maybe you should tell us the whole story, Daphne,' JD said quietly.

Daphne did, relating the lie perpetrated by Clay's ex-wife until her deathbed confession, the sacrifices made by Donna's husband, Frederick Dawson, and the disbelief of Taylor herself, followed by the plan she'd made to meet her father and judge his character for herself.

When Daphne was finished, there was a moment of silence.

'Wow,' Thorne said, his normally booming voice muted.

Gwyn snorted a laugh. 'Wow?' she repeated with a shake of her head. 'Mr Defense Attorney, king of the courtroom, and that's all you have to say?'

Daphne made a face. 'He is not king of the courtroom. Maybe a baron. Or a viscount.'

'Jester,' Joseph grumbled, and Daphne lightly smacked his arm.

'Stop. You're just mad that Taylor's stepdad outsmarted your background check.'

Which JD would ask Joseph about later. 'How is Clay taking it?' JD asked instead.

'I don't know,' Daphne murmured. 'I wasn't there. I heard about it from Maggie and went to talk to Taylor myself after Clay and Stevie had left. Maggie said he cried.'

Another moment of quiet. All of them knew how hard Clay had searched for his daughter and how devastated he'd been every time he'd come up empty-handed.

The baby fussed and Lucy rocked to settle her down. 'How did Stevie take it?'

'Again I wasn't there,' Daphne said, then shook her head. 'But not so good. Maggie said she was furious with the girl, but that Taylor gave it right back to her. She'd been lied to for her whole life, but she came to find the truth. I was satisfied with Taylor's story, as was Maggie. Clay was simply overwhelmed that she was there at all. I imagine Stevie will come around.'

'How do you know she's telling the truth? That she's really his kid?' Gwyn asked, her voice brittle. Bitter. 'People can say they're a certain person all they want, but they lie.'

Thorne put his arm around her shoulders in a platonic gesture of support. They made an odd picture, Gwyn at five-foot even and Thorne at six-six. 'It's a fair question,' he said.

'She looks just like him, when you know what to look for,' Daphne said. 'I can't believe I missed it. Maggie's known from the get-go. She was waiting for Taylor to show her hand.'

The baby's fussing grew urgent and Lucy stood up. 'I have to nurse her. Gwyn, can you give me a hand with Jeremiah? Maybe run him a bath and clean his face? I have a suspicion JD's going to be busy discussing cop-stuff.'

Gwyn picked Jeremiah up, tickling him when he complained about leaving his toys behind. 'Do we have time?' she asked Thorne. 'I'm supposed to be on stage soon.'

'Yes. Go on. I'll let the club know we'll be a little late.' Thorne turned to Joseph and JD. 'What does Clay's daughter have to do with Gage Jarvis's daughter?'

Joseph gave JD a questioning look. JD shrugged. 'I asked him for information on Jarvis,' he said, then explained that Taylor was so important because she'd gotten Jazzie to open up.

Thorne's dark brows rose. 'Very convenient timing.'

'I thought the same,' JD agreed.

Daphne looked doubtful. 'I don't believe Taylor has any agenda other than meeting her father. And I certainly can't imagine how she could be connected to Valerie's killer, now that we know who she really is and why she's here. But we're talking about the life of an eleven-year-old girl, so I'll hold my vote for a while.'

'Does Clay know that Taylor is meeting Jazzie tomorrow?' JD asked.

'He does,' Daphne said, 'but I'm not sure that he knows the details. Be prepared for a shit fit when he finds out you've planned the meet for Giuseppe's. Especially given the fact that Valerie Jarvis's murderer has already killed three other people to keep his secret.'

'I'll go out to the farm tomorrow,' JD decided. 'I'll meet her for myself. Until then, tell us what you know about Gage Jarvis, Thorne.'

Thorne leaned back into the sofa cushions and regarded them all levelly. 'Five years ago, I was approached by Cesar Tavilla.'

JD, Joseph and Daphne all blinked in unison. 'The head of the ST clique?' Daphne asked, surprised.

'Shit, Thorne,' JD said quietly, not even wanting Tavilla's name to be spoken in his home. The head of Baltimore's Los Señores de la Tierra gang was a bloodthirsty thug masquerading as a legitimate businessman. Even their name was a mockery. *Lords of the Planet, my fucking ass.* 'He's building ST's Baltimore clique, bent on making it even stronger than MS-13 in DC.' Although the notorious MS-13 gang was much stronger in LA and San Francisco, it had been the largest in the Washington area for years. Tavilla was looking to upset that apple cart, then blow it sky high. Turf wars were coming, and every law enforcement officer knew and dreaded the bloodshed that would undoubtedly result. 'Why would *he* approach you?'

'He wanted me to handle his son's case,' Thorne said gravely. 'The son had been accused of murder. Tavilla had tried to bribe the victim's family to make it all go away, but the family wouldn't accept a payoff. They wanted justice.'

187

'Go figure,' Daphne said sarcastically. 'Sorry, go on. I remember that case. You didn't defend him.'

'No, I wouldn't,' Thorne said, then waited as Daphne's eyes widened.

'Gage Jarvis,' she murmured. 'He took the case.'

Thorne nodded. 'Yeah, and he got the kid off. Hung jury. There was speculation about a few of the jurors. I think Gage bought them off or threatened them with something. He was a dirty piece of work.'

'And so?' JD prompted.

'And so, a year ago, Tavilla's kid gets himself arrested for murder again. Gage Jarvis isn't around anymore. Rumor had it that Jarvis had smacked his wife around, got arrested, but was never charged because she withdrew her complaint. Then he left his firm. Company line was that he quit "to pursue other interests", but most of us knew he'd been forced out. I heard that he was last seen partying in Florida. That was a couple years ago. About five weeks ago – again, according to the rumor mill – Tavilla is in Miami having a working vacation. He gets a visit from Gage Jarvis.'

Joseph's brows shot up. 'You have a very good rumor mill.'

Thorne lifted a shoulder. 'I pay very close attention to Tavilla, because when his kid fucked up for the second time last year, Tavilla again asked me to defend him. Again I said no.'

'Because the kid's a punk?' JD asked.

'Most of my clients are punks,' Thorne admitted with a shrug. 'Doesn't mean they're guilty, even though most of them are that too. In either case they're entitled to a fair trial and I do my best by every single one of them. But I have my limits. I couldn't have lived with myself if I'd taken on Tavilla's kid. Plus, I didn't want to be in his pocket, and once you do a job for him, you are.'

'Is Jarvis in his pocket?' JD asked.

'He is now.' Thorne pulled out his cell phone, then looked all three of them in the eye, one at a time. 'I'll voluntarily send you the photo I have, but I want your promise that you won't use this to try to get a warrant to search the rest of my phone. I'll wipe it clean faster than you can get a judge's signature.'

188

'Of that I have no doubt,' Joseph said dryly. 'You have my word.'

'All right. Texting the photo to JD now.' Thorne gave JD a sideways look. 'This was taken a few hours ago.'

JD's phone buzzed, and when he opened the photo, he saw red. It showed Gage Jarvis, dressed to kill, sitting next to Tavilla, eating a lavish meal. 'Motherfucker. Kills his wife and a cop and two other people who had nothing to do with this and then drinks wine like he's Don fucking Corleone.' He passed the phone to Joseph, who sighed.

'You said we'd see Gage Jarvis surface within a few weeks, JD,' Joseph said. 'I truly thought it would be a little longer.' He gave Thorne a sober nod. 'Thank you. Did your rumor mill know what they were meeting about?'

'Seems like Gage Jarvis called in a marker.'

Daphne was studying the photo over her husband's shoulder. 'For getting Tavilla's kid off on the murder charge?'

'Quid pro quo,' Thorne said lightly, but his eyes were angry. 'Why did you mention Gage's daughter before?'

JD and Joseph exchanged a long glance. 'We believe she saw her mother's killer,' Joseph said.

Thorne's brow instantly furrowed. 'Why the hell isn't she in protective custody?'

'No one knows that she saw anything,' JD said. 'Only us, Hector Rivera, Agent Brodie, our forensic specialist, and Quartermaine, the ME. And her aunt and little sister, of course, because they found her hiding behind a chair at the scene, in shock.'

Thorne frowned, and JD could almost hear the wheels turning before Thorne's eyes popped wide. 'Oh my God. You have a leak. Don't worry, I won't mention this to anyone. You have my word.'

'Thank you,' Joseph said again. 'You don't have to answer this question, but I'll ask it for my own conscience. I know that Tavilla's son is serving time for his latest offense. I assume you have someone inside Tavilla's organization, since you were informed so quickly tonight. I'm assuming you've done that to protect yourself against a specific threat, made by an angry father who feels his son is in prison because you refused to defend him.'

189

'What's your question, Joseph?' Thorne asked, slightly mockingly, telling JD that Joseph had guessed exactly right.

'Are you in any current danger from Cesar Tavilla?' Joseph asked bluntly.

Thorne's lips quirked. 'Agent Carter, I almost think you care.'

'I do,' Joseph said seriously. 'You're an honest man, Thorne. I hate to see honest men targeted by scum like Tavilla.'

Thorne looked surprised. 'Thank you.' He recovered his trademark nonchalance. 'Tavilla's made some threats in the past. Nothing concrete. Always veiled and ominous. I had a few near misses after I turned him down. I wanted to know when he gave orders to have me . . . taken care of, so that I could watch my own back. And no, I do not want your help. I can't think of a better way to both end my career and paint a giant target on my head.' He got up, tugged at his suit coat. 'I need to get Gwyn to the club now. Let me know how it ends up, especially for the little girl.' His eyes grew distant for a moment before clicking back to the present. 'Tell Gwyn I'm waiting for her in the car.'

Gwyn came down the stairs a minute after Thorne left. 'Thanks for delivering the dresses, Daphne,' she called, waving to them as she opened the front door. 'JD, your son's face is now clean. I read him a story and he's asleep.'

'Thanks, hon. Thorne's waiting for you in the car,' JD said.

'I know. He texted me from your front porch. See you tomorrow at the rehearsal dinner.'

When she was gone, JD rubbed his throbbing temples. 'Damn, all this and Clay's daughter too?'

'I don't think Taylor has anything to do with this,' Daphne said again. 'I think she was the voice Jazzie needed to hear at the moment she needed to hear it.'

'I hope so,' JD said glumly. 'I'd hate for Clay to finally find his kid only to have to visit her in prison.'

Twelve

Hunt Valley, Maryland,
Saturday 22 August, 11.15 P.M.

Clay woke to a dark room and a warm, solid weight on his chest. Hands cradling his face and a soft mouth kissing him. *Stevie.* Her scent filled his head, her hair falling in a curtain around them. Cocooning them. He hummed into the kiss and swept his hands up her bare back, exploring his way back down to find nothing but silky skin.

'Hmm, my favorite outfit on you,' he murmured.

She didn't say a word in reply, kissing her way down his neck to his chest, grasping his hands in hers when he tried to roll her to her back.

'No,' she whispered. 'Let me. Tonight, just let me.'

There was something in her voice, an urgency that had him narrowing his eyes as he stared down at the top of her head. 'Let you what? Stevie?'

'Hush. Please.' Her hands gripped his, holding his arms at his sides when he tried to move. He could have easily wrestled from her grasp, but her tongue flicked his nipple and he sucked in a sharp breath as a shudder raked across his skin.

'Wait.' Something had happened. He blinked hard, trying to clear the fog from his brain. They'd been talking about Cordelia. Stevie had gone to tuck her in. He glanced at the clock on the nightstand. That had been hours ago. He must have fallen asleep waiting for her to come back. 'Stevie? Honey, what is this?'

191

'Sshh.' She slid down his body, dropping kisses across his chest. 'Be quiet, Clay.'

And then she gave him no choice but to obey, short-circuiting his brainwaves by taking him into her mouth and sucking him deep. He hissed, his back arching off the bed.

'*God.*' Curse or prayer, he didn't know and didn't care. '*Stevie.*' He pulled his hands free, shoving them into her hair, and thrust his hips, needing more.

Digging her fingers into his hips, she pressed him back down into the mattress, releasing his cock long enough to look up and whisper, 'Let me take care of you.'

Clenching his jaw, he spread his arms wide and grabbed handfuls of the sheets, anchoring himself while she went back down on him. Closing his eyes, he . . . let her. And let her. Until his body was stretched taut as a bow and he could feel the orgasm tingling at the base of his spine.

Suddenly, he didn't want to be taken care of alone. He caught her under her arms, pulled her up his body, flipped her to her back, and filled her in one hard thrust.

She gasped, then yanked his head down for a hot, open-mouthed kiss, hooking her ankles around his calves and bucking her hips up into him. He found her hands and threaded his fingers through hers, holding on tight as they slammed their way toward climax.

So close. He wasn't going to last much longer. Sweat dripping down his forehead, he ripped his mouth from hers, met her eyes in the darkness. 'Now,' he gritted. 'Come for me. *Now.*'

She threw her head back into the pillow, her scream utterly silent. He wasn't far behind, the climax so powerful that for a moment all he could see was white light. Spent, he fell against her, burying his face in her neck. He was breathing hard, his lungs struggling for air. Her body settled beneath him, her hands still gripping his.

'Oh my God,' he said when he could form the words. 'Stevie.'

'Told you to let me take care of you,' she murmured smugly, and he laughed.

Pushing to his elbows took the last bit of his energy, but he knew he had to be crushing her so he forced himself to move. She was smiling up at him.

'If this was a dream,' he said softly, 'don't you dare wake me up.'

She brought their joined hands to her lips and kissed his knuckles. 'It's no dream.'

'I didn't hurt you, did I?'

'Of course not. It's nice to know I can still make you lose control.'

He rolled to his side, taking her with him. 'What did I do to deserve that? Because I will totally do it every damn day.'

She chuckled, then the smile on her lips faded to something more serious. 'I just . . . I just needed to show you what you mean to me.'

He raised an eyebrow, about all the movement he still had strength for. 'Was this makeup sex?'

'Partly.' She sighed quietly. 'I talked to Cordelia. She told me about her nightmares.'

His good humor fled as he watched the myriad of emotions flicker across her face. 'Should I have told you? She asked me not to. I've been so . . . torn.'

'No, not if she asked you not to. She said she figured that if her father was still alive he'd want her to keep me safe from the nightmares. She said that by telling you, she was doing exactly that.' A small smile lit her eyes. 'She said that she thought her father would really have approved of you. That if he couldn't be here, he'd be glad you were because you take care of us.'

Clay's throat grew tight. 'I love her like she's my own, Stevie.'

'She *is* your own, Clay.'

'Is she worried I'll love her less because Sienna's turned up?'

'She doesn't seem to be. We mostly talked about her nightmares, though. I made sure that she knew that I would never regret my decision to leave BPD, that I did it for all of us.' She sighed again. 'God, Clay. Her nightmares are far worse than I ever thought they could be.'

'They do seem to be getting a little better. At least that's what she tells me.'

'She said she wasn't keeping anything from you, so that's good.

She's just sorry that you've had to carry her bad dreams around in your head along with your own.'

Clay touched his forehead to Stevie's. 'But isn't that what parents do?'

'That's exactly what I told her. I held her until she went to sleep, and I must have dropped off too. When I woke up, all I could think of was how damn lucky I am and how much I love you. I couldn't handle this on my own.' She drew a deep breath. 'On the bright side, I think we've both learned enough to do all this better with the next one.'

'I hope so,' he said fervently. 'Sienna's carrying an incredible burden on her shoulders.'

Stevie shook her head and said nothing. Just studied him in the darkness.

He frowned. 'Sienna's not carrying a burden?'

'Oh, she is for sure. But I'm not talking about Sienna.'

His frown deepened. 'Then wh—?' And then he understood. His mouth went dry, his heart stuttering in his chest. *The* next *one? Oh holy hell.* 'You're . . . ? You and me?'

She nodded carefully, showing nothing in her expression.

A surge of new energy blasted through him and he sat up, staring down at her. 'We're having a baby?' He grinned, his face practically cracking with it. 'Really?'

She smiled then, relief filling her eyes. 'Really. So . . . you're okay with this?'

He slid back down to lie beside her, running his hand down her arm and threading their fingers together again. 'Hell, yeah.'

'Some of my reaction tonight . . .' She grimaced. 'My bitchiness? I'm going to blame it on hormones, if that's okay with you.'

He brought their joined hands to his lips. 'Anything you say. When did you know?'

'Last week, when you were away. I was going to surprise you with it tonight, and then all the drama happened. I wanted to wait until things calmed down, but . . .' Her smile was shy. 'Like I said, I got kind of overwhelmed with how much I love you, and then I couldn't *not* tell you. Besides, I think if I waited to tell you until we were drama-free, the baby would tell you himself, right after he asked for the keys to your car.'

'He?'

'I had to pick a gender.' She grinned cheekily. 'I defaulted to the one you hadn't had yet.'

'I don't care if it's a he or a she,' he said fiercely. 'I get to be a dad from the ground up this time. The pregnancy and the birth and the diapers and the first steps. First words. Bedtime stories. First day of school. Everything I missed with Sienna.' Because Donna had stolen those things from him. 'I get to have it all.'

She traced his lips with her finger. 'Yes, you do,' she whispered back, her voice breaking.

He blinked hard, unashamed when two tears ran down his face. 'When?'

'Next April. I'm barely a month along.' She pressed her finger to his lips. 'So we shouldn't tell anyone just yet.'

'You've got to be kidding. You honestly expect me to keep this a secret?'

She laughed. 'No, not really.'

He couldn't have held back the laugh that bubbled out had his life depended on it. 'That's good, because I don't think I'll be able to stop smiling.' He hugged her, pressing a kiss to the top of her head. 'I love you.'

'Good, because I love you too. Now go to sleep. We're meeting Sienna early tomorrow.'

He lay there for a long time, holding Stevie until she went to sleep, his heart still racing. All he'd ever wanted from life was a family, children, of his own. When he'd returned from the camping trip this afternoon, he'd had that – a wife who loved him and a nine-year-old stepdaughter who called him Dad. If he'd lived the rest of his life just like that, he could have been content. Not complete, because this afternoon he'd still believed Sienna was lost to him. Still, he could have been content.

But now . . . now he was truly complete. He'd found Sienna. Or, more correctly, she'd found him. *After all this time.*

And he was going to be a father again. His mind still reeled at the thought. He gave in to the need to touch Stevie, carefully spreading his hand over her stomach. His baby was growing in there. *My child.* He and Stevie had made a child. He let himself imagine holding their baby in his arms, while Stevie and Cordelia watched with big smiles.

Sienna wasn't in that little imaginary family portrait, because she didn't seem entirely real yet. Yes, he'd held her in his arms. Heard her voice. Stroked her hair. Still, her arrival felt more like a dream – a beautiful dream.

But it wasn't a dream, he told himself. *Sienna came to me. She sought me out.* He'd searched for her for so many years. *And now she's home.* He sighed quietly. No, she wasn't home. Reality was that her home – and her stepfather – was three thousand miles away. She wasn't planning to stay forever. She'd made that perfectly clear.

But for now, she was here. This was a start.

He pushed away the doubts and the fears and let himself feel complete. And happy.

Baltimore, Maryland,
Sunday 23 August, 2.20 A.M.

Gage knew a lot of truly bad people. Violent, dangerous thugs. It was an occupational hazard of being a defense attorney. He supposed he'd now be considered one of those violent, dangerous thugs himself. That fact hadn't seemed to bother Tavilla. His new boss had only been concerned that he covered his tracks and didn't get caught.

It was good when a man's goals were consistent with those of his employer.

Gage pulled into the parking lot of an old church, quietly closing the door to the junker he'd been driving all day. Like Cleon Perry's money and coke, the car now belonged to Gage. He'd changed out the license plates for a pair he'd taken from a car up on blocks in a weed-infested alley behind one of the boarded-up row houses he'd passed while fleeing from yesterday morning's crime scene. Cleon's old Chevy looked like every other banged-up junker. No one would pay him or the car a bit of attention.

He'd buy another car as soon as he got a few paychecks under his belt – maybe a Mercedes sedan. He'd always gone for the flashy sports cars in the past, but he'd have to be more discreet in this new life of his.

He moved quietly in the shadows behind the church, hyper-aware of his surroundings – and of the gun in the shoulder holster beneath his suit coat. The pistol was a piece of shit, but it had done its job Friday night, keeping Toby Romano quiet until he was sedated, and again tonight when Gage had relieved a man at an ATM of his cash. Gage had parked out of sight and worn a ski mask, so even if the cameras caught him, he wasn't worried that he'd be recognised. He was more worried that the damn gun would jam. Plus, it had no silencer, and that limited its use.

Gage was hoping to significantly upgrade his arsenal tonight. Even if it turned out that Jazzie really had seen nothing and all his ends were snipped, his new job required certain accessories. A discreet car, nice suits and very powerful weapons just in case he ever needed to defend himself.

Rolling his eyes, he started down the gravel path that led through a patch of woods to an old cemetery. The particular violent thug he'd come to see had a flair for the dramatic.

He turned when he heard footsteps on the path behind him. Keeping his hands visible, he nodded once to the man standing before him. 'Reverend.'

Reverend Blake nodded back. 'Mr Jarvis. It's been a long time.' Blake was about sixty, with deceptively kind eyes and a set of muttonchops that had grown far more salt than pepper in the years since Gage had represented him in an intent-to-distribute trial. Blake had been as guilty as sin, but Gage had been a damn good lawyer. The kindly-grandfather look had been Gage's idea, and it had made the difference with the jury. Nobody wanted to put a nice old man in prison.

Blake had ridden the wave of his acquittal, claiming to have found God, and had become a reverend. Of what kind of church,

197

Gage had no idea, and he was sure that Blake didn't either. It didn't matter. The reverend get-up had been the downfall of those stupid enough to try to steal from Blake. Under those clothes was a ruthless killer, and Gage, for one, was not going to forget it.

They regarded each other warily, then Blake smiled and stepped forward to give Gage a man-hug, slapping him hard on the back. When he stepped back, his bushy white brows were lifted. 'You're carrying. Why are you here, then?'

'Because I'm carrying shit,' Gage said, aware that the hug had merely been an excuse to check him for weapons. 'My situation has changed.'

'Oh, I know. I know. You have supper with Cesar Tavilla and word gets around quick. So . . . What are you looking to acquire?'

'Depends on your prices.' Gage was four thousand dollars richer than he had been a few hours ago. The ATM in his old neighborhood attracted exactly the kind of victim he'd been seeking – a man withdrawing cash at an hour when well-behaved men should be in bed, keeping their wives awake with their snores. But this guy had been groomed to the hilt and dressed to pick up chicks. He'd been driving a Bentley and had withdrawn a grand from the ATM, indicating he had a high-limit credit card, then had proceeded to sit in the drive-thru line and count his money with the window still down. It was no effort at all to take his wallet and all his cash.

Gage's luck had continued, because the guy actually had several high-limit credit cards and had written the PIN numbers on a scrap of paper he'd kept in his wallet. An hour later, Gage had collected the maximum cash advance from each card, hitting a different bank's ATM for each withdrawal. He'd worn a mask every time, but he'd been lucky not to have been caught, and he knew it.

Fortunately he'd gotten enough cash that he wouldn't have to pull any more ATM jobs.

'I'd like a rifle with a scope, a semi-auto pistol that's been converted to full. Or which I can easily convert myself. A pair of night goggles. Some tear gas.'

'Not much, then,' Blake said, amused. 'Come with me.'

Gage didn't move. 'How much will it be? Because if I can't afford you, I don't want to waste your time.'

'You kept me out of jail, Mr Jarvis. I think I can swing you a discount.'

'Excellent.' Gage fell into step with the man, who gave him a curious sideways look.

'You're going to work for Tavilla, really?'

'Yep.' Gage wasn't stupid. He knew that once he started working for Tavilla, he'd be the man's sword and shield for the rest of his career. 'I've done worse.'

'I know. But you may want to consider buying a passport under a different name. Just in case you find yourself at odds with your new employer.'

'Not a bad idea. Can you acquire one?'

Blake huffed. 'Only the very best quality.' He led Gage to a nondescript sedan and opened the trunk, which was filled with enough rifles and guns to fuel a revolution. 'After this, we're square. We never spoke. I don't even know you.'

Gage didn't take his eyes off all that firepower. 'Whatever you say.'

Thirteen

Gage stood in the lobby of the apartment building across the street from his sister-in-law's address. He knew that Lilah would emerge any minute. An avid jogger, she made a habit of running before the sun rose during the summer months.

It was important that he call his mother when Lilah wasn't home, otherwise the bitch would interfere and stop Ma from agreeing to give him access to the girls.

He needed to see Jazzie for himself. Needed to see her expression when she looked at him. If she'd seen anything, he'd know. And if she'd said anything to the therapist, they'd both need to be dealt with. At this point he was hoping for the best and planning for the worst.

The door across the street opened and Lilah appeared, stopping under a street lamp to stretch. *Hurry. For God's sake, hurry.* She finally set off down the street and Gage dialed his mother's cell phone. A light came on in Lilah's apartment and a moment later he heard his mother's voice for the first time in over a year.

'Hello?' she said, her voice throaty.

'Ma? It's me. Gage. Your son,' he added with an edge when she said nothing.

His mother exhaled on a sob. 'Gage. I knew it was you right away, but hearing your voice after all this time . . . it took my breath away. Oh my Lord, it's really you. Where are you, son?'

'Back in Baltimore, Ma. I've been gone a while.'

200

'I know,' she whispered. 'Where have you been?'

'All over, but most recently Texas. I . . . I wanted to come home, Mama.'

'Oh sweet Jesus,' his mother crooned through her sobs. 'I hate to tell you, Gage . . . Bad things have happened here. Terrible things.'

'I know, Mama.' He pitched his voice low, made his tone quietly devastated. 'I heard it on the news when I was in Texas. I . . . was in a bad way that day. Coming off of a high. But then I saw on the news about what happened to Val, and I knew the girls would need me.'

'They did, Gage. They still do. But . . . where have you been for the last month?'

Wait for it. Wait for it . . . 'In rehab, Mama. I knew I had to fight this devil inside me so I could take care of my girls. I finally went to rehab, Mama, and I finished it. I've been clean for thirty-three days now. For the girls.'

His mother laughed with joy. 'Oh, son, those words are music to my ears. I knew you could if you really wanted to. I'm *so* happy right now.'

'Me too, Ma. I want to see my girls. I've missed them so much. I don't want to wait another day. Can I come over?'

He had to hold his breath a few beats longer than he'd expected as he waited for her to answer, because she hesitated. His temper flared, but he fought it back. *You lose it now and she will never trust you.* 'Ma?' he prompted. 'Can I?'

'Well, they're sleeping now,' she said. 'And I'll have to get them up for church in an hour. You can come to church with us.'

There was a hopeful note in her voice that irritated him. 'I don't have any church clothes,' he lied.

'God doesn't care what you wear, Gage.'

'Ma.' He tried to make his voice reasonable but vulnerable. 'That's a lot of people in one place. I'm working myself back up to being comfortable in a crowd. Trying to manage my stress, y'know. Just until I've been sober a little longer.'

'That makes sense,' she said slowly.

Good. She was coming around. *Now for the* coup de grâce. *Careful* . . . 'Seeing my girls would really help me, Ma. Can I come over this morning?'

'I told you, Gage, we're going to church.'

'They can miss church once, Ma. This is important.'

Another hesitation, this one longer and more deliberate. 'We've got a routine,' she repeated firmly. 'They need stability. I'm afraid this morning won't work.'

His temper began to bubble. When the fucking hell had she grown a goddamned backbone? 'I just want to see them, Ma,' he said from behind clenched teeth.

His mother drew a breath that he knew meant she was counting to ten. He'd blown it. *Goddammit to fucking hell.*

'Your babies have lost their mama, Gage. It was terrible. And they saw her like that, all bloody and beaten. I know you need to see them. But Janie and Jazzie need stability right now. It's important for us to take care of them. You don't know what they've been through. Your needs have to come second.'

He forced his voice to remain calm. 'All right. I understand.' Like hell he did. *Fuck their needs.* He had needs too. He *needed* to find out what Jazzie had seen. 'Can you tell me about them at least? How are they?'

His mother sighed. 'Sad. Scared. Jazzie hasn't said a word since they found Valerie. She has bad dreams but won't talk about them. Janie's a little better. It's Jazzie that worries me the most.'

'Is she seeing anyone?' *Tell me about this fucking therapist, Ma. I'm not getting any younger here.* 'A counselor or anything?'

'Oh yes! She has a new therapist who's been working on drawing her out of her shell.'

'That's wonderful,' he said, oozing sincerity. 'Where did you find this miracle worker?'

'At a farm up in Hunt Valley. It's a program for kids who've been victims of serious crimes. It's all free, which is a relief. They do therapy with horses.'

'I'm glad. But is this therapist qualified?'

'Very much so,' his mother gushed. 'Maggie VanDorn has been

doing therapy with kids for decades, but it's a much younger woman that Jazzie's latched onto. Taylor Dawson is her name. She's new to the farm. Just graduated from college, I think. In fact, she's taking Jazzie out for ice cream today, on her own time, even. Taylor's a good girl. Very smart.'

Too bad for Taylor Dawson. In her case, smart just might mean dead. 'Can I come over before the ice-cream date?'

'I think that would be nice, Gage. Lilah and Jazzie plan to leave for the restaurant at a little before four this afternoon. You could drop by the apartment at two.'

'I'll do that, Ma.' Actually, he wouldn't, because Lilah would be there. He had to get them away from Lilah or he'd be fucked before he even started.

'Wonderful, son. Just wonderful! Have you talked to your brother yet? He'd love to know you're in town.'

'Actually, I did. He was the one who told me that you were living with Lilah now. I called his house last night, looking for you. We talked for a long time. By the time we were finished, it was too late to call you. So I'll see you all at two.'

'I'm so happy you got clean, Gage. I am the happiest, proudest mama on the planet right now. Now you can be the daddy your girls need you to be.'

He rolled his eyes and bit the words back before they slipped off his tongue. *Yeah, whatever, Ma.* He didn't need to be a daddy. He didn't want to be a daddy. He'd never wanted either of those kids. What he wanted was to be left alone. But he injected a healthy dollop of humility into his tone. 'I aim to do it right this time, Ma.'

'I know, Gage. I love you, son.'

He grimaced at having to say the words back. 'Me too, Ma. Listen . . . I want to start over with the girls. But I'm aware that Lilah doesn't approve of me.'

A carefully drawn breath. 'She didn't approve of the drugs, Gage. It wasn't you.'

The hell it wasn't. 'Well, whatever her reasons, she doesn't like me. I think the girls and I would have a better chance at reconciliation if Lilah isn't around when I visit. Can you maybe bring them to the park?' He held his breath when his mother went silent. 'Ma? You still there?'

'I don't know, son. I don't think Lilah will like that.'

He barely stopped himself from growling. 'I'm their father. I have rights.'

'I know,' she said quietly. 'But Lilah is their legal guardian because no one could find you when Valerie was murdered. And I can't have her mad at me. This is where I live now.'

'How could she be declared their legal guardian already? Valerie's only been dead for a couple of weeks.'

'A month, Gage. A very long month.'

He didn't like her tone. She was starting to sound irritated with him. He needed to pull her back into sympathy mode. 'I'm sorry, Ma. I've been trying to get clean and sober. I just need to see my kids.' He wobbled his voice for effect. 'I need to see my girls.'

'I know,' she said again, and her voice had softened. 'It's just that we've been trying to keep Jazzie close to home.'

Shit, damn, fuck. His brother had been right. The kid had seen something and his mother knew it or at least suspected it. But nobody knew exactly what Jazzie had seen, because if they did, his face would be plastered across the news as a wanted man. 'But you said she goes to a farm and rides horses,' he said, trying to sound bewildered and not infuriated. 'What's so different about the park?'

'She gets therapy at the farm.'

'How do you know that seeing me might not be therapy too? I've changed, Ma. I promise. Please. They need their father.' He forced a small sob, knowing his mother could never resist him when he cried. 'And I need them.'

She took a deep breath, exhaling sharply. 'All right. I'll bring the girls to see you in the park. I'll think of something to tell Lilah.'

'Thanks, Ma. You're the best. I'll see you at two.' He clenched his teeth and summoned the words he knew she wanted to hear. 'I . . . I love you, Ma.'

Her sniffle was audible and genuine. 'I love you too, son. So much.'

He ended the call and blew out a breath. So far, so good, but Lilah would be back soon. He slipped out of the lobby, pausing a moment to check for any joggers, then took off down the street and into the alley where he'd left Cleon's car.

He abruptly ducked below the dashboard when Lilah appeared at the alley entrance. *Shit.* But she just jogged by, not looking his way. She was faster than he remembered.

He pulled on a cap, tugging the brim low to hide his eyes, then cautiously pulled out of the alley in time to see Lilah jog around the corner of the next block. He realized she hadn't gained any speed at all. She'd merely shortened her route by going around her immediate block.

So she can stay near Jazzie. Ma wasn't kidding when they said they're keeping the girl close. Shit. He hoped Lilah didn't interfere with Ma bringing Jazzie to the park later. He was running out of time.

At least he had more information now. The equine therapy was run by Maggie VanDorn and the therapist was just out of college. Taylor Dawson should be easy to find. College kids had the whole social media thing down to a science.

Hunt Valley, Maryland,
Sunday 23 August, 5.55 A.M.

Taylor crept down the stairs, trying not to make any noise. Sunday was Maggie's day to sleep in, and she wanted the older woman to get her rest. It wasn't quite dawn, the house and the land quiet and still.

She got to the kitchen door without making a sound, then muffled a startled yelp when the floor behind her creaked. She whirled, her fisted hands reflexively coming up to protect her face, then shuddered out a breath at the sight of Ford in the doorway to the living room.

His hands were up too, palms out in surrender. 'I didn't mean to scare you.'

Taylor sucked in another breath, pressing one fist to her chest where her heart raced. Then the breath she held slowly seeped from

205

her lungs. Ford was shirtless and shoeless, his hair tousled and his unsnapped jeans riding low on his lean hips.

He was . . . golden. Simply golden, his skin kissed by the sun. She'd known he was solid – she'd felt it when he'd held her the night before. But this . . . *Oh my God*.

His chest was perfectly muscled and lightly furred, the blond hair narrowing to a treasure trail that disappeared behind the zipper of his jeans. Which bulged. A lot. She swallowed hard.

Wow. Just . . . wow.

'Um, thanks?' he murmured, and her eyes shot up to his face. He was blushing, and in another hard beat of her heart, so was she.

She crunched her eyes closed, wishing she could run back upstairs and start the morning over again. 'I said that out loud,' she muttered. 'Didn't I?'

'Yeah.' He sounded amused, so she took a chance and opened her eyes in time to see him fastening the top button of his jeans and pulling them an inch higher on his hips.

Damn.

'Okay.' She cleared her throat, forcing her gaze back up to his face, where one side of his mouth lifted in the smallest of grins. *Which would be the only thing small about him.*

Taylor! Well, it's true. She bit back a sigh. *Hell.*

'What are you doing here?' she asked, desperately trying to regain at least a shred of her dignity. She looked past his shoulder to the living room, frowning at the pillow and blanket on the sofa. 'Did you sleep there last night?'

'Yes.'

'Why? You have a room of your own here.' Maggie had told her so when she first moved in. Taylor narrowed her eyes when the answer came to her, unbidden. 'You were guarding the doors.' His flinch was microscopic, but confirmed her suspicion. 'Did you think I'd run away?'

'No,' he said steadily, 'but Clay was worried that you might. I promised him I'd make sure you were here when he came back this morning.'

Her jaw tightened, anger obliterating any residual lust. 'I said I'd stay. I don't lie, Ford.'

'I know,' he said quietly. 'But I promised.'

She rolled her eyes and unlocked the back door. 'Whatever.'

He was across the kitchen in two strides, lightly grabbing her arm before she could open the door. 'Where are you going?' he asked.

She jerked her arm free and he immediately let her go. 'To clean stalls,' she snapped.

'It's not even dawn.'

She shrugged. 'I couldn't sleep.' She'd stared at the ceiling most of the night, her thoughts bouncing wildly from her father's devastation to Clay's hope to her mother's betrayal. When she'd finally slept, she'd dreamt of Ford, waking up even more unsettled. And needy. Really, really needy, but there wasn't a damn thing she could do about that other than pleasuring herself. Which she'd tried, but ended up feeling even more restless – and lonely – than she had before.

So she'd rolled herself out of bed and gotten dressed, determined to work off the frustrated buzz that filled her mind. Just like she did back home. Except now the buzz had a name. And a face. And a chest to die for. 'I might as well be productive.'

'I'll help you.'

He was too close, his scent filling her head. He smelled too good, tempting her to step forward, to close the gap between them. But he'd turned her down the night before and she wasn't going to give him the opportunity to do it twice. Her ego wasn't strong enough to take another rejection, even if it was given for honorable reasons.

She took a step backward, but the door blocked her retreat. His chest filled her field of vision and she snatched her fingers back before they could find out if the blond hair was soft or coarse. Once again she forced her gaze upward and found him staring down at her, his blue eyes darkly intense. Her mouth went dry.

'You don't have to do that,' she said quietly. 'It's my job. I can do it myself.'

'I know you can.' His murmur was low and . . . intimate. 'But I couldn't sleep either.'

207

A shiver slithered down her spine. 'I guess not,' she said, nerves making her voice warble. 'The sofa isn't too comfortable. I fell asleep on it once myself.'

He leaned in, lowering his head until his nose brushed against her hair. 'That wasn't why.'

She swallowed back a whimper. 'I really need to go. I've got work to do.'

'It'll keep for another minute or two,' he whispered, his breath warm on her ear.

Closing her eyes, she flattened her hands on the door behind her. 'Don't tease me, Ford.' She'd intended the words to be sharp and powerful, but they came out soft and pleading.

'I'm not. I'm . . .' He chuckled self-consciously but didn't move a muscle. 'I'm trying to be smooth, but apparently it's not working very well.'

She blinked up at him, the sudden lift of her chin bringing her lips even with his jaw. A slight turn of his head and he'd be kissing her. 'But last night you said—'

He turned his head, and whatever she'd planned to say fled her mind because his mouth was finally on hers. He tilted his head one way, then the other, keeping the kiss sweet. Light.

Too light. More, was all she could think. He still hadn't touched her anywhere else, and she needed him to. She needed to touch him. Her palms came off the door and she reached for his chest, tentatively petting the hair with her fingertips.

Soft. It's so very soft. She started to pull away, gasping in surprise when he gripped her wrists gently, pulling her hands back to his chest.

'Touch me,' he whispered hoarsely, resting his forehead against hers. 'Please.'

A thrill ran through her as she obeyed, raking her fingers through the light fur, then sweeping her palms across the solid bulk of his pecs to his shoulders. He exhaled on a rough sigh that sounded relieved.

'Last night you said you wouldn't do this with me,' she murmured.

'Because you'd had a shock and I was trying to do the right thing. But then . . .'

'But then?' she prompted breathlessly when he didn't finish.

'But then this morning you looked at me like you were so damn . . .' He brushed his lips over hers, tantalizing her. 'Hungry,' he whispered.

She shuddered, her knees going weak. 'I was,' she whispered between his light, plucking kisses. 'I am.' She drew a breath for courage, then ran her hands up his shoulders, following the muscles to his neck until she could dig her fingers into the hair at his nape, all thick and wavy. 'I dreamed about you.' She pressed her body closer until she could feel that enticing bulge in his jeans, hard and pulsing against her abdomen. 'About this.'

His hands gripped her shoulders so hard it almost hurt. She braced herself for another, hotter kiss, but his body had frozen, his shoulders and back going rigid. His jaw was clenched so tightly that a muscle in his cheek twitched. He was holding back, maintaining a fierce control that had him trembling. A control she wanted to shatter. So she leaned up on her toes to whisper in his ear, 'I dreamed you were there, in the bed with me. And I woke up so damn hungry.'

A growl deep in his throat was her only warning before he stepped forward, pushing her into the door. His mouth ground down on hers, hard and satisfying, while his hips began to rock up into her, harder and even more satisfying. Except that it wasn't. The more he rocked into her, the more she wanted. The more sensation she craved.

Her breasts felt heavy, her nipples suddenly sensitive against the cotton of her bra. She moved experimentally, twisting her upper body, dragging her breasts across his chest, whimpering in surprise at the jolt of electricity that shot from her nipples straight down between her legs. It felt so good that she did it again, wishing that there were no layers between them.

He growled again, his mouth almost punishing, his thrusts harder. Faster. More insistent. His hands slid up and down her sides restlessly, his fingers digging into her back, his thumbs

209

brushing the sides of her breasts only. She wanted more. Too much more.

It's not going to be enough, she realized dimly. *Not here anyway.* Not up against Maggie's back door. But she couldn't seem to stop herself from kissing him. Or touching all that golden skin. Or from trying to pull herself up higher against him, to get that hard bulge closer to where her body clenched and throbbed so hard it was a physical ache.

Please, please, please. She wasn't sure what she was even asking for, but he seemed to know because his hands slid to her butt and he hoisted her up with effortless ease. She wrapped her legs around his hips, locking her ankles behind him, letting her head fall back against the door. *Yes. This.*

'Yes,' she hissed. Finally. She could feel him right where she ached. But still not enough. He pressed a hard kiss to her neck, just behind her ear, before licking his way down her throat. *More, more, more.* She bucked her hips in time with the chanting in her head.

And then he swiveled his hips, ripping a raw moan from her throat that was startlingly loud in the quiet of the kitchen. *Oh my God. In the kitchen.* A flicker of awareness shocked her milliseconds before her feet were lowered to the floor. She flattened her palms against the door behind her to remain upright when her knees threatened to buckle.

Wow. She'd nearly come right there against the door. She should probably be embarrassed, but she wasn't. Her body was revving like a racecar. She'd never felt so good in her entire life.

Still . . . in the kitchen. Where anyone could come in and see them going at it like weasels. *Don't be stupid. Nobody's here yet.* And Maggie slept like the dead. *Don't be a prude, Taylor.*

Ford stepped back and closed his eyes, his chest working like a bellows. His hands clenched into fists at his sides and he hung his head while he huffed like a bull in the ring. 'What do you want, Taylor?' he gritted out.

'More than this,' she whispered, grateful that he'd had the self-control to stop, because she wasn't sure she'd have been able to. 'But not here. Not like this.'

'No, not like this.' He shuddered out a breath, then stepped closer, lifting her chin with one finger, so gently that tears stung her eyes. 'I'll be your first?'

She grimaced, her face growing hot for all the wrong reasons. 'Sorry.'

His eyes flashed, suddenly as intense as they'd been before. 'Don't be. Please.'

'It's just . . .' She rolled her eyes, totally mortified by her inexperience. 'I'm twenty-three years old, for God's sake. I should be—'

'Sshh.' Pressing his finger to her lips, he hesitated, his brow furrowing as he seemed to think hard. 'You'll be my second,' he finally said. 'I'm not Mr Experience myself.'

Her eyes widened. *Oh. Wow.* That meant he hadn't had anyone since Kimberly. *No pressure, Taylor.* 'What happens next?' she murmured against his finger, then kissed it.

He cupped her jaw, his eyes remaining intense while his expression softened to something tender. 'We take it slow,' he said quietly. 'Although slow might just kill me.'

She rubbed her cheek against his palm. 'Me too.'

He suddenly grinned, bursting the bubble that had cocooned them. 'Good. It's only fair that both of us should suffer.'

She laughed, and it felt so good. 'Go put on a shirt, Ford.'

His blue eyes crinkled at the corners as his grin turned smug. 'I don't know. Maybe I like the way you look at me.' He surprised her again by wrapping his arms around her, drawing her close. This embrace was different from the others. Last night's had been about comfort. Up against the door just now had been about lust. This was . . . sweet. 'Just so you know, I like to hold you like this too,' he said huskily, resting his cheek on her head. 'I don't want to pressure you.'

She melted into him, sliding her hands up the smooth skin of his back and holding on. 'And if I pressure you?'

'That would be more than okay.'

They stood there together, in the quiet of the kitchen, as the seconds ticked away. Slowly, inevitably, reality began to intrude. 'I don't want to hurt anyone, Ford,' she whispered.

'I know.'

'But I'm going to. Whichever way I turn, I'm hurting someone. If I stay, I break my dad's heart. If I go home, I hurt Clay. And you.'

Ford stroked her hair. 'What about you? What do you want?'

That he hadn't denied her words ratcheted him up in her esteem. That he zeroed in on the one question she couldn't answer made her want to cry. 'I don't know. For so long I wanted to be invisible. I'm not sure I know what to do now that everyone can see me.'

'You're here for another month. Why not cross that bridge when you get there? Maybe by then you'll know.'

She nodded, breathing him in. Letting herself pretend for just a minute that everything could turn out all right. That she'd be able to have her cake and eat it too. 'Okay.'

'Whenever I get all wound up in my own head, I go for a ride. It helps. Have you had a chance to do that yet?'

She shook her head wistfully. 'No. I've been doing classes and therapy sessions nearly every day. Maggie's been too busy to go with me on my days off, especially when Dillon was away on his bachelor trip. We were short-handed so I pitched in. She didn't want me riding off alone until she showed me the trail at least once.'

'Then today you and I will ride together and I'll show you the rest of the farm. Then I'll help you get your chores done before Clay gets here.' He cupped her face in his hands and dropped a soft kiss on her lips. 'I'll get dressed and meet you in the barn.'

Hunt Valley, Maryland,
Sunday 23 August, 5.55 A.M.

Gage rolled his eyes as he drove past the gated entrance to the equine therapy center where Jazzie had made her apparent connection with therapist Taylor Dawson. *Healing Hearts with Horses. God.* Could the place *get* any sappier? *Spare me the bleeding hearts.*

Except they weren't just any bleeding hearts. Way out in the country, it should have been easy to slip through the farm's front gate and take the therapist out, but this was no ordinary farm.

It was managed by Maggie VanDorn, but it was owned by

212

Daphne Montgomery-Carter, the bitchiest junkyard dog of a prosecutor that Gage had ever gone up against in his years as a defense attorney. And, he hated to admit, smart. She'd bested him in court more often than he'd bested her. She was, unfortunately, honest. He'd never tried bribing her, because others had and had ended up disbarred or even serving time.

The Carter part of her name was new. She hadn't been married when he'd left Baltimore three years before. But when she'd married, she'd gone large. Special Agent Joseph Carter, FBI.

Fuck it all, anyway. Gage's research into Taylor Dawson and Healing Hearts had turned up a wealth of information on the program itself, but not one thing on Taylor Dawson. Not one article, no photographs, no high school awards, no social media. Nothing. It was like the woman was a ghost.

The program was free to children who'd been victims of violence, its operating costs covered by donations. Lots of fund-raising dinners. Lots of photos of Daphne herself and a few of her and Agent Carter, usually at black-tie events. Even in a tux, the man looked dangerous.

There were several pictures of Maggie VanDorn, the head therapist. Precious few of Clay Maynard, Daphne's head of security. The man looked even more menacing than Carter.

Gage only knew Carter and Maynard by reputation, but he knew better than to cross paths with either of them directly. Carter was a James Bond type. Maynard was Daphne's male junkyard dog equivalent. Fortunately, Gage wasn't interested in eliminating either of the men. Just one young therapist. But he didn't even know what *she* looked like.

Thus this reconnaissance trip. Horses had to be cared for – fed, stalls cleaned, that kind of thing. Somebody would be going to the barn at some point soon. Hopefully it would be Taylor Dawson.

He'd learned from the employment opportunities on the website that the interns were housed on the property. It was a perk, because the job paid next to nothing. *Bleeding hearts.*

He pulled his car onto the shoulder about a quarter-mile from the front gate, and grabbed his night goggles and the rifle he'd purchased from Reverend Blake. If nothing else, he could test the rifle's sight and trigger and make sure he could hit where he was aiming.

Dressed all in black, he hung to the other side of the road as he walked toward the gate, stopping occasionally to peer through the goggles. He could just barely see the fence that lined the property. It was mostly obscured by trees, but he could see cameras mounted at regular intervals.

It was what he'd expected when he'd heard Maynard and Carter were part of the enterprise. He suspected the fence was equipped with motion detectors, too. He wouldn't be able to get too close. This would have been easier in the winter, when all the leaves were gone, he thought sourly. He squinted through the night goggles, marginally satisfied when he was able to glimpse the barn through the trees. He might see Taylor Dawson if she came out. At least he'd know what she looked like.

Headlights suddenly appeared when a car came round the bend in the road, and Gage flattened his body to the ground, fixing his goggles to the car's interior as the vehicle slowed to turn into the farm's driveway. Two people. Man and a woman. Both looked young. Could be Taylor . . .

Gage had his rifle positioned on his shoulder as he studied the pair, then lowered it. The couple appeared to have Down syndrome. Probably not the therapist.

The car stopped and the driver lowered the window to punch a code into a security panel. But the panel was truly secure. The driver had to slip his hand up under the cover to get to the keypad. Dammit. There was no way to see the code he had entered.

Once the car had entered, the gate closed behind it and Gage settled in to wait, watching the barn carefully through the goggles. A few minutes later, a woman walked into his line of sight – tall, fluid, long black hair pulled into a ponytail. Blindly he reached for the rifle, but he could see her only from the back, dammit. *Turn around. C'mon, sweetheart. Just a little.* But she didn't, walking briskly, with purpose. By the time he'd gotten the rifle on his shoulder and aimed, she was out of sight.

He breathed out a frustrated sigh. *No worries,* he told himself. *She's got to come out sometime.* Hopefully it would be before the rest of the farm woke up. Shooting her before dawn was risky enough. With all those cameras, he'd be spotted once the sun came up, and he really did not want to tangle with the Healing Hearts security team.

Fourteen

Ford didn't think he'd ever gotten dressed so fast. He took the back stairs in two big jumps, then ran to the barn. He and Taylor were going on a ride and he knew exactly where he'd take her. He'd discovered the little clearing near the stream when he was twelve years old, and it had been his meditation spot ever since.

He'd never taken anyone there. Certainly not Kimberly. She'd been terrified of little wiener dogs, much less horses. Thank God for that, because he would have surely shown her his clearing. And then it wouldn't be special for Taylor. He wanted it to be special for Taylor.

He grimaced, not sure how he was going to manage doing the chores with a massive hard-on, but he'd figure it out. Wasn't like he hadn't done it before. But it had definitely been a while. Kimberly had seen to that. She'd knocked him down and left him numb. Inside and out. Yesterday had been the first time he'd felt truly alive in too long.

Enjoy it while it lasts. His step faltered and he stumbled as he approached the barn. It was going to hurt like hell when Taylor left. Because she would, eventually. She'd go back to the father who'd raised her, to the sisters who still needed her. She was too loyal not to.

Ford could almost hear her logic in his mind and knew which choice she'd make. Frederick Dawson's wife was dead. His oldest daughter was dead. His middle daughter was a recovering alcoholic

216

and his youngest had special needs and would depend on him every day for the rest of her life. Dawson had given up his career and his friends, moving to the middle of nowhere to keep Taylor safe.

What would the man do if she chose to stay in Baltimore?

Clay, on the other hand, would survive. He'd visit his daughter on birthdays and major holidays. For the rest of the year, he had Stevie and Cordelia. He had his security business and he had a ton of friends.

Ford knew in his roiling gut what her decision would be. He also knew that he was getting far too emotional about a girl he'd just met. They'd have some fun. Maybe a lot of fun.

And then she'll leave. And I'll be alone again.

But that's a month from now. He'd follow his own advice and cross that bridge when he got there. At least he didn't have to worry about mucking out stalls with an erection anymore, he thought grimly. Just thinking about going back to the numb loneliness of the past year and a half had taken the starch right out of his sails, so to speak.

But, he repeated to himself, *that's a month from now.* Pasting a smile on his face, he steeled his spine and opened the barn door. And stopped short when he heard an angry female voice that did not belong to Taylor.

Hurrying inside, Ford blinked at the sight of Dillon and his fiancée, Holly, standing in the aisle between the rows of stalls, blocking Taylor's path. Holly was doing the talking, arms crossed tightly over her chest, a mutinous expression on her normally smiling face. Dillon stood behind her, looking generally miserable.

And exhausted, Ford noted as he drew closer. Neither Holly nor Dillon looked like they'd slept. *Join the club.*

'You used him!' Holly was saying angrily. Shaking her forefinger, she got up in Taylor's face, no small feat considering Taylor was nearly six feet tall with her boots on. Holly was only four foot ten, but she made up for it with a powerful personality.

Taylor took a step back, her hands out in a gesture of surrender. 'I didn't. I swear it.'

Holly advanced another step, poking that finger of hers into

217

Taylor's shoulder. 'Your swears don't mean anything. You just pretended to like him so that you could get information about Clay.'

Ah. This was about the conversation on which Ford had shamelessly eavesdropped the day before. He approached carefully, having been on the receiving end of Holly's wrath before. Normally easy-going, she was also fiercely loyal, and nobody messed with the people she loved.

'What's going on here, Holls?' he asked, even though he already knew.

Holly glared at him. 'None of your business, Ford. Go away.'

'C'mon, Holly,' Ford cajoled, but Holly was having none of it.

'I mean it, Ford,' she snarled. 'We don't need you here. Go the hell away!'

Taylor gave Ford a helpless look before turning her focus to Dillon. 'I didn't use you, Dillon. And I didn't pretend to like you. I *do* like you,' she said earnestly. 'That's why I trusted you to tell me the truth.'

Dillon shook his head, hurt in his eyes. 'You came here on a lie. You lied about your name, you lied about who you were. Everything you said was a lie.'

Taylor sighed wearily. 'No. I didn't lie. My name really is Taylor Dawson. I really did come from California. I never wanted to hurt you, Dillon, and I'm sorry that I did.'

Dillon's chin lifted. He had his pride, Ford knew. Dillon had steadfastly refused financial help from Holly's wealthy family because he wanted to provide for her himself. He'd worked hard, here in the barn and bagging groceries at the local market, saving every penny until he and Holly had a nest egg big enough to get an apartment and a car of their own.

With single-minded determination, Dillon and Holly rejected the notion that having Down syndrome meant that they had to be dependent on their families for the rest of their lives. Ford was damn proud of them. But at this particular moment, Holly's single-minded determination was leading her down the wrong path.

Holly stepped in front of Dillon, forcing Taylor to look at her. 'You think that because he has Down syndrome he can't lie,' Holly said bitterly. 'You think he's a big dumb kid you can trick into telling you everything you want to know.'

Taylor shook her head, panic in the movement. 'I never thought any of that. Not even once. Dillon, please, hear me out. Please.' She waited until Dillon moved so that he stood at Holly's side rather than behind her.

His expression was stony. 'I can lie. I'm not a little kid. I'm not . . . simple.'

Taylor flinched as if she'd been slapped. 'I know you're not! I know you can lie. Everybody can lie, but I didn't think you had any reason to.' She dropped her gaze, her shoulders sagging. 'I'm not the best judge of character, though. My own mother lied to me for my whole life and I never suspected a thing. She told me terrible things about Clay. I believed her because she was my mom and I was a little kid. But I'm not a little kid anymore, either, and I'm really tired of being lied to. I figured if you didn't know who I was, you'd have no reason to lie.' She squared her shoulders and met Dillon's gaze, which had softened considerably. 'I'm sorry I deceived you. I didn't mean to hurt you or anyone else. I'm just trying to find my way to the truth.'

Dillon held her eyes for several heartbeats, then gave her a nod and a small smile. 'Okay.'

Relieved, Taylor's knees wobbled. Ford put his arm around her waist to help her stay upright, his heart giving a little kick when she leaned into him.

'Thank you,' she whispered to him, then cleared her throat. 'What are you two doing here so early?'

'Same as you,' Dillon said with a sideways grin. 'Shoveling shit. Holly came to keep me company.' He lifted his brows. 'And to yell at you.'

Taylor warily met Holly's eyes. 'Are we good, Holly?'

Holly's glare had melted away, leaving her normal smile in its place. 'Yes.'

Taylor smiled back. 'Is my invitation to the wedding still good?'

Holly nodded. 'Of course. Unless you hurt his feelings again, and then I will kick your ass.'

219

'And she can kick ass pretty well, actually,' Dillon added proudly. 'She takes karate.'

'From Paige,' Taylor said.

'Clay's other business partner,' Ford supplied.

Taylor's smile was rueful. 'I know. I read about her, too. She's also married to your mother's boss, Grayson Smith. I had to make a spreadsheet to keep all Clay's interconnected friends and their husbands and kids straight in my mind.' She turned back to Holly and Dillon. 'I'll be sure to behave myself in the future. Thank you, Dillon, for telling me about my father. I tried to learn about him before I came, but there wasn't much online.'

Ford wondered if she'd called Clay her father to keep from angering Holly and Dillon further, or if she'd even realized she'd done so.

Dillon had become serious. 'I'm glad I could tell you good things. They're all true.'

'I know. I could have asked a lot of people about Clay when I first got here, but I didn't know who to trust. I don't trust many people, but I trusted you. I hope we can still be friends.'

'Yes,' he said simply. 'I'll take you home now, Holls, then I'll come back to work.'

Holly grabbed Dillon's hand and faced Taylor straight on. 'I don't understand why your name isn't Sienna, but I guess I do understand why you lied. You were scared. But please don't lie anymore. Dillon is a sensitive guy. You really hurt his feelings.'

Dillon rolled his eyes. 'Holly, be nice. Please.'

'I won't kick her ass,' Holly said. 'That's all I'll promise for now.' She pointed her finger back at Taylor, her eyes suddenly sober. 'Don't hurt Clay's feelings either. Or . . . you know.'

'Ass-kicking will happen,' Taylor said dryly. 'Got it. Although I suspect you'll have to get in line behind Stevie and a bunch of other people.' She sighed. 'I will do my very best not to hurt him.'

Holly's chin jutted out stubbornly. 'That's not good enough.'

Dillon tugged on his fiancée's hand. 'Holly,' he said quietly. 'She said she'd do her best. That's all she can promise. That's all you can ask.'

Holly looked up at her man, her expression settling to one of love, contentment and a pride so fierce it made Ford's heart hurt. *That's what I want. Someone to look at me just like that. Like I'm everything they need.*

'You're right,' Holly murmured and patted Dillon's cheek. 'Take me home now.'

The couple left, hand-in-hand, and the barn was suddenly too quiet, the only sounds those of horses shuffling in their stalls.

'He's right, you know,' Ford said into the quiet. 'Dillon, I mean. All any one of us can ask is that you do your best. Whatever happens.'

'I know,' Taylor whispered. 'In my head I know. It's my heart that's being difficult.'

He lightened his tone. 'Then let's get your ass in a saddle so that your head can whip your heart into line.' He swatted said ass and she blinked up at him, clearly caught off guard.

Then she laughed, making him feel invincible. 'Okay. Let's get my ass in a saddle.'

Hunt Valley, Maryland,
Sunday 23 August, 6.35 A.M.

Gage waited for Taylor Dawson to leave the barn, ducking once again when the car with the couple with Down syndrome exited the property. Then he positioned his rifle so that he had the barn door in his sights, aiming for where the black-ponytailed young woman's chest would be. Once she appeared through the door, he'd have only a few seconds to make the shot before she walked out of his field of vision.

She was still in there, along with the young man who'd entered the barn a few minutes after she had. Gage was pretty sure the man was Ford Elkhart. He'd briefly seen his face as he followed the same path the ponytailed girl had. His research on the therapy program and Daphne Montgomery had yielded lots of photos of her son, who'd been on the receiving end of extensive media coverage after he was kidnapped. It made sense that he would work the farm. Again, Gage had no beef with Ford Elkhart. He just wanted the girl.

221

But what if the girl wasn't Taylor Dawson? Yes, she was about the right age, but what if she wasn't the right girl? Then he'd have to find another way to get to her.

And if Denny and Ma were both wrong and Jazzie didn't see anything? Even if this young woman is Taylor Dawson, it doesn't mean she knows anything. Mentally he shoved the doubts away. Taylor Dawson was a potential loose end. Yes, it would be a shame for her to die if she didn't know anything, but it would be a bigger shame if she did know something and told the cops. And if Jazzie hadn't said a word yet, she never would if her therapist was dead. Either way, the benefits far outweighed the risks.

And he'd already killed three other people who hadn't been involved at all. What was one more? Especially one who presented an even greater risk.

I'm going to work for Tavilla. I'd better get used to killing for the sake of expediency.

His arm muscles began to cramp as the minutes ticked by, but he gritted his teeth and maintained his position, resolving to do more upper-body strength training in the future. After about ten minutes, Ford and the ponytailed woman left the barn – but on horseback. *Dammit.* Her chest was no longer in his sight. It had moved several feet higher.

His arm, stiffened from the cramped muscles, jerked upward to adjust his aim, but by then, the girl and the horse were no longer visible. *Fuck, fuck, fuck.*

Time to pack it in. The sun was fully up now and he was a sitting duck, dressed head-to-toe in black the way he was.

At least he knew that Taylor Dawson had long black hair – if that young woman had been her. Chances were better than decent that she had been, so the trip out here hadn't been a total waste of time. He jogged back to his car, stowed his rifle and had just pulled away from the shoulder when he saw a truck approaching. He tugged the brim of his cap down, his jaw clenching when he realized that the driver was none other than security man Clay Maynard. *Shit.* Had he been seen? *Damn, damn, damn.*

Coming out here was a stupid thing to do. Stupid. Don't flinch. Don't cringe. Don't even notice the other car. Just keep your eyes straight ahead and drive.

Their vehicles passed each other and Gage glanced in his rearview, relieved when Maynard just kept driving the other way. *God. That was close.*

Hands shaking, he tightened his grip on the steering wheel and headed back toward his rented room. On the way, he turned onto a side road, pulled a small bag from under the seat, and prepared a nice long line on the piece of mirror he'd carried around for years. And inhaled.

There, he thought with a sigh of relief. *Better now.* He could think again. And he needed to think. Needed to plan. Needed a way to clean up the mess the kid had made, if she *had* somehow seen him. Only one solution would truly take care of the problem.

Three can keep a secret if two of them are dead.

The old Ben Franklin quote popped into his mind and he wanted to scream. It hadn't been three people at first, only two. *Just Denny and me.* But if Jazzie had seen . . . and if she'd told the therapist . . . he could be up to four. Four people who knew his secret.

You're talking about killing Jazzie. You know that, right? You're talking about killing an eleven-year-old girl who used to call you Daddy. Can you actually do that? Can you kill a child?

Could he? He'd never thought he could kill at all. Then he had. But he'd never thought he could kill a child. Never even considered the question.

Maybe he was getting all upset over nothing. Maybe Jazzie hadn't seen a thing.

But . . . *hell.* He closed his eyes on a sigh. The not-knowing was making him crazy. In the end, he'd do what he had to do. No more, no less. And he'd know what that was soon enough.

Hunt Valley, Maryland,
Sunday 23 August, 7.45 A.M.

Ford had been right, Taylor thought as they brushed the horses down after their early-morning ride. She'd needed the quiet so that her head could clear. Unfortunately, her head still hadn't had that talk with her heart, and she lingered longer than she needed to, giving the horse one last stroke down its neck and one last flake of hay.

'You're stalling, Taylor,' Ford said softly, putting his hands on her shoulders and turning her gently towards the open barn door. 'Clay, Stevie and Cordelia will be arriving any minute and I promised I'd make them breakfast.'

Taylor looked over her shoulder with a wince. 'Stevie's coming?'

He nodded. 'Maggie texted me when we were out riding to give me the heads-up. Stevie and Cordelia will eat breakfast with us, then they'll go for a ride.'

'Clay and Stevie made up, then?'

'It appears so. Why are you stalling, Taylor?'

She closed her eyes and let herself lean back against him. 'Because I'm scared.'

He wrapped his arms around her middle and kissed her temple. 'Of hurting Clay?'

She gave a nervous laugh. 'Well, Holly did threaten me with an ass-kicking.'

He began swaying side to side, rocking her. 'What else are you afraid of?'

'I don't know,' she whispered. 'I had this tidy little life in the middle of nowhere, Ford. My biggest exposure to people was when I finally got to go to college. It was a small school and I lived at home. I didn't socialize. I didn't even drive myself back and forth every day.'

'And you had a bodyguard, you said. One of your father's ranch hands.'

She huffed an empty chuckle. 'The son of Dad's foreman, actually. At least Jacob got a psych degree out of it, since he took the same classes I did. But even with him next to me, I was . . . afraid. I didn't make eye contact with anyone. The people sitting all around me could just as well have been mannequins.'

'It was impersonal. No need to form connections. You just existed among them without being part of them.'

'Exactly,' she said, relieved that he understood. 'But now . . .'

'Now you've met your bio-dad and he's got this huge circle of friends. And they're going to put you under a microscope.'

'Like a bug,' she said glumly. 'I hope I don't get squashed like one.'

He chuckled. 'It won't be that bad. Holly and Dillon have probably already vouched for you to Joseph's family. It won't be long before the grapevine heats up.' He kissed the side of her neck, sending a shiver down her back. 'It's just breakfast. Waffles and bacon.' He released his hold, then took her hand. 'Come on. You have a few minutes to wash up before they get here.'

She put one foot in front of the other and focused on his hand holding hers and not the people who'd be waiting for her. 'Thank you for the ride. I did need it.'

'So did I. I hadn't gone riding in over a month, and I missed it.'

She chanced a glance up at his face, her heart stuttering a little in her chest. He was a good guy. Handsome. And she certainly hadn't forgotten what was going on under the T-shirt he wore. But now she studied his face, happy to see him looking a lot more relaxed than he had before. 'Why haven't you?'

'Just busy at work. I was trying to get a few projects closed out before taking two weeks off. I wanted to spend time with Dillon and the others on the camping trip and I promised Maggie I'd help her with the horses while Dillon and Holly are on their honeymoon.'

Yep. A truly good guy. And, she thought, as lonely as she was, which was mystifying. She had to wonder at the women he knew, that one hadn't already snapped him up.

'Where do you work?' she asked as they crossed the yard, still hand-in-hand. 'I thought you'd just finished college.'

'I did. I've been interning for Joseph's father's company for a few years. Mr Carter was good enough to offer me a full-time job whenever I finished school, but I knew I didn't want to go for my masters. At least for now.'

'So you accepted his offer?'

'Yes. It's really amazing work. I'm lucky I got in on the ground floor the way I did.'

225

She looked up at him and smiled. He looked like a kid at Christmas. 'What is it?'

'Prosthetics,' he said with satisfaction. 'Revolutionary stuff that'll change the quality of life for a lot of people.'

Yep. A really good guy.

He squeezed her hand as they approached the house. 'That's Clay's truck. They're early. You ready?'

She gave a hard nod. 'As I'll ever be. You did say there would be waffles?'

'And bacon.' He smacked his lips together, making her laugh again just as they climbed the back stairs and entered the kitchen.

She had not a single doubt that he'd specifically timed it so that she'd enter laughing.

Clay and Stevie were already sitting at the table with Maggie, drinking coffee and talking. A glance into the living room revealed Cordelia on the sofa watching cartoons. Clay immediately stood, a huge smile taking over his face even as his eyes flickered with what looked like relief.

He thought I'd bolt, Taylor thought sadly, but she kept her own smile on her face. 'Good morning,' she said, tempted to grab at Ford's hand when he released hers and took the stairs two at a time, presumably to wash up before he cooked breakfast.

'Good morning.' Clay took a tentative step forward, uncertainty chasing the relief away.

That uncertainty broke Taylor's heart a little more. Surprising herself, she closed the gap between them, giving him a hard hug. 'I went riding with Ford. I didn't run away from you. I wouldn't do that.' Her smile became rueful. 'Now that I've met you, anyway.'

His big chest rose and fell as he whooshed out a breath. 'I knew you wouldn't.'

She had to grin at his obvious lie. 'No, you didn't.' From the corner of her eye she saw Stevie roll her eyes and knew she was right.

Clay grinned back. 'Okay, I didn't. But I hoped. Hard.'

Maggie pointed to the empty chair next to Clay's. 'Have a seat, Taylor.'

'Give me a few minutes to wash up so that I don't smell like a horse. I'll be right back.'

Taylor rushed through her cleanup, coming out of the bathroom at her end of the hall just as Ford came out of his bedroom, freshly showered. And shirtless. Again. He was toweling his hair with one hand while the other held a clean T-shirt. She stopped and stared. Again.

With a grin, he spread his arms wide and waggled his brows at her, making her chuckle. He'd planned this, the jerk. 'Now you're just being mean,' she whispered loudly.

He met her in the middle of the hall and quickly kissed her mouth. 'Nope. Just trying to take your mind off your troubles for a minute or two, since your head and your heart still aren't on speaking terms.'

She looked up at him wistfully, wishing she could touch all that pretty golden skin the way she wanted to. 'You want to be their mediator?'

In answer he put his arms around her and cradled her like a child, tightening his hold when she shuddered against him. 'It'll all be fine,' he whispered in her ear. 'You'll see.'

'Ford!' Maggie called loudly. 'We're about to expire from hunger down here. Leave the girl alone and get yourself downstairs and start cooking.'

Taylor jerked out of his arms, her face on fire, but Ford just laughed. 'I'm coming, Maggie,' he called down affably. 'No need to dig out your whip.' He pulled the T-shirt over his head, tugged it into place, then skipped down the stairs, throwing a wink over his shoulder.

Fifteen

Hunt Valley, Maryland,
Sunday 23 August, 8.10 A.M.

Taylor was still blushing as she took the chair Maggie had indicated, grateful that someone had put a full cup of coffee at her place. She took a big gulp, wincing when it scalded her mouth. Still, it was a welcome distraction from the unwanted attention from the three adults at the table, who stared at her, then Ford, then back at her.

But no one said a word and Ford got busy cooking.

Stevie rolled her eyes again, but this time in an uncomfortable, self-deprecating way. 'Before anyone says anything, I need to apologize. I was rude to you yesterday, Taylor, and I'm very sorry. My daughter was right. You were very brave to come here and, based on what you were told, very smart to take the precautions you took. Regardless of where you choose to settle permanently – here or California or anywhere else – you are always welcome in our home.'

Taylor felt like a weight had rolled off her shoulders. 'You had every right to protect your husband. But thank you. Apology accepted.'

Clay smiled at his wife, something warm and lovely passing between them. Obviously they'd kissed and made up from the night before, which was another weight off Taylor's shoulders. She hadn't wanted to come between them.

'I told them about your adoption,' Maggie said. 'So you don't have to go through it again.'

'Thank you,' Taylor said fervently.

'I have to say I'm relieved,' Clay said. 'I've felt so incompetent all these years, not being able to find my own child when I make a living helping other parents find theirs.'

'My dad in California is a smart guy.' Taylor hesitated. 'I really think you'd like him.'

Clay's smile was gentle. 'I think I would too. I'm not happy that we were apart for so long, but I can understand his reasons. But enough about what's past. I want to know everything that's going on in your life now. College and hobbies and all of that.'

The rest of breakfast was relaxed. Ford set big platters of food on the table, then took the empty chair on the other side of Taylor. The conversation flowed naturally as Taylor and Clay simply got to know each other. Stevie and Maggie added details when Clay's recitation of the facts was too sparse, like the way he'd saved his fellow soldiers in Somalia, ending with his being awarded the Purple Heart and the Silver Star. And the way he'd courted Stevie for years before she'd finally said yes.

The stories painted a picture of a truly good man, and too many times Taylor mentally cursed her mother for denying her this relationship.

As she ate, she also found herself worrying about who she'd choose. It seemed that Ford could read her mind, because every time her thoughts wandered, he'd squeeze her hand, bringing her back to the present. The past was done. The lost years couldn't be recovered or relived. The future . . . Taylor still didn't know what she'd do, but she found herself enjoying the present almost enough to stop worrying about how it would all end. Almost.

Finally, when the waffles were eaten and the bacon was history, Clay pulled an envelope from his wallet. 'You haven't really asked about my family,' he said.

She'd told him all about her family. Her sisters. Her dad. But she hadn't asked Clay anything about his. *My grandparents.* 'I'm sorry. That was rude of me.'

Clay tapped his finger over her lips. 'Hush. I don't want you to say you're sorry anymore.' He handed her the envelope. 'Pictures of my family. *Your* family.'

229

Taylor took the photos out with fingers that trembled, then sucked in a startled breath. The one on top was old and worn around the edges, clearly taken decades ago. The woman had long black hair and Clay's eyes.

My eyes. And my face. The resemblance . . . *My God.* It was like looking in a mirror. This was her grandmother. *Goddammit, Mom. How could you?*

The woman – *my grandmother* – smiled at the camera, so worry-free and happy that tears filled Taylor's eyes, blurring the photo in hands that no longer merely trembled, but shook so hard that she could barely see even after blinking the tears away. Impatiently she wiped her cheeks with a napkin before raising her gaze to Clay's.

'I . . . I look like her,' she whispered.

Clay smiled at her. 'Yeah, you do. I saw it right away. She was eighteen in that picture.'

Maggie leaned over Ford's shoulder to look, then whistled. 'Taylor's the spittin' image of your mama, Clay,' she said. 'No wonder you knew her as soon as you walked into the room.'

Clay's smile turned wry. 'For a moment I thought I'd seen a ghost.' He gave the edge of the photo a brief caress, his eyes growing shiny, his smile becoming so damn sad. 'She would have loved to know you,' he whispered, meeting Taylor's gaze once more. 'She made me promise to never stop looking until I found you. It was one of the last things she said.'

Taylor stared at him, stunned. *She's dead. My grandmother's dead and I never got to meet her. She's dead and he grieved for her. He still does. Just like he grieved for me.* A sob barreled up and she shoved it back down, but it got stuck halfway, clogging her throat.

'What was her name?' she asked hoarsely.

Beside her, Ford stroked her back, giving her silent comfort. But her eyes stayed locked on Clay's. He swallowed hard, then swallowed again, audibly.

'Nancy,' he finally whispered.

Nancy. My grandmother was Nancy and she would have loved me. 'Dammit,' she whispered, the photo growing blurry again. Ford slipped a tissue into her hand, but it was too late. The sob escaped,

230

and then she was in Clay's arms, crying so hard she couldn't breathe.

The photos were gently pried from her hand as her body shook with grief. *Ford*, she thought dully. But it was Clay who held her, rocking her like a baby. Somehow she was sitting on his knee, her arms around his waist, her face buried against his neck.

Eventually her weeping ceased and she could hear his gentle shushing. He hadn't stopped rocking her and she wondered if he would have rocked her to sleep at night when she was little and scared. Of course she wouldn't have been scared of the same things. She wouldn't have been scared of him. She would have had a normal childhood. A normal life.

A grandmother who looked just like her. 'How long ago?' she asked, her voice like gravel.

'How long ago did she die?' Clay asked, and she nodded. 'Four and a half years. But at the end of her life, she was thinking of you. And me.'

'I wish I could have known her.'

'Me too, baby,' he murmured, laying his cheek on the top of her head. 'Me too.'

Taylor heard a chair creak and remembered where she was. At a table surrounded by people who'd seen her fall apart twice in as many days. Embarrassed, she sat up, shielding her eyes with her hand because the light coming from the small chandelier over the table was way too bright. Her face hurt. Her head hurt even worse.

'I hate to cry,' Cordelia said matter-of-factly from the other side of the table. 'It sucks ass.'

'Cordelia!' Stevie exclaimed, but it sounded like she was trying not to laugh.

'Well, it does,' the girl said.

'I didn't say that in front of her, Stevie,' Maggie said defensively.

'Of course you didn't,' Cordelia said, sounding way older than nine. 'It was Mom.'

'I know,' Maggie said in a stage whisper, and Cordelia giggled.

'You okay now, Taylor?' Cordelia asked.

Way older than nine, poor kid. 'I will be.' Taylor slid back into her

231

own chair, and instantly Ford's scent filled her head. He was still there. Her lips curved in spite of her headache. Of course he was. The guy was solid like a rock.

Ford opened the fist she hadn't realized she'd clenched and dropped two white tablets onto her palm. 'Just normal over-the-counter stuff,' he said softly.

'Thanks.' She popped the pills and chased them down with coffee that had grown cold. She grimaced, both at the cold coffee and at the thought that Ford was seeing her face when it looked like ground beef. But a glance up revealed him holding a bag of frozen peas. 'What the heck, Ford?'

'For your eyes,' he explained, and she laughed up at him.

'You're kidding me.'

Ford grinned. 'Nope. It'll help. Don't ask me how I know.'

'Fair enough,' she said, and slapped the bag over the top half of her face. 'Oh. That feels good. Thank you.' She kept it there just long enough to dull the throb, then tossed the bag to the table and turned back to Clay, who was watching Ford with something between amusement and dire warning. 'Tell me about your mother,' she said softly. 'Please.'

Clay picked up the photos, his expression growing instantly softer. 'My mom was the very best. She was a single mom for the first few years of my life, that is, until she met my stepfather, Tanner St James. This is them on their wedding day.'

The bride and groom were smiling at each other, while each held the hand of a small black-haired boy. 'This is you?'

'Yeah,' he said, and it was obvious that the memory was a sweet one. 'My mom was always worried that she'd never meet anyone who wanted someone else's kid, but Tanner did. He's always been the dad he didn't have to be, just like your stepfather was for you.'

'Is Tanner still . . . here? Still alive, I mean?'

'Yeah,' he said again, his mouth curving in a smile that made her smile back. 'And he wants to meet you so badly. I could only make him promise to wait until dinnertime before he drove over. He's got a place in Wight's Landing, on the Chesapeake Bay. He's hoping you'll come out to see it before you go back to California.'

'It's peaceful there,' Stevie added. 'Sometimes I go out there all by myself, just to think.'

'Grampa's got dogs,' Cordelia chimed in. 'Lacey and Columbo. I got one of Lacey's babies, but Mannix isn't little anymore. You like dogs, right? Even big, hairy, slobbery ones?'

'Love them,' Taylor assured her. 'The bigger, hairier and slobberier, the better.'

'You'll be fine, then,' Stevie said wryly. 'Because Mannix is all of the above.'

'And you spoil him with treats when you *think* nobody's looking,' Cordelia said archly.

'Busted,' Maggie said in a sing-song voice, and she and Cordelia bumped fists.

'Boom,' Cordelia said, and Taylor laughed again.

'I can't wait to meet him,' she said, then made a face. 'Tanner, I mean, although I'm sure I'll like the dogs too.' Cordelia smiled, making Taylor smile back at her. 'But I have an appointment in the city this afternoon. Jazzie Jarvis and I are meeting for ice cream.'

Clay nodded. 'I know. I'm going with you.'

'Oh, right.' Taylor's conversation with Maggie in the barn office seemed like years before. 'That's how all this started yesterday. You're my security.'

'Damn straight,' he muttered. 'I'll have Dad come to our house at six.'

'Although he'll get there earlier,' Stevie said fondly. 'He won't be able to wait.'

'He can watch a movie with me before Taylor gets there,' Cordelia said. 'Because he's gonna want to spend all his time with her after.' The words were spoken without rancor or ill will, but they still got Taylor's attention.

'You know I'm not here to steal him away,' Taylor said softly. 'Right?'

Cordelia's nod was sage. 'I know. It's not a contest, Taylor. He can love us both the same. So can Clay.' She lifted her brows. 'But I think Ford's gonna love us very different.'

Ford barked a startled laugh. 'You little shit.'

233

Cordelia giggled delightedly and made kissy noises. 'Yep.'

Taylor's cheeks heated in a blush that totally gave her away. Avoiding Clay's eyes, she angled Cordelia a sharp look. 'You sure you're only nine, kid?'

Stevie ruffled her daughter's hair affectionately. 'Going on forty. And it's different*ly*.'

Cordelia frowned. 'Are you sure?'

'Very sure. In that sentence, "love" is a verb. It's something that you do.' Stevie smiled at Clay, then at her daughter. Grabbing her cane, she pushed herself to her feet. 'C'mon, short stuff. We have horses waiting to be ridden.'

Taylor marveled at the change in Stevie, then glanced at the time. 'Oh crap. I've got kids arriving soon for therapy sessions. I've got to get the horses tacked up.'

Ford pressed her shoulder down when she would have risen. 'Stay here and look at the rest of your pictures. I'll get the horses ready.'

She took his hand from her shoulder and gave it a grateful squeeze. 'Thank you, Ford.'

Maggie followed him out, leaving Taylor alone at the table with Clay. *My father. My father who missed so much of my life.* She drew a breath. *My father*, she thought again. And the words weren't so scary any more.

He cleared his throat, breaking the silence. 'So . . . you and Ford?'

Her cheeks, which hadn't completely cooled from Cordelia's teasing, heated right back up. 'He's been very kind. And I think we're both a little lonely.'

He nodded with a sigh. 'He's a good young man. Been through a lot.'

'I know. I read about it.'

'Just . . .' He shook his head, his smile rueful. 'Am I allowed to tell you to be careful?'

'Yeah. I think you've earned that, at the very least.'

His eyes narrowed a fraction, clearly confused. 'What does that mean?'

Unable to look at him, she poked at the bag of peas, no longer frozen. 'It means you're my father, but you were denied the most basic of parental rights through no fault of your own. It means we have a lot of catching up to do. And that there is no reason for you not to behave like a father while we're doing it.' She swallowed hard. 'It means I don't have any idea what to call you, because you don't deserve to be called by your first name by your own daughter but I can't make myself call you "Dad", which just *sucks ass*. And it means I have no idea what the ever-lovin' *hell* I'm going to do when this internship is over,' she finished thickly. She dropped her chin to her chest and sighed heavily. 'That was kind of a lot. I'm sorry.'

His hand slipped under her hair to cradle the back of her neck. It was a tender touch and she leaned into it. 'You don't need to worry about any of that today,' he murmured. 'Especially what you'll do when your time here at the farm is finished.' Then he pulled her close and kissed her temple. 'Let's look at the rest of those pictures, okay?'

She rested her head on his shoulder and it felt . . . good. It really did. *Which is not a betrayal*, she told herself, trying not to see her *other* father's face in her mind. But of course her mind did see Frederick Dawson's face while it replayed his breaking voice from their phone call the night before. Still, this moment here with Clay was too sweet to deny. *To either of us.*

'Looking at pictures sounds like a good plan.'

He reached around her to grab the stack of photos from the table. The next picture showed a sturdy man with graying hair smiling from the deck of a boat that had *FIJI* stenciled on the front end. 'That's my dad, Tanner St James.'

'He looks happy.'

'He should look exhausted,' Clay said dryly. 'He's got himself a new wife who's not that much older than I am.'

'Oh,' she said, then the true meaning of his words hit her and she laughed, which she suspected had been his intent. 'Ohhhh myyyy.'

'"Oh my" is right.' He went on to the next photo, which showed his father with a pretty blonde wearing a police uniform. 'This is Nell.'

'She's a cop?'

'A sheriff's deputy, there in Wight's Landing. And, um, her boss is my ex-fiancée. Pre-Stevie, of course.'

'Of course,' Taylor said, amused and entertained. 'Does Stevie know her?'

'Who, Nell or my ex?'

'Both.'

'Knows and likes Nell. Knows and tolerates Lou. Most of the time,' he added with a little wince. 'Sometimes they . . . well, let's just say they sharpen their claws on each other.'

'Me-ow,' Taylor said, and he chuckled.

'Yeah. That's when the men run and hide.'

'Cowards,' she teased.

'And not ashamed to be.' The next photo showed a much younger Clay in his Marine Corps uniform with his arm draped over Tanner's shoulders. Neither man was smiling. Tanner's jaw was clenched in anger. Younger Clay simply looked numb. 'I was just a little younger here than you are now,' he said quietly. 'And I'd just found out I had a daughter.'

'Oh.' More tears stung, but she willed them back. 'How did you find out?'

'Saw some of the guys from my old high school when I was home on a furlough. They told me that Donna had married her old boyfriend, the one she was trying to win back by . . . flirting with me.' He looked uncomfortable at the topic of the bout of sex that had been her conception, a blush staining his rugged face. 'Yeah. Anyway, they told me that the guy "didn't even mind that she already had a kid". I was shocked. Then I did the math and it kind of hit me like a brick that she'd lied. She'd told me that she'd miscarried. I immediately went to her parents' house to find out where she was so that I could confront her, but she was already gone. Her parents were . . .' He hesitated. 'Not forthcoming with details. Threatened to have me arrested if I didn't back off and leave her alone. Her father . . .' He shrugged. 'He actually hit me. I wanted to hit him back, but I figured I really would get arrested. I found out that she'd already divorced the old boyfriend – turned out he was abusive. I didn't have time to even look for you at that point. My furlough was over and I had to report back or be counted AWOL.'

Her heart hurt yet again for the young man he'd been, bewildered and used and betrayed. He must have been so angry. His stepfather – *my grandfather* – certainly appeared to be so in the photo. 'Was Tanner angry with you?' she asked tentatively.

'Oh no, honey. Not *with* me. *For* me. He went looking for you. At first because I was deployed and I wasn't even in the country. Then later, when I was a cop in DC, he and I searched together sometimes, and sometimes separately. He went to California twice a year before he retired from the force, and more often after. He looked for you when I'd all but lost hope.' An audible swallow. 'He has always been there for me. He's my father in every way that matters. So I get your feelings for Dawson. More than you know.'

She couldn't say a word. Her heart was too full. She pressed her cheek harder against his shoulder and he stroked her hair, seeming to understand.

'Sometimes I call Tanner Dad,' he went on when she said nothing at all. 'And sometimes I call him Tanner.' He rested his cheek against her hair. 'When I was really little, I called him Uncle Tanner, until one day, about six months after he and my mother got married, I just started calling him Dad. He never pushed it. He waited until I was ready. I'll wait until you're ready, Taylor. You call me Clay until you're ready to call me something different. And if you're never ready, that's okay too. I don't want you to have to choose. I just want to be part of your world.'

'Thank you,' she said hoarsely. He'd called her Taylor. Not Sienna. It should have been a relief, but for some reason it made her sad. Like he'd relinquished his dream. Like he was willing to settle for whatever he could get. And that wasn't fair. *None of this is fair.* 'You don't have to call me Taylor.'

'I know. But I will, because that's your name.' He gently shrugged the shoulder on which she leaned. 'I didn't name you Sienna either, you know, so I'm not exactly tied to it. Actually, I kind of like using the name Dawson picked instead of the one your mother chose.'

'But . . . it hid me from you. You lost . . . you lost all those years.'

'I know,' he said again. 'But you're here now and we're starting fresh. Right?'

She gave a hard nod. 'Right.'

'Good.' He was quiet for a long, long moment. 'You seem to think you owe me something, Taylor. You don't. None of what happened was your fault, and when you realized the truth, you came to me. I'll always be grateful for that, and I will always love you, because you are my daughter. Sshh,' he said gently when she tried to blubber a response. 'I'm not quite finished yet. You also seem to think you owe your stepfather something. I don't believe for one moment that he thinks you do. From everything you've told me about him, including the lengths he went to just to keep you safe, Frederick Dawson loves you. The love a parent gives a child is free, Taylor. *Free*. Nothing owed. No paybacks required. Just love him back. That's all he wants.'

Her tears began to fall again. 'Did Tanner teach you that?'

'Yeah, he did. Because for a long time I thought I owed him. I thought that if I wasn't the perfect son, he'd leave and my mom would be lonely again. When he finally realized it, he took me aside and said the exact same words I just said to you.'

'I wish . . . I wish you'd been in my life all along.'

His chest expanded and he carefully released the breath. 'Me too, baby. Me too.' He slid the photos back into the envelope. 'We can look at the others later. Now dry your eyes and go take care of your kids, or Maggie'll have my hide.'

Sniffling, she dried her eyes. 'I need more frozen peas. The kids will know I've been crying.'

Clay huffed a laugh. 'Here. Wear this.' From his back pocket he pulled a black baseball cap with *M&B* stitched in gold on the front. He snugged it on her head and pulled down the brim to hide her eyes. 'There. Nobody'll know. If you sound stuffy, blame allergies. Stevie does it all the time when she cries. And yes, I'll deny I ever said that until the day I die.'

She smiled at him. 'I won't tell. I know M&B Security is your business name, and M is obviously for Maynard, but what does the B stand for?'

238

'You didn't find out in your research?' he asked teasingly. 'I'm going to have to show you how to dig a little deeper on the Internet. Which really means I'll have one of my college-aged assistants show you.' He tugged the brim again. 'It's for Buchanan, my first partner. Ethan left the firm when he got married and moved to Chicago, but we're still tight. We visit each other on holidays and birthdays and christenings. He's going to want to meet you too.'

'I look forward to it.' She stood reluctantly. 'I'd better go do my lessons.'

'Take your time. I'll be here when you finish.'

Impulsively she leaned down to kiss his cheek. 'See you later.' She let a beat pass. 'Pop.'

She was at the door when he snorted a laugh, as if the name had just sunk in. 'Absolutely not "Pop",' he stated baldly. 'No way. Stevie will never let me hear the end of it.'

She just threw him a grin over her shoulder and let the door slam shut behind her.

Hunt Valley, Maryland,
Sunday 23 August, 10.30 A.M.

JD parked his SUV between Clay's truck and the farm's main barn, but didn't turn off the engine. Made no move to get out.

I so do not want to be here.

It wasn't just that he wished he were home with Lucy and the kids, even though of course he did. He did not want to meet Clay's daughter, knowing first-hand as he did how much pain her absence had caused one of his most trusted friends.

He certainly didn't want to face Clay, to see the hope on his face when JD had such serious doubts about the timing of the re-appearance of his infamous long-lost daughter. He *really* didn't want to face Stevie. Daphne had said that Stevie hadn't taken Sienna's 'homecoming' well. JD didn't want to be the one to turn the screw, to heap even more stress and disappointment on his former partner and her family, because Stevie was far more to him than his

239

former partner in the homicide department. She was the sister JD had never had.

And I'm acting like Jeremiah when he doesn't want to try a new food. Stop pouting. Go observe the intern therapist in action. If she's real, she's your best chance at getting Jazzie Jarvis to talk.

He forced himself to get out of the SUV and walk to the training ring. He'd called Maggie the evening before, after Daphne and Joseph had left. He'd grilled her for information on her new intern. Sounding exhausted, Maggie had told him to come by after Taylor had finished her therapy sessions, so that she could introduce them, but JD had purposely come earlier to observe.

There she was. Sienna Maynard, aka Sienna Smith, aka Taylor Dawson. She was dressed practically in a plain white T-shirt and jeans that weren't too tight. Her long black hair was in a ponytail and she wore a black ball cap. One of Clay's caps, actually. The young woman didn't look like she could hurt a fly.

Like she would actually look *menacing*, he mocked himself. Taylor had slipped through Joseph's background check and had lied about her reason for being here for two weeks. She was far too skillful a liar to take at face value.

Liar or not, Taylor was currently working with a little girl who looked to be about five years old and terrified of the small horse on which she sat. Terrified, but determined. Taylor was patient with the child, leading her around the ring again and again. She was patient and . . . competent. And compassionate. By the end of the session, the child wasn't completely fearless, but she'd laughed and patted the horse's neck, seeming to relax more with each moment that passed. When the session was finished, Taylor held out her arms and helped the little girl from the saddle, lowering her gently until her feet touched the ground.

'Mommy, Mommy!' the girl cried joyfully. 'Did you see me?'

A woman stood on the other side of the fence on the far side of the ring, putting on a brave face where she'd been wiping away tears minutes before.

'She's good,' Stevie murmured from beside him, and JD jumped, startled.

'Where did you come from?' he demanded, and she laughed up at him.

'The barn. I was riding with Cordelia, but I've been standing here for the past two minutes. Helluva detective you are,' she added with a grin. She had one arm curved around the fence post, leaning into it, while the other hand clutched the handle of her cane. Anyone who didn't know her would think her pose casual, but JD saw her white knuckles and the slight pinch of pain around her mouth, even though she smiled. She rode horses with Cordelia because her daughter loved it, but the activity wasn't a comfortable one for her.

'You're hurting,' he said, more sharply than he'd intended.

'Totally worth it,' she said without hesitation. 'What are you doing here this morning?'

JD lifted his brows and Stevie breathed out a sigh. 'Oh,' she said quietly. 'You obviously know.'

'Word travels fast. You know that.'

'Oh, I do,' Stevie said with a nod. 'Daphne?'

'Of course. She and Joseph stopped by last night. They wanted to give everyone a day to get the oh-my-Gods out of their systems so that Holly's wedding isn't overshadowed.' He frowned at Taylor, who was earnestly talking with the five-year-old's mother and didn't seem to notice him or Stevie standing there. 'Selfish of her to pop out of hiding two days before the wedding.'

'I think she would have kept it a secret much longer had it been her call,' Stevie said thoughtfully. 'She's . . . a little shy. Probably because she lived in a small community for the last ten-plus years. She's not comfortable in large groups.'

JD stared down at her. 'You sound like you're defending her.'

Stevie glanced up, then blinked. 'Oh for God's sake. Daphne told you guys that I was mad? That was wrong of her. I just needed time.'

'She didn't say you were mad. I just heard you hadn't taken it well. And Daphne only said it because Lucy asked. Because she was worried about you.'

'I was upset, more for Clay because I've seen up close and personally how much his fruitless searches have hurt him. But

Taylor seems real, JD. And she seems like a good person. Did you really come out here just to gawk at her?'

'No. I came to talk to her. She agreed to have a one-on-one session with one of the program kids who hadn't bonded with anyone else. I wanted to see what was so special about Miss Dawson that the little girl in question talked to her when she hasn't talked to anyone else for an entire month.'

He gave her the Cliffs Notes version of Jazzie's story and watched Stevie's brow furrow as she put the pieces together. Her ability to make sense of chaos was one of the things he admired most. And missed the most. Hector was a good cop, but he was no Stevie Mazzetti.

Stevie pursed her lips. 'Well, JD, there's a few things you need to know. First, Clay's going to hit the fucking roof if you involve his daughter in anything remotely dangerous.'

'I wouldn't do that,' JD said, feeling a little hurt. 'I thought you knew me better.'

'I do. It's Clay who'll be threatening to rip your head off and use it as a soccer ball.'

JD winced. 'Okay. I'm warned. But Joseph and I have set this up in the safest possible environment. We've got Jazzie's safety to worry about, too.'

'I hear you. I'm just sayin'. The second thing is that Ford has a thing for Taylor, and after Clay rips your head off, Ford will be the one to kick it through the goalposts.' She pointed to the barn door, where Ford was barely visible, standing in the shadows. Watching Taylor Dawson with near adoration. And a great deal of lust.

JD groaned. 'You've got to be kidding. All this time Ford goes without a girl and he's suddenly infatuated with Clay's daughter?' Then he pictured it, and his lips twitched despite his doubts about Taylor's sincerity. 'I will love to see how that plays out. Ford having to deal with Clay when he takes Taylor on dates.' He chuckled darkly. 'This could be totally entertaining.'

Stevie socked his arm, hard. 'Be nice. Ford's had a hard time. He's . . . vulnerable. And so is she.'

'I thought you didn't like her,' JD said with another frown.

242

'I didn't at first. I'm still a little skeptical, because there are so many unanswered questions, or questions she didn't answer with what I wanted to hear.'

'Like?'

'Like what took her so long to come to Clay after her mother's deathbed confession.' She shrugged. 'But Cordelia schooled me. Told me that it's harder for some people to break through their fears than others.'

'Ouch,' JD murmured.

Stevie shook her head. 'You knew about the nightmares, too?'

'Yeah. I'm her godfather. I buy her ice cream. She tells me stuff. I take it she told you too.'

'Eventually, yes. And I'm okay with it. I'm okay that everyone knew but me, because I know why Cordelia couldn't let me know. I get it. I guess I'm a little unrealistic in my expectations when it comes to how other people deal with fear.'

'Because you have none. And you need some.'

'Workin' on it. Baby steps, JD. Baby steps.'

And for some reason that made her smile. But before he could ask her why, his cell buzzed. 'Maggie,' he said, reading the text. 'She says the next session's canceled because the kid has a cold. Taylor will be free for the next twenty minutes. I'm going to the office to meet with her now, to make sure she's willing to do the one-on-one with Jazzie.'

Stevie threw a cautious look over her shoulder toward Maggie's farmhouse. 'I'll come too. Once I have all the information, I'll relay it to Clay.'

'My head thanks you,' JD said dryly. 'Lucy likes it connected to my neck. So maybe we can keep it there.'

'That's up to you, Detective.' Stevie headed to the barn, leaning heavily on her cane.

'You gonna be okay, Stevie?'

She nodded. 'Just sore muscles because I haven't ridden in a while. Although it might be a while before I ride again. Come on. I'll introduce you to Taylor.'

243

Hunt Valley, Maryland,
Sunday 23 August, 10.45 A.M.

Taylor found herself sitting in front of Maggie's desk for the second time in less than twenty-four hours. And feeling almost as nervous as she had last night. This was a different kind of nerves, though. Last night was all oh-shit-I'm-busted. But today . . . it would be the first time meeting one of Clay's friends, now that they knew who she was.

Detective JD Fitzpatrick wanted to meet her because she'd be meeting with Jazzie later today. But it was more than that and Taylor knew it. It was important that JD approve, because he was important to Clay.

'Relax,' Maggie murmured.

'Easy for you to say,' Taylor muttered. 'You're not the one under the microscope.'

'True, but I don't think anyone will judge you.' Maggie smiled. 'And if they do, they'll answer to me.'

Taylor wanted to smile back, but she couldn't force her lips to curve. 'These people are all important, Maggie. I mean, Fitzpatrick is Clay's friend. He was Stevie's partner when she was a cop, right?'

'Yes.' Maggie's voice was calm. 'But JD and Stevie go back much farther than that. He's Cordelia's godfather, and Stevie is godmother to JD's son.'

Taylor groaned quietly. 'God, this just gets worse. Stevie's barely over wanting to kick my ass back to California. This Fitzpatrick guy better like me or she might change her mind.' She was being overly dramatic, she knew. She hoped, at least. *God.*

Maggie chuckled. 'I'll risk sounding like a cliché by telling you to just be yourself.' She reached across the desk to pat Taylor's hand. 'It will be fine. This isn't about Clay and it's not really about you at this point.'

'It's about Jazzie.' Taylor sat up straighter. 'Getting her to talk. Keeping her safe.'

Maggie's nod was approving. 'Exactly.' Someone knocked on

her office door and she glanced at the monitor on her desk. 'It's JD, and Stevie's with him. Can I tell them to come in?'

'Of course.' Taylor stood up and schooled her expression to one of cordial interest. *Not about you*, she reminded herself. *This is for Jazzie.*

Stevie came through the door first and dropped into one of Maggie's club chairs. She looked a little pale. She was followed by a man Taylor recognized from a few of the newspaper articles she'd studied. Homicide Detective JD Fitzpatrick was Clay's height, but lean where Clay was bulky. Maybe a few years younger than Clay. He appeared to be unaffected by the heat, despite wearing a navy-blue suit and a tie. His dark hair was threaded with silver at the temples. His eyes were dark blue, darker even than his suit, and laser-focused on her face. His mouth curved into a polite smile as he stuck out his hand in greeting.

'I'm Detective Fitzpatrick. I'm investigating the murder of Valerie Jarvis.'

Taylor blinked, hiding her surprise. *Oh.* She'd expected first names. *Okay. Formal it is then.* She shook his hand. 'I'm Taylor Dawson. It's good to meet you.'

'Likewise,' he said, then gestured to the chair in which she'd been sitting. 'Please.'

Taylor sat gingerly. Warily. This hadn't started as she'd expected. A side glance at Maggie confirmed that the older woman was also surprised.

Stevie heaved a sigh from the chair. 'For God's sake, JD, be a human being. Taylor, this is JD. JD, Taylor. Clay's daughter.'

Fitzpatrick's cheeks actually reddened. *Why?* Taylor wondered. Embarrassment? Annoyance? Anger? It was hard to tell.

'Of course, Stevie,' he said. 'You're right. It's very nice to meet you, Taylor. You'll have to excuse me. I was anticipating meeting the intern therapist, but instead I find myself meeting Clay's long-lost daughter. I'm still processing that information.'

Annoyance *and* anger, Taylor decided. *And no, sir, I won't excuse you.* But she'd be polite. For Clay. She'd opened her mouth to speak when Stevie chuffed in irritation.

245

'JD, I thought we'd settled this. Clay is over the moon about Taylor being here. I am too. I am not upset. Therefore you are not allowed to be upset. Okay?' Without waiting for a response, Stevie turned to Maggie. 'I could really use some water and crackers if you have them.'

'Are you all right?' Taylor asked, concerned because Stevie was still very pale.

Stevie waved her hand. 'Fine. Just overheated.'

Maggie supplied the items, her grey brows lifted, apparently not convinced, but she didn't push it. 'So, JD, we're here about Jazzie?'

'Yes.' He smoothed a hand over his tie. 'What have you been told, Taylor?'

Taylor met Fitzpatrick's eyes unflinchingly. If they were going to have a less-than-friendly relationship, she didn't want to start off looking weak. Frederick had taught her that, long ago. 'I know that you believe that Jazzie saw her mother's killer. I know that your primary suspect is Jazzie's father. I know that you've kept it a secret because you're worried he'll find out Jazzie was a witness and try to kill her too. I know that Jazzie hasn't spoken in a month, except for saying "thank you" to me yesterday. And I know you're hoping I can draw her out of her shell and get her to reveal what she actually saw. I'm not certain that's a reasonable expectation, but I will do my best to get her to talk. That's all.'

He nodded once. 'What you also need to know is that we believe this man killed three other people yesterday morning – a homeless addict, a dealer and a police officer. We believe the addict's murder was planned. He'd been framed so that it looked like he killed Valerie Jarvis. The officer was murdered because he surprised the killer while the killer was dumping the addict's body. The dealer was killed to provide a suspect for the officer's murder.'

Holy fucking shit. The man Fitzpatrick sought had murdered four people? But Taylor kept her expression neutral. 'I understand,' she said evenly. 'That means if he's cornered, he'll strike out, and he's unconcerned with collateral damage. If we draw his attention this afternoon, he will not hesitate to act, given the opportunity. He could easily kill again.'

Fitzpatrick looked reluctantly impressed. 'Exactly. I need to be sure you understand that although we will keep you protected at all times, there is still an element of risk.'

Taylor considered his words carefully. 'And if Jazzie does reveal what she saw that day? What then?'

'It depends on what she says.'

Taylor frowned at him, not bothering to hide her impatience. 'Detective Fitzpatrick, you have just told me that this man has killed four people. Don't play games with me, please. If Jazzie IDs her father, what will you do? I assume you don't know where he is, because if you did, you'd have brought him in for questioning. Will you put his face on the news and say he's a wanted man?'

Fitzpatrick held her gaze. 'Probably.'

'That would make Jazzie a target,' Taylor said.

'And you also, Taylor,' Maggie said, sounding troubled.

Taylor glanced across the desk. Maggie was watching the security camera feed, but she flicked her gaze back to Taylor. 'Are you comfortable with that?' Maggie added.

Taylor turned it over in her mind. Her father would freak. *Both* of her fathers would freak. *I should be freaking.* But she wasn't. In fact, she felt pretty damn calm. *Go, me.* 'I'm not sure. What protection do you plan to provide, Detective Fitzpatrick? And for how long?'

Fitzpatrick didn't blink. 'We'll provide security here at the farm and at the apartment where Jazzie lives with her aunt. The farm is very secure already. You won't have to worry.'

Taylor smiled tightly. 'Oh, I think I will. Worrying is my best skill. So basically I'd be stuck here, on the farm, for the duration of my stay?'

He lifted his brows. 'Is that a problem?'

'Not for me. I came here to work.'

'No,' Fitzpatrick corrected in a tone that scraped, 'you came to observe Clay.'

Taylor drew a breath. Let it out. *Stay cool. Stay calm.* 'That, too. But I am also here to work. So far I'm doing lessons every day. I don't see that changing, unless Maggie becomes dissatisfied with

my work, but that would be between Maggie and me. I am more concerned about Jazzie at this point. Will you put her in a safe house?'

'If I find that it's required, of course I will. For now, we plan to
keep her in her aunt's apartment, in the environment where she
feels most comfortable. We will provide security so that she is safe.
And if anyone comes after her, we'll be ready for them.'

Oh. Taylor's eyes widened, her temper abruptly flaring to an
instant boil as the detective's meaning became suddenly clear.
*Sonofafuckingbitch. He's using Jazzie for bait. Me too, to a lesser extent,
but I'm an adult. I can choose this.* But Detective Asshole wasn't giving
Jazzie any choice. Taylor had opened her mouth, was trying to form
words that didn't include profanity when the office door flew open,
banging into the wall.

JD jumped up, hand on his weapon, but dropped his hand to his
side when Ford stormed in. '*You sonofabitch,*' Ford snarled, his eyes
flashing with fury. He got in JD's face. 'You're using them for *bait*.
For fucking bait! No way. *No. Fucking. Way.*'

For a long moment, Taylor could only stare, stunned. And also
captivated. Ford was . . . electric. Energy was coming off him in waves
as his body vibrated with rage. *God.* He was absolutely gorgeous.

And one breath away from punching Fitzpatrick in the face.
Stowing her own rage for the moment, Taylor leapt to her feet and
grabbed Ford's arm, pulling him away from the detective. Ford let
her move him, stepping backward until the back of his thighs hit
Maggie's desk.

Taylor got in front of him, wrapping the fingers of one hand
around his hard bicep, which continued to flex as he clenched and
unclenched his fists, still at his sides. Her other hand she laid flat on
his chest, gentling him. 'Relax,' she murmured.

He stared down at her, his blue eyes as intense as the inside of a
flame. 'You will not be bait.'

'You will not curse loudly in a barn full of child victims,' she
returned, patting his chest softly. It was heaving with the harsh
breaths he drew. 'You'll scare the kids, Ford.'

He swallowed hard, his throat working. He shuddered out a
breath. 'You will not be bait,' he whispered. 'No.'

'I won't be.' Her jaw tightening, she threw a baleful glare at Fitzpatrick. 'Jazzie will be. Which is *not* okay.'

'You will be, too.' Ford was no longer huffing like a bull. The fury in his eyes morphed into something else. It looked like pain, but she couldn't be sure, because he jerked his gaze away from hers and stared over her shoulder at Fitzpatrick. 'No bait.'

'You're not in charge here, Ford,' Fitzpatrick said mildly. 'But I get that you're upset.'

Ford gritted his teeth and his fists clenched again. 'Do not patronize me, JD,' he growled.

Taylor glanced over her shoulder to see Fitzpatrick holding out his hands like a traffic cop. 'We'll discuss it further,' he said. 'For now, Taylor and Jazzie are just meeting for ice cream. If Jazzie doesn't tell us anything, nothing changes. Neither Jazzie or Taylor is in any more danger than they are right at this moment. If Jazzie does talk, and if she saw her father, we will catch him before he can hurt anyone else.'

'You cannot promise that,' Ford said through clenched teeth. 'Shit happens. You know this.'

Fitzpatrick's eyes softened. 'Yeah, I do know. We'll deal with it when we know more. Okay?'

Ford said nothing. His seething was almost audible.

Stevie cleared her throat and pushed to her feet, using her cane for balance. 'I'm going to let Clay know what's going on. I'll smooth things over as best I can, JD.' She paused next to Taylor and smiled. 'Nice job, kid. You held your temper and calmed this one down.' She tilted her head toward Ford, then met Taylor's eyes, her own grown serious. 'This is totally up to you. Nobody will blame you if you say no.'

'She says no,' Ford muttered.

Taylor shook her head. 'She says yes,' she said, moving her hand from his chest to cover his mouth. 'Go on in the house, Stevie. We'll be there in a few minutes.'

When Stevie was gone, Fitzpatrick closed the door. 'So your answer is yes?' he asked.

'Yes.' Taylor gritted her teeth, allowing some of her temper to surface. 'Even though as plans go, yours truly sucks. She's just a little girl, Detective.'

'And if we do nothing, she might not live to be a big girl,' Fitzpatrick said seriously.

Taylor jerked a single nod. 'I know. That's why I say yes. She deserves a life – one without fear.' She then leaned sideways to look at Maggie. 'I assume you were watching your monitor because Ford was eavesdropping outside.'

Maggie's lips twitched. 'Yes. I'm really surprised he lasted as long as he did before charging in here.'

Taylor sighed. 'Can you guys give us a few minutes? Please?'

Maggie pushed away from her desk and walked around to where Fitzpatrick waited silently. The detective had gotten what he'd come for, so Taylor was sure he was keeping his mouth shut so as not to mess it all up. He and Maggie left, leaving her and Ford alone.

Taylor patted Ford's chest again and squeezed his arm. 'Look at me.' She waited until he had, his blue eyes still intense and angry. Impulsively she leaned up on her toes and pressed her lips to his, meaning just to give him a peck, but he growled against her mouth, his hands sliding around her waist to cover her butt.

He lifted her effortlessly and in a few long strides had her back against the door. He took over the kiss and it was . . . Her brain short-circuited and she couldn't think about anything but getting closer to him. She lifted her arms, locking them around his neck, and then her legs, gripping his hips, and she kissed him back. He licked her mouth and she opened for him, greedy for more.

Hot. God, he was hot and he made her burn. *Everywhere.*

He thrust against her and he was hard between her thighs. She closed her eyes and would have moaned, but he was still kissing her, like he was ravenous. Because he was. He'd had no one to give him affection, to touch him, in so long.

She dropped her arms from his neck and tugged at the hem of his shirt, yanking it up when he bowed his back to give her space. Flattening her hands against hard muscle, she stroked his chest with wide, sweeping motions, then flicked at his nipples with her thumbs.

That amped him higher and his thrusts became urgent. He

grabbed the fabric of her sleeve in one hand and yanked it down, baring her shoulder, then tore his lips from hers and kissed his way down the side of her neck until he got to her bra strap. Letting go of her shirt, he pushed the strap down and fastened his open mouth to the skin where the strap had been, sucking hard.

Hard. So hard she'd have a bruise. And there didn't seem to be a reason for that to make her throb between her legs, but it did. She arched, pushing against him, feeling his hard length pushing back. And then he shoved his hand down her shirt to cover her breast with his palm, and she could feel his heat through the thin cotton of her bra.

Her head fell back against the door and she closed her eyes, drinking in the feeling. 'So good,' she whispered. 'That feels so damn good.'

He straightened, leaving her shoulder to return to her mouth and his kiss was all grinding motion and stark demand. 'I want you,' he groaned into her mouth, his voice low and gravelly. 'God, I want you.'

'Yes,' she whispered back, but she wasn't sure what she was agreeing to. At the moment, she didn't care.

He moved the hand that cupped her breast, stroking up to pause at the edge of her bra, and she held her breath, waiting for him to delve inside, waiting for his touch against her bare skin. But he didn't. For a long, long moment he hovered there, frozen, his eyes clenched shut. Then he exhaled on an almost silent groan, and moved his questing hand to her hip.

Pressing his lips to the skin he'd sucked, he kissed her there, softly. Tenderly even. 'Not here,' he whispered. 'You deserve more than this.'

She lifted one trembling hand to his hair, sifting the soft strands through her fingers. He stood stock still, his lips still touching the place he'd sucked so hard. He was panting and so was she.

'I do not want you to get hurt,' he whispered against her shoulder.

She wasn't sure if he meant Gage Jarvis physically hurting her, or himself wounding her heart. Either was a fair concern. 'I know,' she murmured. She kept stroking his hair until he pulled his lips from her skin and set her bra strap and shirt to rights. Then he straightened his back and she let her legs slide down his until her feet touched the floor.

'I have to try to help Jazzie,' she said softly.

'I know.'

'I'm not foolish. I'll do what Fitzpatrick tells me to do. I won't take chances.'

'No,' he murmured. 'You won't. I'm going with you.'

'But Jazzie—'

He cut her protest off by gently covering her mouth as she'd done his. 'I know I can't be in the room with you two. I know she's scared of men. But I will be there. I have to be there.'

She gently pulled his head down for one more kiss, this one sweet. 'I get it. Promise me you won't hit Fitzpatrick. I don't want to have to bring you a cake with a file in it.'

He snorted a laugh. 'Okay.'

And just that fast, they were. Okay. She smiled up at him. 'Ready to go into the house and watch Clay yell at Fitzpatrick?'

His grin was quick and wicked. 'Yes, but not just yet. I can't . . . I don't want your father to see me like this. Just give me a minute to think deflating thoughts.'

Her cheeks heated and he laughed softly, kissing her, first one cheek then the other. He took a step back and walked around the small office, picking up tools and books until he drew a somewhat normal breath. 'Okay. Let's go to the house.'

Sixteen

Hunt Valley, Maryland,
Sunday 23 August, 11.00 A.M.

Clay was sitting at the table when Stevie came back from her ride, his throat still thick. And he was still chuckling. *Pop. As if.*

But if that was what his daughter wanted to call him, he'd take it. Except that he could hear Cordelia picking it up. And then the new one would, too.

Their new baby, his and Stevie's. No way was his baby calling him Pop.

'What are you grinning about?' Stevie asked, dropping into the chair next to him, then rubbing her behind with a pained expression. 'Ouch.'

'Been a while since you were in the old saddle, huh?'

'Shut it, Maynard,' Stevie said mildly. 'Cordelia and Maggie have already both laughed and lectured me for letting too much time pass between my rides.' She reached over and ran a finger over his lips. 'Seriously, you were grinning like crazy in here. What gives?'

Pop. Not. 'I was thinking about you-know-who,' he said, reaching over to give her stomach a gentle poke. 'And what he will call us.'

Stevie blinked at him. 'Mommy and Daddy?'

'That's much better.'

One of her dark brows arched. 'Than?'

'Than nothing,' he lied smoothly, and her lips twitched.

'You keep your secrets, *Daddy*. It's okay with me.' She took his hand when he offered it and let him pull her onto his lap. 'You

253

were in here with Taylor for a while. Did she see the rest of the pictures?'

'Not all of them yet. We had a chat about Tanner. It seemed to help both of us.'

'Good.' She kissed his jaw. 'I talked to JD a little bit ago, by the way. He'll be taking you and Taylor to the meet with the little girl. Jazzie.'

That Stevie and JD Fitzpatrick had already talked this morning came as no surprise to Clay. The two had been friends for years, back when both were married to their respective spouses. They'd supported each other emotionally when those spouses died, and later were teamed up as partners in the homicide department.

JD was Cordelia's godfather and Stevie was godmother to JD's toddler, Jeremiah. Clay didn't think a day had gone by since Stevie's retirement that she and JD didn't talk at least once, and it was usually about the job. JD was one of Stevie's best resources when it came to the cases she investigated for their business.

'What did he say about the investigation into Jazzie's mother's murder?'

'He thinks Jazzie knows who killed her mother. He's also nervous that there's a leak in the department. That's why he's suppressed some of the evidence from the filed reports.'

Clay frowned. 'What makes him think that?'

'The estranged drug-addict husband's alibi is . . . convenient. The husband – Gage Jarvis – was a shark defense lawyer with a slick firm downtown and the husband's brother Denny is a defense attorney in the Legal Aid office.'

Clay's knee-jerk reaction was to hate defense attorneys, but he knew at least one who was decent, so he shrugged. 'Doesn't mean they're dirty, just deluded.'

'Husband's alibi came unsolicited from a deputy sheriff in Texas, less than a day after JD noted that husband was a suspect. This morning, JD went through Denny's old court cases. The deputy sheriff's wife has a cousin who escaped a lengthy jail sentence. He was repped by Denny Jarvis.'

'Okay,' Clay conceded. 'The alibi does seem convenient. But I'm still not getting the need to suppress evidence or the logic for a leak in the department.'

'Denny Jarvis's wife works in the prosecutor's office as a clerk. For Daphne.'

'Fuck.' The wife had access to case details before they ever ended up in a final BPD report.

'Exactly. Denny's wife knew about Daphne's therapy program and begged her to take Jazzie and Janie. The program is filled to capacity. Maggie squeezed the girls in.'

'Does JD think Denny's wife is involved?'

'He doesn't know. Daphne doesn't think so, but she's taking no chances. Everyone was hoping the program would help shake Jazzie's secrets free so that they could put out a BOLO and pull Gage's ass in for questioning.'

'Where's Gage Jarvis now?'

'He hadn't been seen since the day of the murder, when he was allegedly in Texas, but as of yesterday, he's back in Baltimore.'

Clay frowned, troubled. 'If the husband did it, he won't want to leave a witness.'

Perched on his knee, Stevie looked him in the eye. 'If you're asking if anyone else suspects that Jazzie saw him, the answer is "I don't know". If you're asking if JD is worried that Jazzie's father will hurt her, the answer is "he's arranged for Jazzie to meet Taylor in the private room at Giuseppe's".'

Clay felt the color drain from his face. Giuseppe's restaurant was a secure place that the Feds and BPD used when they wanted to control every aspect of a meet. The place was wired for sound and video and had hiding places for half a dozen cops.

This had abruptly escalated way past a casual chat with a little girl over ice cream.

He shook his head adamantly. 'No. No way. Taylor's not doing this. She didn't know how serious this was when she agreed to meet Jazzie.'

'Yes, Clay, she did. Maggie told her. So did JD. JD told her everything I just told you.'

'When did JD talk to Taylor?' *Without me?*

'We discussed it in Maggie's office. Just now.' Stevie rested her forehead against his. 'For what it's worth, Ford's more upset than you are.'

Clay shook his head. 'Whatever. That's not even the point here. Taylor is not getting involved in JD's investigation. No ifs, ands, or buts. She's—'

'Stop right there.' Stevie gave him a quelling look. 'If you're planning on saying that she's too young to know her own mind or – God help you – that she's too delicate or too much of a girl to do this, you'd better rethink.'

His mouth opened and closed like a fish as he tried to find words that wouldn't piss off his wife. 'She's been sheltered, Stevie.'

'Yes and no. It's true that she grew up isolated from other kids, but she also grew up looking over her shoulder and expecting a monster to jump from the bushes.'

He winced. 'Dammit, Stevie.'

'Dammit, Stevie, nothing. She is hyper-aware of her surroundings. And if you're worried she can't defend herself, ask Ford. Did you see the bruise on his jaw?'

'Yeah. Figured he and Cole mixed it up.'

'No.' Stevie grinned. 'He approached your daughter from behind yesterday and didn't announce himself. She spun around and decked him. Ford says she's got a sneaky right hook. She knocked him on his ass.'

Clay sat back in his chair, stunned. And totally proud. 'Really?' Taylor was no petite violet, but Ford had six inches and at least seventy pounds on her.

'Really. And she knows how to shoot, too. Dawson taught her. She and Maggie went shooting last weekend. Maggie said she can hit the bullseye at a hundred yards.'

Clay's pride bloomed so big that he didn't know if his chest could contain it. But not enough to change his mind. 'No. She's not putting herself in jeopardy.'

'What jeopardy? You'll be there. So will JD. And I'm thinking you'll have to chain Ford to the barn wall to keep him from tagging along with you.'

'We both know these things can hit the crapper in a blink.'

'We do,' she said calmly. 'But we also know that Jazzie is suffering. She needs to talk to someone and, like it or not, she's picked Taylor.'

'*Not*,' he snarled.

Stevie took a breath and slowly released it. 'What if it were Cordelia? Would you want her walking around with this secret on her chest? With no one to help unburden her?'

His lungs emptied in a hard whoosh. 'Dammit, Stevie.'

Her lips curved sympathetically. 'I get your fear, Clay. I really do. But I trust JD with my life. I trust him with Cordelia's life. If he says this is safe, it'll be safe. It's just ice cream. This little girl has started to open up to your daughter. According to Maggie, Taylor has a certain something around the kids. She's rock-steady and sweet. They love her.'

He closed his eyes. 'I have no right to feel this proud. I didn't contribute anything to her growing up. That was Dawson.'

'You can still feel proud, Clay. Don't make her defy you on this, because I have a feeling that she will. She feels strongly about helping this child get past her fear.'

Clay shook his head, desperation making his heart beat harder. 'And what if this child does spill her guts? Jazzie *and* Taylor will be wearing giant targets for a drug-addicted murderer.'

'Who JD will then catch,' Stevie said calmly.

Clay went completely still as understanding abruptly dawned, followed by fury that roared through him like a goddamned freight train. 'They're *bait*? Are you fucking *kidding* me, Stevie? Are you trying to tell me JD is using *my daughter* as fucking *bait*?'

She continued to sit on his knee, cool as a cucumber, which just made him angrier. Carefully, very carefully, he scooped her up and set her back on her own chair, then straightened his spine. She still watched him, almost expressionless.

Except for her eyes. They flickered and flashed with emotions that he was too angry to parse. 'When did you know JD wanted to use Taylor as bait?' he asked quietly.

'About three minutes before I walked through that door.' She pointed to her cane. 'Took me that long to hobble in here from the barn.'

His shoulders relaxed a fraction. She'd come to tell him right away. Actually, she'd come to *brief* him right away, letting him come to his own conclusions. That way she was loyal to both him and JD.

JD. *That motherfucking bastard.* How *dare* he put Taylor in danger like this?

Stevie still watched him, her eyes a little less intense now. She was clearly waiting for him to decide what he wanted to do about the situation.

'My gut instinct is telling me to go out there and break JD's neck,' he admitted.

'Understandable,' she said evenly. 'But not advisable.' One eyebrow rose. 'I already told him that you'd rip his head off and use it as a soccer ball, but I don't think you really could. He's younger than you are. You might break him, but he'd damage you first, and I happen to like you just the way you are.'

More tension flowed out of him. Okay. She was pissed, too. But she wasn't freaking out and threatening to castrate JD, so she obviously agreed with at least some part of her former partner's plan. 'What do you think about this?'

'I think you're giving me a crick in my neck. Sit down, Clay.' She switched her tone to one that was light and teasing. 'Breathe, baby,' she said. 'Breathing is good.'

He did what she asked, lowering his body into the chair. That tone was the same one he used on her when he was stretching her out after one of her physical therapy sessions. It had been a year and a half since she'd been shot in the leg in the line of duty, but she still required regular therapy and exercises. She complied with a lot of bitching and complaining, because it was still painful, but he was usually able to make her feel better afterward by stretching her and applying pressure to the muscles she'd punished.

Then they made each other feel better in other, much more pleasurable ways.

She was his partner, in business and in life. She had his back.

And she was less emotional than he was at the moment. *Cooler heads prevail*, his dad had always said.

'What do you think about this?' he asked again, more calmly this time.

She smiled at him then, a smile of love and pride. Clay was glad he was already sitting down, because that smile made him feel as weak as a kitten.

'First of all,' she said, 'I think that this whole thing sucks. But I also think that JD has turned over every damn rock he can find looking for Gage Jarvis and he's getting desperate.'

'Which one is getting desperate – JD or Jarvis?'

'Both.' She hesitated. 'Gage Jarvis framed someone else for his wife's murder a month ago – a homeless addict. That addict was found dead yesterday morning.' She drew a breath. 'Along with two other people. One of them was a cop.'

Clay hadn't thought he could be any more terrified, but he found that he could. 'He's escalating.'

'Yes. And JD knows that if Jazzie's father was the one who killed her mother, it's only a matter of time before Daddy Dearest becomes twitchy about leaving a witness alive. Besides, Jazzie can't keep carrying this around inside her. It's eating that little girl alive from the inside out.'

Clay dragged his palms down his face. An hour ago his daughter had kissed him on the cheek. Now she was walking into possible danger. *Not if I can help it.*

'Tell me more about the husband, his brother, the victim and the crime,' he said.

Stevie gave him a nod of approval. 'The victim, Valerie Jarvis, was beaten to death. Her killer used his fists. He then stole some of the contents of her jewelry box. A few items have been recovered, but nothing was worth any money. Apparently she'd sold off all her expensive jewelry to help pay her bills after her husband disappeared. His former boss said he left voluntarily, but JD thinks the guy was covering his ass, that Jarvis was fired after his wife filed domestic assault charges, which she later dropped. There was drug use also – coke. According to the victim's sister, the drug use was major and

259

the domestic assault had happened frequently. Jarvis's mother says his drug use wasn't that bad and the assault never happened, that the victim was a liar.'

The kitchen door opened and JD came through, his expression wary. 'You gonna hit me, Clay?'

'Thinkin' about it,' Clay told him honestly. 'Sit your ass down, JD, and convince me that the daughter I just found after twenty-three fucking years won't be a pawn in a clusterfuck.'

JD obeyed, folding his arms over his chest, his biceps straining the sleeves of his suit coat. *Hell*, Clay thought with a wince. *Stevie was right. I might be able to get in one good punch, but he'd clean my damn clock.* Except, if it came to that, Clay would be fucking furious and that gave a man strength.

'I was wrong,' Stevie murmured. 'Even odds. But don't let it come to that.'

'Even odds to what?' JD asked suspiciously.

Clay shook his head. 'Never mind. Do you think Denny's wife is using her access in Daphne's office to feed her brother-in-law information?'

'No. But Denny might be using her access.'

'Has Denny had any contact with Gage?' Clay asked.

'Not that I've seen, but I wasn't tailing him twenty-four seven.' JD grimaced. 'Plus, there's all the red tape with going for any kind of warrant against an attorney. And don't even think of requesting a wire tap, not with all that legal confidentiality shit.'

Legal confidentiality shit that won't stop me. Clay's IT assistant, Alec, had hacked into phone records on several previous occasions. Not that Clay was about to admit that to JD, even though JD was well aware. 'So you haven't checked Denny's phone records?'

JD gave him a placid look. 'Nope. Not yet. But if I did, this is the number I'd be looking at.' He slid his own phone across the table. On the screen were his case notes. Highlighted and bolded was a phone number.

Clay keyed it into a text message addressed to Alec, followed by a second text. *Run this as fast as you can. However you must.* He hit SEND, then looked up. 'What else?'

'Tell him about Grandma, JD,' Stevie said quietly. 'I was just getting to her.'

JD sighed. 'Gage's mother, Eunice, lives with the girls and their aunt Lilah, who is their mother's older sister. Eunice lived with the girls and their mother, Valerie, before the murder. She'd moved in with Valerie because she'd mortgaged her house to the hilt to send Gage to rehab – which he never finished – and the bank foreclosed. I interviewed Eunice as part of my investigation and she's . . . well, calling her an enabler is an understatement. She had only good things to say about Gage, even though he bankrupted her.'

'What about her other son?' Clay asked. 'Denny, the Legal Aid guy?'

'Eunice treats Denny like a failure.' JD shrugged. 'Says he works for Legal Aid because it was the only job he could get after barely graduating law school and barely passing the bar. None of which is true. Denny graduated high in his class. He was with the public defender's office for years and was well-respected there. He's well-respected at Legal Aid now. Denny is definitely Eunice's second choice, but he is a doting son. Gives her pocket money to spend and pays her share of the expenses at Lilah's place, plus groceries for the two girls.'

Clay frowned. 'Doting? Or needy?'

'More the second one,' JD said. '"Doting" was Grandma's word.'

'You think Grandma knows where Gage is?'

'She's not a good liar, so I don't think so. She really believes he's somewhere in Texas.' JD rolled his eyes. 'Anyway, we've been watching her too, but until we have solid proof that either she or Denny has either helped Gage or knows his whereabouts – or that Gage was involved in his wife's murder, for that matter – we don't have grounds for warrants.'

'Unless Jazzie identifies her father as being at the scene of the crime,' Clay murmured.

JD's nod was grim. 'Exactly. And until now, she hasn't said anything to anyone.'

'But she only said a few words to Taylor. I'm not sure why you think she can get this child to spill her guts over a sundae.'

261

'She might not,' JD agreed reluctantly, 'but at this point I don't have a better idea, and if my gut is right and her father is guilty and he's getting twitchy, then I don't have much more time.'

'Is Gage still listed as a suspect?' Stevie asked.

'With me? Yes. But for the purposes of the report that's visible in the database, he is no longer a person of interest. I wanted him to feel confident enough to poke his head out of his hidey-hole. The murderer didn't leave any evidence behind in Valerie's apartment. Not a single fingerprint, and we dusted every square millimeter. All I have is a flimsy alibi and my gut.'

'And Jazzie,' Clay said with a sigh of his own. 'Okay, JD, what's your plan to get my daughter and this little girl in and out of Giuseppe's in one *undamaged* piece?'

Baltimore, Maryland,
Sunday 23 August, 2.05 P.M.

She was late. Standing behind the large hedge that bordered the park, Gage glanced at his phone for the tenth time in as many minutes. *Dammit, Ma, you'd better be coming. And you better have the kid. I need to know one way or the other.*

He tapped his foot impatiently. Then his foot went still and he looked around suspiciously. Could she have called the police? Led him into a trap?

No. His mother would never do that. *She loves me. And trusts me.* Which was her mistake, he supposed.

Ah. There she is. She was walking hand-in-hand with the girls. *They've grown*, he thought. Which was understandable. It had been a few years. He only hoped he'd brought enough sedative for their increased body weight. Just in case Jazzie freaked out and he had to quiet her down. He had enough for his mother, however. She was the same size she'd always been.

He could tell when she'd spotted him at the edge of the hedge, because he could see her eyes growing brighter, even from this distance. She leaned down and said something to the girls, prompting Janie to run to the swing sets shouting for her sister to

262

push her to the sky. Jazzie followed more cautiously, her eyes darting everywhere. The girl was spooked. That didn't look good. Of course, it could simply be that she'd discovered her mother's body after he'd been long gone. He'd know for sure in a few minutes.

He stepped out from behind the hedge and waited for his mother.

'Gage!' Eunice Jarvis looked every one of her sixty years, plus a couple of dozen more. She walked stiffly to where he stood and wrapped her arms around his neck. Because she was short, he bowed down, taking her plump body into a hard hug.

'Mama, you look terrific.' Of course she didn't, but what was one more lie?

She was crying and patting his back. 'My baby. My baby's finally home.'

Let her believe it a few seconds longer. 'Did you tell Lilah you were bringing the kids?'

An audible swallow. 'No. I sent her to the mall. Told her that Jazzie needed art supplies.' Her chuckle was forced. 'That girl goes through pencils and sketchpads like nobody's business. Especially since . . . well, since they found Valerie like that.'

He feigned a sorrowful sigh. 'I'm sorry I wasn't here for them, Ma.'

'You're here now,' she said firmly. 'And that's all that matters.'

He felt a twinge of remorse as he pulled the handkerchief from his pocket. In a quick move, he pressed the ketamine-laced cotton to her face, leaving it there as she struggled. Not for long, though. He counted down the seconds. 'Dream nice dreams,' he murmured into her ear. 'Dream you saw your son again.' Her body went lax in his arms.

Studies had shown that ket users were open to suggestion before the administration of the drug. The studies were usually in a surgical setting and had to do with whether the patient would dream pleasantly while under ketamine sedation versus the terrifying hallucinations that were common. He'd cited one such study years ago while defending a date rapist who'd used ket to render his victim unconscious. He'd painted the victim's broken memory of the assault as a bad ket dream. His client was guilty, for sure, but the young man had cleaned up well, and could feign earnestness in a truly sociopathic way – and the young woman had a history of partying. The jury had bought the bad-dream defense.

Gage personally had never remembered anything after coming down from a ket high, not in all the many times he'd used the drug. Hopefully his mother's physiology would be the same and she'd simply wake to a blank slate.

He carefully lowered her to the ground behind the hedge. Hopefully he'd sedated her for nothing. Hopefully Jazzie's fright was simple trauma from finding her mother. If that was the case, he'd watch the kids until she came around and tell her that he'd found her passed out. She wouldn't question him, nor would she tell Lilah, because she'd have to admit to Lilah that she'd lied, and his mother never admitted she'd been wrong.

It was how she'd been able to overlook his sins all these years.

And if Jazzie *had* seen him? He'd grab both kids and then . . . Well, first he'd have to find out how much she'd seen. Then he'd have to get an alibi. Denny would be good for that. He'd talked big the day before, but there was no way he was telling the cops the truth. He'd lose everything. Denny wasn't that brave.

His mother wouldn't wake up for an hour, at least. He quickly searched her enormous handbag for her phone and wallet, pocketing them. Mostly to make it appear she'd been mugged in case she was discovered before she woke up, but partly because she always carried a little cash and he knew all her PIN codes. She never changed them, using his birthday, Denny's birthday, or the day her husband died. *Good riddance*, Gage thought bitterly, having spent his entire life becoming the success that his father had always been too drunk to even dream about.

He rooted around in the handbag for another few seconds. A plastic baggie filled with pill bottles was the only other thing of value. The pharmacy labels had her name on them, so he took the bottles, too. He'd sort the pills later to see if there was anything worth selling.

He didn't want anyone identifying her if she was found before she woke up. They'd call the cops, who'd call Denny. He didn't want Denny knowing his mother had been drugged. Not until Denny had provided his alibi. Denny could be unpredictable when it came to their mother. It would be best to let him think she had passed out from heat stroke. It was certainly hot enough for that to be a believable possibility.

He hesitated, then placed her empty handbag under her head, feeling another twinge of remorse. But it was done now. He had no choice but to push forward.

Turning away from the hedge, he spotted the girls. They'd left the swings, and now Janie was climbing up the steps to the slide, Jazzie right behind her. Janie was smiling. Jazzie was not. She didn't look like she wanted to play.

She looked . . . shell-shocked. But she hadn't seen him yet. And he couldn't have scripted this moment any better if he'd tried. He waited until Janie had started to slide down, then started running. He grabbed her as she got to the bottom and spun her in a circle before she had a chance to even squeak. 'Janie, baby! It's Daddy. Daddy's come home.'

Janie struggled, then recognized him, likely from the photos that Valerie had kept in her apartment. 'Daddy!' Her cry was one of pure joy, and for another moment he felt the briefest of twinges. *Regret.* He'd once had this welcome every evening, but it hadn't been real. The girls weren't his. Valerie had lied and ruined all their lives.

Jazzie had frozen at the top of the slide, her face growing white as a sheet. Her mouth opened and she drew a breath, like she wanted to scream.

Shit. Shit, shit, shit. He realized at that moment that he'd still harbored a little hope that she hadn't seen him in her mother's apartment. But she had. She knew. *Walk away now. Right now.*

But if he did, he'd be a hunted man for the rest of his life. Forever looking over his shoulder. He swallowed hard. As Janie tightened her little arms around his neck and buried her face in his shoulder, Jazzie stared at him in horror, frozen in place.

Prison, asshole. That little girl staring at you like you're Frankenstein's monster could send you to prison for the rest of your fucking life. That cannot happen.

265

That *would* not happen.

Holding Janie with one hand, he reached into the pocket of his suit coat and pulled out his gun, just far enough for Jazzie to see it. He put it back in his pocket, but kept his hand on the barrel.

'Come along, Jazzie. Let's take a walk.' She was eleven and smart. Smart enough to understand the threat to her sister. Smart enough to obey.

Which was what she did. On shaky legs, she climbed back down the ladder and approached him like he was a snake, coiled to strike. *Yep. Smart girl.*

Jazzie's eyes were wild, her lips a tense line. Anyone looking at her would know she was fucking terrified.

Janie lifted her head from his shoulder. 'Where's Grandma?'

'Grandma went to the store,' he lied smoothly. 'She wanted to give us some time alone. To get to know each other again.' The words were for Janie. It was clear that Jazzie didn't believe him. 'Let's go get some ice cream.'

'Ice cream!' Janie said happily. Jazzie said nothing, and Janie patted his shoulder. 'Don't mind her. She's been like that since Mama . . .' Her face crumpled, tears rolling down her cheeks.

'I know, honey,' he said, keeping his eyes on Jazzie's face.

Jazzie's eyes flashed, the set of her mouth downright hostile. He'd seen that look before, on Valerie's face when he'd forced his way into her apartment a month ago. She hadn't worn that look for long. He'd beaten it off her.

Along with her face. Jazzie knew he'd done that. So yeah, he could understand her hostility. But anyone looking at her right now would call 911.

'Smile,' he said, giving Janie a little boost to sit higher on his hip. 'I mean it, Jazzie.'

'She won't,' Janie confided loudly. 'She's sad and mad and cranky all the time.'

'Well, ice cream might sweeten her up,' he said to Janie, gesturing to Jazzie with the gun in his pocket. 'My car is this way.'

He led them to the car, put Jazzie in the back seat and closed the door. Not trusting the child lock to keep her in, he'd removed the handles from every door but his own. Jazzie's lips began to quiver, and once again, he felt that goddamn motherfuckin' twinge. Resolutely he pushed it away.

He put Janie in the front passenger seat and belted her in. 'I'm not supposed to sit up front,' she informed him, her eyes wide. 'On account of the car bags.'

'The airbags?' He hoped like hell Jazzie was smart enough not to try to run. He didn't want to hurt her. But he would if he had to. *Don't make me, Jazzie.*

'Yeah, those. Aunt Lilah says they can explode and break my nose.' She leaned forward. 'Or maybe even kill me,' she added in a stage whisper.

'You don't have to worry about this car. It's too old to have airbags.'

Janie's eyes popped wider. 'Then it's not safe!'

'It'll be fine. Not everyone has money like your aunt Lilah,' he added, hearing the note of bitterness in his own voice. *Stop it. Back to the plan.* From the small cooler at her feet he took the cup of juice he'd prepared and gave it to her. 'Drink this, honey. It's a hot day and this car doesn't have A/C either.'

In the back, Jazzie opened her mouth as if to warn Janie not to drink, but Gage stopped her with one look.

'Okay,' Janie said cheerfully. 'I like grape juice.'

'I remember.' He didn't really remember. Valerie had handled all the kid shit, but the children's liquid Benadryl was grape-flavored, so he figured the juice would mask the taste.

Janie guzzled it down, then handed him the empty cup. 'Yum!' she pronounced. 'That was good. Can I have more?'

'Maybe with your ice cream.'

He got in the car and started it up, only to see Janie looking over her shoulder, her expression stricken. 'Jazzie's crying. You forgot to give her juice. Her feelings are hurt.'

'I did forget. I'll give her juice in a little while.' He had questions to ask her first. He pulled out of the parking lot and exhaled quietly. He had them both now.

But what were his next steps? They'd seen his face. They couldn't live. He hadn't thought about how exactly he'd . . . *God*. His hands clenched the steering wheel. He hadn't planned exactly how he'd kill them. It would have to be painless. *More sedative*, he thought. He'd give them sleeping pills and they'd go to sleep. *No pain*.

By the time they were halfway to his rented room, Janie was sound asleep. 'It was just Benadryl,' he told Jazzie, which was the truth. 'Neither of you will get hurt if you cooperate and do everything I say.' Which was a dirty lie.

Jazzie was shaking like a damn leaf. In the rear-view mirror, he watched as her chin lifted and she swallowed hard. 'W-where is G-Grandma? R-really?'

Shit. Gage had hoped she'd grown out of that stutter. 'Back at the park.'

'D-d-d-dead?' A thread of hysteria wound through her stuttered syllables.

'No, just asleep. I gave her medicine to make her sleep, just like Janie. She's not dead, I promise.'

'I . . . I d-don't believe you.'

He shrugged. 'Whatever. Believe what you want. Just don't try anything crazy or Janie won't live to see six.'

'I h-hate you,' she said, all on one huff of air. 'I w-w-wish you w-were d-dead.'

He couldn't blame her. 'Get in line, kid. Look, I just want information. I'm not gonna hurt you.'

He felt the change and checked the rear view to see a little of the tension seeping from her bony little shoulders. 'Y-y-you're not g-gonna k-k-kill us? R-really?'

'If you do what I say, I won't hurt you or Janie.' God, he was convincing. He almost believed it himself.

She nodded uncertainly. 'O-k-kay.'

'What I want to know is who you've told.'

'N-nobody.'

'Not even your aunt Lilah?'

'Nnnn . . .' She gritted her teeth in frustration. 'No.'

'Why not?'

She closed her eyes, her jaw set. 'P-p-pencil, p-p-please.'

That was a better plan. Her stuttering was irritating him. He was stopped at a light, so he rummaged through the glove box, hoping the car's previous owner had left something to write with. He found a stub of pencil and a yellowed vehicle registration card.

He handed the card and the pencil back to Jazzie with a stern look. 'Don't try anything funny, or you'll make me mad. You won't like me when I'm mad.' He lifted his brows menacingly. 'In fact you've already seen what I can do when I'm mad.'

She nodded tremulously as she took the items from his hand. The kid had guts, he had to admit. The light turned green, so he started driving again. 'I want to know why you didn't tell.'

He drove in silence until he was stopped at another red light. He looked behind him. Jazzie was holding out the card. *Because I was afraid you'd find out and kill me*, she'd written in one of the margins. He handed it back.

'Smart girl. Who is the therapist you've been seeing?'

An indrawn breath from the backseat had him turning to look at the stubborn jut of her jaw. 'Don't even think about lying to me,' he snarled. 'See, now you're starting to make me mad. Write it, dammit.'

Traffic began to move, and he made his way through the streets to his rented room. He parked the car behind the rooming house and held out his hand for the card. 'Taylor Dawson,' he read aloud. 'Good choice, Jazzie. Very good choice. See, I already knew her name. I was just testing you, to see if you'd tell the truth or if you were a little liar.'

Her eyes flashed in anger. 'I . . . I d-d-don't l-l-lie.'

'I hope not. What did you say to the Dawson woman?'

She dropped her gaze to the card, wrote two words, then handed it back to him. 'Thank you?' he read, puzzled. He looked back at her. 'You're welcome?'

She rolled her eyes. 'Th-that's w-what I s-s-said. Th-thank you.'

'What else?' he demanded.

'Th-that's all.'

She'd lied about not lying. She must have. *She lies nearly as well as her mother, in fact.* 'Two words? That's all you said to her? You expect me to believe that?'

She turned her head deliberately to stare out of the car's window. 'It's t-true.'

'Yeah, right.' He ground his teeth, willing his fists not to clench. He could beat it out of her. But he really didn't want to have to do that.

He let out a breath. He'd been her father once. He'd rocked her to sleep, been there for her first steps, read her bedtime stories. Sometimes. When he'd gotten home from work in time.

He had to stop thinking about that. He needed to know who she'd told about him. He considered the options, then tried another tack. 'That's not what your uncle Denny said. He said you'd told them everything.'

Her gaze shot back to him, wide and alarmed. And hurt. 'Uncle D-D-Denny knows?'

'That I have you? No. That I beat the ever-loving shit out of your mother because she defied me and humiliated me? Yeah, he knows.'

Betrayal flickered in her eyes and, dammit, there was that little twinge again. He knew how that kind of betrayal felt. After all, he was looking right into the eyes at the consequences of a betrayal that was even worse. Or at least just as bad.

'He t-told y-you? About my th-therapy?'

'Yep. Not because he wanted me to silence you forever, of course. He wanted to scare me into leaving town.' He was done talking. He was done listening. And he didn't want to look into her wounded eyes another second. He took another cup from the cooler, then got out of the car, went around to her side and opened the door. 'Drink it.'

She pursed her lips, so he pried her jaw open, poured some in her mouth and held her nose and mouth closed until she swallowed it. She choked, gagging and coughing and giving him a killing glare. 'B-bastard!'

He sighed. 'Jesus, kid, you're making this hard. You do not want to make this hard. Trust me. Will you drink the rest or do we have to rinse and repeat? It's just Benadryl.' He pulled the bottle from his pocket to prove it to her. 'It will make you sleep for a little while. That's all. I swear it.'

Her laugh surprised him. It was adult and full of contempt. 'S-s-so you can h-hurt us in our s-s-sleep?'

'I said I wouldn't hurt y— Oh.' He grimaced when he caught her meaning, then bristled with irritation that she'd even think it. He gripped her chin and forced her to look at him. 'I am many things, Jasmine Marie Jarvis, but I have never and will never rape a child.'

She didn't blink. 'J-just k-kidnap and d-drug us,' she said bitterly. 'Th-that's okay then.'

'It's for your own good, kid,' he said, making his voice softer. More cajoling. It had always worked on her mother, but from the hard look in Jazzie's eyes, it wasn't working on her. 'Look, I really don't want to hurt you. But I will. You know I will. And then I'll run and Janie will be here all alone. You don't want that, right?'

Jazzie finally looked away, but not before he saw the tears in her eyes. Straightening her shoulders, she drained the cup and handed it back to him with the manners of a queen.

Yeah, she was a lot smarter than her mother had been.

'If you try to run, I will stop you,' he said. 'And once I've stopped you, there is no good reason for me to keep your sister alive. You got that?'

She nodded. 'W-w . . .' She blew out a breath and he waited for her to finish, because he figured she'd earned it. 'One more qu-question. Did G-Grandma know, too?'

Her eyes were flat now, and he recognized the look. She knew the answer already but needed to hear it out loud. At the same time, she was shielding herself from heartache. More heartache, anyway.

'Yeah,' he said, and watched her close her eyes, her flinch unmistakable. 'She knew she was bringing you to see me. But she thought I just wanted to talk to you.'

'S-s-stupid woman,' she said, and he shrugged.

'She just really wants to believe I'm a good person.'

Jasmine scoffed and looked away. 'R-right.'

Fair enough. 'If it's any consolation,' he said quietly, 'your uncle

Denny only helped me because I threatened his wife and kids.' That wasn't true, not at first. But he figured he owed it to her to salvage some of her disappointment in the adults who were responsible for her well-being.

It was the least he could do.

She gave him a disbelieving look that was far too grown-up. 'W-whatever.'

He stepped back and allowed her to get out of the car. 'I'm going to get your sister now. Do not try anything. Please.'

She folded her arms over her chest and looked away while he lifted Janie out of the front seat and retrieved the cooler from her feet, then she followed him into his room.

Seventeen

Gage closed and locked the door to his room, then put Janie on the bed, covering her up before turning to look at Jazzie. 'Get in the bed with her. You'll be asleep soon enough.'

Jaw clenched, chin lifted, she gave him a wide berth as she walked to the other side of the bed. She sat on the mattress and pulled her sleeping sister onto her lap, smoothing Janie's hair from her forehead, looking at him as if she had something to say.

'Are y-you m-my r-r-real f-father?'

'I thought you said that last question was your last question.'

'I l-lied.'

His lips twitched. 'You said you didn't lie.'

She shrugged. 'Are y-you?'

'No. Does that make you feel better?'

Hate glittered in her eyes. 'Y-yes.'

It was fair, he supposed. 'I'm not Janie's father either.'

Her arms tightened around her sister protectively. 'G-g-good.'

'Your mother apparently got lonely when I was in law school, studying all the time. She tried to pass you off as mine. Then she got lonely when I made partner in the firm and tried to pass Janie off as mine.'

Understanding glittered in there with the hate. 'Th-th-that was wr-wrong of h-her.'

'Yeah. Neither of us were the best parents in the world.'

273

She shook her head, struggling to keep her eyes open. 'M-M-Mom wasn't a g-good w-wife, but she w-was a good mom. Sh-she was th-there for us. Y-you w-weren't.'

That was fair, too. 'I have one more question for you now. Where were you that day?'

She closed her eyes then, flinching from the memory. 'Behind th-the ch-chair. I c-came home from s-school. And s-saw her there. I heard you. In the closet.' Her stutter was lessening as the Benadryl began to take hold. 'I s-saw you.'

'I figured that out myself,' he said, feeling his eyes burn. He did not want to kill her.

No. No. You will not change your mind. She will send you to prison.

He sat down in the chair and tried to think, to plan. He needed sleeping pills. Powerful ones. He'd crush them and put them in . . . what? Applesauce? He'd read that somewhere once.

He knew dozens of dealers who kept sleeping pills. He just needed to pick one. And then . . . 'Fuck,' he muttered. He didn't just need an alibi. He needed to find someone to blame for the disappearance of two young girls. He might have used Toby Romano. *But I fucking killed him already. Goddammit.*

He shoved his fingers through his hair and yanked hard in frustration. This was bad. Really, really bad. Whoever he picked, it needed to fit. All the pieces would need to fit, starting with Valerie, all the way to Jazzie, or the cops would be on him like white on rice. Who? Who would make sense?

Oh. Okay. The panic receded as the answer became obvious. *Denny.* Denny would be the perfect fall guy. And it would kill two birds with one stone, because Denny was his last loose end. He'd figure out another alibi. That would be simpler than presenting a plausible explanation for the murder of two children.

'How did you know?' Jazzie asked sleepily, breaking into his thoughts.

'Know what?' he replied gruffly, realizing that there was no trace of her stutter left.

Her eyes were closed, her voice a little slurred. 'That we weren't yours.'

For some reason he found himself telling her. 'Janie got hurt when she was two.'

'I remember. The dog jumped through the glass door. She got cut up.'

'Yeah, that was the day.' The damn dog was trying to run away from an outside bath into the house, and it had run right through the glass, shattering it. The dog ended up without a scratch, but Janie had been in her walker and had nearly lost an eye.

He also keenly remembered waking up that morning as the father of two little girls and the husband of a woman who loved him. He'd gone to bed that night . . . changed. 'Janie needed blood and I offered mine. Your mother tried to get me not to volunteer, but I was insistent. Janie was my baby and she was hurt.' He paused. 'But then I found out she *wasn't* my baby.'

'Wrong blood type?' Jazzie slurred.

He was surprised. 'How do you know about that?'

'We learned about it in science class. Some types can't mix to make other types.'

Smart kid. 'Exactly. Your mother and I were both type A. You and Janie had to be either A or O. But Janie's B. You're type O. But I suspected by then, and I did paternity tests on both of you. Both of you came up as not mine. I confronted your mother, then went out and got stoned.'

'And stayed that way,' she whispered.

Also fair. He felt a twinge of regret that the kid knew what it meant to be stoned. He'd been a live demonstration during the final days that he'd lived with them. 'Pretty much.' He'd done coke in the past recreationally, or to stay awake when he had an important case, but he hadn't *needed* it. After finding out his kids weren't his . . . he'd needed it then.

'Why did you get fired from your job?'

'They found coke in my desk drawer. That was after your mother accused me of hitting her.'

'You did hit her,' she said sleepily. 'I was hiding behind the chair then, too.'

'Yeah, well.' He didn't have the energy to argue with her. 'The

275

firm found coke in my desk and fired me. I wasn't an addict. Close, but not.'

'Are you now?'

'No. I can stop. I have stopped in the past.' For weeks at a time. When he'd used again, it had been on his own terms. 'I use when I want to now. Not when I need to.' *Except when you're tired and about to meet your new boss, or you need to wake up, or your hands shake.* He pushed the doubts aside, because that was situational. He'd be fine once he was working steadily again.

'One . . . more.' Jazzie blinked hard, struggling to keep her eyes open. 'Why no divorce?'

He frowned at her. 'What do you mean, why no divorce?'

'We're . . . not yours. Why . . . did you run away? Why not stay and get a divorce?'

Again he was impressed. 'That is an excellent question, Jazzie. Really excellent.'

'Answer. Please.'

He pinched the bridge of his nose. 'The night I hit your mother, your aunt called the cops on me. If I'd been tried and convicted of assault, I'd have been disbarred. That basically means I'd have lost my job.' Which he'd ended up losing anyway. 'Your mother agreed not to press charges if I agreed not to divorce her and to continue paying the mortgage.'

Jazzie giggled quietly.

'What the fuck is so funny?' he demanded.

'Grandma did the same, backwards.' She sighed. 'Knew Mama was cheating. Didn't know about us not being yours. Told her she wouldn't tell if Mama didn't press charges.'

'How do you know that? Hiding behind the chair again?'

'No. Was listening outside the door that time.'

Shit. The kid made a habit of spying on people. 'Go to sleep, Jazzie,' he said sharply. 'I have work to do.'

He was pissed about everything in general. Valerie had manipulated him, but the kids hadn't asked for any of this. They hadn't asked for their mother to be a fucking whore. They hadn't asked that he turn out to be no blood kin. They hadn't asked to be here, drugged up and sleeping on a filthy blanket.

Feeling twitchy, he got up to at least take off their shoes. They might as well be comfortable as they slept. Seeing as how they'd be sleeping for a long time.

He set Janie's little sneakers on the floor, then pulled off Jazzie's.

And froze. Jazzie had hidden a business card in her shoe. And not just any card, either. It was one of Taylor Dawson's cards, with her cell phone number on the back. The card was soft around the edges, like it had been handled a lot.

Jazzie *had* been talking to the therapist. She'd *lied*. Furious, he grabbed her shoulder and shook her. 'Wake up!'

Jazzie pulled back with a shocked whimper and he let her go. 'You hurt me,' she whispered. 'You promised.'

He shuddered out a breath. He had. He'd promised. But she'd lied. *Because you pointed a gun at her little sister. Duh. What did you think she'd do?* He drew a breath, knowing that as furious as he was with the girl, he was more furious with himself for being taken in by her lies.

'What did you tell the damn therapist?' he growled.

Her eyelids fluttered. 'Nothing.' She blinked rapidly. 'N-nothing. I s-swear.'

She was lying. She'd told the therapist, who'd probably involved the cops.

The cops already are involved. They had been ever since he'd left Valerie in a pool of her own blood. But they'd accepted his alibi. They'd accepted that Toby Romano had killed Valerie. Denny knew this for a fact, and Denny was far too stupid to lie.

Gage glared down at Jazzie, who stared back up at him with glassy fear in her eyes. Fear that hadn't been there when she was fully awake. Denny could take some lessons in lying from this eleven-year-old girl.

He held up the business card. 'What did you tell her?' he asked quietly, menacingly.

Jazzie was trembling, clutching her sister in her arms. Good. She needed to be very afraid. So afraid that she lost her little mind.

'N-n-n . . .' She clenched her eyes shut.

'Tell me the goddamn truth!' he thundered, raising his hand, but checked the movement when Jazzie began to sob.

'P-p-please. D-don't hurt us. I'll t-tell you. Wh-wh-whatever you w-want.'

He drew a breath, tried to calm himself. Or he'd kill her. And he didn't want to do that, not with his fists. With pills. Pain-free. They'd just go to sleep.

Damn you, Valerie. Damn you and your whoring lies. You did this to me. To us. To our family. Which had never, ever been his.

He kept his voice icy cold. 'Good. Tell me what you told the therapist.'

She was sobbing so hard that he was seriously afraid she'd choke. She spoke gibberish.

'Jasmine!' His voice cracked like a whip, but he didn't realize he'd slapped her face until he felt the stinging in his palm. 'Stop crying and tell me what I want to know or I'll hurt your sister next.' He raised his hand again threateningly. 'Tell me what you told the therapist. *Now.*'

Jazzie shrank back against the pillow. 'E-everyth-thing. I t-told her everything. D-don't hit J-Janie. Please.' She rolled on top of her sister to shield her, willing to take the pain so that Janie didn't suffer, and for a moment Gage was her father again. For a moment he was back *there*, in the life he'd left behind. For a split second he wanted to soothe. To comfort. To promise her that nothing bad would happen.

Then he saw himself in prison, and his stomach roiled. Prison could not, would not happen. Whatever it took. He steeled his spine, hardening himself to Jazzie's tears. 'Everything?'

She nodded miserably. 'P-p-please don't hurt Janie.'

'I won't. For now.' He added the last as an afterthought, to keep her frightened enough to obey. 'Where were you going to meet the therapist for ice cream?' he asked.

'A r-r-restaurant. Gi-Gi . . .' She gritted her teeth. 'Seppe's.' She forced the word out.

'Giuseppe's? The Italian place?' It was an odd choice for ice cream, he thought. He'd been there when he'd lived here before. He knew the layout, the location. He knew exactly where he could set up and how to get away once the deed was done. He was glad he'd bought the rifle. He'd need it because of the distance he'd have to put between himself and the front of the restaurant, but it would be a clean, unobstructed shot, unlike this morning at the horse farm.

'Wh-what are you doing?' Her eyes widened in terror when he took the rifle from his closet and checked the barrel. Still loaded. 'You s-s-said you w-w-wouldn't hurt us!'

'I'm not going to shoot you.' He looked at her squarely. 'I'm going to shoot your therapist.'

Jazzie's mouth fell open. 'No! Y-y-you c-can't! She p-promised n-not to t-t-tell. The th-therapist. Y-you d-don't n-need to hurt her.'

'She'll tell. She has to if she thinks you're in danger.'

'No! P-p-please d-don't! I lied. I d-didn't say anything to h-her. N-nothing! I s-swear!'

He looked up from shoving ammo in his pockets. 'Then why did you say you did?'

'S-so y-you wouldn't h-hurt J-Janie.' Tears were streaming down her cheeks.

'It doesn't matter at this point, Jasmine. I can't believe anything you say, so I have to assume the worst.' If the therapist knew anything, of course she'd tell the cops. It was likely that she already had.

Fuck. What if she *had* told them? *Breathe, relax,* he told himself. He'd defended plenty of clients who'd actually committed the murders of which they'd been accused, but there had been no witnesses, so there had been no trial. Of course they'd killed all the witnesses themselves, but the end was the same. No witnesses, no trial. Everything would be fine.

But . . . if Jazzie had already told the therapist everything, why have this little meeting?

He narrowed his eyes as realization dawned. The ice-cream date was a setup.

Denny. Hell. Never gave you credit for this. It was Denny who'd told him about the therapist. About their Sunday appointment over ice cream. Denny who knew Gage wasn't running away.

It's a fucking trap. They'd hoped to lure him in, then take him away. Put him in a cage.

'Did you know?' he asked Jazzie.

She was still sobbing. 'Kn-know what?'

'That they were going to use your little ice-cream outing to bring me out into the open?'

Her head wagged harder than the rest of her body shook. 'No.'

The single word made him see red. 'Liar,' he said coldly. 'Just like your mother.'

They couldn't take him if he got them first. He made sure he had sufficient ammo for the rifle before checking the clips for his new Glock. He dropped the filled clips in his pockets, then from the top shelf of his closet he pulled out the rope he'd bought to secure the girls. It was soft rope. It wouldn't chafe them too badly. *No pain.* He didn't want them to feel any pain.

Bile rose to burn his throat as he bound Jazzie's wrists and feet. *Thanks, Valerie. Just . . . thanks. You fucking bitch. If you'd just been the wife you were supposed to be, it never would have come to any of this.*

He positioned a strip of cotton in her mouth before tying it around her head. He wanted her to be able to breathe. Just not scream. Then he did the same to Janie, who thankfully slept through the whole thing. By the time he'd finished, his hands were shaking too.

'I'll be back,' he said thickly as he gathered his things and put them into a duffel bag. He closed the door behind him, locked it, then made his way to the car and started for Giuseppe's Italian restaurant, knowing he'd hear Jazzie's frightened whimper in his head the whole way.

Maybe for the rest of his fucking life. *But at least I'll have a life.*

Baltimore, Maryland,
Sunday 23 August, 3.40 P.M.

Taylor's skin itched and she squirmed in the front seat of Clay's truck as they drove to the ice cream parlor where she was to meet Jazzie.

Clay glanced away from the traffic long enough to give her a sympathetic grimace. 'Nervous too?'

'Too?' She lifted her brows. 'You? Nervous? Say it isn't so,' she deadpanned, because Clay had been a live wire ever since he'd learned of JD Fitzpatrick's plan. He'd railed and ranted, calling the detective every name in the book, and then some that Taylor had never heard. Fitzpatrick seemed immune, though, sitting through the rant with an expression that was a mix of boredom and weary agreement as Clay bellowed all the things that Taylor herself had considered saying, just not for the same reason.

Taylor had been furious that Jazzie was being used as bait. Clay was furious about that too, but protested far more vocally that *his daughter* was being used as well. His tirade would have made Frederick Dawson proud.

She frowned. *Dad.* Would have made her dad proud. When had she come to think of him by his given name? He'd always been Dad. Always would be.

But Clay was quickly assuming an equivalent position. She'd known him less than twenty-four hours, and already he'd taken the seat next to her dad in her heart and mind. *Aren't I the loyal one?*

Clay's eyes had narrowed at her sarcastic reply, and from the backseat Ford snorted a laugh. 'Damn, she's your kid, Clay.'

Clay's glare softened at that. 'Yeah. So it would seem,' he murmured.

'It's ice cream,' Taylor insisted. 'This is going to be all right.'

'Then why are you twitchy?' Clay asked.

'Because this Kevlar itches!' She tugged at the collar, pulling at the mock turtleneck that hid the skintight vest. Both the vest and the sweater belonged to Paige, who'd donated to the cause. The sweater was a lightweight, sleeveless cotton blend, so at least Taylor wasn't going to roast. Sweaters in August, for God's sake. Her father's business partner had been sympathetic as she'd helped Taylor get dressed.

Paige herself had not been what Taylor had been expecting. She bore a mild resemblance to Taylor herself, and by extension, to Clay's mother. Clay had told her that he'd trusted Paige at first sight, and Taylor silently wondered if the resemblance to his mother had entered into that, at least on a subconscious level. But no one else seemed to notice, so Taylor kept it to herself.

'That itchy Kevlar could save your life,' Clay muttered. 'It's saved mine.'

Taylor frowned. 'That's upsetting. That your life would need to be saved, I mean. How often do you get shot at?'

'Not that often,' Clay replied carefully.

Ford snorted again. 'Not that often this week,' he said, shaking his head.

'Not true,' Clay said calmly, but aimed a glare at the rear-view mirror. 'Shut up, Ford.'

Ford spread his hands, palms out. 'I just calls 'em like I sees 'em.'

'Well, you need glasses, then,' Clay grumbled. 'I'm not reckless.'

'Never said you were,' Ford said seriously. 'But you put yourself in dangerous positions. So does Stevie. And Paige, too.'

'Not lately,' Clay insisted.

Ford rolled his eyes. 'Because Paige is pregnant!' He met Taylor's gaze when she looked over her shoulder in surprise. 'Nobody's supposed to know yet, but we all do. It's hard to keep secrets in a group this tight knit. Especially the really good ones.' He gave Taylor a lascivious wink, and she blushed furiously and looked away.

Clay winced. 'Jesus, Ford. Really? You do realize that her father is sitting *right here.*'

Ford was unfazed. 'And that your personal weapons arsenal rivals that of several small countries? And that you can break my neck with your pinkie? Yeah, I realize all of that.'

'And?' Clay demanded.

'And I've behaved myself. For the most part,' he added wickedly.

Clay huffed an exasperated breath. 'God.'

'So . . .' Taylor lifted her chin and pretended like her cheeks weren't on fire. 'With Paige being pregnant, does this mean you and Stevie will have to take her workload? Does that mean more exposure to people with guns?'

'Not for Stevie,' Clay said firmly, then winced.

Ford's fist pumped the air. 'Yes! I was right.'

Taylor's cheeks had cooled enough that she felt safe looking at him again. 'About what?'

'That Stevie's pregnant too,' Ford said, his eyes sparkling. 'Maggie thinks so, too.'

Taylor's gaze whipped to Clay's face just in time to see him school his expression from fierce joy to mild surprise. 'Why would you two think that?' he asked Ford.

'Because I heard her puking her guts up in the bathroom in the barn,' Ford said wryly. 'And she ate half a sleeve of saltine crackers in Maggie's office this morning.'

Clay shrugged. 'She could just be sick.'

Except that the joy he'd tried to quench came through, the small lines at the corner of his eyes crinkling in a smile even though his mouth didn't curve an iota.

'She is, isn't she?' Taylor asked.

Clay opened his mouth. Closed it again. 'If she is?'

Taylor felt a settling in her chest. A peace. If she left him to go back home, he'd be all right. He'd have another child to love. 'I think that's lovely,' she said quietly, and meant it with all her heart. 'Congratulations.'

His brow crunched in consternation, his joy abruptly gone. 'That doesn't mean that I don't need you or love you, Taylor.'

'I know.' She expected his frown to melt away, but it became even more pronounced. 'I'm thrilled for you, Clay. Really.' She smiled at him uncertainly. 'So . . . why are you scowling at me?'

He didn't reply or even smile back as he circled the restaurant's parking lot, looking for a space. The lot was surprisingly full for a Sunday afternoon and the street directly in front was a no-parking zone. Remaining troublingly silent, he parked the truck in the first legal space on the street, more than a block away.

He switched off the engine, then turned to look her in the eye. 'You think that because I'll be a dad again that I won't need you. That you can go back to California and be Dawson's daughter and that it won't break my heart.'

'I . . .' She had no idea what to say to him.

He took her chin gently between his thumb and forefinger. 'Now you listen to me, Taylor, and listen well. I would be the happiest father on the planet if you stayed here, but I know you have a life there and someone who loves you as much as I do. If you do leave, I'll miss you. I'm not gonna lie. I just found you and I want more time to get to know you. But planes fly both ways. You can come back to visit and I'll fly out there whenever I can, and that's a promise. Because, bottom line, I just want to be part of your life, however that happens.'

'But a new baby will help, right?' She studied his face anxiously. 'You'll be so busy you won't have time to miss me.'

There was sadness in his eyes, even though he smiled back, as if he knew that she'd made up her mind. But had she?

'I will be busy, that's true.' He leaned a few inches closer, his dark eyes intense. 'But I will still miss you. And I'll always have time for you. Always.'

'Thank you,' she whispered.

He let her chin go and straightened in his seat. 'You'll be a big sister, so you'll have responsibilities too. You'll have to come back to visit. Now, let's have some ice cream.'

He got out, but Taylor didn't move, her attention suddenly riveted to the back seat. Ford was sitting so still, his expression flat and unreadable. 'Ford?' she said tentatively. 'Look, I like you. A lot. More than a lot, actually. I don't want to hurt you either.'

Ford sighed. 'I'm not trying to make you feel guilty, Taylor. I'm just disappointed. I knew this was the choice you'd make. I just hoped you wouldn't make it for a few weeks yet. Or at least not say it out loud.' He hesitated. 'I haven't been with anyone since ... Kimberly. I haven't wanted to be. Until you. I'd just hoped we'd have a little more time. And speaking of time . . .' He glanced at his phone. 'We're way early, but that's okay. Giuseppe should have the private dining room cleared out by now. We can wait while JD gets everything set up. At least we can get out of the heat.'

He climbed out of the truck, opened her door, and helped her down, trapping her between the truck and his hard body. His chest was now covered with a white button-up shirt, but Taylor remembered how his skin had felt under her fingertips. And how solid he'd been when she'd needed to lean on him.

So she did that now, resting her forehead against the hard muscle of his chest, sighing when his arms came around her to hold her closer. She gripped the back of his shirt, silently cursing the Kevlar that Clay had made them all wear that kept her from touching him.

Of course, not touching his bare skin was probably a good thing, considering they were standing in a public place. The last time, she'd ended up against a door, being kissed within an inch of her life. She wanted that again. Desperately.

She wanted to tell him that it would work out. That it would be fine. That she wouldn't hurt him. Or leave him. That they could have all the time they needed to see if this . . . chemistry between them went anywhere. But she couldn't promise him any of those things, so she simply held his hand tightly as they followed Clay up the sidewalk.

Put your game face on, she admonished herself. *You're here to help a little girl identify a killer.* It wouldn't bring Jazzie's mother back, but at least the child wouldn't have to live with the constant fear of being the next victim.

'Ready?' Clay asked her, his expression so very kind it made her want to cry.

She made herself smile. 'Ready as I'll ever be, I guess. This will feel very silly if all Jazzie says is "thank you" again.'

Ford squeezed her hand. 'That'll still be more than she's said to anyone else, right? This may be a multi-step process. And it could be a lot worse. At least you're eating ice cream. It could be Brussels sprouts or something.'

She chuckled, her forced smile becoming real. 'Little blessings.'

Ford bumped her shoulder with his. 'Exactly.'

Eighteen

Baltimore, Maryland,
Sunday 23 August, 3.42 P.M.

Taylor Dawson kept a damn low profile, Gage thought with a scowl. He'd been sitting in Cleon's car, tucked back in an alley about a half a block from the restaurant where Jazzie was to have met her therapist. Once again he'd combed through Facebook and the rest of the Internet looking for a photo of the woman, but he'd found nothing. Not even a mention of her. She'd gone to college somewhere, but it must have been a nunnery, because there were no party pics, no nothing. All he knew was that she had long black hair.

He shifted in the driver's seat, sweat beading on his forehead. He was hot. He was hungry, and he so needed a hit. He looked down at his hands to see them shaking. Fuck it. He wasn't going to be steady enough to fire the fucking weapon when Taylor Dawson, whoever the fuck she was, finally walked into target range.

Just a little. Just enough to take off the edge. *So I can think.*

Taking the baggie from his pocket, he quickly prepared a line and snorted it up, then breathed deeply, feeling the shakes subside almost instantaneously. Now he could think.

He put his phone in his pocket when a group of three got out of a pickup and began walking toward the restaurant. There was a woman in her early twenties and two men, a blond about the same age and a black-haired guy closer to forty. The woman had long black hair and was the same size as the girl he'd glimpsed that morning at the farm, but two other women who'd walked into the restaurant while he'd been waiting outside had also matched her description.

The blond man looked like Ford Elkhart and the fortyish guy looked like Clay Maynard, but Gage couldn't shoot until he knew for one-hundred-percent sure. It would bring the cops, and if that black-haired woman was not Taylor Dawson, then Taylor would know she was a target and would hunker down and hide – going even more low-profile than she was now, if that was even possible. Any more under the radar and he'd wonder if she was in witness protection.

But he was ninety-nine-point-nine percent sure, so grabbed his rifle, placing the three in his crosshairs as they looked around, as if meeting someone. Then the young woman waved.

At Lilah, who'd been parked around the corner, out of his view, and now was walking briskly toward the three people on the sidewalk. That would be the therapist then. Taylor Dawson.

That's all I need to know.

Baltimore, Maryland,
Sunday 23 August, 3.50 P.M.

Ford forced himself to smile at Taylor as she walked beside him, managing not to wince even when she held his hand so tightly that he thought she'd break his fingers. *She's leaving. You knew that.* The situation was no different than it had been yesterday.

Except that twice now he'd tasted her mouth, heard her moan. Felt her up against him. And he'd watched her face relax as they'd ridden through the woods. She'd found some peace in the clearing that had always been his favorite place. And they'd sat together in the morning quiet with very little conversation at all.

He wasn't sure he'd ever met anyone with whom he had shared such a comfortable silence. And then . . . God, the look on her face when she'd seen that photo of her grandmother.

Ford thought it was probably that moment when it finally hit her exactly how much her mother's lies had cost *her* – Taylor herself. Not Clay. Not Frederick Dawson. Up until that moment her concern had been about everyone else. But when she realized that she'd lost

287

the opportunity to know the grandmother who would have loved her, her tears had broken his heart.

As had the look of helpless frustration on Clay's face. Twenty-three years. Stolen from them both. Stolen from Clay's mother, who hadn't lived to meet her only granddaughter.

At least Clay's dad was still alive. The gruff retired cop, who ran a fishing charter service when the mood struck him, had all but legally adopted Ford and the other younger members of their circle of family and friends. *Tanner St James will love her.*

I, on the other hand, he thought grimly, *won't get a chance to find out.* Unless a month was enough time to know if someone was 'the one'. Because a month was all they had.

Nothing has changed, he reminded himself again. But he was lying to himself. He'd hoped deep down that he'd have a chance to change her mind. That maybe she'd stay. For Clay and for Tanner. *And maybe even for me.*

Taylor rested her head on his shoulder for a few steps. 'I'm sorry.'

He smiled down at her. 'For what? You have nothing to be sorry for.'

'And you're a really bad liar,' she said softly, her smile even more forced than his. 'But we'll go with that if it makes you more comfortable.' She blinked hard and gave her head a shake. 'Jazzie,' she murmured, as if to remind herself why they were there.

'Right,' he echoed. 'Jazzie.'

Taylor paused, her gaze focused up the street as a lone figure came around a corner, approaching them. 'There's Lilah. But she doesn't have Jazzie.' A heavy sigh. 'I bet Jazzie had second thoughts. Detective Fitzpatrick won't be happy.'

Clay glanced at her over his shoulder. 'No, but I have to say I'm relieved. This idea of JD's was ill-conceived. All we needed was a sociopathic killer showing up to eliminate his witness and you getting caught in the crossfire. This was a stupid plan.'

Taylor huffed impatiently. 'Are you always going to be this way?'

'Which way?' Ford asked lightly. 'Overbearing, crass, bossy, negative? Stevie says those are his good qualities.'

Taylor laughed but Clay did not look amused. 'Watch it, kid,' he said grumpily.

'Miss Dawson.' Lilah stopped on the sidewalk in front of them, breathing hard. 'Mr Maynard.' Her eyes narrowed slightly when she looked at Ford, as if trying to place him.

'I'm Daphne Montgomery's son, Ford.'

Lilah smiled, but it was a stiff bending of lips. Not a true smile. 'Is Jazzie here yet?'

Ford stiffened. Something was wrong. Taylor had gone very still beside him, studying the older woman's face.

'Is something wrong, Miss Cornell?' Taylor asked before Ford could.

Clay was already scanning the area, back on alert.

'No, no,' Lilah said. 'The girls' grandmother and I may have had a mix-up in plans. I went out to the mall, and when I came home, they weren't there. I figured she was bringing Jazzie here. Let me call her and—'

'Let's get inside,' Clay interrupted. He stepped in front of Taylor, taking her arm and hustling her toward the restaurant's front door.

The first burst of gunfire took Clay down like a ton of bricks, and after that everything went into slow-mo. Lilah screamed and ran back in the direction she'd come. Taylor went to her knees, dragged down by Clay, who hadn't released her arm, despite the fact that his leg was shooting blood like a damn geyser.

Ford dropped to his knees next to Clay's leg. The wound was bleeding faster than he had thought possible. 'Dammit, Clay. That's gotta be an artery.'

Clay grabbed Ford's shirt. 'Go. Get her out of here.'

Ford gave her a push. 'Taylor, run!' he ordered, but he didn't move from Clay's side. *Stop the bleeding*, was all he could think. He ripped at the buttons of his shirt as he looked up at the rooftops, scanning for a person, a shadow, a gun. Anything. But there were no shooters, no guns, not even any metal glinting in the sunlight.

Totally ignoring Ford, Taylor shoved her phone at him and took Clay's arm, wrapping it over her shoulders. 'You call 911,' she said.

'I don't know exactly where we are.' She dragged Clay to his knees. 'Dammit, Ford, help me get him on his feet. We need to get him inside and he's heavy as hell,' she said through her teeth, her jaw clenched as she struggled to lift him.

The street between Clay's truck and the restaurant was a fire zone. There was no cover. Not a tree, not a parked car, nothing. *Where the fuck is JD?* Ford fought back his panic, fought to stay calm. JD was in the restaurant, too far away to hear if they yelled for help.

Hooking one arm under Clay's armpit, Ford stood up, hefting the older man to his feet. He and Taylor took off running, Clay hopping on one foot, but mostly being dragged between them.

'Call JD,' Clay commanded harshly.

But Ford didn't know JD's number and didn't have time to search for his own phone. He'd started to dial 911 on Taylor's phone with his free hand when pain ripped into his back, a second shot splitting the air. He stumbled, going back down to his knees, and the phone flew forward, landing somewhere in the street. For a moment he knelt there, the breath knocked out of him. He reached behind him to touch his back, relieved when his hand came away free of blood. His own, anyway. Clay was still spurting blood like a fire hydrant, and it had splashed onto Ford's jeans and the front of his shirt.

He grabbed for Clay, but a third shot was fired, nicking his own thigh, followed by a fourth, which brought a pained grunt from Clay and another rapidly spreading red stain, this time on Clay's arm.

Ford looked around, panic clawing up his throat. Nothing to hide behind. *Dammit.* 'Where the fucking *hell* is JD?'

'Get inside, Taylor,' Clay ordered, but weakly. His face had paled, his skin growing gray at an alarming rate. 'Now.'

'Not leaving you,' she gritted through clenched teeth. 'Shut up.'

He's bleeding to death, Ford thought, new horror spurring his muscles to move, and he crawled over to crouch next to Clay's leg. Dipping his head low, he presented his back to the shooter, using his body to shield Clay and Taylor.

'Dammit, woman, get inside!' Ford yelled at Taylor, shrugging out of his shirt so that he could wrap it around Clay's leg. 'Go get JD.

290

Get some help.' Luckily he'd ducked, because a spray of bullets came whizzing past his shoulder, hitting the restaurant wall, spraying concrete shards onto their heads. The next bullet hit Ford in the back again, but he was prepared. He rocked forward with the momentum, then gritted his teeth and straightened back up.

Clay grabbed the collar of Taylor's turtleneck and tried to shove her away, but he'd lost too much blood to budge her. 'He's shooting at you, Taylor. For God's sake, take cover.'

Once again Taylor ignored them both, going into what Ford could only describe later as robot-ninja-warrior mode. She pressed Clay's chest until he lay back against the pavement, sliding backwards on her stomach in the same movement so that her body was flat to the ground.

Before Ford realized what she intended, she'd unsnapped Clay's holster, pulled out his gun, racked it and started shooting back as two more shots were fired from across the street, both going over her head.

She fired twice, the first shot shattering glass, the second producing a blood-curdling scream. She took a microsecond to adjust her aim, then fired a third time before calmly putting Clay's gun aside, whipping the belt from her jeans, wrapping it around Clay's leg above the wound and cinching it tight.

All while Clay stared in open-mouthed disbelief at his daughter.

Ford was mesmerized as well, but for very different reasons. *Oh my God.* That had been amazing. *And hot. So damn hot.* He took a deep breath to control the sudden jolt of adrenaline mixed with the most potent arousal he'd ever experienced. *Don't get a hard-on. Not now. Not in front of her father. Later. Now, save Clay or Stevie will beat you senseless.* Although no one could blame him for being aroused. Taylor Dawson was fucking hot.

You know, California really isn't that far. And they have companies to work for there, just like here. He shook his head hard. *Dammit, boy, focus.*

Somewhere a door slammed and three suits came running around the restaurant from the rear exit, led by JD Fitzpatrick. 'What the hell?' JD shouted, taking in the scene. 'Holy God. Oh shit. *Clay.*'

He radioed for an ambulance, while sending the other two cops to the car in the alley across the street.

'Tell the paramedics to hurry before he bleeds to death,' Ford snapped, then forced his attention back to Clay's leg. Balling up the body of his shirt, he pressed it against the wound, then wrapped the sleeves around the leg and knotted them tightly, securing the makeshift bandage until the paramedics arrived.

'How bad's he hurt?' JD asked anxiously.

'I'll live,' Clay said irritably.

'The bleeding has slowed down,' Ford told JD, ignoring Clay. 'Partly because Taylor applied a tourniquet and partly because he's lost so much blood already.'

Clay snorted weakly. '*He's* right here and *he's* still conscious, so how bad could *he* be?'

JD dropped to a crouch beside them. 'What just happened here?'

'Give me something to wrap his arm,' Ford said tightly, ignoring the question for now. 'He can't lose any more blood.'

A cop rushed up, a first-aid kit and towels in his hands. 'Towels are clean, Detective. Restaurant owner gave them to me.'

'Thanks. Go back inside and maintain crowd control. Keep everyone away from the windows,' JD said to the cop, immediately beginning to wrap the wound on Clay's arm. 'This one doesn't look as bad as the leg wound. You were damn lucky to make that shot after getting hit in the arm.'

Clay shook his head, his eyes sliding closed. 'Not me,' he protested, his voice thin. 'Ford shielded me and Taylor took care of the shooter. Hell of a shot, baby,' he added proudly.

With a double-take, JD looked across the street to where the two other detectives had already stretched crime-scene tape across the alley entrance. The front of a rusty vehicle was visible, its side window completely shattered.

'*Taylor* made that shot?' JD asked in disbelief.

Clay nodded, his eyes still closed. 'Hell, yeah. Probably saved our lives.'

I didn't even see the car, Ford thought, stunned by the knowledge that he never could have made a shot like that, even under the controlled conditions of a target range. But Taylor had simply . . . acted. *Wow.* Now that what she'd accomplished was sinking in, he found himself more than a little intimidated as well. And still far too aroused for his own comfort.

Stunned, JD shook his head. 'Okay, let's start from the beginning. What *exactly* happened here?'

'We were approaching the restaurant and he opened fire,' Clay said. 'He's either dead or he's run. All I know is he stopped shooting.'

'He was standing behind his car door,' Taylor said, her voice nearly as thin as Clay's.

It was then that Ford realized that Taylor was too still, her face way too pale. She was sitting back on her heels, her body slack, her dark eyes gone glassy. *Adrenaline crash*, he thought, coupled with the reality that she'd just shot a man.

'He had a rifle with a scope,' she went on tonelessly. 'That's what I first saw – the flash of sunlight off the scope. He had dark hair. Don't know his height. He was bent forward with the rifle balanced on the top of the open car door, so that's where I aimed.'

JD pushed to his feet. 'Thank you. Stay here while I check it out.' He jogged across the street, leaving the three of them in a bubble of eerie quiet.

'Taylor?' Ford reached across Clay to touch her arm, and she flinched.

Clay tried to pull her close with his uninjured arm, but she shook her head silently. 'Taylor?' he asked roughly, his voice strained with pain. 'Are you okay?'

'Did I kill him?' she asked, sounding hollow.

Ford knelt beside her and pulled her into his arms, rocking her gently. She went limp, like a doll. 'I don't know,' he murmured into her hair. 'But no one can blame you if you did.'

Baltimore, Maryland,
Sunday 23 August, 3.58 P.M.

Taylor shivered despite the blazing heat of the August day, and Ford tightened his arms around her. *No one can blame you if you did.*

Well now, Taylor thought numbly, that was where Ford was wrong. *I can blame me. If I killed that man, I will blame me. Because I pulled the trigger. Nobody else but me.*

She'd heard his scream. Seen him fall. Watched the rifle he'd aimed at them slide out of his hands to clatter to the asphalt. When she closed her eyes, she saw it all again, in a never-ending video loop.

Please don't let him be dead. She hadn't been aiming to kill him. She'd just wanted to disable him. But years and years of intense training had taken hold of her mind, moving her limbs like a marionette on a string. Muscle memory, her father had called it. He'd started teaching her to handle a gun from the very first day they'd moved to the ranch. He'd trained and tested her skills, then trained and tested some more. A laugh bubbled out of nowhere, coming out hysterical and shrill. 'He taught me because of you.'

'Who taught you?' Ford asked softly. Carefully. Like she was fragile glass that would shatter into pieces any moment. *Maybe I will.*

'My dad.' She tried to swallow, but the gulp stuck in her throat and it hurt to breathe. 'My other dad. He taught me to shoot.'

'Because of me?' Clay's question was raw and sharp and filled with the same hurt that was squeezing her chest like a vise.

Can't breathe. Can't breathe. Black spots floated in front of her eyes and she clenched them shut. *Panic.* This was a panic attack. She'd had them before. But not like this. Never like this. *Duh. You never killed a man like this.* She pressed her face into Ford's chest. *You don't know that he's dead. Maybe you just wounded him.*

Please don't let him be dead.

Through the curtain of panic she heard a high-pitched keening sound and nearly laughed again. *Me. That's me. Goddammit, Taylor. Stop this. Right now.* But she couldn't stop. Couldn't breathe. Like running down a hill, faster and faster, until her feet wouldn't *stop.* Couldn't stop.

'Ow!' A sharp pain in her scalp abruptly yanked her out of the panic. Another hard tug had her turning in Ford's arms to see Clay still holding her hair with his uninjured hand.

Her father was watching her through narrowed eyes. 'You back with me, Taylor?'

She scooted out of Ford's hold, instantly missing his warmth. She pulled her hair from Clay's hand with a frown. 'That hurt.'

'I know. You were spiraling into a panic attack and your hair was all I could reach.'

Taylor rubbed her scalp. He hadn't pulled any of her hair out by its roots, but it still smarted. 'Gonna make me bald,' she grumbled, then sighed. 'But thanks. Mostly.'

'You're welcome.' Clay's gaze was still narrowed. 'Dawson taught you to shoot like that? What was he? Special Forces or something?'

'Or something,' Taylor murmured. She knew her dad had been a soldier, long ago. She'd asked once and he'd become uncharacteristically broody for days. So she'd never mentioned it again. 'He wanted me to be ready in case you came to grab me when he wasn't home.' She hunched her shoulders forward. 'I never thought I'd actually shoot someone.' She closed her eyes, her heart beginning to race again. 'What if I've killed him?'

Clay grabbed her hair again, tugging lightly. 'Look at me, Taylor. *Now.*'

The barked command stopped the panic attack in its tracks and she met his eyes, dark and intense. *Like looking in a mirror.* 'I'm okay.'

'You're more than okay,' Clay said, his fierce pride on full display. 'You saved our lives, because that asshole was going to keep shooting.'

'And I don't know how many more hits I could have taken,' Ford confessed.

That got her attention. Taylor swung her gaze to Ford's. 'How many hits *did* you take?'

'Two to the back,' he said, 'but the Kevlar stopped them. Still hurts like a bitch.' He pressed his fingers to the side of his upper thigh and pulled them back covered in blood. 'And apparently one to the leg.'

Taylor stared at his bloody fingers for a heartbeat, then reached for one of the towels and the first-aid kit that had been brought from

295

the restaurant. She wiped the blood from Ford's hands, then pressed the towel to his thigh. Now that she was focused, she could see the dark stain on his black jeans, but thankfully it wasn't very large.

From the back pocket of her own jeans she pulled the Swiss army knife her other dad had given her for her thirteenth birthday. Flipping it open, she sliced away the torn fabric of Ford's jeans until she could see the wound.

'It's small,' she said. 'Barely a scratch.'

Ford sat placidly, allowing her to check out the wound, and all at once she realized that this was his equivalent to Clay pulling her hair. It had distracted her from her panic.

She glanced up, saw his tolerant expression. 'You knew it was only a scratch, didn't you?' she asked. When he only nodded, she smiled ruefully. 'Thank you.'

'You're welcome. It's okay to be shaken up, Taylor. I've never had to shoot a man before. Came close a few times, but I never had to do it.'

Back when he'd been abducted, Taylor knew. She'd read the entire account in the court transcripts. He'd done what he had to do to get away. To survive.

'You had to,' Ford went on, his voice calm. Rock-steady. 'There's no shame in post-adrenaline jitters. And whether he lives or dies, that's not on you. He shot at us. And if he's who I think he is, he killed Jazzie's mother and he would have killed Jazzie if she'd been here.'

Detective Fitzpatrick rejoined them, looking grim. Taylor's heart sank.

'I killed him,' she whispered. 'Shit.'

'No,' Fitzpatrick said unhappily. 'He got away.'

Taylor sucked in a breath that was both relieved and horrified. *I didn't kill him. But he's still out there.* She did a visual scan of the street, but didn't see anything suspicious. *You wouldn't see him. He'd make sure of that.*

Ford swore. 'Where?' he demanded. 'How?'

'He left a trail of blood in the alley that ended abruptly at the other end.'

'He stole a car,' Clay muttered.

A scowl twisted Fitzpatrick's face. 'Or he can fucking fly. I've called in additional units to canvass the neighborhood. We need to know who was parked there and what they were driving. One of my guys is doing a door-to-door in the building on the other side of the alley right now.' He glanced at Taylor. 'One of your shots hit his tire.'

She nodded with numb satisfaction. 'Good.'

'The third shot,' Ford said, marveling again. 'You were aiming for the tire?'

His open amazement made her uncomfortable. 'Yes. I didn't want him to be able to get closer to us with the car. You know, to do a drive-by.'

Fitzpatrick's brows rose. 'You thought of that,' he murmured, as if to himself, then gave a half-shake of his head. 'That's why he left the car there. That and the shattered window, of course. He would have been noticed and stopped once the BOLO went out. It's a lucky break for us. Hopefully we'll get prints or something else that IDs him.'

'It was Jarvis,' Ford bit out, his blue eyes now flashing fury.

Fitzpatrick nodded. 'Probably. But I want a positive ID.'

Clay lifted his head and squinted at the rusty car the shooter had left behind, then blinked hard several times. 'Sonofabitch. Is that pile of rust a Chevy Malibu?'

'Yes,' Fitzpatrick said, his brows crunching in a frown. 'He stole it from Cleon Perry, the dealer he killed yesterday. Why?'

'Because he was at the farm this morning,' Clay said through clenched teeth. 'I passed that car about a quarter-mile from the main gate. I should have checked the security tapes, but I was in a hurry.'

'To see me,' Taylor murmured.

Clay turned his head to glare at her. 'He came to kill you this morning, Taylor.'

She nodded, the fear in her gut collapsing into a cold, hard ball. 'I understand that,' she said, trying to keep from panicking again. 'But you have fences and alarm systems. He couldn't have gotten in.'

'But if we'd ridden a little further, he could have seen us from the road,' Ford said hoarsely. 'And he had a rifle. Jesus.'

'We'll look at the tapes,' JD promised. 'Along with all the security tapes in the vicinity. For now, I've put a BOLO out.'

'Is he still armed?' Ford asked, his voice steady again.

'We're assuming so, although he left his rifle on the ground and his handgun in the car. He also left a hundred rounds of ammo for the gun and another hundred for the rifle. He'd prepared for a firefight. He was going to kill you.'

'How badly is he wounded?' Ford asked.

'Not enough that he couldn't drag himself off, but he lost a lot of blood in the alley. I'd say that Taylor hit something vital for sure.'

Taylor straightened her spine, prepared for the consequences. 'Will you arrest me for shooting him?'

'Fuck, no,' Clay blurted out, moving like he was going to try to get up.

Fitzpatrick shushed him. 'Stop, Clay. I'm not arresting your daughter. We'll do an investigation, but it'll be paperwork. Just dotting the i's for the bureaucrats. You know the drill.'

'Okay,' Clay said grudgingly, settling down as sirens whined in the distance. 'They took long enough to get here.'

'It's been less than five minutes,' Fitzpatrick said mildly.

Seemed like five hours, Taylor thought wearily.

'Then what the mother*fuck*,' Clay said, every word sounding like he'd forced it out, 'took *you* so long to get out here?'

'We were in the listening room, which is soundproofed. We were prepping for Taylor's chat with Jazzie, who thankfully didn't show up today or he might have shot her too. And it wasn't that long, Clay. Less than two minutes in total. Giuseppe ran in to tell us, and as soon as he opened the door, we heard all the screaming in the restaurant.' He glared at Clay. 'We came out the *back* door, which was the door you were *supposed* to come *in*. You would have been covered there. Not fodder for some lunatic killer on the goddamn street.'

His voice had risen with every word, and Taylor was ready to tell him to shove his anger when she recognized it for what it was – true fear for his friend.

Clay exhaled heavily. 'Oh shit,' he whispered.

'Oh shit is right,' Fitzpatrick spat. 'What the hell happened, Clay? Why didn't you follow the goddamned plan?'

Hesitating, Clay gave Taylor a worried glance. 'I forgot,' he mumbled. 'Just . . . forgot.'

Fitzpatrick blinked. 'You just forgot? You don't just forget, Clay. You don't ever just forget. Especially plans that keep your family safe.'

Ford's jaw had tightened. 'He was distracted, JD, okay? Let it go.'

Taylor frowned. Distracted? By wha— And then she remembered what they'd been talking about when Clay had parked the car in the wrong place.

'Distracted?' JD echoed. 'And no, Ford, I won't just let it go.'

'He was distracted by me. Again,' Taylor said quietly, wishing like hell she could go back and rewind the past hour. She'd all but told Clay she was going back to California. He'd seemed so . . . okay with it. Hurt, but like he'd make the best of it. Obviously he'd been a lot less chill than he'd wanted her to believe. 'We were talking about my plans to return home. I didn't realize how distracted he was. I didn't know.'

Clay winced. 'Way to go, boy genius,' he muttered sarcastically to Ford.

'She would have figured it out,' Ford snapped back.

'This isn't your fault, Taylor.' Clay reached for her hand and she held his tightly. 'This is my fault and only mine. You better not feel guilty for any of it.'

Taylor could only sigh. 'Pot, meet kettle?'

Ford rolled his eyes. 'That's the understatement of the goddamn century.'

Fitzpatrick held up his hands like a traffic cop. 'Okay, okay, I get the picture. Who's going to tell me what happened next?'

'I will,' Ford said, and quickly relayed the entire scene, including their belief that something was wrong with Lilah before the shooting even started.

Taylor twisted around to look toward the restaurant. She'd forgotten all about Jazzie's aunt. 'What happened to Lilah?'

Fitzpatrick frowned. 'No idea. She didn't come into the restaurant, through either door. I'll have someone go by her apartment and make sure she and the girls are okay.'

An ambulance and several BPD cruisers arrived, lining the street.

'*Now* there's cover,' Ford said with a shake of his head.

Two paramedics lifted Clay onto a stretcher. Even though they were as gentle as possible, pain tightened his features, his eyes appearing alarmingly more sunken in the seconds it took to settle him. His whole body seemed to shrink on itself and suddenly he was . . . *frail. My God. He looks so frail.*

Taylor rose on shaky legs to hold his hand while the medics hooked him up to an IV. 'You stay with me,' she ordered, grateful her voice was stronger than her legs. 'Your hair is too short to pull or I'd be returning the favor right now.'

A ghost of a smile quirked Clay's lips. 'Smartass.'

She cleared her throat, grateful when Ford moved to stand behind her, holding her upright when her knees wobbled. 'You got that right, Pop,' she said, keeping her tone light.

Clay winced. 'Dad. Father. Pa. Know-it-all old man.' He drew a labored breath that scared the shit out of her. 'But not Pop.'

She leaned down to kiss his cheek, shoving her fear deep down. 'We'll negotiate later.'

The paramedics had started wheeling him toward the ambulance when a different kind of panic gripped her. She didn't want him to be alone. 'Can I ride with him?' she asked. 'I'm his daughter,' she added before they could ask.

Both medics avoided her gaze and her heart dropped to her gut. This was bad. Very bad. When one of them looked at Fitzpatrick and shook his head, all the blood in her head drained to her feet and she felt herself sway. Ford gripped her shoulders, continuing to keep her upright.

'Breathe, Taylor,' he whispered in her ear. 'Just breathe.'

She tried. She honestly tried, but her fear had burst from its cage, clawing at her throat. 'I can't lose him, Ford. I just found him.'

JD sent a cruiser to escort the ambulance. 'Just in case Jarvis tries shooting at them en route,' he said, then pointed to the remaining squad cars. 'You two get in one of those. I'll get you a ride to the hospital.'

Ford led Taylor to the cruiser. 'Clay's a tough son of a gun. He's fought through far worse.' He gently pushed her so that she sat sideways on the rear seat, then lifted her chin, and forced her to meet his eyes. Steady and honest and blue. 'And don't forget, he's just found you too. He'll fight as hard as he needs to. He has a family to live for, you included.'

Fitzpatrick followed them to the squad car, his big body throwing a shadow over them. 'Anything either of you need before you go to the ER?'

'Stevie,' Taylor said, frowning. 'I need to call her. What happened to my phone?'

'I'll call her,' Fitzpatrick promised. 'And I'll find your phone and have someone bring it to you at the hospital. Ford, you will let them check your leg, won't you?'

Taylor was annoyed with herself for forgetting Ford's leg wound so soon. Even a scratch could become infected. 'He's right. Dammit.'

'Don't agree with him,' Ford said, trying to tease her. 'He's already got a big head.'

'Don't start with me, kid,' Fitzpatrick warned, but it was only more teasing. They were both trying hard to keep her from falling apart.

When Fitzpatrick's shadow disappeared, Taylor's body sagged as if the detective had taken her bones with him. She wanted to believe the day couldn't get worse, but she knew that it could. *Clay could die. Oh God.* And the blame would fall squarely on her shoulders.

Ford slid her over so that he could sit next to her. 'You realize,' he said softly, 'that this very moment Clay is lying in that ambulance thinking the same thing you are, that this is his fault. Except he'll think it an octave or so lower, because, you know, mega-buckets of testosterone left over from being a Marine.'

She huffed a tired chuckle. 'You're right. I've known him less than twenty-four hours and I can hear him thinking it right along with me.'

'You're not doing each other any good feeling guilty,' he continued mildly. 'So stop it.'

She leaned forward and rested her forehead against Ford's. 'I shouldn't say that I'm glad you're here, because you got hurt. But I'm so damn glad you're here.'

Baltimore, Maryland,
Sunday 23 August, 4.15 P.M.

Goddammit. That bitch. She just grabbed that gun and fired it. Like a fucking soldier. *What the hell kind of therapist shoots like that?*

Apparently Taylor Dawson did. At least he'd hit the two men she was with – Clay Maynard and Ford Elkhart. He'd hurt Maynard pretty badly, but Elkhart was just a graze. The men had formed a protective shield around Taylor and they wore Kevlar, meaning they'd come expecting trouble.

Gage had failed. Spectacularly. He'd left DNA all over the damn place. *Fucking bitch.* He'd bled all over the alley and the car he'd stolen from the old lady who'd been hobbling toward it, her keys clutched in an arthritic hand.

Now he'd ditched that car because it was new enough to have GPS and was looking for another. He'd have to zigzag his way back to his place. And not leave any more blood for the cops to find.

I need to get out of here. Out of the city. Out of the fucking country. This was it. He'd completely messed up.

He sidled toward a car that had been left with its engine running. The windows were up, the A/C blasting so that the window glass was cold. A small dog sat on the front passenger seat, snarling. A bumper sticker proclaimed that the owner loved his shih-tzu.

Gage rolled his eyes, tempted to shoot the barking little fucker. He'd left the new semi-auto and rifle behind, but he still had his piece-of-shit pistol. He used the butt of the gun to break the passenger window, then took the shirt he'd wrapped around his bleeding shoulder, reached through the broken glass, and shoved it over the dog's head, scooping the dog up and tossing it to the ground. He shook the shirt to get rid of the broken glass, then balled it up. He'd toss it in a dumpster somewhere along the way. Unlocking the driver's side, he slid behind the wheel.

He took the car as far as he dared, then ditched that one too. He filched a few shirts from a clothesline, using one to pack the wound and shrugging into the other as best he could. It was several sizes too big, but it would do for now. His shoulder still bled, but it had slowed to a seep versus the gush it had been.

He'd need stitches. *Fuck.* He'd stitched himself up once before, when he'd been sliced with a broken bottle in a bar fight. He could do it again. He'd have to.

He was only a few blocks from his rented room when his cell buzzed in his pants pocket. Only two people had his number – Denny and Cesar Tavilla. It was Tavilla.

'Yes?' Gage answered, hoping he didn't sound too weak.

'You said there would not be any repercussions, Mr Jarvis, but not even twenty-four hours later, I hear your name is being broadcast over the police radio. You're wanted for a shooting in front of Giuseppe's restaurant.'

Gage didn't know what to say, so he simply sighed wearily. 'I figured as much.'

'Our business association is terminated. It will be only a matter of time before your face is all over the television. One of your victims is the son of a prosecutor in the DA's office. That was particularly bad judgment on your part, Mr Jarvis. I suggest you run very far, very fast.'

Gage heard the click as Tavilla hung up on him. 'Yeah, I'll do that,' he muttered, barely able to stay on his feet. 'I'll run like the fucking wind.'

He made it to his room and staggered through the door, closing it and throwing the deadbolt. He wasn't sure if he'd been followed, but he had to rest. If they came after him, he had the kids as hostages.

At least he now knew that Denny hadn't set him up to be caught at the restaurant. It had been way too easy to shoot at Dawson and the two men. If it had been a setup there would have been snipers on the rooftops, and there hadn't been. At a minimum, there would have been cops out in front of the restaurant, and that hadn't happened either.

He sat in the one chair in the room and closed his eyes, so damn tired. He needed food, water, money, and stitches in his god-damn shoulder. Not necessarily in that order. He still had about twenty-two hundred left in cash.

And he had a passport, courtesy of Reverend Blake. He wiped his bloody hand on his pants and pulled the passport from his pocket.

Ronald Lassiter.

He drew a ragged breath and let it out, choking back a sob. He was not going to break down. He did not have enough time.

Neither did he have nearly enough money. Two grand and some change wouldn't get him very far, even if he lived on the cheap, under the grid. *Need to get out of the country.* And go where? *Anywhere they don't extradite for murder.*

'Focus,' he snarled. He needed to get more money and fast, before he was tracked here.

His gaze landed on the two girls in the bed, still bound and gagged. He might use them as bargaining chips, but to do that he'd have to get close enough to the cops to be within the sights of their snipers. The kids were too small to be much of a shield and he could only keep hold on one at a time with his shoulder messed up.

But . . . One side of his mouth lifted. Lilah had money, and she loved the kids.

It was really the best of both worlds. He could get the money he needed and not have to kill the children. He wasn't going to make it too complicated. He didn't have the time or the concentration. He was becoming light-headed from loss of blood.

He stood up to get a glass of water and a sheet of paper. He'd make a list of the things he'd need to do and then he'd call Lilah.

He caught a glimpse of his reflection in the cloudy mirror over the dresser. 'Hi, Ronald,' he murmured to himself. 'Nice to meet you.'

Baltimore, Maryland,
Sunday 23 August, 4.20 P.M.

JD pulled a uniformed officer aside, and squinted at the man's badge. 'Officer Nelson, I need those two taken to the ER.' He pointed to Ford and Taylor. 'She was the intended target of this attack, so use all caution and for God's sake make her keep her head down. Him, too. He'll try to protect her.'

JD was downright rattled, in a way he hadn't been since . . . God, not since Stevie'd been shot a year and a half ago. He drew a breath, trying to calm down enough to think clearly.

'Are they under arrest?' the officer asked.

'No,' JD answered automatically, but once again he was wondering about Taylor Dawson. Either she had the worst luck ever or she was not as innocent as everyone else thought she was. Ever since she'd turned up, it had been one fucking disaster after another. Most of which were probably not her fault, he reasoned. But still. 'Watch the girl. I think she's okay, but . . . Just watch her. And when you get to the ER, stand guard until Agent Carter arrives. He's the boy's stepfather.'

'Yes, sir,' the officer said, and JD realized that the man wasn't much older than Ford, who JD had just called a boy. *God. When did everyone get so young?*

He pulled out his phone and flipped to the photo of Gage Jarvis that Thorne had given him the night before. He manipulated the photo so that only Gage's face could be seen. 'If you see this man, call for backup.'

Officer Nelson studied the photo, then looked up at JD with a hard nod. 'He's the shooter?'

'Most probably. Thank you.' JD waited until the officer had walked away before placing the call he dreaded like the plague. From his favorites, he tapped 'Boss', and told himself to breathe once again.

'Hey,' Joseph said when he picked up. 'What's up?'

'Where are you?' JD asked, instead of answering right away. 'And where is Daphne?'

305

'At my sister's event hall,' Joseph grunted. 'We're setting up for the rehearsal dinner.'

Goddammit. Holly's wedding had completely fled JD's mind. 'We've had a situation. A shooting. Clay was hit.'

Joseph sucked in a breath. 'How bad?'

'Bad. Bullet to his femoral artery.'

'Again?' Joseph gritted out, his voice as angry as JD had ever heard it.

'He's in the ambulance on his way to the hospital right now.'

'God. All right, so where's the shooter now?'

'Escaped, but he's bleeding too. Taylor shot him.'

'Taylor?'

'I know, right? I'm frankly amazed. Maggie said she could shoot, but this was a shot *I* might not have been able to make, and I was a sniper.' He could hear the distrust in his own voice and didn't care. 'She's not what she seems, Joseph.'

'All right,' Joseph said again, and it was clear he was trying to calm himself just like JD was. 'We'll deal with the puzzle of Taylor Dawson later. Was Gage Jarvis the shooter?'

'I think so, but I'm not sure. I'll have officers round up any security tapes that are available and we'll check. He left his car behind. Taylor shot it as well. It matches the description of the car that Cleon Perry drove, though license plates are different. Probably stolen.'

'I want Jarvis's face out on a BOLO. Yesterday.'

'I've already put his description out on the wire. I'll crop the photo Thorne gave me so that Tavilla's face doesn't show and I'll put it out there also.'

'Good. Now, you told me Clay was hurt and that Taylor shot the shooter. You haven't mentioned Ford and I know he was there. So . . .' Joseph's voice cracked. 'Tell me.'

'He's okay. He was shot. Three times. Twice in the back, but the Kevlar stopped it. Once in the leg, but it's barely a scratch. I doubt he'll even need stitches. He will need a clean shirt. He used his to stop Clay's bleeding. Probably saved his life. I just sent Ford and Taylor to the ER in a squad car. The officer driving them knows what Gage looks like. He'll stand guard.'

'Good work, JD.' Joseph cleared his throat roughly. 'I'll tell Daphne. Have you called Stevie yet?'

'No. She was my next call.'

'I'll take care of it. She's here, decorating with us. You get confirmation it was Gage Jarvis. Then crawl up Tavilla's ass and find out if he knows where Jarvis is hiding out.'

'Will he go to his brother, Denny?'

'If he does, we'll know. I put a tail on Denny and his wife, remember?'

'Right,' JD said, mentally kicking his brain to get the fuck into gear. 'I'll call you when I know anything.' He almost ended the call, when his brain finally engaged. 'Wait. Tavilla. If I'm able to contact him, I'll need to tell him how I knew to call him. I can't connect Thorne to this. Any ideas?'

Joseph paused for several seconds. 'It's unlikely, but not impossible, that Gage would tell his mother that he's got a job here in the city. Tell Tavilla that his mother gave you his name. We'll pick her up and put her in protective custody until we know what her connection is to all this. She might have been the one hiding him, after all. Good thinking, JD. We don't want to put Thorne in danger.'

'Because this is enough of a clusterfuck already,' JD muttered, hearing Clay's voice so clearly in his mind. *What's your plan to get my daughter and this little girl in and out of Giuseppe's in one* undamaged *piece?* 'We can't reverse it. We can only contain it now.'

'And in that vein,' Joseph added, 'don't use the photo that Thorne gave you. My gut says that Thorne's got someone inside Tavilla's organization. We might need that person someday, so don't compromise their cover. Find another photo. Did Gage have a mug shot taken when he was arrested for the domestic abuse charge?'

'I'll find something. I need to go now. Call me if you hear anything. I'll do the same.'

Nineteen

Taylor couldn't hold back her worried sigh when she gave Ford back his phone. They were sitting together on a bed in the ER, his arm around her shoulders, holding her tight. 'I'm sure your dad is fine,' he assured her in that rock-steady voice on which she'd come to depend in a rather terrifyingly short period of time. He kissed the top of her head. 'Both your dads.'

Taylor cuddled against his chest, frowning her worry even as she appreciated the warmth of his arms around her. The ER was freezing cold and she'd been shivering, which was how he'd convinced her to climb up on the bed with him and keep him company while he kept her warm. But really they were cuddling, and it was so very nice.

Except that Taylor hadn't been able to reach her dad in California all day. 'I'm afraid he's going to hear about all this on the news and think I'm hurt. I wish Detective Fitzpatrick would bring me my phone. Dad may have left me messages.'

She'd given Ford her phone to call 911 when Clay had first been shot, but the shot that had hit Ford in the back – she still hadn't gotten over the scare of that – had knocked him to his knees and her phone had flown out of his hand, landing somewhere at the crime scene.

'If JD finds it, he'll send it here. He promised, and he keeps his promises.'

Ford had said this to her twice before, but he still sounded

308

patient. 'I'm sorry,' she said. 'I know I'm OCD'ing on you.'

He rested his cheek against her hair. 'No apologies or I'll be forced to pull your hair like Clay did.' He tugged a handful playfully. 'Okay?'

'Yeah.' And then she sighed, thinking about Clay for the thousandth time in the last five minutes. They'd been told that he'd been taken up to surgery and that it could be hours before they heard anything.

She glanced up at the institutional-looking clock on the wall. The hands were moving painfully slowly. She and Ford had been there for about a half-hour. The doctor had dressed the graze on his leg with a bandage and recommended ice packs for his bruised back. From a medical standpoint he was free to go, but the police had asked them to stay in the ER wing until someone came to escort them home.

Not that they planned to leave the hospital while Clay was still in surgery. *Which is not my fault.* Or so she kept telling herself. She was trying not to take the blame for this, but it was hard to break habits ingrained over a lifetime.

'No, it's not your fault,' Ford murmured, stroking her hair.

She winced. 'Did I say that out loud?'

'Yep. Shhh. Just relax.'

'Easy for you to say,' she grumbled without heat. 'They gave you a painkiller.' Because the bullet graze on his leg wasn't very long, but it was deep. And because his back was a mass of bruises from the bullets caught by the Kevlar.

'And it's working. They offered you one. You should have taken it.'

Actually they'd offered her a Valium, because she'd had another mild panic attack when they'd arrived in the ER, but she'd declined. Still, she tried to relax for Ford's sake, matching his deep, even breathing. He continued stroking her hair lazily, and the combination had her drifting off, until two familiar twangs outside the curtain jerked her awake.

'Nooo,' Ford said sleepily, reaching for her when she scrambled off the bed. 'Don't go. Not yet. Not ready for you to go yet.'

Taylor kissed his forehead. He was a little loopy and she wondered if he meant now or in a month from now. 'Sshh. I'm not going anywhere for a while,' she whispered, and he settled. 'Your mother is here. Sounds like Maggie, too.'

''Kay,' he murmured.

The curtain was whisked back, revealing an anxious crowd – Daphne and Maggie, but also Joseph, Ford's half-brother Cole, and Holly and Dillon. An older woman who Taylor had never met before was hanging on to Maggie and all four women had clearly been crying.

Taylor was instantly alarmed. 'Did they give you news about Clay? Is he . . .' *Still alive?* 'Still okay?'

Daphne rushed to the bed and Taylor tried to step aside, only to be gathered up in a hard hug. 'No, no,' Daphne said hoarsely. 'Nothing new. It was just . . . Stevie and Tanner are in the waiting room. We went there first. They're both just wrecked.'

Taylor felt ill. Meeting her grandfather for the first time was to have been a joyous, happy occasion, but now it would be tense and sad.

Awkwardly Taylor patted Daphne's back when the woman didn't release her from the hug. 'Well, I'll just step outside to get out of your way. I know you want time with Ford. He really is okay, by the way. He's just sleeping because they gave him a pain-killer.'

'I'm not asleep,' Ford mumbled, his eyes still closed. 'Wish I were, but so not asleep. Let Taylor go, Mom. You're suffocating her.'

Hiccupping a laugh, Daphne released the hug, but held on to Taylor's arm. 'I know you're okay, son, largely due to this young lady.' To Taylor she added, 'I'll hug him to make sure and I'll cry some more and he'll be completely mortified, but I'll fall apart on him in a minute.'

'Thanks for the warning, Mom,' Ford said with affectionate sarcasm.

'Hush, son. Taylor, my mother wants to meet you. Mama, this is Clay's daughter. Taylor, this is my mother, Simone Montgomery.'

'It's nice to meet you, ma'am.' Taylor held out her hand but found herself engulfed in another tight hug. Daphne's had been hard and fierce, but Simone's was warm. And she smelled like chocolate cookies, as if she'd been baking.

'You saved my grandson's life today,' Simone said emotionally, her accent sharper, more pronounced than Daphne's. 'Clay's life too. JD told us all about it. Thank you, child.'

More awkward back-patting. Until Taylor remembered that her own grandmother, Clay's mother, had died before Taylor could hug her. So she took what this woman offered, sinking into the hug. 'You're welcome,' she said. 'But it wasn't like I meant to do it. It just seemed like the right thing to do at the moment.'

Simone let her go, cupping her cheeks with her palms, a lovely smile on her face. 'There was no "just" about it. It was amazing, child. Don't you hide your courage under a bushel – or your skill. Do not minimize the value of the lives you saved.' She smiled fondly at Ford, then dropped her hands from Taylor's face and frowned at her grandson in a quicksilver mood change. 'You shielded them with your body, Ford? Really? Are you *insane*? Kevlar is not foolproof, you silly boy.'

'My sentiments exactly,' Daphne said, hugging her son as hard as she'd hugged Taylor, eliciting a grunted curse. 'But I'm still proud of you, sweetheart.'

'Bruises, Mom. Watch the bruises on my back.'

Taylor tried to ease her way out of the room, but Maggie slipped an arm around her waist. 'Stay. You're not in the way. You're Clay's daughter and that alone makes you family.'

Everyone started talking at the same time then, and Taylor felt the panic rising. Surprisingly, it was Joseph who took pity on her.

'I need to ask Taylor a few questions,' he said brusquely. 'We'll be in the waiting room down the hall.' He led the way, with Cole and Dillon joining them. The women stayed to fuss over Ford.

Dillon collapsed in one of the waiting-room chairs. 'Too many people,' he huffed. 'Makes me nervous.'

'I agree,' Taylor said, leaning on the door frame. 'I'm still not comfortable with crowds. I lived in the middle of nowhere for too many years.'

311

'I like the barn better,' Dillon said. 'The barn is quiet. Hospitals are not quiet.'

She smiled at him. 'No, they're not,' she agreed. 'And yes, I like the barn better too.'

Cole was studying her carefully, and Taylor was once again surprised that the young man was only fifteen. He looked Ford's age, but it was largely due to his size.

'Did you really make that shot?' he asked suspiciously.

'Yeah,' she said unhappily. 'And now that I've had time to think about it, I wish I had killed him. Then he wouldn't still be out there.'

'If you'd killed him,' Joseph said dryly, 'there would have been a shitload of paperwork. But I understand the sentiment.'

'Did you really have questions for me?' she asked him.

He shook his head. 'Not really. You just looked like a wild animal ready to chew off its own leg to get away. I did want to talk to you, though. Maggie and Daphne passed on everything you told them. I would like to meet Frederick Dawson someday. He sounds impressive.'

'He is.' Taylor bit at her lip. 'And he's not answering my calls. He's going to be worried sick over me. I wish I had my phone.'

'Oh.' Joseph took a plastic evidence bag from his pocket, along with a pair of latex gloves. 'Fitzpatrick found it. It's still evidence, but you can check your messages and call logs to see if he's called you. I'll need it back after you're done, though.'

'Thank you.' Relieved, Taylor donned the gloves and checked her messages. Nothing from her dad. She tried dialing, but still no answer. 'He's not picking up on the house line either.' She tried her sister Daisy's phone with the same result. She handed the phone back to Joseph. 'Something's got to be wrong.'

'Don't borrow trouble,' Joseph suggested kindly. 'We've got enough of that to spare.'

'That's the truth,' Taylor murmured, then startled when the ER doors flew open. A medical team pushed a stretcher past the waiting room and Taylor narrowed her eyes when she saw the victim's face. When she *recognized* the victim's face.

She turned to Joseph once the stretcher had disappeared into an exam room. 'Joseph, that's Jazzie's grandmother. I'm almost sure of it. I've only seen her a few times, but she has the same color hair. It's dyed bright red. Kind of unforgettable. And kind of coincidental, too, especially with Lilah acting so strangely this afternoon. She was asking if the girls' grandmother had arrived with them, said they'd had a miscommunication over who would bring them to Giuseppe's for ice cream. But it was Lilah and Eunice who set the meeting up. They were the ones who made Jazzie's little two-word conversation with me into this raging big deal. Well, Jazzie did cry all over me, too, and I don't think she'd done that with anyone since her mother died. But still.'

Shut up. Stop talking. It was the nerves. She was running on fumes and the words kept spewing out. She snapped her teeth together to make herself stop, shrugging fitfully when Joseph gave her a speculative look, like he was doubting her sanity. 'Or maybe I'm just being ridiculous,' she said, embarrassed now. 'It's okay. My nerves are all jangled up and I know I sound crazy. You can say it.'

His lips quirked up, making him a very handsome man in a dangerous, brooding kind of way. Not Taylor's cuppa, but she could certainly see why Daphne was attracted. Taylor had had enough of danger and of looking over her shoulder to last a lifetime. She thought of Ford lying in the bed just a few minutes before, holding her. Grounding her.

Give me slow and steady as a rock any damn day of the week. Blond worked, too.

'Actually,' Joseph said, shocking the hell out of her, 'I was thinking that you sound perceptive. Let me check it out.'

'But it's Detective Fitzpatrick's case,' Taylor said with a frown. 'Is the hospital even allowed to talk to you?'

Joseph looked amused. 'Don't worry. They'll talk to me.'

Cole leaned on the side of the door opposite Taylor when Joseph was gone. 'Joseph is JD's *boss*,' he murmured.

Taylor shook her head. 'Can't be. One's FBI, the other BPD. One's federal, one's local.'

313

'But he is. Joseph heads up a joint task force. Violent Crimes . . . somethin' somethin'.' Cole waved his hand vaguely.

'Enforcement Team,' Dillon supplied, then rolled his eyes when Cole looked surprised. 'I read the news, Cole. Plus, he's gonna be my brother-in-law and he used to scare me to death, so I learned about his cases to impress him.' Dillon winced. 'So he wouldn't kill me.'

Cole smirked. 'He only wanted to kill you because he caught you and Holly makin' out the first time he met you.' He winked at Taylor. 'I heard that their clothes were flung all over the living room and poor Dillon here was bare-assed.'

Dillon gave a moan of embarrassment, his cheeks turning red. 'I was *not* bare-assed. Not completely anyway. And please don't remind me.'

Cole patted his shoulder. 'Well, all your hard work paid off. He doesn't want to kill you anymore.'

'You should read the paper too, Cole,' Dillon said seriously. 'He's your dad now. Read about his cases. If I could read fast like you, I'd read even more.'

'I will,' Cole promised, but Dillon rolled his eyes again and Taylor wondered how often they'd had similar conversations.

Joseph returned looking very troubled. 'She was brought in as a Jane Doe. A lady walking her dog discovered her on the ground under some shade trees in a park a few blocks from Lilah's apartment. She had no ID and no phone, but her head was pillowed on her empty handbag. She may have been drugged, but right now she's suffering from heart failure. They were using the defib paddles and it did not look good.'

Taylor sank into the chair next to Dillon, the sick feeling returning to her stomach in force. 'Lilah said that the girls were with her. If Granny is here, where are Jazzie and Janie?'

Joseph was already dialing his cell phone. 'Good question. I'm calling JD.'

monster in the closet

Baltimore, Maryland,
Sunday 23 August, 5.10 P.M.

Gage snapped a photo of the sleeping girls, then checked his list again. He'd prepped everything he needed to make the ransom call to Lilah. This was actually going to be . . . fun. Lilah had started this whole mess by pushing Valerie to report him for domestic abuse. It was only fair she pay for the cleanup.

On his phone's browser, he brought up a spoofing website and entered his mother's number as the caller and Lilah as the receiver. Lilah would answer a phone call from his mother.

'Eunice?' Lilah said, picking up on the first ring. 'Where are you? I got home from the mall and you and the girls were gone. You weren't at the restaurant and I've been looking for you everywhere.'

He said nothing, waiting for her to shut the fuck up.

'Eunice?' Lilah said uncertainly. 'Are you all right?'

Showtime. 'I have your girls,' he said calmly, not trying to disguise his voice. He wanted her to know who he was, because she'd know what he was capable of doing. She'd empty her bank account to keep the girls from ending up like their mother.

His declaration was met with silence. Dead silence. Finally, Lilah spoke. 'Who is this?' she asked quietly.

He smiled. It was her tell, going all quiet when she was one breath away from panic. She knew exactly who she was talking to. She was just stalling for time. 'If you want to see them again, you'll do exactly as I say.'

'Gage,' Lilah whispered. 'Why are you doing this?'

'I'm losing patience with you. If you want to see your nieces alive, you will go to your online bank account and move fifty thousand dollars into their grandmother's account. I'll take it from there. When I'm satisfied that I have the money in my possession, I will tell you where to find the girls. Do you understand me?'

Another stretch of silence. 'Where is Eunice? She was with the girls.'

'She's alive. The girls won't be if you don't obey. If you tell anyone, I will kill them. And know that if they die, it's on your head.'

315

'How . . .' An audible swallow. 'How do I know they're still alive?'

He knew she'd ask. He already had a separate website loaded on his phone's browser that would allow him to spoof a text, again from his mother's phone number as the sender. He attached the photo he'd taken of the sleeping girls and hit SEND.

He knew the moment Lilah received it. She uttered a hoarse cry followed by a sob. Several shuddering breaths. 'You . . . sonofabitch. You tied them up. They're just little girls. You're a monster.'

'You have one hour. Fifty thousand. Now, go.'

He hung up, satisfied that she'd honor the demand. He really needed three or four times that amount, but he'd have to make do. Live simply. Quit using.

Giving up coke would save a bucket of bucks right there.

He choked on the sharp suck of air that seemed to stab his lungs from the inside out. *Goddammit. Breathe in, Gage.*

He closed his eyes. *Not Gage anymore. Not Gage ever again. I'm Ronald.* Ronald Lassiter.

Breathe out, Ronald. Think about something else. Think about what you'll do next.

Because Lilah would give him the money. She'd be too scared not to.

Once she had, he'd stash it in the offshore account he'd set up years before to hide assets from Valerie. Getting into his mother's accounts would not be a problem because, like her PIN numbers, she never changed her password. It was always his father's name with the years he was born and had died.

He'd have to open another account in Ronald Lassiter's name and transfer it all. And then he'd get the hell out of the country and hightail it somewhere else. Somewhere warm and sunny.

He was thinking Mexico. From there, he'd make his way into Nicaragua, which had no extradition treaties with the U.S. His Spanish wasn't too bad. *And coke is probably cheaper there. Wouldn't have to completely quit. Just cut back. Use recreationally. You've done it before.*

And if he needed a job, there were always the cartels.

He had one more call to make. He dialed Denny directly, not bothering with the spoofing site.

'I thought I told you not to call me anymore,' Denny stated, bypassing any greeting.

Ma hasn't called him yet. Nor had he seen the news. If either had happened, Denny would have been too furious to speak coherently, but he didn't sound angry at all. 'I just wanted you to know that I'm leaving town later tonight. I've got a ride that leaves after sundown.'

'How very Wyatt Earp of you,' Denny said sarcastically. 'Goodbye, Gage.'

'Just a minute,' Gage snapped. 'I just wanted to be sure you know that if I see any cops sniffing around my place before sundown, the deal is off.'

'What deal?'

'The deal that I stay away from your wife and kids.'

Denny huffed like a bull. 'Don't you dare touch them.'

'I won't. Not unless you break your end of the deal. At any time. Now or in the future.'

'I *said* that I *wouldn't*.'

'And I want you to remember that, little brother. You say one word about me and everything you are, everything you own, and everyone you love will unravel before your eyes.'

Denny sighed wearily. 'Fine, fine. I hear you, Gage. I hear you and I fucking tremble. Is that why you called?'

It didn't sound like Denny was actually trembling, but the resignation in his voice would have to be enough. 'It'll do, little brother. It'll do.'

Gage hung up and went over to the bed. Janie was still snuffling softly in her sleep, but he could tell Jazzie was awake even though she was pretending to be asleep. He'd seen her flinch a few times during his conversation with Lilah. 'You might as well open your eyes,' he said caustically. 'I know you're awake.' He fumbled with the knot he'd tied in the soft rope he'd bound them with, trying to loosen it one-handed. He finally managed it, then removed her gag. He left the bonds on Janie in case she woke up. 'Get up and help me.'

Cautiously Jazzie got up and stood next to the bed, as far away from him as she could. Her eyes grew wide when she saw the blood. 'W-what h-happened to you?' she whispered.

'None of your business.'

She was trembling so hard he could see it from across the room. 'Is T-Taylor d-dead?'

'Yeah,' he lied flatly. 'Sorry, kid. Get over here and help me.' He threw a threatening look at Janie. '*Now.*'

Jazzie took stumbling steps, clearly willing her feet to move. Damn, the kid had guts. Too bad she wasn't his.

He sank into the chair. 'Help me take off my shirt. I need to clean the wound so that I can stitch it.'

Her expression grew even more horrified. 'You m-mean I have to t-touch it?'

He might have laughed if he didn't hurt so damn much. 'Yeah. This ain't no picnic for me either, kid. Now do it!'

She jumped, closed her eyes, pursed her lips, then deliberately opened her eyes and dropped her chin so that she looked only at the buttons. Her skinny, trembling fingers loosened them one at a time. She stepped back when she was finished, staring at the blood-soaked shirt he'd taken from the clothesline to put pressure on the wound.

She was cringing. 'It's bloody.'

'That's because I got shot,' he snapped. 'You're supposed to be smart. Now pull it off. Gently!' he hissed when her shaking hands yanked at the balled-up shirt. He'd nearly passed out when he'd pressed it to the wound. He hadn't expected taking it off to be even worse, but it was.

Jazzie gagged when she saw his shoulder.

Again, he couldn't blame her. He clenched and flexed his fingers. At least there was no nerve damage. But the bullet was still in there. *Shit, damn, fuck.* This was going to be really bad. 'In the drawer. Get the bottle.' He'd grabbed the whiskey when he'd raided Val's liquor cabinet after he'd killed her. He didn't actually like whiskey, so he'd drunk everything else first and had even bought more of what he liked, leaving the whiskey largely untouched. There should

318

still be enough to get him hammered so he could get the fucking bullet out.

Jazzie obeyed, still shaking so hard that she looked like a walking marionette. The amber liquid sloshed in the bottle when she brought it back to him. He took a few healthy swigs, then wiped his mouth with the back of his hand.

'Okay. Here is what you're gonna do. Are you listening?'

She nodded like a timid mouse, arms crossed over her chest. She looked like she was going to throw up.

'You better not hurl, kid, because you'll be cleaning it up. Yours and mine.' Because he was having to grit his teeth against the nausea as it was. He dug in his pocket for his blade and she whimpered when she saw it. 'Shut up,' he snarled. 'I'm not going to use this on you. Not if you shut the fuck up. I've got to get this bullet out of my arm. While I'm doing that, you're going to be my nurse. Got it? You're going to fold those towels up and press them against the wound to soak up the blood.'

He only hoped he had enough towels.

She swallowed hard and nodded.

'And Jazzie?' He stared into her terrified eyes. 'Do not try anything. I will do what I need to do to get away from here alive. Do you understand me?'

A flash of fury cut through her fear. 'Yeah,' she whispered, and he was impressed that she could imbue one little word with so much hate.

'Good. Now go into the bathroom and find my shaving kit.' His old man's shaving kit was the one thing he'd actually kept during the past three years living on his own. She obeyed silently, returning to hand him the kit with an angry set to her mouth.

'Good for you, kid. Keep that piss and vinegar. It'll help you when everything gets real.'

Although this here was about as real as it got, he supposed. Still, it wasn't bad advice for a guy to give a kid who wasn't even his. He took another few swigs of whiskey to calm the twitching in his hands, then dug out a little pre-packaged sewing kit, an amenity from a hotel stay a million years ago. In another life.

He looked at his arm and cringed. Digging out that fucking bullet was going to fucking hurt. He wasn't drunk enough for this yet.

Stalling for time – yeah, he was man enough to admit it – he checked Eunice's bank account on his phone and a grim smile twisted his lips. Lilah had moved fifty grand into it. Promptly. So promptly that he realized he should have asked for more.

He eyed the kid. She was watching him like he was a snake, poised to strike. 'I'm going to make another phone call. I'm counting on you continuing to behave intelligently. You will say nothing that I do not tell you to say. Got it?'

She nodded jerkily, her eyes filling with tears. 'Y-y-yeah.'

'Not that I really need to worry,' he taunted, twisting the metaphorical blade while holding the real one with a steadiness that surprised him. *Huh. Whiskey really works.* He'd have to keep that in mind. 'Before you got out the second "h-h" in "h-h-h-help", I'd have more than enough time to hang up.'

She flinched. 'I . . . *hate* you.' She'd expelled the word on a harsh breath, and he smiled at her.

'That's a good technique, kid. You should remember that. Now keep your trap shut or Janie's face won't be so pretty anymore.' He had no intention of touching Janie with the knife or anything else, but the threat had an immediate effect on Jazzie.

She went so white that he thought she'd pass out. 'Y-y-you're a v-very bad man.'

'And don't you forget it, kid,' he said soberly, a surprise considering how much whiskey he'd just chugged.

Using Ma's spoofed number, he called Lilah again.

She picked up before the first ring ended. 'Eunice?' she asked tentatively.

'No,' Gage said.

A sob. 'I gave you what you wanted. I transferred the money to Eunice's account.'

'And I'm grateful,' he said mildly.

'So tell me where I can find them. You promised.'

'Oh, I will. But not just yet. The girls are okay. Not terribly happy at the moment,' he said, looking Jazzie in the eye, 'but okay. If you want them to stay okay, you'll make another deposit into my ma's account. Make this one an even hundred.'

Another gasp. 'A hundred thousand dollars! I don't have that much.'

'I think you do. You're a fuckin' spinster whose idea of fun is a jog around the block.' He realized that *fuckin'* and *spinster* were probably oxymoronic, but he'd blame that on the whiskey too.

'The police are looking for—'

'You called them?' Gage snapped.

'No!' Lilah cried. 'You told me not to so I didn't. I've done what you said to do. Everything. I didn't have to say a word to them. They know that you were the shooter today. Your face is all over the news. You won't—'

Gage forced his body to relax. He believed her. She hadn't told. Besides even if she had, they didn't know where to find him. Only Denny did and he would not risk his family's safety. He woudn't tell. *So I'm okay. For now anyway.* 'Please tell me you're not about to say that I won't get away with this,' he interrupted, making his tone bored. 'Yeah, the cops are hunting me. Which means I have absolutely nothing to lose.' He let the words hang, satisfied when she exhaled in defeat.

'Okay. But this is all I have and that's the honest truth.'

'Okay,' he said agreeably. It might be all she had in a checking account, but she had more. It might be tied up in stocks or property, but it was there somewhere. 'Five minutes. Or . . . this.'

He snapped a photo of his knife at the sleeping Janie's throat, and texted it, still spoofing his ma's phone number. Lilah's strangled cry was music to his ears.

'You *bastard*. You really are a monster.'

'Yeah, yeah, yeah. You forgot "evil",' he deadpanned. 'Five minutes, Lilah.' He hung up and put the phone securely back in his pocket, because Jazzie was watching it like a hawk. *She's planning her escape.* Damn, the kid had guts.

He was relieved he wasn't going to have to kill her.

Baltimore, Maryland,
Sunday 23 August, 6.15 P.M.

The ER waiting room was so tensely quiet that Ford found himself fidgeting in his chair like a kid in church. Once he'd been officially released from the ER, almost everyone had gone to the OR waiting room to sit with Stevie and Tanner. His mother, Maggie and Joseph stayed with him and Taylor in the ER, waiting for JD to arrive.

Maggie had officially identified Eunice Jarvis and the hospital had called Lilah to inform her. They'd wanted to call Denny Jarvis, the younger of her two sons, but Joseph asked them to hold off on that because nobody knew what Denny's role was in all this. It had pained Joseph to do so, especially after the doctor told him that Eunice's prognosis was not good at all, but the lives of two girls might lie in the balance.

Taylor was slouched in the chair beside Ford, hands folded over her stomach, her eyes closed. She needed some rest, but Ford knew better than to hope she was asleep. Her body practically vibrated even though she sat statue-still.

Ford got up and walked to the open doorway of the waiting room, checking the hallway once again. No Lilah. He turned back to find his mother watching him with concern, and it made him surly. Because he knew she looked at him that way often, ever since he'd been abducted over a year and a half before. It made him feel suffocated. Like she was waiting for him to fall so that she could bandage him up.

She didn't mean to, and under the circumstances, she was probably entitled. Still, it made him itch for some space. *Some room to breathe.*

Shit. Taylor's panic attacks were apparently catching. He forced his mind elsewhere. 'Who's got Cordelia?' he asked.

'I dropped her off with Lucy,' Maggie answered. 'She was going to take all the kids to the aquarium. We, uh, didn't tell Cordy about Clay. They wouldn't have let her in the waiting room and it seemed cruel to make her suffer without Stevie.'

'That makes sense,' Ford said, his chest hurting for the little girl.

322

Cordelia had been through so damn much. *Clay has to be okay, God. You can't take him away from that child*. He closed his eyes, another thought hitting him hard. 'Stevie's pregnant.'

Maggie and Daphne shared a sigh. 'We know,' Daphne said. 'We were with her when Joseph told her about the shooting. The first thing she did was spread her hand over her stomach and say "Not again."'

Because Stevie's first husband had been shot and killed while she'd been pregnant with Cordelia.

'It's not going to be an issue, because Clay will be okay,' Daphne said firmly. But her lips quivered, ruining all that wonderful, if not bogus, optimism.

Ford kissed his mother's cheek, then returned to sit next to Taylor. He didn't ask her how she was, because he hated it when people did that to him. So he just held her hand, unsurprised when she squeezed so hard that a few bones audibly popped.

The silence was broken by the trill of a cell phone – his mother's. She frowned at the screen for a moment. 'I have to take this,' she said. 'It's work,' she added when both he and Taylor tensed. She got up and moved to the window, where the signal was better, her quiet murmur nearly inaudible. She obviously didn't want them to listen, so Ford attempted to distract himself and Taylor.

'Clay will be okay, y'know.' Ford repeated his mother's words, understanding that he needed to say them as much as Taylor needed to hear them.

She opened her eyes and met his. 'He knew we'd be there,' she said quietly.

Ford frowned, confused. 'Who? Clay?'

'No. The shooter. Who may or may not have been Jazzie's father.'

Joseph looked up from his laptop to give Taylor his attention. 'It was definitely Gage Jarvis. Detective Rivera got the security tapes from area businesses and he's positively ID'd Jarvis fleeing the scene.'

'Poor Jazzie,' Taylor said softly. 'I was kind of hoping it wasn't her dad, you know?'

Joseph's smile was kind. 'Yeah, I get that. By the way, Gage is hurt pretty badly. The footage showed that you got him in the right arm. He was bleeding a lot.'

'Good,' she said fiercely. 'He knew we'd be there meeting Lilah and Jazzie. He opened fire as soon as Lilah started talking to us.' She drew a breath. 'He was shooting at me. He shot Ford and Clay because they were blocking his line of fire.' The look she gave Joseph was self-deprecating. 'But you've already figured all this out.'

'That Gage knew you were coming, yes,' Joseph said. 'But keep going.'

'Well, he knew we'd be there, and when, but I don't think he knew what I looked like. He had to wait until Lilah spoke to us. If he'd been targeting Jazzie, he wouldn't have shot until she arrived, because once he started shooting, he'd have shown his hand and Jazzie would have been whisked away. Not only did he know we were coming, I think he knew Jazzie *wasn't*.' She grimaced. 'Because maybe he's already got her.'

'Unless Jazzie wasn't a target,' Joseph said.

Taylor scoffed. 'Why wouldn't she be? If she saw him either killing her mother or afterward, why wouldn't he want to silence her?'

'Okay,' Joseph said, 'let's assume she *is* a target. Why wait until today?'

'She's been watched pretty carefully,' Ford said. 'Maybe he didn't have a chance.' And then Joseph's meaning clicked in his head. *Oh.* 'JD said they'd kept it out of the press and the police reports that Jazzie was hiding behind the chair and had seen her mother's killer. Maybe he just found out.'

'All right,' Joseph said. 'Who told him?'

Taylor puffed out a breath. 'The only people – other than us – who knew that Jazzie found her mother's body first were Lilah, Janie and maybe Eunice. I'm not clear on how much Lilah might have told her, but my money's still on Jarvis's mom. I'm betting Lilah wouldn't give him the time of day.'

Joseph nodded. 'I agree. But Lilah hadn't told Eunice that Jazzie was hiding behind the chair. She didn't trust her not to blab it to everyone and put Jazzie in danger, even if it was inadvertently. How would Eunice have known?'

Taylor bit at her bottom lip. 'Lilah was so excited that Jazzie talked yesterday. She probably told Eunice that.'

'She did,' Maggie confirmed. 'Lilah called me after she left with the girls yesterday. She wanted to make sure that I'd heard about Jazzie's breakthrough. I could hear Eunice chattering in the background. They were both so excited.' She frowned, concentrating. 'Eunice was on the phone, too, I think. Her voice is loud, so I heard her talking, but there were gaps, like the person at the other end of the line was talking too. She was telling someone that this was a huge breakthrough.'

'That might have been enough,' Taylor said tentatively. 'If Gage learned that Jazzie was talking and that Lilah and Eunice were heralding it as a huge deal . . .' She trailed off, clearly discomfited by Joseph's even gaze. She swallowed hard and continued. 'Gage is smart, right? Fitzpatrick told us this morning that he framed that homeless man – what was his name? The one who was murdered yesterday morning.'

'Toby Romano,' Joseph told her.

'Yes, him. How exactly did Gage frame him?'

Joseph hesitated, contemplating, then shrugged slightly. 'Gage left a brooch where Romano could easily find it. Romano was picked up after trying to pawn it, but Fitzpatrick didn't believe Romano was guilty. Gage became impatient because Romano hadn't been arrested yet, so he upped the ante by planting some of Valerie's stolen jewelry in Romano's pockets so that it would be found with his body. That's the theory, anyway.'

Taylor leaned forward, her expression intense. 'Well, if I were Gage, and I was impatient that Romano hadn't been arrested, and all of a sudden people are excited about Jazzie's talking when she hasn't since the murder, I'd worry. I'd wonder what Fitzpatrick knew that I didn't. I'd be afraid of what Jazzie knew – and what she'd said to her therapist.'

Joseph nodded. 'So would I.'

'And,' Ford said, pushing back the anger that once again roared

325

to life inside him, 'he was waiting for Taylor, not Jazzie.' Anger mixed with sick dread. 'He has his daughters, Joseph.'

Joseph exhaled a weary sigh. 'I'd have to agree. With all of it.'

'What are the odds those babies are still alive?' Maggie asked, voice trembling.

'Not good,' Joseph admitted.

Ford felt the shudder that passed through Taylor and he squeezed her hand. It wasn't fair. Jazzie was just a little girl and none of this was fair. Then again, the bad things that had happened to him and Taylor weren't fair either.

'And now Gage's mama shows up in the ER after being abandoned in a park,' Taylor murmured.

Ford knew the park where Eunice had been found. 'That park has a huge playground.'

Taylor flinched. 'My God. Lilah said the girls had gone out with Eunice. That woman delivered her granddaughters to him. What kind of person does that?'

'Eunice never thought Gage was guilty,' Maggie said quietly. 'She didn't think he was capable of the violence used against Valerie. But she loves those girls. She wouldn't have just delivered them to him like lambs to the slaughter. Gage must have gotten to his mother. Manipulated her into bringing the girls to him.'

'Guess Eunice figured out her mistake a little too late,' Ford said bitterly, thinking of how frightened the girls had to be. If they were still alive. *Please let them be alive.* 'But . . . the hospital told Lilah that Gage's mother was here, that she was in critical condition, that the girls weren't with her in the park. Why hasn't Lilah called the police?'

'I think *that* is the question we need to focus on,' Joseph said. 'Lilah doesn't strike me as an irresponsible woman. Either the girls are safely with her, or something else is going on.'

Ford was about to ask what Joseph's team was doing to find out when a creative curse uttered loudly by the window had the four of them turning toward his mother, who was still engaged in a conversation on her cell phone that had suddenly become intense.

Taylor glanced at the clock on the wall. Clay had been in surgery for almost two hours. 'Is Daphne discussing Clay? She looks upset.'

Joseph shook his head. 'No. She's still dealing with her office.'

Taylor watched Daphne warily, as if she didn't believe Joseph's claim. Joseph, to his credit, didn't seem rattled, but that was just the kind of guy he was. Ford was happy his mother had found someone to take care of her. For just a little while, he'd thought he might have found that for himself. *You still might. She hasn't gotten on that plane back to California yet. And planes do fly both ways. And they have engineering firms in California too.*

'Your mom fell apart when I told her about Clay,' Joseph murmured, cutting into his thoughts. 'And when I told her that you'd been shot? I thought she was going to pass out.'

'I'm all right,' Ford said, quietly but firmly.

'She knows that. That's what's keeping her going right now.' Joseph cleared his throat, then continued at a normal volume. 'And I'm keeping our promise to Clay. JD promised that he'd keep Taylor safe. I'm your personal bodyguard until he gets here.'

'When will that be?' Taylor asked.

Joseph's slight smile was enigmatic. 'When he gets here.'

Baltimore, Maryland,
Sunday 23 August, 6.20 P.M.

JD was losing his patience and his temper. He knocked hard on Lilah Cornell's apartment door – for the umpteenth time. 'Miss Cornell, this is Detective Fitzpatrick. Please open this door! I need to speak to you.'

He knew she was in there. Or somebody was in there. He'd seen the slight movement of the drapes in her living-room window, and her car was parked out front. But she refused to answer his attempts – or those of anyone else – to communicate with her.

The hospital had called her cell and home phones to tell her about Eunice. She'd answered neither and they'd left messages. She'd called back almost immediately, telling them that she'd be there as soon as she could. But she hadn't shown up, and both he and Joseph were concerned. JD had called her, but she hadn't answered his calls either. So he'd come by in person. And now the seconds were ticking away in his head as he knocked, called Lilah's phone, and cajoled through the door.

If those little girls had been taken by their asshole father, their time was quickly running out.

That their asshole father was hiding in their apartment was a real possibility. That Lilah was in there hurt was also a possibility. No one had seen her get hit by any of the bullets, but nor could anyone say with any certainty that she hadn't been. It had been too chaotic.

He knocked again. 'Miss Cornell, if you do not open this door, I'll be forced to break it down. I'm concerned that you were injured in the shooting.'

'I'm fine, Detective,' she said through the door. 'Everything is fine.'

JD frowned. 'And the girls?'

'They're fine too, but they're exhausted. They're sleeping – or trying to. You're making enough noise to wake the dead.'

His frown deepened. 'Can you please let me in? I'd like to check on them.'

'I can assure you, Detective,' she said, her tone abruptly changing from that of the caring aunt he'd spoken with over the last month to one that was commanding and more than a little harsh. Suddenly she sounded like the attorney she was. 'I know when a child simply needs sleep. Eunice took them to the park to run off some energy because Jazzie was nervous about meeting with Miss Dawson. Janie said that Jazzie had a panic attack when they couldn't find their grandmother, that she was terrified. They thought that maybe she'd lost them too and had gone home, thinking that was where they'd go. They had no idea that she'd collapsed.

'They walked home, and Jazzie was in a near emotional meltdown by the time they got here, terrified that she'd been abandoned. Plus the heat didn't help. They were overheated and dehydrated. When I got back, they were both in the living room, cooling down and dozing off. Janie told me what had happened. Jazzie wrote on her notepad that she didn't want to see Miss Dawson today. I put them to bed and took a bubble bath myself. That is why I didn't answer your calls or your banging on my door. Now you're up to speed, Detective.'

She spoke too carefully and he wished he could see her face, because he did not believe a word she said. It was too pat. Too rehearsed. 'I'd like to see you for myself, ma'am.'

'Oh, for the love of—' She jerked the door open, just a crack, but it was enough to see that her expression was annoyed and she wore a filmy robe that left very little to the imagination. Startled, he yanked his gaze back up to her face, which was now grim. 'There. Now you see me. Are you satisfied, Detective? Now please. You need to leave me alone. Jazzie does not want to talk to Miss Dawson. You need to respect that.' She started to close the door, but he held it open with the palm of his hand.

No, he was not satisfied. She was lying. She hadn't once asked about Eunice or the aftermath of the shooting. She hadn't asked if anyone was hurt. The woman he'd dealt with for the last month would not be so callous and cold.

Her expression appeared to be annoyed, but her eyes and the set of her mouth were grim. Plus, she hadn't taken a bubble bath. If she'd just gotten out of the tub, he would have detected some scent, and there was none, but he did smell sweat. The room behind the front door was cool. He could feel the temperature difference from where he stood. She shouldn't be sweating. The robe was a ruse, intended to startle him into leaving. She was terrified and hiding it well, no doubt thanks to her experience prosecuting criminals.

JD wondered if she was being held at gunpoint, or if Gage was threatening the children to ensure her cooperation. He leaned forward, trying to see as much as he could of the apartment through the cracked door. It was impossible to know if anyone was there.

'Miss Cornell, your brother-in-law Gage Jarvis was the shooter this afternoon. He was trying to kill Miss Dawson. He nearly succeeded in killing Healing Hearts' head of security. Mr Maynard is in surgery. He may not make it.' Even as he said the words, JD prayed he was wrong, but he wanted to paint the most accurate and frightening picture for Lilah Cornell.

329

She drew a breath. 'I'm sorry to hear that,' she said quietly. 'I'll pray for him.'

He gave her an intense look and silently mouthed, 'Is Gage in there with you?'

She shook her head. 'No,' she said aloud. 'There is no one here but me and my nieces. Now I need you to go. If you continue to knock on my door, I'll file a complaint with BPD.'

JD ground his teeth, beyond frustrated. 'If he calls you, please let me know.'

'I will.' She started to close the door.

'Miss Cornell,' he said urgently. 'He was shot this afternoon. He's wounded. He may come to you for help.'

Her laugh bubbled out, just shy of hysterical. 'I can assure you that Gage Jarvis will not be asking me for help. Now, good day.'

She closed the door with a snap and he could hear the deadbolts being turned.

He stood there for several seconds, breathing evenly and attempting to stem his frustration. He needed a better plan. He needed to see inside that apartment. He needed to know if those girls were really safe or not.

His gut told him they were not. For now, he'd have to treat this as a hostage situation until he knew more. He sent a flurry of texts to Joseph, updating him on the status and recommending a hostage retrieval team.

Joseph texted back right away. *Agree. Will send agents to maintain surveillance on LC's apt and all exits. U focus on finding Jarvis in case he is not inside. Might be somewhere else with easier escape route. Also his wound is bad, he will need med attn.*

That was true, JD allowed. This apartment building would be hard to escape from, and Gage had shown a talent for planning. If he were hurt and bleeding, Lilah Cornell would be the last person he'd allow to take care of him.

Any sign of Gage at Denny's house? JD texted.

None yet, came Joseph's reply. *Will assign Hector to head HRT.*

That was a good choice. Hector had been trained in hostage retrieval. *Okay. ETA and ID of surveillance agent?*

Ingram is 15 min out.

Excellent, JD thought. Agent Ingram was new to their team, but had proven himself to be a good cop. *Okay. Will keep u up to speed.*

Pocketing his phone, JD leaned on the wall outside Lilah's door and waited, listening for any sound of life inside, but he heard nothing. Her apartment was as quiet as a tomb.

Baltimore, Maryland,
Sunday 23 August, 6.25 P.M.

Ford and Taylor both jumped when Joseph's phone started buzzing like a swarm of bees. They'd been sitting silently, hand-in-hand, waiting for news of some kind. Maggie had gone back up to the surgery waiting room to sit with Stevie, and Daphne was still on the phone, her tone alternating between whispered conversation and loud cursing. Whatever she was talking about, it didn't appear to be good.

Taylor opened her mouth, no doubt to ask if he had information on either Clay or the little girls, but Joseph shook his head before she could speak.

'These are all from JD,' he said. He fired off a series of responses, then looked up to meet their expectant gazes. 'He's spoken to Lilah Cornell and she claims the girls came home from the park on their own and were sleeping. She would not allow him to come in and he doesn't believe her story.'

'Could Gage be inside?' Taylor asked.

'Possibly. I'm assigning a hostage retrieval team.'

Taylor chewed on her lower lip. 'She accepted a call from the hospital, but won't accept calls from the police?'

'Technically she didn't accept the call from the hospital,' Joseph corrected. 'They left her a message to call them back and she did.'

'Did they tell her in the message that Eunice was here?' she asked.

Joseph shook his head. 'No. They just told her to call back. Why?'

'Calling the hospital back makes it sound like she was worried that someone might be hurt. Like maybe the girls. Because she didn't

331

know. They're not there with her.' She shrugged. 'Lilah's not going to talk to you, but she did try to talk to the three of us earlier – Ford, Clay and me. Maybe she'll talk to Ford and me if we go over there.'

Joseph laughed, and it wasn't a pretty sound. 'And there I was thinking you had an actual brain in your head. One of your trio is fighting for his life right now. In what parallel universe did you actually think I'd let either of you do that?'

Taylor didn't flinch and Ford respected the hell out of that. He also agreed one hundred percent with Joseph that Taylor shouldn't be anywhere near Lilah, proximity-wise, but talking to her? Yeah, that seemed like a better idea than having JD bang his head against a wall.

'In the universe where two little girls have likely been taken by a killer,' Taylor said evenly. 'You can try to force Lilah to talk to you, but she won't. Not until she knows the kids are safe. Or dead. One or the other.' She stood and looked at her clothing, spattered in Clay's blood. 'I'd like a shower and a change of clothes, but what I need is to go to the OR waiting room now and sit with Stevie. And meet my grandfather. I've put it off long enough.' Her smile had a razor-sharp edge. 'I think I have enough of a brain to find the surgery floor without help, as long as it's safe to travel across the hospital. But of course I'll follow your wishes.'

Joseph's voice was mild but his eyes were narrowed. 'You'll need an escort. I'll get an officer to walk you up.' He typed a text into his phone and hit SEND. Within a minute, a uniformed policewoman stood in the doorway.

'What do you need, Agent Carter?' she asked.

'This witness needs to be escorted to the OR waiting room. Taylor, stay with Officer Meyer. Please.' Joseph waited until Taylor was gone. 'Will she do as we ask, Ford? Please tell me she's smart enough not to try leaving the hospital to talk to Lilah herself.'

'She is,' Ford said. 'She won't like it, but she'll be safe for Clay's sake.' *And I'll make sure of it.* He'd follow her up to the surgery waiting room after he found out who his mother had been talking to. He'd heard Daphne say the words 'IT' and 'breach', and neither sounded good.

His mother finally finished her call and came to sit next to Joseph. 'Damn stupid phone. The only good reception is next to the window.'

'Well?' Joseph asked.

'The silent alarm that IT put in the police report database was tripped. Someone accessed Valerie Jarvis's murder file an hour ago using Missy Jarvis's account.'

'Denny's wife, the woman who clerks for you?' Ford asked, staying calm on the outside, but inside he was snarling. *That's the connection.* JD had known that Gage was getting insider information through either Denny or his wife. Or if JD hadn't known, he'd at least suspected. Yet he'd still sent Taylor into what had become an explosively dangerous situation. And now Clay was fighting for his life. *Sonofabitch, JD.*

Ford wanted to hit something. Hell, he wanted to hit JD, but he forced the fists he'd clenched to relax. JD had to be feeling like shit. *As well he should.* Still, getting angry with him on Taylor's behalf wasn't going to make matters any better and it was in stressful times like this that people said things they couldn't take back. So he bit his tongue and waited for his mother's answer.

Daphne nodded, troubled. 'Missy's account was used, yes, but the access was established remotely from her house. She's been at her sons' softball games all afternoon. Her husband's at their house right now and has been all afternoon. Alone.'

Ford was surprised. 'You put a tail on him?' That was a cop thing. Not a prosecutor thing.

'Joseph did. On both of them. I'm glad we know for sure that Missy didn't do it.'

Joseph sighed. 'It's safe to assume that her husband somehow got access to her codes. Let's hope she didn't give them to him willingly.'

'I never liked that man,' Daphne stated baldly. 'Denny was always . . . weaselly. Like a kid who was proud because he thought he'd gotten away with something.'

'At least now we'll have cause to get a warrant for his phone records,' Joseph said. 'Before this we didn't. If he's been in contact with his brother, we'll find that out.'

'How long will it take?' Ford asked. 'If Gage has Jazzie and Janie . . .' He didn't want to think about that. He knew the terror of being abducted, and he'd been twenty at the time. Jazzie was only eleven. Janie was only five. *Poor babies must be simply terrified. If they're still alive.* And even if they were dead, there was still urgency. 'Not to mention that Taylor's a target until this guy is caught.'

Joseph's expression remained resolute, but his eyes revealed that he was more affected than he let on. 'I know that. I know all of that. I'll make it happen as quickly as possible.' He lifted a brow. 'If you leave right now, you can catch up to Taylor and Officer Meyer. Make sure Taylor knows that I'll have her followed too if she's foolish enough to try talking to Lilah Cornell on her own.'

Ford's temper bubbled. They hadn't thought her foolish this morning when she'd agreed to JD's crazy scheme. He was about to open his mouth to say so when his mother broke in.

'"Foolish" is a harsh word, Joseph. Taylor seems like the kind of young woman to overplan everything.' His mother spoke softly, derailing Ford's temper. 'She's abundantly cautious. But she's been put through an emotional wringer and she might be . . . less cautious. And if that happens? Ford, you may be the only voice of reason she'll listen to. You may need to be wise enough for both of you.'

Ford met his mother's eyes, gave her a nod. 'I won't let her be "less cautious", Mom.' But the next person who called Taylor foolish or stupid or who questioned her brain would hear all the words he was holding back.

Twenty

Baltimore, Maryland,
Sunday 23 August, 6.40 P.M.

'Hold the elevator, please!'

It was Ford's voice, so Taylor stopped the elevator doors, allowing him to slip through and ignoring the scowl on Officer Meyer's face. 'He could have been the guy who shot at you,' Meyer scolded. 'I can't keep you safe if you allow just anyone this close to you. Next time, let him wait for the next elevator.'

Taylor supposed she had Joseph to blame for Meyer's condescending attitude. *Actual brain, my ass.* She managed not to roll her eyes at Meyer, smiling sweetly instead. 'I'm sorry. I'm a little new at being the target of a homicidal maniac. I don't know all the rules yet.'

Beside her, Ford snickered, and Meyer frowned at him too. 'Kids,' she muttered.

Taylor felt her cheeks heat in anger. 'I'm twenty-three, Officer Meyer,' she said coldly.

'Then stop taking stupid risks or you won't live to see twenty-four,' Meyer retorted.

Ford had gone too still. 'Her biggest stupid risk was an op sanctioned by the FBI/BPD taskforce that promised to keep her safe while dangling her as bait for a killer,' he snapped.

Taylor squeezed his hand. 'It's okay, Ford.'

'No, it's not,' he said, visibly struggling for control of his temper. 'I didn't see them questioning your intelligence when you agreed to their ridiculous scheme.'

She leaned up on her toes to kiss his cheek. 'Calm down,' she said softly. He jerked a nod, saying nothing more as they exited the elevator and walked to the OR waiting room hand-in-hand, Meyer bringing up the rear.

'I thought you'd agree with Joseph,' Taylor murmured.

'No. Well, yes, that it's dangerous, but not about the brain thing. Joseph can be an arrogant prick sometimes, but he is damn good at his job. The way I see it, they involved you when they made you bait. Which *I* was against, if you recall.'

He hadn't just been against it. He'd nearly busted Maggie's office door in after listening in on JD's conversation with her and Maggie that morning, his fury reminding her more of a charging bull. 'I recall quite clearly,' she said.

'Good,' he said with a nod. 'Involving you – emotionally and physically – means that they owe you the right to be part of the resolution. Talking to Lilah is a good idea. There may be another way to make that happen that doesn't put you in Gage Jarvis's cross hairs again.'

She chanced a look up at his face and caught her breath. His eyes were sharp, intense. Like a live wire daring her to touch. 'How?'

'I'll tell you once we've settled inside.' He started to walk in the door to the OR waiting room, but Taylor held back, hesitating. It was noisier in there than the ER waiting room had been. Lots of people. All of Clay's friends, most likely. And his stepdad.

No, her heart corrected. *Tanner is his dad just like Frederick is mine. His father in every way that matters.* Clay had said so, just that morning. Tanner was her grandfather.

My grandfather. The sudden, overwhelming need for Tanner to accept her morphed into another wave of panic, and she dug her heels in, pulling back when Ford would have led her into the waiting room.

'Wait. I'm not . . . I can't . . . Just wait.' She started to rub her sweaty palm on her jeans, then remembered her jeans were still stained with Clay's blood. Her other hand, sweaty or not, was being firmly held by Ford, and when she tried to tug free, he just tightened his grip.

'It's fine,' he whispered in her ear. 'They will like you. Tanner will love you.'

He didn't force her, though. The noise abruptly quieted when he cleared the threshold alone. 'Hi,' Ford said quietly. 'Any news?'

'No, son. Not yet.' It was a man's voice. Older. Worried. Then almost pitifully hopeful. Eager, even. 'Where is she? Did you bring her with you?'

The 'she' needed no clarification. Ford tugged Taylor's hand, pulling it into the room while the rest of her remained frozen in the hallway. Ford gave her an exasperated look over his shoulder. 'She's here. She's shy.'

'Tell her to come in, Ford.' It was Stevie, and she sounded so tired it hurt Taylor's heart. But there was dry humor in her voice when she added, 'And Taylor, I swear to God if you say you're sorry even once, I'll take away your iPad and send you to bed without your supper.'

That sent a chuckle through the room, and it was on that sound that Taylor stepped over the threshold and found herself face to face with Tanner St James.

He was closer to her height than to Clay's, his gray hair still sporting a few strands of red. His shoulders were broad without being bulky. His eyes were blue, although bloodshot at the moment, with smile lines at the corners. But he wasn't smiling now. He was staring at her – just as Clay had stared twenty-four hours before – with reverential awe and a healthy portion of disbelief. Like she was a ghost or some trick of the eye.

'Oh my God,' he whispered. 'He told me that you resembled her, but . . .' He gave himself a little shake, regaining his composure. 'I'm sorry, Taylor. Forgive an old man's ramblings. But you . . . you could be her.'

'Nancy,' Taylor said quietly. 'My grandmother. I never knew.'

He drew a deep breath and let it out, and it was like he'd shed the weight of the world. 'Well, now you do. Now you're home.' He wrapped his arms around her and she breathed him in. A little salt, a little sweat. And just a hint of Old Spice. 'Welcome home, Taylor,' he whispered fiercely, tears in his voice. 'It doesn't matter where

337

you live or who you live with, or how often you visit us or for how long. We're part of you now. Part of your heart. You'll take us with you wherever you go. And we will always be your home.'

Somehow, some way, he'd known exactly what she needed to hear. She wasn't sure how long they stood there, holding each other tight. She knew she cried and she knew he did too. When they finally stepped apart, a smile lit his face like the Fourth of July.

'Come, sit a bit,' he said, leading her to an empty loveseat and settling in with his arm around her shoulders like he'd known her forever. 'You'll have to forgive me if I stare. We've waited a long, long time for you to come home.'

It was then that Taylor noticed the other faces in the room. She knew about half of them. Holly and Dillon and Cole. Paige, dozing on the shoulder of a huge dark-haired bruiser of a guy who Taylor assumed was Grayson Smith, Paige's husband and Daphne's boss.

Stevie was sitting with an older couple and a slightly younger version of herself. 'The Nicolescus, Stevie's parents,' Tanner told her. 'Emil and Zina. And that's her sister, Izzy.'

Stevie caught Taylor watching her and gave her a smile that was a little too bright. 'He'll be fine. Don't worry.'

'I can't promise that I won't worry,' Taylor said honestly. 'I'm really good at it.'

Stevie sighed. 'Fair enough. Then we can worry together.'

Izzy's smile was easy and warm. 'We'll all be on our best behavior and not swarm you. I don't want Clay waking up to find out we scared you back to California.'

Taylor found it impossible not to smile back. 'Thank you. It is a little overwhelming to meet all these people.'

A bright-eyed blonde came into the waiting room, carrying a huge bag from a local sub shop. Her gaze immediately found Tanner, her eyes widening when she saw Taylor.

'My wife, Nell,' Tanner said, standing up to receive a hug and a kiss and the bag of food. 'Nell, this is Taylor.'

Taylor hoped her surprise didn't show, because Nell was *really* young. *You go, Grandpa.* 'It's nice to meet you. Clay speaks highly of you.'

'We're glad you're here,' Nell said warmly. 'You've made my guy here very happy.' With a nod, she became briskly businesslike. 'I brought sandwiches. And don't tell me you're not hungry, Tanner St James. You know you need to eat. Have you checked your blood sugar?'

'Yes, dear,' Tanner said patiently, then rolled his eyes. 'I have diabetes. She worries.' He broke a sandwich in half and gave Taylor a piece. 'Help a grandpa out here.' He glanced at his wife, who'd already begun passing out sandwiches to the others in the room. 'Just don't tell Nell.'

Taylor smiled. 'One day and you're already corrupting me.'

Nell took some sandwiches to the small table in the corner where Ford and Alec, who was Clay's IT assistant, were hunched over Alec's laptop. They looked up to thank her, then bent back down to stare at the laptop screen.

Tanner's eyes narrowed. 'What are those two up to? They look way too serious.'

Taylor figured this was what Ford had referred to in the hall, his way of contacting Lilah that was less dangerous than Taylor's more direct knock-on-her-door approach. Either way, she wasn't certain that Tanner wouldn't report them to Joseph, so she just shrugged. 'Probably playing a video game. I'll go find out.'

She joined Alec and Ford, peeking at the laptop, which did not have a game on its screen. 'Can I play too? I'm a whiz at League of Legends.'

Alec grinned at Ford. 'She's a gamer too? Awesome,' he said, his speech a little off.

Taylor had met Alec on her first day at the farm, but he'd been busy and had greeted her with a quick handshake before hustling off to work on the camera systems. Now she had a chance to really look at him, specifically at the hardware behind his ear. It was some kind of hearing aid, neon green just like his high-top sneakers.

Ford gave her his seat next to Alec, then moved behind her chair, leaning over her shoulder to see the laptop screen. 'Taken,' he said lightly, and Alec rolled his eyes.

'Figures,' he said, then tapped the device behind his ear. 'Cochlear implant. Saw you looking.' He lowered his voice. 'I can hear you whisper, so please don't shout.'

'Wouldn't think of it,' Taylor whispered back, studying what filled Alec's screen. It was a list of dozens of phone numbers, each with a time, date and duration of the call. Ford reached over her shoulder, casually putting his phone into her hand.

The guys talked as if they were playing a game while Taylor read the flurry of texts they'd sent to each other after she'd left the ER waiting room with Officer Meyer.

Ford: *Where r u?*

Alec: *OR wait room. Where r u?*

Ford: *OMW now. U have ur laptop?*

Alec: *Duh. What u need?*

Ford: *Phone records for Denny Jarvis. First name Dennis? Def atty. Bro of shooter.*

Alec: *Have it. Clay asked this a.m.*

Ford: *Yessss. Need records for Eunice Jarvis too.*

Alec: *Her number?*

Ford: *IDK.*

Alec: *I'll try.*

Alec scrolled to the top of his laptop screen, showing the name Denny Jarvis, then opened another document – Eunice's phone records – and arranged the two side by side.

Alec opened a text window on his laptop and began to type. *They share an account.* He hit SEND, and Ford's phone buzzed in her hand.

Ah. Taylor realized that the two had been communicating via text under the noses of everyone in the room. *Denny pays for his mom's phone,* she read. *Piece of cake to break in.* Alec rolled his eyes. *His password was his children's names.*

Taylor studied the columns of numbers, quickly seeing the patterns. 'There,' she said, pointing to a number that was common to both. Denny had called and received calls from the number several times over the last month. Eunice had received only one call – early that morning. *That was when he convinced her to bring the girls to the park,* Taylor typed into Ford's phone.

340

'Yep,' Ford said aloud.

Taylor sighed and continued typing. *If we call Gage, he'll just be alerted and he'll run.*

Ford took his phone back and typed for a few minutes. When he hit SEND, the new text appeared on Alec's laptop.

Joseph has a tail on both Denny and his wife. If Denny gets a call from this number – with the right bait – he might go to Gage. His tail follows him to where Gage is. If he still has the girls, hopefully they are there too. Either way, we get G.

Alec gave Ford a dark look. *The COPS get him. Not WE. Not U. Right?!?*

Ford nodded seriously. 'Of course,' he said aloud, but spoke very quietly.

Taylor reached for Ford's phone. *How do we call from this phone number? It's Gage's phone and we don't have that.*

Spoofing sites, Alec typed. *Messes with caller ID. You can pick the number you're pretending to be.*

Taylor frowned. She'd never heard of such a thing. *Okay,* she typed. *Offer me as bait. It brought him out today.* She didn't intend to be literal bait, of course. She'd heard Joseph's warning and as much as his condescension had rankled, she knew he'd been right. She wasn't going to leave the hospital. But Gage didn't know that.

'*No.*' Ford's spoken reply was nearly silent, but he didn't need to shout for Taylor to know he was furious. She could hear him grinding his teeth. 'No fucking way. I . . . I forbid it.'

Forbid? Really? Taylor turned around in her chair to face him, delaying her explanation that she really wasn't going to *be* bait. This attitude of his *had* to be nipped in the bud. *Right. Frickin'. Now.* 'Forbid? You are not my fa—'

She was cut off by the sudden greetings that erupted from everyone in the waiting room for a man who had just come through the door holding a suitcase with one hand and a pretty redhead with the other. The man was young, but he had a head of white hair and hadn't removed his wraparound sunglasses even though he was indoors. And he had a presence. Even from the back of the room Taylor could sense his energy as he strode in like he owned the place.

341

The atmosphere had abruptly changed. Become charged. Spines straightened, shoulders lifted and smiles lit the faces of every single person. 'Deacon!' they all called out, just like the folks at the *Cheers* bar greeted Norm.

'Deacon' would be FBI Special Agent Deacon Novak. Taylor had read about him in the transcripts for the trial of Ford's abductors. Novak had worked with Joseph to bring Ford home. He had been transferred somewhere in the Midwest nearly a year ago. To Cincinnati, Taylor recalled. Obviously he was a family favorite.

Ford's reaction was different to that of the others. He called out Deacon's name like everyone else, but his shoulders sagged as some of the tension in his body melted away before her eyes. He looked . . . relieved, like the cavalry had finally arrived.

Holly was first to run to the door, launching herself at Novak. 'Deacon! You're here!'

Novak caught her around the waist, spinning her once before carefully setting her feet on the floor. 'Of course I did. There was no way I'd miss your wedding.' He looked around, sobering when his gaze settled on Stevie. 'You doing okay there, Mazzetti?' he asked softly.

One side of Stevie's mouth lifted. 'Not really. But I am glad you're here.'

'Wild horses couldn't have kept me away,' he said gently, then perked back up, rubbing his hands together. 'Where is Joseph? Dillon's still alive, so I assume he's not on the lam for murder.'

'He doesn't want to kill me.' Dillon's grimace was cute. 'Not anymore, anyway.'

Novak winked at him. 'Good to know. I could take him in a fight, but it wouldn't be pretty. For an old guy, he's got some serious moves. So where is he?'

'Joseph and my mom are down in the ER, waiting for a potential witness,' Ford answered loudly, then leaned down to whisper in Taylor's ear. 'We are *not* finished with this conversation. You will *not* be bait again.' He strode across the room and pulled Novak into a hard hug, the two pounding each other's backs.

Beside her, Alec sighed quietly. 'Not a smart move, Taylor. Don't push him on the bait thing. He was abducted as bait to draw his mother out. He won't let you do that to yourself.'

Shit. 'I hadn't thought of it that way,' she murmured.

'Well, do. If you care anything about anyone in this room, you'll find another way, because nobody's gonna want to explain to Clay how they let you get hurt once he wakes up. And he *will* wake up.' Alec's voice had gone hard when he spoke of Clay waking, but his eyes were filled with devastation and Taylor sensed he was simply trying to keep it together. 'Clay . . . he's like my dad. Which might be awkward for you because he really is your dad, but . . .' He trailed off helplessly.

'It's all right,' she said as gently as she could. 'I didn't know you two were so close. I knew he was your boss and maybe your mentor, but that's all.'

'Yeah, he's those things too,' Alec said gruffly. 'But he saved my life, you know.'

Taylor blinked, startled. 'No, I didn't know that.'

'I was kidnapped when I was a kid, just like Ford, only younger. I was twelve. Ford and I . . . we became friends because we had too much shitty past in common not to. We've stayed friends because we have too many good things in common not to.'

'How did Clay save your life?'

'He was the one who found me, pulled me out of the rat pit where I'd been stashed, all drugged up and close to . . . Well, if he hadn't found me when he did, I wouldn't be here today.' Alec turned to her, his expression fierce. 'He has waited for you, looked for you, *loved* you for as long as I've known him. Do not make him grieve for you. Please.'

Now Taylor felt even worse. 'I really didn't mean I'd actually *be* bait, you know. I just meant that we could offer it. Make it an opportunity Jarvis couldn't refuse.'

'Okay, I get it. But Ford? I think all he can see is you getting shot at again and maybe not being so lucky a second time.' He hesitated. 'I've seen him at his lowest. Sat with him when he was so depressed by what Kimberly did to him that he couldn't bring himself to even speak. She stole more from him than his safety. She stole his light.

But when he looks at you, I see that light again. Be careful with him, that's all I'm saying.' He put his laptop aside and stood up. 'I'm gonna say hi to Deacon. You coming?'

Taylor shook her head. 'No, it's okay. I'll stay here.' She was far more comfortable observing than participating, especially since she didn't know the man.

Everyone in the room had gathered around Novak, giving him hugs and handshakes. There were smiles and . . . hope. Deacon Novak, she thought, had delivered the hope that Clay's friends and family had so desperately needed. That Ford had needed.

Novak stepped back to draw the redhead to his side. 'Everybody, this is my fiancée, Faith Corcoran. Faith, this is just part of my Baltimore family.'

Poor Faith looked as overwhelmed as Taylor felt, but waved gamely. And then Novak saw Taylor and went still, causing everyone else in the room to fall abruptly silent. As one, they followed his gaze.

'Is that her?' he asked Ford. 'The one who shot the shooter? Clay's daughter?'

Baltimore, Maryland,
Sunday 23 August, 6.45 P.M.

God. Gage's hand shook as he pulled the last stitch taut. It was done. Finally. It had taken for-fucking-ever, because he kept nearly passing out from the pain as he'd dug out the bullet. He'd tried to get Jazzie to do the stitching but her hands shook worse than his did and he was afraid she'd rip the wound bigger, even if she didn't mean to.

That her fear was real had never been in doubt. He eyed her carefully, wondering if he could trust her to cut the leftover thread that dangled from his arm. He decided not to risk it, because she was green and trembling. All he needed her to do was accidentally rip the sutures from his arm or . . . *God.* Throw up on him. She looked like she was on the verge.

He slapped a gauze pad on his arm, yelping at the pain that shot through his body. His movements were jerky and less controlled than he would have liked. He'd drunk a *lot* of booze, the two empty bottles on the table testament to the fact. His stomach churned and his vision blurred.

He handed Jazzie the roll of tape. 'You should be able to tape the gauze at least.' He gave her what he hoped was a menacing glare. 'Do not hurt me or I will end you and your sister,' he growled. 'Do you understand me?'

She nodded, her eyes glassy and her skinny body shaking like a leaf, and he felt a wave of shame. *Some man you are. Bullying a little girl.*

A little *lying* girl, he reminded himself. He gritted his teeth as she wound the tape around the bandage. She looked at the scissors on the table, glancing up at him, her lower lip caught between her teeth.

He barked out a bitter laugh. 'No, thank you. You'd stab me with those scissors. Or try to. You don't have the muscle to jab hard enough to make it hurt.' She tightened her jaw, confirming his suspicions. 'Use your teeth to cut the tape.'

Wordlessly she obeyed. 'Good,' he grunted. 'Now get on the floor next to the bed.'

She sucked in a breath, eyes darting toward the door. 'W-w-why?' She took a step back. 'W-what are you going to do?'

Her stutter was back, annoying him further. He rolled his eyes and was instantly sorry he had, because the room tilted. He was fucking smashed. 'I'm going to tie you up, you little bitch. Then I'm going to sleep. Then I'm going to leave. If you don't try to cross me, you'll be back with your precious aunt before breakfast.' *Tuesday morning,* he added silently to himself.

He'd wait until he was safely in Mexico before calling Lilah with the girls' location. They'd be hungry and thirsty, but otherwise unaffected. Physically at least. They'd be emotionally scarred forever. Which was not his fault.

Isn't it? He lurched to his feet, giving his asshole conscience a hard shove. 'On the floor, Jazzie. Now. Put your hands behind your back.'

Still shaking, she obeyed. He took a few stumbling steps toward the bed and dropped heavily to his knees, fumbling with the rope. He tied it around her hands, her ankles, then stuffed the gag back in

345

her mouth. Noted the tears coursing down her cheeks.

'I wouldn't cry,' he ground out, hating the way his voice slurred. 'Your nose'll get stopped up and then you won't be able to breathe.'

He lifted Janie off the bed and put her on the floor next to Jazzie. Gently, he realized. He'd handled the child gently. So he wasn't totally a monster. *Just ninety-nine-point-nine-nine percent.*

He straightened his back abruptly, disgusted with himself. Whether the disgust was because he was a monster or because of the gentleness he still apparently possessed, he wasn't entirely sure.

Fuck. Oh fuck. He'd straightened too quickly and his churning stomach began to heave. He barely made it to the bathroom before he puked his guts into the toilet.

At least that would help him sober up faster. He'd just hurled what felt like half the booze he'd guzzled. He sank to his knees, tempted to sleep right here on the floor, but knew his back would go out if he did that. He had a long, long day tomorrow.

According to Google Maps, it was a twenty-six-hour drive to Laredo, Texas, where he'd need to find an unguarded border crossing. Just as Tavilla had predicted, Gage's face was all over the news. He'd have to stay under the radar as he made his escape, so it might take even longer. He didn't need the complication of an out-of-whack back on top of everything else.

He needed the bed. He grabbed the sink, pulling himself to his feet. A few steps later his body hit the mattress face first and he welcomed the blackness of sleep.

Baltimore, Maryland,
Sunday 23 August, 7.10 P.M.

Ford looked across the waiting room to where Taylor sat alone, her expression one of extreme discomfort at suddenly being the center of attention yet again. He knew he should hold out his hand and draw her over to where the rest of them stood, but he was still too shaken at the ludicrous, infuriating notion of her making herself bait. Again. He couldn't trust himself to be gentle, or even civil. Not just yet.

Tanner's wife, Nell, got the conversation going again, bless her.

She took Faith by the arm and introduced her to everyone, taking the focus off Taylor. Taylor slumped into her seat wearily, her eyes closed. Ford's heart squeezed hard with compassion, but the fear did not subside.

Bait, my motherfucking ass, he thought grimly. *Just . . . no.*

But he controlled his voice when he answered Deacon's question. 'Yes,' he said quietly. 'That's Clay's daughter. She's called Taylor Dawson, though. Not Sienna.'

'I see. I haven't heard the whole story yet, but I imagine you'll tell me.' Deacon gave Taylor an appraising look before turning back to Ford, his white brows crunching together in concern. 'After you tell me what the hell's going on with you. Joseph said you were shot.'

'Just a graze and a few bruises. I didn't even need stitches. But Clay . . .' He sighed, glad that Nell had led the group away, leaving them alone to talk. Because his one sigh would have destroyed the positive vibes Deacon had released into the room. Still, he felt better now than he had before Deacon's arrival.

Seeing Deacon again was like a shot in the arm. The good kind of shot. Not the bullet kind that got you bandages and antibiotics. *Or surgery*, he thought, unable to drag his mind away from Clay. Still, Deacon had helped. He'd only got off an airplane an hour ago, and just by walking in the door he'd perked up the whole room.

Of all the cops Ford had met after his escape from his abductor, he'd liked Deacon the best. The man had understood his pain at Kimberly's betrayal and had never minimized the situation by giving him false platitudes, focusing instead on what Ford needed to do next, giving him goals to aim for. They'd simply clicked and they'd been friends ever since.

Of all the cops and ex-cops that Ford knew, Deacon was most likely to approve of their plan to lure Gage Jarvis out. He was a good man to have on your team. For the first time, Ford felt a smidgen of hope.

'Clay will be all right,' Deacon said with absolute certainty.

Holly had wandered back over to them and wound her arms around Deacon in sweet, unfettered affection. 'I hope so,' she said, her voice small.

Deacon kissed the top of her head. 'You'll see. He's too ornery to let a little thing like a bullet take him out. Besides, he has a speech prepared for your reception. He was gonna make everyone bawl their eyes out. Maybe he'll let one of us read it for him.'

Holly's eyes filled. 'He won't be able to come to the wedding. It's tomorrow. He's gonna miss seeing me get married.'

The conversation all around them dulled at Holly's distress. She was so incredibly well loved. No one wanted to see her sad.

'We can video it,' Dillon said, patting her back to comfort her.

'It's not the same,' she cried, turning into Dillon's embrace, leaving Deacon looking as helpless as any of them to fix this for her.

Again the room was quiet until Taylor, still sitting at the back of the room, cleared her throat. 'We can use Skype,' she suggested. 'He can watch you in real time, from his hospital bed. He won't be there in person, but it's the next best thing.'

Suddenly Holly was smiling again. 'Can we, Alec? Can we do that?'

'Absolutely, Holls,' Alec said fondly. 'Good idea, Taylor.' He returned to sit beside her, and Ford tried not to feel jealous when the two of them leaned in to see Alec's laptop screen, their heads nearly touching.

Fucking bait, Ford thought with a snarl. Taylor was not going to make herself bait.

'How long have you known her?' Deacon asked, amused.

'A day,' he snapped.

'Oh, Ford.' Deacon shook his head. 'You got it bad, boy. Puppy-dog eyes and all.'

'Shut up,' Ford said, but without any heat, because it was true. 'Listen, I may need your help. It's important. And maybe dangerous. Two little girls – and one older girl who's too foolish to be allowed to roam alone – might be in big danger, and the clock is ticking.' Yes, he'd used the word 'foolish'. And he wasn't going to apologize. *Make herself bait, will she? Fuck, no.*

'Tell me what you've got.'

He and Deacon went out in the hall, where Ford gave him the abridged version, Deacon nodding in all the right places. 'And now

Taylor wants to make herself bait,' he finished, disgusted. 'Just because he tried to kill her once before, she thinks she should offer herself up again.'

'Well,' Deacon said practically, 'beyond the obvious no-way-in-fucking-hell, her offering herself as bait doesn't make sense. Gage wants to kill her. You want something that tempts *Denny* to roust himself, get in the car and drive to wherever Gage is hiding. Right?'

'Right,' Ford agreed warily.

'Taylor won't tempt Denny because Denny doesn't want to kill her. We tempt Denny with something that's important to *him*.'

Ford nodded. 'That sounds better to me, all the way around.'

Deacon grinned. 'I'll bet it does, Romeo.'

Ford rolled his eyes and ignored his teasing. 'The question is, what's important to Denny? I'd bet anything that Lilah knows what's going on, but she's not telling anyone anything.'

'We'll figure it out.' Deacon sobered. 'But first we tell Joseph your plan. He has to control all communication with anyone involved in this mess.'

'No way.' Ford's temper bubbled up. 'Dammit, Deacon, I thought you'd understand.'

'I do understand. More than you know.' Deacon took off his wraparound sunglasses to squeeze the bridge of his nose, and Ford sucked in a breath. Deacon's odd bi-colored eyes were turbulent and full of grief and pain that made no sense.

Nobody here had died. Not today. Not yet.

Ford gripped Deacon's shoulder. 'Deacon? What's wrong?'

'Look, Ford, I've just finished a hard case in Cincinnati. I've seen more people die the past two weeks alone than I hope you ever see in your whole damn life, so believe me when I say I understand the urgency. I've seen my Faith terrorized by a motherfucker holding a gun to her head – after she *made herself bait*, so believe me when I say I understand your fear.'

Ford drew a breath, surprised to find himself calmed even more by Deacon's burst of anger than by his logic. 'Taylor got wrapped up in the moment, I guess. I'm sorry, D. You're right.' He smiled wryly. 'You usually are, but you didn't hear that from me.'

349

Deacon slid his shades back on. 'Temper happens under stress. To all of us.'

Ford raised his eyes in mock disbelief. 'Even to you?'

Deacon chuckled. 'Yes, even to me, you shithead. The truth is, you've both conducted yourselves admirably considering all the stress and tension of the day. Now, I do agree with you that Joseph is being a little too cautious under the circumstances.'

Ford shrugged, even though Deacon's words warmed him from the inside out. 'He has to be. Otherwise he gets blamed when a judge throws his case out of court and a killer gets away. I get that. That's why I figured we could engineer this so that Gage was flushed out of hiding and right into the arms of the cops who'd followed Denny to his hiding place. Nobody gets blamed and the job gets done. Two kids are safe. If they're not already dead.'

Deacon sighed. 'Let's hope he's holding them for concessions of some kind.'

'Like ransom?' He'd thought it, of course, but it helped his ego that Deacon had too.

'It's not out of the question. You told me that the aunt wouldn't talk to the police. She must believe that Gage is watching her. He's already shown he's capable of murder by killing the kids' mother.'

'And based on the few times I've talked to her at the farm when the girls were riding, she doesn't seem to be the type to shrink away from danger to herself,' Ford said.

'Would she have talked to Taylor alone?'

'Maybe. There's a better chance with Taylor than with anyone. Man, you should have seen the look on Lilah's face yesterday when Jazzie threw herself into Taylor's arms and started to cry. It was like Taylor was a miracle-worker or something. I still think trying to get Lilah to talk to Taylor is a good plan.'

'It's not completely ridiculous,' Deacon admitted. 'Neither is drawing Denny out with a fake message. But the two of you can't be anywhere near Denny if he does go to Gage.'

'I hadn't planned to be,' Ford said honestly, then sighed. 'But I am more than a little emotionally invested, so Joseph's dragging his feet has got me impatient.'

'Of course it has. The bastard shot Clay and tried to shoot Taylor. Of course you're going to be impatient.'

Ford shook his head. 'It's not just that. Mostly it's that those two little girls have been through hell. They found their mother's body, and Gage had beaten her so badly that it's good he left her fingerprints intact, because they couldn't have used dental records for ID. Right now, that guy has those kids. If he hasn't killed them, then they're scared out of their minds. Especially Jazzie, because she knows what he can do.'

Comprehension flickered through Deacon's odd eyes. 'I guess you would relate to the abduction terror better than the rest of us.'

'Except for maybe Alec,' Ford said quietly. 'I was twenty. Alec was twelve. Just a year older than Jazzie. Janie's only five.'

Deacon sighed heavily. 'Okay. We go to Joseph. You tell him what you've told me, and then leave him to me. He'll do the right thing. He always does.'

Any additional discussion was cut off when Ford's phone buzzed in his hand. It was a text from Alec. *Let's talk. Your girl has an idea for better bait. I think you'll be good with this one.* Ford showed the phone to Deacon, who looked pleased.

'Lead on,' Deacon said with a flourish. 'I'd like a chance to talk to your girl, too.'

My girl, Ford thought wistfully. He wished she was. Hoped she'd be. For now, the least he could do was make sure she lived long enough for them to find out.

Baltimore, Maryland,
Sunday 23 August, 7.15 P.M.

Jasmine tilted her head, listening hard. From where she lay on the floor she couldn't see him up on the mattress, but he was snoring loudly and had been for what seemed like hours. But it couldn't have been, because she could still see the sun through the window.

Please let him really be asleep. But she was pretty sure he was. She moved slowly, careful to make no noise, even when she was able to tug her wrists apart a fraction of an inch. She wanted to

351

sigh with relief, but she just exhaled as carefully and quietly as she'd moved.

He'd been so drunk when he'd tied her after she'd bandaged him up. So drunk that she'd taken a chance and held her wrists together at an angle, touching skin only on one side. She'd left a gap between her wrists on the other side, praying that he wouldn't notice.

He hadn't. She'd waited while he put Janie on the floor beside her then run to the bathroom to throw up in the toilet. She'd held herself perfectly still as he'd staggered to the bed and fallen on it, until he began to snore.

Get your hands free. She chanted it inside her mind over and over as she pulled, tugged and twisted her wrists. She visualized her hands behind her, focusing on the feel of the rope as it burned her skin. Otherwise she'd panic and cry and he'd wake up.

He'd said he'd give them back to Lilah, but she didn't believe him. He'd lied about so many things. She couldn't take the chance that he wasn't lying about setting them free.

Baltimore, Maryland,
Sunday 23 August, 7.45 P.M.

JD entered the BPD building wanting to scream. Or throw something. With barely a nod at the security guard, he headed for his office. He exited the elevator into the small bullpen area that Joseph's team occupied. It was nearly empty, with Hector the only other person there.

Hector was sitting at his own desk, his back to the bullpen entrance, arms crossed on his chest. JD briefly wondered what he was doing there, since he'd been tasked to lead the hostage retrieval team and should be either out front of Lilah's apartment building or inside the building itself. Obviously Hector had hit a barrier with Lilah too.

JD was extremely familiar with the barriers Lilah Cornell had erected. The woman's behavior was unacceptable. Both Jazzie and Janie were missing, their grandmother was nearly dead, yet Lilah had ignored every one of his attempts to communicate.

As had Cesar Tavilla, so JD *still* didn't know where Gage Jarvis was hiding.

And Clay was still in surgery. *Goddammit.*

JD kicked a chair, sending it crashing into an unoccupied desk. 'Fuck,' he muttered.

'Did that make you feel better?' a smooth voice asked in a heavy accent.

Not Hector's voice.

JD went still, then looked up as the man in Hector's chair slowly spun around until they were facing each other. He was a suave man in his late forties, impeccably dressed. He uncrossed his arms, then elegantly crossed his legs, idly swinging one foot.

'Mr Tavilla,' JD said with a cool nod, although inside he was far from cool. How the fuck had the bastard gotten in here? He was just sitting at Hector's desk like he owned the joint. Considering that he was here unescorted suggested that he owned at least one cop here in the building. *Fucking shit.*

The man nodded back. 'Detective Fitzpatrick. You've been trying to reach me all afternoon.' He gestured broadly. 'So I am here.'

JD retrieved his chair and calmly sat at his own desk. He took a power bar from his drawer, because he hadn't stopped to eat in hours. He downed the protein, chasing it with a bottle of water while Tavilla sat patiently.

'You could have simply phoned me back,' JD said mildly.

Tavilla shrugged. 'I was in the neighborhood. So . . . why are you looking for me?'

'Gage Jarvis,' JD said bluntly. 'I know he works for you. Where is he?'

'I don't know,' Tavilla assured him, showing no surprise whatsoever. 'And Mr Jarvis never technically worked for me. He was to have started work tomorrow morning, but I fired him today. After that debacle in front of the Italian restaurant this afternoon, I want no part of him.'

Apparently Thorne's rumor mill was very good indeed. 'What did Jarvis say when you fired him?'

A slight grimace. 'Many things that are not appropriate to repeat.'

'I see. Where was he when you fired him?'

'I don't know. I called him on his cell. I cannot give you his location, but I can give you his telephone number.' He withdrew a piece of paper from his pocket and handed it to JD. 'That is the number. I imagine it's a burner, but I hope you can still find it useful.'

Tavilla leaned back in his chair, smoothing his hand down a tie that probably cost JD's salary for a week. The guy's shoes, a detective's salary for a month. Maybe two or three months. An honest detective's salary at least.

The thought struck JD hard as Tavilla simply sat and regarded him through cold, dark eyes. JD placed the piece of paper on the far corner of his desk, closest to Tavilla.

'I'd like nothing better than to sit here and stare you down all day long, Mr Tavilla, but I have things to do, so let's just cut to the chase. What do you want from me?'

Tavilla smiled and JD was glad he'd braced himself, because the man's smile made his blood run cold. He was able to maintain his expression of wary distrust, but only barely.

'I'd like to know how you knew to call me.'

JD feigned reluctance and looked at the piece of paper, letting a trace of his very genuine desperation show. 'He told his mother that he was finally coming home, that he had a job with you. She told us.'

'Why?' Tavilla asked, seeming sincerely curious. 'Why would she tell you? The police?'

'Because she's proud of him. She didn't know about him opening fire on three people in front of that restaurant today. She was barely conscious at the time and we didn't want to upset her. She was bragging about her boy.'

Tavilla sighed. 'Sometimes it's the simplest mistakes that trip one up, no?'

JD suppressed a shiver, wondering if Tavilla was referring to Gage Jarvis or to himself. Making a mental note to warn Thorne, he smiled wearily. 'Sometimes it's the only way we cops catch a break.'

Tavilla's smile was real this time, and humor glinted in his dark eyes. 'I know your record, Detective. You are smart enough to exploit any weakness you see. You don't need the criminals to trip up.'

Oh my, the man was spreading it on thick. JD hid his irritation. *Does the bastard think I'm that shallow? That flattery will get him somewhere?*

'That's where you'd be wrong,' JD said seriously. 'And Gage is smart too.'

'It's why I hired him,' Tavilla agreed. 'Well, I'll leave you to your investigating. It's been a pleasure to finally meet you, Detective Fitzpatrick.'

'Just one more question, if you don't mind,' JD said, and Tavilla paused mid-rise and resettled himself into the chair, lifting a brow in permission. 'Did you seek Jarvis out or did he come to you for a job?'

'Why is that important, Detective?'

'Just trying to trace his movements, to account for the lost time. And to understand why he came back a month ago.'

Tavilla considered, then shrugged. 'He came to me. He looked strung out, thin. Rumor had it that he'd partied hard on money he'd had stashed away, but that his funds had run out and he was reduced to doing odd jobs along the beach. When he reminded me that I owed him a favor, I thought he'd ask for money. But he wanted a job. I could respect a man who wanted to work, so I said yes.'

'Did he ask for anything else?'

'No. He was dressed in a ratty T-shirt, shorts, and flip-flops, but he still had an air of . . .' Tavilla frowned, searching for the word. 'Pride, I suppose. I asked if he had a place to stay in Baltimore and he said he had a house. He got . . . how do you say?' He bowed his shoulders up and thrust his chest out.

'Puffed up?' JD supplied.

Tavilla smiled. 'Exactly. Like an angry bird. Said he was not a beggar. But I got the sense that he was tired of living as a beach bum.' His expression grew thoughtful. Maybe even wistful. 'I think he was simply ready to come home.' He shook his head as if to clear it, then fixed his gaze on JD, eyes cold once again. 'Anything else, Detective?'

'Yes.' JD smiled self-deprecatingly. 'One more question. Who set his starting date? You or Jarvis?'

Tavilla tilted his head, studying him through narrowed eyes. 'Why?'

JD shrugged. 'Curious.'

Tavilla considered him another long moment. 'He did,' he finally replied. 'Said he needed some time to get his affairs in order. I called him on Friday, asked if he was still planning to start on Monday since I had not heard from him since our initial meeting. He said yes, so I set up a dinner meeting with him for last night.' Tavilla's smile was easy but cold. *Predatory.* His eyes narrowed to reptilian slits. 'But I'm sure that I tell you little that you do not already know. Your . . . sources are apparently very well placed.'

JD blinked, covering his dismay. *He knows that I already knew about the dinner.* Tavilla hadn't bought his story about Gage telling his mother about his new job. *Fuck. Thorne definitely needs to know.* JD didn't relish that conversation. Thorne had trusted him. And Lucy was going to be livid that JD had potentially compromised her friend's safety. *Fuck.*

But still he kept his expression neutral, on the off-chance that Tavilla was fishing. 'Well, a man tells his mother things, I suppose.' He shrugged. 'I wouldn't know, of course. My mother's not the chatty type. Jarvis's mother, now? Very chatty. And worried about her son. She thinks he's ill.' He rolled his eyes for show. 'She's got it blown all out of proportion. Thinks he has cancer, for God's sake. How did he seem to you? Still thin?'

Tavilla's eyes relaxed, his expression returning to that of a suave businessman. 'A little, but he looked healthier than he did a month ago. He was tanned. Clean.' He made a face. 'He was not so clean when we met in Florida last month, so last night was an improvement. He had a new suit and he'd dyed his hair darker. Oh, and he had a beard. Not a full beard, but . . .' He stroked his own clean-shaven jaw, searching for the word.

'Stubble?'

'Yes, that's it. He had stubble.' One dark eyebrow arched. 'So you should update the photo you attached to his BOLO. That was the mug shot taken of him three years ago when he was arrested for domestic assault.'

'I'll take care of that directly,' JD said smoothly. They were just dancing around each other now. He'd gotten all he was going to get out of the man. And he knew damn well he hadn't gotten anything that Tavilla had not planned to give him. Except that moment of wistfulness when he'd said Jarvis just wanted to come home.

JD stood. 'Thank you for coming in, Mr Tavilla. I appreciate the information and that you gave it so willingly, expecting nothing in return,' he added pointedly. 'Good citizens are far too rare.'

Tavilla came to his feet too, his lips actually twitching, dark eyes twinkling with amusement. 'It was truly my pleasure, Detective. I hope you catch your prey.'

JD walked him to the elevator and took it down with him, accompanying him to the exit, wondering exactly who had let the man through. That would be a question he'd have to ask later.

He instructed the security guard on duty that the man who'd just left was not to be allowed back in, then went back to his desk, noting that he'd missed two calls from Joseph as he'd been talking to Tavilla. 'I just had a visitor,' he said when Joseph picked up. 'Cesar Tavilla.'

'Oh really?' Joseph sounded surprised, which didn't happen often. 'What did he have to say?'

'That he'd fired Gage this afternoon, and then he gave me Gage's cell phone number.'

'Excellent,' Joseph said with satisfaction. 'Bring it with you. I need you back at the hospital ASAP.'

JD's stomach twisted. 'Clay?'

'Still in surgery. Deacon's here. And apparently Ford, Alec and Taylor have been taking some initiative. They have a plan and Deacon says it doesn't suck. His words.'

JD laughed, the sound startling him in the quiet of his office. 'Of course they're his words. You know, I didn't think I'd miss the white-haired bastard as much as I have.'

Joseph chuckled quietly. 'I know. I'll see you when you get here.'

Twenty-one

Joseph Carter was a hard man to read, Taylor thought, studying him as he sat on the other side of the table that nearly filled the small hospital consultation room in which she, Ford and Alec had shared their plan. Joseph's expression gave no indication whether his response would be open or dismissive. Her four-year degree in psychology was useless against the man's granite mask. Hell, she didn't think a Harvard PhD could see beneath that face of his.

JD Fitzpatrick, on the other hand, was easy to read – or maybe he was simply too tired to be enigmatic. Fitzpatrick had arrived looking dog-tired, overheated and frustrated. He and his team had questioned potential witnesses, analyzed the crime scene, traced the string of cars Gage had stolen during his getaway. But Gage had ditched the last car and had either walked to wherever he was hiding or taken a car that hadn't been reported stolen yet. Either way, they were no closer to knowing his hiding place.

Taylor, Ford and Alec had laid out their plan for Joseph and Fitzpatrick while Deacon Novak and Daphne Montgomery looked on. Daphne was easy to read. She was full of worry. Taylor imagined that in the courtroom she'd have more of a poker face since she was a prosecutor, but here, sitting next to her son, she was all mama bear. *Which is exactly as it should be.*

Novak never took off his sunglasses, so Taylor couldn't get a good read of his face. He seemed onboard. More mildly anticipatory

358

than anything else. Ford and Alec trusted him, so Taylor had no choice but to rely on their judgment.

Fitzpatrick was too hot and tired to care about hiding anything. He was clearly peeved that Alec had compromised Denny's cell phone logs, but mostly because Alec hadn't come forward with them as soon as he'd gotten them. Apparently Fitzpatrick and Clay had an under-the-table agreement about the sharing of ill-gotten information.

Fitzpatrick had obtained Gage's cell phone number 'legally' from 'a source', but Alec had stolen his thunder by getting the same number first. Taylor thought that annoyed the detective the most. He was in a very snarly mood.

And he doesn't trust me. That had come through perfectly clearly in every conversation they'd had so far today. It was obvious in Fitzpatrick's body language as he listened to Ford and Alec speak. Taylor wasn't sure why he didn't trust her, but this meeting wasn't the venue to find out. This was about finding the girls – and bringing Gage to justice. *Not about me.* So she'd remained mostly silent, letting Alec and Ford do almost all of the talking.

Joseph listened stoically until the end, his body completely still except for one hand that spun a pencil through his fingers with a speed and accuracy that suggested he did it often. When Alec and Ford were done, he sat back in his chair.

'So you want to send a text to Denny Jarvis via a spoofing service, so that it looks like it came from the cell number from Denny's log, which we can safely assume is Gage's phone, because it matches the number given to JD. You want this text to be so compelling that Denny leaves his home and immediately goes to where Gage has been living. The officer tailing Denny will follow and tell us where Gage is.' He raised his brows. 'Am I keeping up?'

Ford nodded. 'Yes.'

'All right,' Joseph said in the same even tone. 'You assume that Denny knows where Gage lives or has at least been hiding. And you assume that's where Gage is right now and that he has the children with him.'

'Or at least that we can make him tell us where they are,' Alec said. 'But yes, we realize those are assumptions. I also assume *you* don't have Denny's cell records yet.'

Joseph didn't react to Alec's blatant goading, and Taylor wondered if that meant Joseph was controlling his temper or if he normally displayed no affect at all. 'Not yet,' he said. 'I may not have this information legitimately for a few days.'

Ford glanced at Fitzpatrick. 'You've been on this case for hours. Do you have a better plan?'

'Not really,' Fitzpatrick admitted. 'But if Denny calls Gage back, your trap will be prematurely sprung and you won't even know. That'll just piss Gage off more and he might retaliate by hurting the kids that we aren't even sure he has because Lilah won't fucking *talk* to us.'

Ford and Alec looked at each other blankly. 'Was there a question in there?' Ford asked.

Sighing inwardly, Taylor directed her answer to Alec and Ford. 'I think he means that we've neglected to consider that Denny might respond to "Gage's" text with an *actual voice call*, because we are all under twenty-five years old and never use the phone to actually *talk*.' She rolled her eyes. 'My dad always made Daisy and me call him from college at least once during the day so that he could hear our voices. He worried that I'd be grabbed and that Cl— I mean, the assailant would use my phone to text him that I was okay, and that I could be three states away before he knew I was missing. So we always had to *voice-call*.' She blinked hard because she'd lost her point. *Oh, right*. 'It really doesn't matter either way, though, whether Denny calls or texts him back. If he replies to our text in any way, it will go to Gage's phone, not back to us. Right, Alec?'

Alec nodded. 'Yes, and I did think of that – the text part of the response, anyway. We'd write the message so that Denny would be too upset or afraid to answer.'

'That's a big risk,' Daphne said quietly. 'If one of them smells a trap, they could work together to form an ambush and we wouldn't know. Our people could get hurt.'

'But we would know,' Alec said. 'That communication happened, anyway. Not the content of the communication. We can see Denny's cell account. His provider updates his call log online every twenty minutes or so. I've been watching most of the afternoon.'

Fitzpatrick's brows shot up. 'Why?' he demanded. Alec had clearly crossed a line. 'I figured you'd go in, copy records, and back out. Lurking around all day is not what I signed on for. Why would you take such a risk?'

Alec shot Fitzpatrick a dirty look. 'Partly because I thought that if Gage and Denny called each other again, you might like to know. But mostly because Clay got shot doing *your* dirty work and now I'm losing my fucking mind because he might *die*,' he snarled. 'So pardon me for getting a little obsessed with Denny's call log. And you're fucking *welcome*, by the way.'

Fitzpatrick straightened, stunned. And clearly pissed off. 'Wait just a damn minute, Alec . . .'

Novak and Ford each gripped one of Alec's arms, urging him back in his chair when he would have lurched to his feet. 'Alec,' Novak murmured. 'Whoa. Breathe, buddy.'

Wincing a little, Taylor said nothing, because what could she say? Alec considered Clay's guarding her to be dirty work. That was always *so* nice to hear.

Alec closed his eyes. 'I'm sorry.'

'For what?' Fitzpatrick asked, glowering.

'Not for what I said to you,' Alec snapped, then calmed his voice. 'To Taylor,' he said, and when he met her eyes, he did look apologetic. 'I guess I'm more churned up about the prodigal daughter returning than I thought I was. It wasn't a dirty job. It was a necessary job that Clay wanted to do. Nobody could have stopped him. I hope you can forgive me, because I was way out of line.'

Taylor found a small smile. 'Nobody's killed a fatted calf yet, so I think we're good.'

Alec gave her a nod of thanks, then turned back to Fitzpatrick and Joseph. 'You may not have "signed on" for me to lurk in Denny's account, but will you use this information?'

'Depends on what the message is going to be,' Joseph said. 'But we're still listening.'

Which was at least encouraging, Taylor thought as she pushed printouts of both Denny's and Eunice's call logs in front of Joseph, side by side. 'I've highlighted—'

'Where did you guys find a printer?' Fitzpatrick interrupted suspiciously. 'You didn't give this to anyone here in the hospital to print, did you? Tell me you weren't that stupid?'

Taylor, Ford and Alec took a collective deep breath. Anyone could see that Alec was still holding to his temper by a thread, but he pursed his lips and said nothing. Taylor counted backward from ten. Twice.

Fitzpatrick glared at the three of them when no one immediately answered. 'Well, did you?'

Drawing another deep breath, Ford leaned over to whisper in her ear. 'JD's not usually such a dick. He's scared too.' He cleared his throat. 'No, JD,' he said quietly. 'Alec has a printer in the trunk of his car. He used that. Battery-operated, so we didn't even use the hospital's electricity. No one knows about this except us. Now, as Taylor was trying to say . . .'

Taylor pointed to the pages she'd put in front of Joseph. 'I've highlighted calls from Denny to his mother. Ford and I went down to the ER to visit her while Alec was printing the phone records. And just so you know, we asked Officer Meyer to accompany us. The ER nurses were getting Eunice ready to go to ICU.'

Novak tilted his head. 'Why did you visit her, Taylor? Do you feel sorry for her? Because if Gage has those two kids, it's because his mother delivered them right to him.'

Taylor wished once again that she could see his eyes, because she had the feeling that this was a test. 'Most people would think that Eunice brought her injury on herself by agreeing to meet a known addict – probably in secret, because Lilah didn't know about it and wouldn't have approved if she had known. And,' she admitted with a shrug, 'I'm one of those people, especially because her blind faith endangered Jazzie and Janie. But I can think that and still feel compassion for her. Yes, she allowed herself to be duped, but sometimes the people we love the most are dirty, rotten, filthy liars.' *Right, Mom?* 'But because we love them it doesn't occur to us that they're lying, so we believe them. And even when we find out that we've been lied to, it's hard to just stop loving them or hoping that someday they'll change. So yes, part of me does feel sorry for her. Can you understand that, Agent Novak?'

One side of Novak's mouth lifted. 'Yeah, I can. So, from the look of all the highlighted calls on Denny's phone record, he calls his mama *a lot*.'

She must have passed muster, she thought, absurdly relieved. Or not so absurdly. Novak, Joseph and Daphne were all important to both Clay and Ford. Their approval was damned important. *So far, so good*.

'Denny calls his mother every morning and evening,' she said briskly, 'like clockwork. Three times on Sunday.'

'So Denny's a good son,' Joseph said. 'Or possibly a mama's boy. Either way, you're thinking of using Eunice as the bait?'

Ford nodded. 'Yes. Denny called her this morning and they talked for four minutes, which is the average length of all their calls. He called her again about an hour ago. The call length was just long enough for him to leave her a message. He doesn't know she's here.'

'Or he does and he's not coming,' Joseph countered. 'Lilah could have called him after the hospital called her. If she called his landline, it wouldn't be on those cell records. Some people still have landlines,' he added with a sarcasm so mild that Taylor nearly missed it.

'I think he'd be here if he knew,' Taylor said, trying not to sound stubborn. 'Look at these records. Denny calls Eunice. She never calls him. Their calls are short. She doesn't get chatty with him. She told Detective Fitzpatrick that Denny was basically the loser son. If she told a cop that, she certainly hasn't kept it a secret from Denny himself. There would have been digs through the years. And yet Denny still continues to call faithfully. He wants her to love him. If we make him think she's in danger or sick, he *will* go to where she is.'

Her voice had become passionately loud and now everyone around the table was staring at her. 'He will,' she added softly. Then closed her mouth, pursing her lips to keep herself from babbling further.

Joseph lifted a brow. 'So says your psychology degree?' he asked mildly.

Her spine stiffening, Taylor felt Ford bristle beside her. She patted his knee, hoping he'd get the message and settle down. Joseph was still testing her, maybe testing all three of them, and it was making her frustrated too.

'Just a minute, Taylor,' Daphne murmured when Taylor started to answer. 'Joseph, leave her alone. She's right, you know. Last Mother's Day, Denny's wife Missy got a pretty bouquet of tea roses delivered to her desk. Nothing fancy, but I complimented them and she got this bitter look. She said that if I liked hers, I should see what Denny sent his mother. Apparently he sends Eunice extravagant flower arrangements on all the holidays, but gives Missy much smaller bouquets – and that's when he remembers her at all. Missy started to cry and said she'd always played second fiddle to Eunice with Denny. And Taylor's also right that Eunice made no secret that she never really liked Denny. Gage was her blatant favorite. Denny busts his hump doing things for Eunice. When she still had her house, he mowed her lawn, fixed appliances, generally asked how high when Eunice said jump, and all that when his own home needed repairs. Gage was always too busy working to do his part. And when Gage went off the deep end, Eunice forgave him over and over while making Denny feel like he'd never be good enough.'

Novak's white eyebrows appeared over the top of his wraparound shades. 'Do you feel sorry for Denny, Taylor?'

Because Novak sounded genuinely curious rather than accusatory like Fitzpatrick had been, Taylor answered him honestly. 'I might have if he hadn't aided a murderer. Eunice didn't know that part. Denny did.'

Fitzpatrick nodded reluctantly. 'I have to agree that Denny knew. I was able to connect him with the sheriff's deputy who provided Gage's alibi. The deputy's wife has a cousin who owed Denny for getting him off on what would have been a very long prison sentence. But I can't prove it.'

'You will,' Ford said, 'when you get Denny's cell phone records through your legal channels. Two days after Valerie Jarvis was murdered, Denny placed a call to a Texas area code. It's a diner in the same town where the deputy's wife works.'

'Then I'll make sure the local Bureau field office has that information,' Joseph said evenly. 'They'll investigate. But for now, let's focus on Denny. I also agree. He knew.'

Another test. Once again Taylor pushed her irritation away. 'So, we thought to text him something like this.' She unfolded the paper she'd written it on and read it aloud. 'Met Ma in the park. She followed me back, got overheated. Passed out. Can't call 911. Too many cops looking for me. Ditching this phone, so don't contact me. Come get her.'

Ford opened his phone to the photo he'd taken. 'Then we can attach this picture of Eunice. We snapped it when we went to visit her in the ER.'

'Now *that* makes sense as a reason for your visit,' Novak said. 'But it's not a great picture, Ford.'

'We did it on the sly, D,' Ford said, exasperated. 'It wasn't like we were gonna ask her to sit up and say cheese.' He passed the phone to Joseph. 'We Photoshopped out as much of the tubes and monitors as we could, so Denny won't see them unless he looks hard.'

'You're hoping he's too upset to look closely,' Daphne said, and Ford nodded.

'Whose idea was it to use Eunice as the hook?' Joseph asked, studying the photo.

Taylor had to yank her hand back because she'd started to raise it like a kid in school. 'Mine,' she said flatly. *And he hates it. Wonderful.* 'So if you don't like it, blame me.'

'It's a damn good plan,' Alec muttered, and Taylor shot him a grateful smile.

'So, Joseph,' Ford said warily, 'what do you say?'

Joseph passed Ford's phone to Fitzpatrick and Daphne. 'It's a damn good plan.'

Taylor blinked at him, trying to keep her temper locked down. The man had been wasting their time. Had wasted Jazzie and Janie's time. 'This was a test, wasn't it?'

Joseph met her eyes directly, and a shiver of discomfort raced down her spine. Damn, but the man could be cold.

'Yes,' he said unapologetically. 'If I use this information, I have to

365

be prepared for the consequences if anything goes wrong. I'll call you my confidential informants, but I need to know that my informant network is emotionally mature enough to handle an interrogation without cracking.'

'Are you satisfied that we are?' Taylor asked.

'Not entirely. But enough to consider the logistics of your plan. Are you three planning to text from one of your own phones?'

'I can't, even if I didn't have enough of an "actual brain" to know that was stupid,' Taylor said pointedly. 'You took my phone as evidence.'

A flicker of discomfort appeared in Joseph's eyes, but was quickly extinguished. He inclined his head. 'I'd forgotten that your phone was evidence. My apologies.'

'Accepted,' Taylor said gracefully, wondering if he was apologizing about the phone or for insulting her brain earlier. She figured it was the latter, because Daphne covered her mouth to hide a smile and Ford coughed to disguise a laugh.

'I'm not using mine either, Joseph,' Ford said

'Me either,' Alec said, looking a little confused. 'We'll use a burner phone. I've got at least a dozen in the trunk of my car.'

Joseph sighed. 'Of course you do.'

'I'll get one for you too, Taylor,' Alec said. 'You can go to your online account to forward your calls to your burner number, so you'll know if your other dad calls.'

Taylor's smile bloomed. 'Thank you, Alec.'

Alec shrugged, but looked pleased. 'Least I can do.'

Feeling a bit more in control just knowing she'd have a phone in her hand again soon, she turned to Joseph. 'Are you planning to tell Lilah about the ruse?'

'No, I'm not ,' Joseph said. 'She's been less than honest with us. I don't care why she's holding back. We can't trust her. Why?'

'Because those girls are traumatized, and Jazzie in particular is leery of men. If Lilah's not going to be on hand for them once we get them back, they need someone they trust. They know me.' Taylor held up her hand when the men got all huffy. 'Let me finish, please. I'm not asking to be part of any showdown and I will not touch another gun, but when you do find them, after it's all over, let me at least be nearby to hold them. Please. I'll stay in the car, I'll wear whatever body armor you say. I'll cower on the floorboards. I'll wait three blocks away. I promise.'

Joseph looked at Fitzpatrick. 'Can we keep her safe?'

Fitzpatrick nodded, displeased. 'We can put her in one of the bullet-resistant SWAT vans and park her far enough away. But you have to promise to stay put, Taylor. No getting anyone else distracted so that they forget the plan.'

Stunned, Taylor's eyes widened. *You condescending asshole.* She swallowed hard to keep those words – and others that would have been far worse – from clawing their way up her throat and escaping out of her mouth. *Stop it. They're letting you be on hand for the girls. Don't lose it or they'll change their minds.*

'Thank you,' she said, then pursed her lips to keep from saying any more.

Fitzpatrick frowned. 'You didn't promise,' he said, sounding truly worried.

She made herself smile, drawing on the experience of every one of the years she'd schooled her expression while in hiding so that no one was alerted to how scared and angry she really was. 'I promise,' she said sweetly. 'Sir.'

From the corner of her eye she saw both Novak and Daphne wince. Under the table, Ford squeezed her hand before mercifully taking the conversational baton, because she didn't think she could get another word past the lump in her throat.

'Going back to Lilah,' Ford said. 'Has anyone been able to make contact with her, other than when JD talked to her earlier?'

'Hector did, but only through the door,' Fitzpatrick said. 'She's still claiming that the girls are in the apartment with her. That they're still napping.'

'She's lying,' Ford said, very quietly.

'Of course she's lying!' Fitzpatrick snapped, pinching the bridge of his nose. 'She also knows judges who believe her when she says her two nieces are currently in her care. Expect a call, Joseph. She threatened Hector that she'd report both him and me for harassment.'

'I'll take care of it,' Joseph said calmly.

A muscle twitched in Ford's cheek. 'But Gage could be in her apartment for all we know, holding her and the girls at gunpoint. Can't you just get a friggin' warrant, JD?'

'No, I can't just get a friggin' warrant,' Fitzpatrick shot back. 'Don't you think I would have if I could? Did you *hear* the part about her knowing *judges*? I *tried*. *Twice*. Two different judges. Both said I didn't have enough cause for a warrant. They'll probably call you too, Joseph. I was . . . insistent. They still said no.'

'Still, it would be nice to know if the kids really are missing,' Novak commented mildly, pointedly ignoring Fitzpatrick's irritated glare. 'Before we go to all this trouble. Especially seeing as how Joseph's going to have to act on a tip provided by a confidential informant. This could blow up in his face.'

Daphne drew in a long breath. 'Joseph?' she began uncertainly. 'We want the girls safe, of course, but let's do this wisely, in a way that will let us use whatever evidence you find. If it's fruit of the poisoned tree, we won't be able to charge Gage with kidnapping.'

Taylor's stomach went tight with panic. *Whoa. Wait. Fruit of the poisoned tree?* Alec had hacked into Denny's account, true. And technically Alec had broken the law, so technically anything they discovered from the hacked accounts wasn't useable in court. *But we can use the information to find the girls.* The girls were the priority, weren't they?

Gage had done so many other terrible things. They had good evidence to charge him with the murder of Valerie and those three people the morning before. After they found the girls. They couldn't be going back to the beginning.

Joseph said our plan was good. But Taylor caught the barest flicker of hesitation in his eyes. He was reconsidering. *No, don't. Please don't leave those girls with Gage Jarvis.*

'There is another way to get Lilah to talk to us,' she blurted out.

'I don't like the look on your face,' Fitzpatrick said darkly, and he was definitely not teasing. 'It's telling me that we do not want to hear this other way.'

Taylor flinched, and the tight leash she'd kept on her anger simply snapped. 'I don't give a good goddamn whether you like my look or anything else about me, *Detective*.' Scowling at her, Fitzpatrick opened his mouth to respond, but she waved his words away. 'Have I given you any reason at all to make that statement? *No I have not*,' she barreled on, not giving him a chance to answer. 'What I *have* done is *exactly* what you've asked of me, up to and including making myself goddamn *bait* for a psychopathic *killer*.'

She rose slightly out of her seat, her finger jabbing at the air to underscore the words she could no longer hold back. '*You* recruited *me*. *You* asked for *my* help. *You involved me*. You were all too happy to use me as cannon fodder when it suited you, but the minute the bullets started flying it somehow became my fault. Yes, I distracted my father. And yes, I am *sorry* he's hurt.' Her voice broke. 'I am so goddamn *sorry*. But as sorry as I am, it was *not my fault*. Why didn't you have snipers on the goddamn roof? Why didn't you put anyone outside the restaurant? Because you didn't expect a fucking gunman to be hiding across the street, that's why. And I get that. I do. *I* don't blame *you*, so don't blame *me* when all I have done is *cooperate*.'

She stopped abruptly, suddenly aware that she had the undivided attention of everyone in the room. And that her cheeks were wet. She retracted her pointed finger and let her hand fall to her side. Her heart hammered, her head pounded and her throat burned.

'I shot a man today,' she whispered, then swallowed hard. 'I never shot anyone before, but I shot a man after he shot my father, who might die before I ever get to know him.' She looked down at her jeans. 'I'm still covered in his blood. Because we *cooperated*. So, Detective Fitzpatrick, if I haven't earned your respect, I have at least earned the opportunity to see this through without any of your condescending *bullshit*.'

Wiping her eyes, she lowered herself into her chair. For a second you could have heard a pin drop. Then Ford shifted uncomfortably in his chair, grabbed her hand and squeezed it *hard*. 'Jesus, Taylor,' he breathed in her ear, his words only for her hearing. 'Warn me next time.'

Confused, she chanced a glance up at him from the corner of her eye and quickly understood. His cheeks were flushed, his blue eyes sharp and focused. And aroused. It was all she could do to keep her face blank as she looked back at the other faces around the table, meeting the eyes of each person. But under the table she squeezed Ford's hand back, giving his thumb a caress with her own before letting him go.

Apparently Ford was turned on by a woman who spoke her mind. *Good to know.* They wouldn't last long if he'd wanted a shrinking violet. Taylor might have been sheltered, but Frederick Dawson had always respected her opinions and taught her how to stand up for herself when she expressed them. *Thanks, Dad.*

Daphne looked pleased. Alec grinned in delight, and Deacon simply appeared amused. And shock of shocks, Joseph Carter actually smiled at her.

Fitzpatrick, however, looked stunned and dismayed. 'You're right,' he said. 'But you're also wrong. You *have* done what I have asked. You *have* cooperated. And you've earned the right to see this through. But I *don't* blame you for Clay being shot.'

'You could have fooled me,' she said quietly.

Fitzpatrick sighed. 'I can see how you might think that based on what I said, and I admit I've found the timing of your arrival suspicious, given everything else that's happened. I apologize, Taylor. You haven't seen me at my best today.'

She dipped her head. 'Accepted. Thank you.'

Fitzpatrick gave her a brisk nod. 'Okay. Back to Lilah. Do you want to try talking to her?' That he asked without a hint of condescension went further to soothe her ire than his apology had.

And now Taylor had to pretend that she wasn't aware of the large, aroused man sitting beside her. 'Yes, but if she's not taking calls from the police, there's every chance she won't take mine either. However, if Gage does have the girls, she might take a call from him.'

Nods all around the table made her feel even better. 'You want to call her by spoofing Gage's number,' Joseph said.

Taylor nodded. 'It could backfire on us, of course. Especially if Gage is there with her and sees the caller ID on her phone. But if he's not and I play it right, Lilah might be able to give us details that could save Jazzie and Janie's lives.'

Joseph nodded. 'Let's do it then. Alec, go get one of those burner phones.'

As if on cue, all the phones around the table began to buzz and ding as a series of texts were delivered. The room went suddenly, painfully still. Taylor sucked in a breath and closed her eyes, afraid to look at the phone in Ford's hand. Afraid of what she'd see. There was only one reason everyone was being texted, all at the same time.

Please, please let him be okay. I just found him.

Then Ford's arm was around her shoulders and he was pulling her to him. 'He's okay,' he whispered in her ear as whoops and hollers broke out all over the room. 'He's out of surgery and he's going to be okay.'

Taylor collapsed against him, boneless with relief. She opened her eyes just in time to find herself squarely in the middle of a huge group hug as everyone came together like they were doing a wonderful, disorganized square dance. These people were her father's family and she celebrated with them until, after about a minute, Alec broke away from the huddle.

'I'm gonna go get the burner phones,' he said. 'And we'll get started.'

Baltimore, Maryland,
Sunday 23 August, 9.05 P.M.

Ford was glad when his mother rushed back up to the OR waiting room to sit with Stevie. Because looking your mom in the eye after almost coming during a meeting with cops? Too fucking embarrassing for words.

But he hadn't been able to help himself. Taylor had been amazing. *And she used my words,* Ford thought, pride swelling his chest until he thought he'd bust with it. He hadn't been sure she'd absorbed what he'd told her when Officer Meyer had belittled them earlier, in the elevator on their way to the ER waiting room. That Joseph and JD owed her participation after involving her in this scheme in the first place. She'd been so nervous about meeting Tanner that he

371

hadn't thought she was really listening. But she had listened and made his words her own.

And she'd been breathtaking.

She'd left the room a few minutes before to 'freshen up'. A nurse had brought her a pair of scrubs so that she didn't have to wear jeans crusted with her father's blood. Ford figured his mother had sent the nurse, because that was exactly the kind of thing she did. She was an awesome mother. When she wasn't embarrassing him, anyway.

Deacon settled into the seat next to him, leaning over to bump his shoulder lightly. 'Going to the target range with Faith?' he murmured. 'Best. Aphrodisiac. Ever. Better than oysters. Helluva lot cheaper, too.'

Ford closed his eyes, feeling the heat creep back up into his cheeks. 'Thank you so much,' he said sarcastically. 'Damn, Deacon, now I can't get that picture out of my head.'

Deacon's chuckle was downright wicked. 'Then my work here is done. As long as it's Taylor who stars in your little fantasy and not my fiancée, of course.'

Ford winced. 'Of course.'

Taking off his wraparounds, Deacon leaned his head back with a sigh and rubbed his eyes. 'Damn, I'm tired.'

He looks it, too, Ford thought, suddenly worried about his friend. 'Look, Deacon, I'm sorry I was an ass earlier. I know you get the urgency in these situations. And I'm sorry that you've watched so many people die recently.'

'Thanks. Some of those we lost were important to Faith's people in Cincinnati. It's been rough. A few of the funerals in particular just . . . yanked my heart out. It's hard when you have to tell a stranger that their husband or son isn't ever coming home. But when it's family . . . God.' He hesitated, then sighed. 'And it's not only that. You remember when we found you in West Virginia?'

'Yeah,' Ford said in a *duh* voice. 'Not like I'm ever going to forget any of that. Why?'

'Do you remember when I told you about my sister Dani, the one who was sick because she'd listened to a boyfriend who told her he was disease-free?'

Ford sucked in a breath, remembering the conversation as clearly as if it had been yesterday. Deacon had been gently urging him to get himself tested because Kimberly had been a lying bitch and Ford had been intimate with her. *Because I trusted her.* And Deacon had trusted Ford, with information not everyone knew. It was the moment Ford knew he and Deacon would be friends.

'She's not . . . she's not one of the . . .' *Don't let her be dead.* 'God, Deacon, is she okay?'

Deacon nodded, but his body shuddered. 'I hope so. She was attacked. Stabbed. She made it through surgery and is recovering, but . . . Dammit, Ford, I'm scared for her. She's HIV positive and I'm fucking terrified she's going to get sick. And I can't lose her. I can't.'

Ford drew a breath and realized that no matter how much they'd all needed Deacon here, his friend might have needed them more. He squeezed Deacon's shoulder gently. 'But she's safe for now. Right? You may have to hold on to that today, and tomorrow too. And then every day after that. Worrying about it just wastes time you could be spending with her.'

Deacon's mouth curved up and Ford felt a wave of sweet relief. 'When did you get so wise, kid?' Deacon asked gruffly.

'Watching my mom battling breast cancer,' Ford said honestly. 'I still worry sometimes, but less now. It was Mom who told me to be happy with each day we have. So . . .'

Deacon's lips pursed hard and his throat worked, but at the end he held himself together. 'Thanks, kid,' he whispered, then drew a huge breath, his chest expanding. He relaxed into the chair, then rolled his head, opening one eye to give Ford a puzzled look. 'I'm surprised you didn't read about my case online. It's been national news for the past week.'

'I was camping with Dillon for the past week. No Internet.'

Deacon smirked. 'I'd forgotten about the bachelor party camping trip. Did you take Tanner's RV?'

Ford rolled his eyes. 'Of course. Dillon wanted to sleep in tents because he'd never done it before, but Clay convinced him to use the RV because Tanner was too old to sleep in a tent.'

Deacon snorted. 'Ha. I hope Tanner didn't hear that. Clay just likes having A/C.'

'He wasn't the only one.' Ford grimaced. 'It was hotter than hell. Anyway, I just got back yesterday afternoon.' He rubbed his jaw ruefully. 'And promptly met the business end of Taylor's right hook.'

Deacon grinned delightedly, which had been Ford's reason for telling him. He hated seeing his friend so sad. 'She hit you? Seriously?'

Ford laughed. 'Knocked me on my ass. I learned not to sneak up on her. Which I honestly hadn't meant to do. I thought she heard me walking behind her, but I thought wrong.'

'Damn. And she's a great shot, too. I bet Clay is one proud papa. I hope he wakes up before we have to leave. I want to see his face when he looks at her. I bet he goes to mush.'

'Pretty much,' Ford said quietly.

They sat for a few moments in silence, and then Deacon sighed. 'I gotta say, the past few weeks have been so bad that I almost called Holly and told her I couldn't come to the wedding. I was ass-deep in paperwork and surrounded by too much death. And then with Dani getting hurt . . . I figured I'd only bring the party down. Dani wanted me to go, but I didn't want to. Then Faith forced me to get on the plane, and I'm so glad she did. Seeing you guys was exactly what I needed.'

'What we needed too. The waiting room was like a wake before you showed up.'

The door opened and Alec came in holding two throwaway phones, Taylor close behind him, and Ford found himself sitting a bit straighter. She'd evidently borrowed a hairbrush and some lipstick, and she was all cleaned up and looking . . . gorgeous. *Damn. I do* have *it bad.*

'Aw, shut up,' he muttered to Deacon when the man laughed.

'Got the burners,' Alec announced, and they gathered around the table again. Here's one for you, 'Taylor. Hopefully you can reach your other dad in California.'

She held the phone like it was a precious stone. 'Thank you.'

374

'So how are we gonna play this?' JD asked Joseph.

'Maybe call Lilah's phone and wait to see who picks up,' Joseph said. 'If it's Gage, Deacon, you can pretend to be a telemarketer or something. They spoof all the damn time.' He looked at Taylor. 'Don't take offense, but I don't see you as a bullshitter. Deacon, on the other hand, is the king of the bullshitters.'

'And proud of it,' Deacon said, buffing his nails on the lapel of his suit.

'I have no issues with Agent Novak handling Gage. But,' Taylor added in a gently admonishing tone, 'don't ever underestimate someone who's spent her whole life bullshitting because she thought she had to hide to stay alive. If I didn't have Clay's eyes, no one here would have ever suspected that I wasn't born Taylor Dawson.'

Respect flickered in Joseph's eyes. 'Point taken.'

'Thank you. Now if Lilah answers, I made a note of what I wanted to say.' She pushed the paper across the table so that the cops could read it. All nodded their approval.

'I have the spoofing site open,' Alec said. 'Ready when you are.'

'Let's make the call,' Joseph said, 'then get ourselves over to Denny's house. The officer on surveillance duty knows that Denny is likely to leave quickly and is ready to follow. During the break, I lined up SWAT resources and Children's Services if we need them. I canceled the hostage retrieval team. Hector left Agent Ingram in charge. I want Hector here for this op. Go ahead, Alec.'

Alec dialed and they held their collective breath. The phone rang several times and Ford thought it would go to voicemail, but at the last moment Lilah picked up.

'Hello? Who is this?' She sounded tentative, her voice hoarse and raw, as if she'd been crying. Then a carefully indrawn breath, followed by a whisper. 'Gage?'

Taylor opened her mouth, but Joseph held up his hand, silently asking her to wait. A few seconds passed as his expression tightened with indecision, then he whipped a handkerchief from his pocket, covered the phone, and pitched his voice to a raspy growl. 'Yes.'

Lilah shuddered out a tortured breath. 'Thank God. Where are they? Are they okay? I'll come get them. Just tell me where. Nobody will know, I promise. Just tell me where they are.'

Joseph remained silent, his hand still lifted for Taylor's silence as well.

'No,' Lilah moaned. 'Not again. *Please.* I did what you said. Both times. What can you possibly want now? I cleaned out my bank accounts, so there's no more cash.'

After about ten seconds of continued silence, Lilah began to cry, huge ragged sobs. 'Dammit, Gage, they're just little girls. They're *your* little girls. How can you do this to them? I'm begging you. Is that what you want? You want me to beg you on my knees? I will, then.' She choked on her tears. 'I don't have any pride left. Just give them back to me. *Please.*'

Joseph gave Taylor a nod, and she drew a deep breath. 'It's not Gage. It's Taylor Dawson. Please don't hang up.'

'Oh my God. *Oh my God.*' Lilah just cried harder. 'He has you, too?'

'No, no. I'm safe, completely safe. I know you think this is cruel, and I'm sorry, but I wanted the truth about Jazzie and Janie and you wouldn't answer any of our phone calls. So I tricked the phone into displaying Gage's number.'

'*No.*' Lilah's voice was horrified. 'He'll find out you called. He'll know. What if he has my phone tapped? How could you *do* this?'

Taylor closed her eyes, but not before they'd filled with both pity and panic. Ford covered the hand she rested on the table with his, squeezing it lightly.

'Gage is hurt, Lilah,' Taylor said quietly but quickly. 'He's bleeding heavily. I know, because I shot him myself. He can't go to a hospital, because they'll turn him over to the police. He's going to run or he's going to go under and let his wounds heal. It'll have to be somewhere where he feels safe. He may have already done so. If he dies, no one will know where the girls are. Do you have any idea where he's keeping them? Any clues, background noise or anything?'

'No.' Lilah's voice had hardened to a thin, brittle shell. 'I don't know anything except that if my girls are hurt because he caught me talking to you, you won't have to worry about Gage. *I* will make you wish you were never born. Don't call me again.'

And the line went dead.

Joseph pocketed his handkerchief, worry lines now bracketing his mouth. 'I hope he doesn't have her phone tapped. We've completely shown our hand if he has.'

Taylor swallowed hard. 'I didn't know what to say when she said that.'

'You did fine,' Joseph said, then sighed. 'At least we know that Gage has them.'

'Or at least he *said* he did when he called Lilah for the ransom,' JD added.

'Maybe,' Joseph allowed. 'We also know he's not at her apartment. All we can do for Lilah now is protect her safety. The agent standing guard outside her door will do that. Alec, go ahead and send the text.'

When Alec had done so, Joseph stood up. 'Let's move out. JD, you're with me. Alec, stay here, and watch your phone. I may have to call you if we need additional . . . *unconventionally obtained* information. Ford, Taylor, you're to ride in the rear of the SWAT van and stay the hell down. Deacon, go in the SWAT van with them, if you would.'

Taylor's back stiffened. 'I would have complied with the stated rules even without a federal babysitter,' she said quietly.

'Not a babysitter,' Deacon said kindly. 'More like a bodyguard in case anything goes wrong. So that you don't have to shoot anyone else today.'

She nodded shakily. 'I can appreciate that. Thank you.'

'You're welcome.' Deacon hesitated in the doorway. 'You two coming?'

Everyone else had cleared out, but Ford stayed at the table, his hand on Taylor's knee, silently asking her to stay too. 'Give us a minute,' he said. 'We'll be right down. Promise.'

Twenty-two

Baltimore, Maryland,
Sunday 23 August, 9.20 P.M.

A second after Novak closed the door behind him, Ford pulled Taylor into his lap, shoved his fingers into her hair and took her mouth in a kiss so hot, so hard, so possessive that all she could do was hang on for dear life. It was over quickly, leaving her lips bruised and her heart jackhammering once again. She was shaking and so was he.

'I had to do that just once before we left,' he whispered, his breath warm against her temple. 'To get it out of my system for a little while. You've got me so tangled up that I can barely see straight. And I have to see straight because I can't let you get hurt again.'

'You didn't let me get hurt the first time, Ford,' she said, rubbing her cheek against the unyielding muscle of his chest. 'You protected us. You let him shoot you in the *back*, for God's sake. Don't be a hero again, okay?'

His laugh was unsteady. 'I'll promise if you will.'

'I promise.' She shuddered again, this time with the memory of the shot she'd taken that afternoon. 'I know Gage deserves to be punished, but . . . God. I keep hearing him scream. I can't do that again. I can't shoot a person again.'

'Even if he's shooting at you?'

She pulled back enough to look up into his very sober eyes. 'I don't want to find out.'

The corner of his mouth lifted. 'Me either. So no more heroing for us.'

378

'Amen,' she said firmly and hoped she wasn't telling a lie. Because those two little girls were in danger, and she knew that she'd do whatever she had to do to keep them safe. Even if it meant shooting Gage to kill. Luckily Novak and the others would take care of that task themselves, should it come to that.

She slid off Ford's lap and held out her hand. 'Come on. We need to move out or they'll leave without us.'

He didn't let go of her hand as they rushed to the ground floor, where Novak stood next to a van painted with a plumber's logo, staring at his watch. 'Two minutes thirty,' he said curtly.

'We're sorry,' Taylor said as she climbed into the back of the van.

Novak had finally taken his sunglasses off, and she had only a moment to note the stark contrast between his snow-white eyebrows and his face, tanned a healthy-looking bronze, because she quickly averted her eyes, her cheeks heating at the careful scrutiny he was giving her.

'You need to shave more often, Ford,' he remarked casually. 'You scratched her face. Do I have to teach you everything?'

'Why was I so glad to see you again?' Ford snapped, glaring at Novak.

Novak grinned as he got into the front passenger seat. 'Because I'm amazing.'

'You're something, all right,' Ford muttered as climbed in behind Taylor and pulled the side-by-side doors closed.

'You're full of shit is what you are, Novak,' the van's driver said with a shake of his head as he pulled into traffic. 'I thought we'd seen the last of your scary ass.'

'You missed me,' Novak said with equanimity. 'You know you did.'

'Maybe a little. Like you miss a tooth after it's been yanked out,' the driver admitted, then turned around to look at Taylor. 'I'm Detective Hector Rivera. I work for Joseph and I'll be your chauffeur today. How you doin', Ford? I heard you had some excitement earlier.'

'Hey, Hector. My back hurts and my leg throbs a little, but otherwise I'm fine.'

'Well, let's keep it that way,' Rivera said. 'There are vests and helmets back there. Suit up. Your mother'll have my hide if you get hurt on my watch.'

Ford glanced at Taylor, rolling his eyes as his face turned red with embarrassment. 'I have to get out of this town,' he muttered. 'She'd wrap me in bubble wrap if she could.'

Taylor patted his shoulder. 'I haven't known her long, but I doubt something as paltry as distance would stop her from mothering you.'

The van had no windows in the back, the windows in the front tinted dark. A bench seat lined one wall and a curtain, hanging open at present, separated the front of the van from the back. A monitor was mounted on the opposite wall, attached to a computer and a listening station by a half-dozen cords. A camera attached to the ceiling, periscope-style, had Taylor itching to try it out, but she sat down and obediently put on the smaller of the two vests.

Ford tightened the straps of his own vest with more force than necessary. 'That "mother" is part of "smother" is not a coincidence. I love her, but she makes me crazy sometimes.'

'At least you still have her,' Taylor murmured. 'My mom lied to me for my whole life, but I still miss her.'

Ford flinched. 'I'm sorry, Taylor. I should have thought before I spoke.'

Taylor made herself smile as she put on the helmet. 'It's okay. And anyway, your mom is still better than my dad. He never let me out of his sight, and then only with an escort. Speaking of Dad, I'd like to check my call log again and set up call forwarding to this burner number. Can I use your phone?'

It didn't take her long to set it all up, but once again there was nothing. No calls, no texts. Nothing. Her heavy sigh had Ford leaning over to look at her phone's screen.

'He still hasn't called?' he asked.

She put the phone in the pocket of her borrowed scrubs. 'No, and I'm really worried. It's not like him to give anyone the cold shoulder. He always answers the phone when I call. Something's happened to him.'

Novak turned around to look at her. 'Who?'

'My dad,' she said.

Novak's blink was the only sign that he was startled. 'Did Clay's status change in the two minutes it took you to get down here?' he asked carefully.

'Oh,' she said, understanding. 'No, not Clay. My other dad. In California.'

Ford told him about her stepfather, and Novak frowned. 'If he hasn't called by the time we're finished with this job, I'll make some calls and have someone from the closest sheriff's office go by your house and check on him.'

'Thank you.' She bit her lip. 'He had a few TIAs recently. You know, the little strokes. But one of the ranch hands would help him, so I'm trying not to obsess about it.'

'Good,' Novak said with a nod. 'We need you clear-headed.'

He hadn't been condescending. Just matter-of-fact. There was something about him that she trusted. 'I haven't been clear-headed since I shot Gage Jarvis. I'm not sorry,' she added. 'He had to be stopped.' She shifted in her seat so that she could see his face better. 'You've shot people, right?'

'Too many,' Novak said wearily. 'But all of them needed to be stopped too. Why?'

'How do you put it out of your mind?'

He looked over his shoulder and met her eyes, and she blinked, momentarily shocked. Now she saw what he'd been covering with those wraparounds of his. His irises were both bi-colored, blue and brown. But basic manners kicked in, along with the ability to smooth her expression.

Novak's lips quirked up. He'd noticed her reaction, even though it had spanned only a split second. 'You don't put it out of your mind,' he said, answering her question. 'You will remember Gage Jarvis forever. Maybe not actively, but subconsciously. And one day you'll see or hear or smell something and it'll take you back to the moment you pulled the trigger. Be prepared for that. Figure out how to meditate or how to breathe. Get therapy. Anything that enables you to pack it away again in its little box until the next time it pops up.'

'Like a demented jack-in-the-box,' she said, dejected. She hadn't really expected there would be a magic solution to forgetting what she'd done today, but she'd still kind of hoped.

Novak chuckled. 'I like her, Ford.'

Ford squeezed her knee. 'So do I,' he said softly. Closing his eyes, he settled back in his seat, but his hand stayed on her knee.

They rode in silence for several minutes, then Novak's voice rumbled into the quiet. 'When you can truly forget the person you've hurt or shot . . . or killed . . . then you should be worried. Because that means you've lost part of your soul.'

Detective Rivera cleared his throat. 'Amen,' he murmured roughly.

Taylor swallowed her sigh, feeling as if she'd already lost part of her soul, just by pulling the trigger. She wondered at the cumulative effect of all those pulled triggers on the souls of the two men sitting in the front seats.

And she thanked her lucky stars that she'd never even considered a career in law enforcement. Counseling the emotionally traumatized so that they might pick up the pieces of their lives would be hard enough without having to worry about the fate of her own soul.

But it's the same. The realization stole her breath. If her future clients didn't pick up the pieces, if little girls like Jazzie and Janie never healed and lived full, rewarding lives? She'd care. And she'd remember. Every face and every name. And it would hurt. A hell of a lot. *How do I deal with that?*

Suddenly overwhelmed, she took a deep breath to control her pulse. 'Do you remember the victims, too?' she asked, already knowing the answer.

Novak's lips flattened grimly. 'Every single one. You, Hector?'

'Yeah. Every damned one. The kids are the worst. I hope we get to these girls in time. I got enough baby ghosts floating around inside my head.'

Novak grunted his agreement. 'I'd like to have a few faces in the "win" column to remember when the "lose" column wakes me up at three a.m.'

That's how I'll deal with it when I'm a therapist. I'll remember the wins. Please God, let Jazzie and Janie be a win. Please.

Baltimore, Maryland,
Sunday 23 August, 10.00 P.M.

'Denny stopped near the corner of Edmonson and Appleton.' Joseph's voice came rattling out of the radio up front and Ford twisted in his seat to allow Deacon to pass from the front of the van to sit at the surveillance console in the back. Hector pulled the curtain, blocking their view of the street – and the street's view of them – but seconds later, the street view popped up on the monitor mounted to the wall.

The street was one long row of the connected houses that one saw all over Baltimore. It looked like this section of town had seen far better days, but it could have been worse. It was quiet now, with very little car or pedestrian traffic. Which was good, Ford thought. If Gage started shooting again, there wouldn't be anyone caught in the crossfire.

Deacon put on headphones and did a camera sweep. 'We've got video and audio,' he said. 'We're a block behind you. Once you've got the kids, we'll approach.'

Gage's brother Denny had immediately taken the bait, driving away from his house like a bat out of hell. Joseph and the others had been worried that the man would be stopped by a cop before he got to his brother's hiding place.

'He's going into one of the row houses,' Joseph said.

Deacon flipped a switch and the monitor split, one side showing the street where they waited and the other side a rundown row house. 'We've got your feed. Standing by.'

'What next?' Ford asked.

'We cross our fingers that Gage didn't come back here after Taylor shot him,' Joseph answered, 'and that Denny either comes out when nobody answers or he manages to open the door to Gage's room and finds the girls himself.'

'That would save some paperwork,' Deacon said dryly. 'Considering the source of your tip.'

Ford hadn't fully considered the risk to Joseph when he accepted the phone numbers Alec had found through his hacking. But Joseph *had* considered the risk and had come anyway. *Mom chose well*, he thought.

'But what if Gage did come back?' Deacon countered. 'What if he's there now? We know he's got access to weapons.'

'Then we call for backup and follow hostage protocols,' Joseph said grimly. 'Priority one is to get the girls out safely. We'll deal with the fallout later.'

'I hope I hurt Gage so bad that he couldn't get back here,' Taylor whispered fiercely. 'Maybe he's bleeding in an alley somewhere.'

Ford grasped her hand tightly and held on, his eyes glued to the monitor. 'Me too.'

Baltimore, Maryland,
Sunday 23 August, 10.00 P.M.

Lying on the floor, Jasmine kept her eyes closed, concentrating on taking slow, deep breaths, matching the rhythm of her breathing to his so that she wouldn't startle him into waking up. She needed him to think she was asleep, for just a little longer. She didn't want him to hear her breathing fast or hard. Didn't want to call his attention to the fact that she hadn't been lying still, that she'd been squirming and shifting – first her hands, then her entire body.

It had taken a while and her wrists were now burning and bloody, but she'd succeeded. Her hands were free! She'd wanted to scream with joy, but she'd stayed quiet, making sure he still slept. Then she'd contorted, bending her body in half so that she could pick at the knots on the ropes at her ankles. That hadn't taken quite as long, but it had required her to stop and breathe more often. She'd left the gag in, thinking she could roll to her back to hide her freed hands if he woke up long enough to peer down at her.

But that hadn't happened. He'd continued to snore and her feet were now free as well. She'd started on Janie's ankle ropes next, but that had her breathing hard too. He hadn't been drunk when he'd tied Janie's ropes, and they were really tight.

She hadn't given up, though, and had managed to loosen Janie's knots, but not completely, because he'd double-tied them.

Through all of it, Janie hadn't woken up, and Jasmine was starting to panic about that. Janie was a heavy sleeper normally, but she hadn't stirred even when Jasmine had needed to dig her fingers into her sister's skin to get at the knots.

What if Janie was drugged too much? Could someone die from Benadryl? What if she never woke up? *What if I have to carry her?* Jasmine wasn't sure that she could.

I'm so tired.

She'd needed to rest for just a minute, so now she lay on the floor, stretched out next to her sister, trying to regulate her own breathing. Trying to pretend to be asleep, without actually falling asleep. That would be the worst if that happened. *He'd kill me.* Jasmine had not a single doubt. *He'd kill me, then he'd kill Janie.*

The pretending-to-sleep wasn't hard to do. She'd had lots of practice, after all, pretending to sleep when Aunt Lilah came in to check on her, because if Lilah saw she was awake, she fussed, plumping pillows and asking if Jasmine wanted warm milk.

Warm milk? Really? Jasmine wanted to hurl. It was the thought of warm milk, she assured herself. It had nothing to do with his blood that had dried on her clothes after she'd helped him. Or of her own blood drying on her skin. *Think of cute puppies, of art class, of warm milk even.* Anything but the smell of his blood.

Because she couldn't throw up. She needed to get away. She needed to get Janie free without getting caught. And then? Well, then the plan was super-simple.

Once Janie could walk, Jasmine would grab her and run as fast as she could. Out the door and into the street. Someone would help them. *Someone* has *to help us*, she thought desperately.

She wondered if anyone was even looking for them. She'd heard him talking to Lilah, heard her aunt promise to not call the police. She hoped Lilah wasn't stupid enough to really not call the cops. She hoped someone had found Grandma, that she was okay. Even though she'd basically handed her own granddaughters over to a crazy man.

I should have told Lilah what I saw that day. I should have said that I saw him, that he killed Mama. I should have said something to someone. Why didn't I? Why was I so stupid?

385

Because you were afraid out of your mind, dumbass. Not the same as being stupid.

Which didn't change anything, because she was still here, lying on a dirty floor next to her sister, trying to figure out how to get away. *Just stay asleep, you bastard. For God's sake, don't wake up!*

A racket in the hallway had her stiffening, listening. She opened her mouth and drew a breath, trying to decide if she should scream for help. But if anyone lived here, they were probably drug addicts like him. They wouldn't help her and she'd just make him mad. So she closed her mouth, praying they'd be quiet and let him sleep.

So I can run. Please. Please, just let him stay asleep.

Her hopes were dashed when someone jiggled the doorknob and cursed. The door creaked when whoever was outside threw themselves against it, trying to break it down.

Above her, the bed pitched as he rolled over. *He's awake. Dammit.*

'Go away,' he slurred. 'Jus' go the hell away an' leave me alone.'

'Gage?' The voice was low and urgent. *Uncle Denny.* 'Open the door.'

Jasmine's heart leaped, then fell with a hard thud that felt like somebody'd punched her. Uncle Denny had known her father was here. Denny had been a part of this. *Can't trust him.*

No, she corrected herself, Gage Jarvis was *not* her father. He was a killer. *Not my father.* And for that she was grateful.

Gage didn't stir from the bed, moaning another plea to be left alone, but Denny began banging on the door.

'Open up! Open this door or I will turn your fucking ass in, and I am not kidding!'

'Shut the fuck up! I'm coming!' The bed creaked as Gage hefted himself to his feet. He staggered to the door, nearly tripping over Jasmine and Janie. 'Goddammit,' he snarled, and kicked at them. The toe of his shoe caught Jasmine's hip, but he'd thrown himself off balance and it didn't really hurt. Not like it might have.

He made it to the door, his back to them now. Covering Janie's sleeping body with her own, Jasmine looked around frantically. There was just one door, and the window was stuck shut. She knew that because he'd complained when he'd been unable to open it himself.

Think. Think. Janie was still tied. *I shouldn't have stopped. Shouldn't have rested.* She'd never get past them. Not if she was carrying Janie. *But I'm not leaving her behind.* No matter what.

Gage opened the door a crack. 'What do you want, for God's sake?' he hissed.

His back was to them, so Jasmine sat up and pulled Janie's feet close, frantically yanking at the knots. *Just a little more.* A sob was building in her throat. *Don't cry*, she told herself. *He'll hear you. He'll kill you both and Uncle Denny won't help you.*

'I'm here for Ma,' Denny said in a *duh* voice. 'You told me to come get her.'

'You're hallucinatin',' Gage said, shaking his head. 'And *I'm* the drunk one.'

'Let me in. I'll take Ma home and you can go your merry way.' The door moved as Denny tried to force it open.

Gage shoved it back. 'And I'm telling you she's not here. She's at the fucking park.'

'Right now? It's dark outside.'

'How should I know where she is right now?' Gage spat back belligerently. 'Last time I saw her she was in the park. That was this afternoon.'

'This afternoon?' Denny echoed, panic edging into his voice. 'Why would she go to the park in the first place? It's over a hundred degrees out there.'

Gage sighed heavily. 'Because she met me there, okay? She was still there when I left. I'm sure she's fine.'

But even Jasmine could hear the uncertainty in Gage's voice.

'What have you done, Gage?' Denny asked, the panic in his voice becoming fear.

'Nothin'. And I got nothin' more to say to you,' Gage said thickly. He tried to close the door, but Denny pushed harder.

'But *you* texted *me*,' Denny insisted. 'Here, look at my phone, at this picture.'

'I did not send you any text. Get your phone out of my fuckin' face.' He was still a little drunk, but mostly he sounded sleepy and grumpy. From the corner of her eye Jasmine saw him push Denny's hand away. 'Look at the picture yourself. I need to sleep.'

Her heart pounded in her throat as her fingers scrabbled with the rope, but it finally – *finally* – loosened and she flung it away. Janie stirred, also *finally*, but her eyes were wide and glassy. Like Gage, she was still half asleep.

Jasmine put her finger over her lips and Janie closed her eyes again with a smile.

'Oh no,' Denny said quietly. 'Oh God. This picture wasn't taken in your room. It was taken at the hospital.' He sounded even more panicked now, his voice lowering, like he was talking to himself. 'I didn't see the tubes before. She's in the hospital, hooked up to machines.' His voice grew louder, desperate. 'You didn't send this picture. Ma really isn't here, is she?'

'I told you that, fuckwad. Now leave me alone. I'm going back to sleep.' Gage leaned on the door, but stumbled back when it flew open abruptly.

Denny charged in, his shoulder down like a football player, knocking Gage across the room. Jasmine quickly dragged Janie under the bed to get out of his way.

This is it! We have to run – now! She shook Janie's shoulder. 'Wake up!' she whispered. 'Janie, wake up.'

'She's not here!' Denny cried, and the bed bowed down as he and Gage fell on it.

'What the fuck, Denny?' Gage sputtered. 'Dammit, you're hurting me.'

'I'll do worse, you sorry sonofabitch. She's not *here* because she's in the fucking *hospital*.'

'Let *go* of me.' There was the crack of a fist hitting bone, and the bed dipped again. They were rolling around up there. Fighting. And not paying attention to her and Janie. 'Denny . . .' Gage's voice was rough and all gaggy, like he was being choked.

This may be our only chance. She shook Janie's shoulder again, harder. 'Wake up,' she begged. 'Please.'

'I ought to fucking kill you,' Denny gritted out. 'Ma's in the hospital with an IV in her arm. I didn't see it in the picture before, but now I do. It's there. What did you do to her?'

'I gave her a little something to make her sleep,' Gage said hoarsely. 'That's all.'

The bed rattled and the choking sounds got louder. 'You gave her a *sedative*? Then left her in the park . . . *alone*? In this heat?' Denny roared like a lion. 'You moron. She's got fucking *Parkinson's*. You put her in the hospital! Look!'

Another pause. 'Where did you get this picture?' Gage asked, suddenly sounding a lot more sober.

Run. Run. Carry Janie if you have to. Jasmine edged out from under the bed, dragging Janie with her. Her sister's eyelids fluttered open and Jasmine pressed her finger to her lips, trembling with relief. 'Quiet,' she mouthed, and Janie nodded, still groggy.

At least I don't have to carry her now. Jasmine hadn't been sure how she'd have managed that. Janie was really heavy for a little kid.

'*You* texted it to me,' Denny yelled. 'Are you that damn drunk that you don't remember?'

'Are *you* that damn *stupid*? You've been *played*. You *moron*.' The bed began to shake again and Jasmine could see their feet change position as they rolled. Gage had control now, and she flinched at the sound of more punching and Denny's grunts of pain. 'The cops tricked you. They faked my number to get you to come here.'

'No. It's not possible. Nobody followed me. I was careful.' Denny sounded terrified.

'What you are is a fuckup, and I'll be goddamned if you take me down with you.'

A sharp click followed, and Denny started to babble. 'Gage, no! No! Put the gun down. Please. Think about this. I *helped* you. I *helped you.*'

That's it. We have to go. Jasmine grabbed Janie's hand and pointed at the door. 'Run fast,' she mouthed. 'Don't stop.' She drew a breath, said a prayer, then leapt up and ran.

The door was still open a little. As she dragged Janie through, she could hear Denny begging.

'I won't talk, Gage. I promise. I wouldn't, because I'd go to jail too. Just let me up. We'll get away. I'll help you get away.'

'No,' Gage said. 'I've got leverage. You're a liability, Denny. Sorry.'

Leverage? Halfway down the stairs, Jasmine froze, her hand clutching the banister. *That's us.* We're *the leverage.* But they weren't in the room anymore. *He'll be mad. So mad.* And Jasmine knew what he could do when he was mad. 'Hurry, Janie,' she urged, half lifting her sister so that they could run down the remaining stairs.

He'd discover they were gone any minute. *Think, think.* He would catch them. He was faster. He was coming down the stairs. She looked right, then left. Two doors. Front and back. *Trick him and hide.* The front door was closer. He'd think they'd gone that way. She grabbed one of her shoes and threw it toward the front door, then dragged Janie to the back. *Where's the door to outside? Where's the—*

It was in the laundry room. The handle turned, and Jasmine could feel the heat of the outside on her face. It was dark when they burst through the door.

If the police had followed Denny, they were here somewhere. She had to find them. *I should have gone out the front. They're probably there.* At least that was where they waited on TV. She and Janie were standing in the middle of a long line of houses. Row houses, all connected. No alleys to cut through to get to the street. *I should have gone out the front.* Now they had to run all the way to the end. Which way should they go? *Which way?*

She picked the right and started to run, dragging Janie, but the sound of gunshots made her stumble, her feet freezing in place. Two gunshots.

Janie tugged her shirt. 'Jazzie? What was that?'

'He shot Uncle Denny,' Jasmine whispered, jolted out of her shock. That Denny had shot Gage was too much to hope for.

'Daddy?' Janie asked, confused. 'Daddy shot Uncle Denny?'

Not our daddy. But she'd deal with that later. 'Run, Janie. Fast as you can.' Forcing her feet to move, she ran, dragging Janie with her.

Baltimore, Maryland,
Sunday 23 August, 10.03 P.M.

'He's been in there for three minutes,' Joseph said over the radio. 'Probably long enough to know his mother isn't there. I'm going in. JD, you take—' Two sharp *cracks* in rapid succession interrupted him.

Taylor flinched. *Oh God.* Somebody was shooting. And the girls . . . She'd been praying they were in there. Now she was praying they weren't. That they were okay. Still alive.

'Shit,' Joseph spat. 'Shots fired. Hector, call for backup, and then the two of you get up here. Leave the van where it is. Ford, do not leave the vehicle. JD, let's go.'

Taylor stared at the TV monitor in horror as Detective Rivera and Agent Novak followed Joseph's orders, leaving her alone with Ford. 'How many shots?' she asked hoarsely.

'Sounded like two,' Ford said, his jaw set. 'Doesn't mean Gage shot the kids, Taylor.'

'I know. He may have shot Denny.' She couldn't rip her eyes from the screen. 'If Denny's dead, we led him into the trap. His blood's on our hands, Ford.'

'Denny knew who he was dealing with,' Ford said stubbornly. 'He knew what Gage did and he protected him. Hell, Denny may have fired the shots himself. It could be Gage that's down. You don't know. But whatever happens, Denny knew the score going in.'

'True,' she murmured, hoping that someday she'd believe it.

She watched Joseph and Rivera enter the front of the building while Fitzpatrick and Novak circled around to the back. It was a long row of houses and the one Denny had entered was towards the middle, so Novak and Fitzpatrick had to run up one side and down the rear. *Hurry. Hurry, dammit.*

Her thumb suddenly burned and she realized she'd bitten the nail past the quick. She folded her hands in her lap and returned her gaze to the monitor. The view of the house was static. Nothing happening, no movement.

But on the other side of the split screen . . . *What the hell?* She

391

stood up and leaned close to the monitor, not believing her own eyes. 'Ford, look.' She pointed at the edge of the building nearest them, where two small figures had appeared, running as fast as they could.

It was Jazzie, dragging Janie behind her.

'Oh my God,' Ford whispered, horrified. On his next breath he was moving, yanking the van's side door open. He shoved his phone at Taylor. 'Call Deacon. Tell him to hurry.' Then he was out of the van, running toward the children. 'He's on my favorites,' he called over his shoulder.

Taylor fumbled the phone, her hands shaking. She'd just found Novak's name when another person rounded the corner. Big, male and carrying a gun, which he pointed at the two girls.

Oh God. Novak wasn't going to be able to get there in time. She was out of the van and running after Ford before she'd consciously made the decision.

'Jazzie!' Taylor shouted. 'This way!'

The expression of relief on Jazzie's face would go a long way to erasing the memory of Gage's scream when Taylor had fired that afternoon – and any residual guilt that came with it. Jazzie made a sharp turn and Janie stumbled, pulling her sister down with her.

'Miss T-Taylor!' Jazzie cried. 'H-help us, p-please!' Falling to her knees, she looked over her shoulder in a panic, then scrabbled back to her feet and started running again, never releasing her sister's hand. 'He's chasing us! He has a gun! He's coming!'

Turning on the speed, Ford reached the girls and grabbed them, one under each arm. 'Follow me,' he shouted to Taylor, 'and be ready to pull those doors closed.'

Or this will all be for nothing, because Gage will kill us all.

Taylor ran after Ford, but even with his wounded leg he was faster, his stride longer, and he had the girls in the back of the van more quickly than she could close the distance between them.

Only a few more . . . Pain exploded in her thigh and she cried out, her voice tinny and shrill to her own ears. He'd shot her. Just like he'd shot Clay. Gage went for the legs, not the Kevlar. *Should have remembered that.*

She half hopped, half dragged herself toward the van, frowning when something large sailed past her, roaring with rage. She turned her head just in time to see Ford tackle Gage to the ground, grabbing him by both wrists. 'You motherfucking bastard,' Ford snarled. 'You think you get to hurt whoever the fuck you want?' Using the tactical helmet he still wore, he head-butted Gage hard enough to make the older man grunt with pain.

Good, Taylor thought. *Hope it hurts, asshole.*

Ford was squeezing Gage's wrist, trying to get him to drop the gun, but Gage was surprisingly strong for a man who'd been shot in the shoulder. For a few seconds Taylor watched through bleary eyes, trying to think through the pain to figure out what she was supposed to be doing. *Oh yeah. Help Ford.*

She dragged herself over to the two men and dropped to her knees, gouging the knee she could actually control into Gage's gun hand. Wrenching the weapon from his grip, she rolled away, coming up on the good knee to point the gun at his head.

'I will end you,' she told him quietly. 'And you know I can shoot.'

Gage turned his head, his eyes cold and full of hate. 'You cunt,' he spat.

Ford head-butted him again, harder this time, the dull thud of helmet against skull audible. 'Call her that name one more time and I'll let her shoot your miserable head off. Shut your fucking mouth, Jarvis. You're done.'

That last blow to the head appeared to have knocked Jarvis out, but because the man was a snake, Taylor didn't take her eyes off him. So she heard Novak coming around the corner before she saw him.

'What the ever-loving *hell*?' Novak shouted. 'You were supposed to stay put!'

Ford rolled off Gage and rose stiffly, pointing at the open van where the two girls huddled, sobbing as they clutched each other. 'You weren't here,' he said with a shrug. 'He was seconds away from getting them.'

'We're not sorry, either.' Taylor gritted her teeth against the waves of nausea rolling through her. The gun was shaking. *No, that's you, Taylor.* 'But I would appreciate someone taking over covering him, because I think I'm going to throw up.'

Ford took the gun from her hands while Novak cuffed Gage and bound his feet with a zip-tie, neither done too gently. Ford lowered her to the ground and ripped at the bullet hole in the borrowed scrubs she wore until he could see the wound. 'She needs an ambulance,' he told Novak tersely, his hands shaking. 'Are you hurt anywhere else?' he asked her.

She swallowed hard. *Do not throw up. Not on Ford. Because that would be . . . awkward.* The absurdity of the thought made her laugh, which told her that she was closer to going into shock than she'd thought. 'No. He's a creature of habit. Got me in the leg, just like Clay.'

'Well, you're not gushing a bloody geyser like Clay was,' Ford said, relieved.

'I didn't think so.' She gripped his shoulder and tried to stand. 'Help me to the van, please,' she said, then sucked in a startled breath when he lifted her in his arms and carried her, just like in the movies. She slid her arm around his neck, holding on for the ride, which was a little bumpy because he was limping. 'Remind yourself to do this again when I'm not about to hurl, okay? Because it's pretty damn impressive, I gotta say.'

He chuckled, his breath warm on her ear. 'Yes, ma'am.' He deposited her carefully on the floor of the van. 'I'm going to get the first-aid kit. I'll be back.'

She threw him a grateful look, then held out her arms for the two girls, who threw themselves against her, both still sobbing. 'Hey,' Taylor said softly, hugging them tightly. 'It's all over now. You guys are safe.'

'He shot Uncle Denny,' Janie wailed.

Taylor looked up at Novak, her brows raised in question.

'He's not dead,' Novak said with a grimace. '*Yet,*' he mouthed.

Taylor sighed. 'I know he did, Janie. He's not a good man.'

Janie raised her eyes to stare beyond the van door at Gage, who was now surrounded by Joseph's team and a few uniformed officers who'd arrived as backup. 'But he's my daddy,' she whispered, sounding so very lost.

'N-no, he's n-not,' Jazzie said with sad certainty. 'N-not to either of us. He t-told me.'

Janie turned her helpless, confused stare on her big sister. 'But he . . .' Whatever she saw in Jazzie's expression had her swallowing hard. 'Then who *is* our daddy?'

'I don't know,' Jazzie told her. 'M-Mama knew. But we m-might never f-find out now. B-because *he* killed her,' she added, spitting the last sentence out bitterly.

Confusion clouded the younger girl's face. 'Who did? Who killed Mama?'

Jazzie lifted a still-shaking hand to point to Gage.

Pain filled Janie's eyes. 'Daddy killed Mama?' she asked, her whisper nearly soundless, and Taylor's heart broke a little more.

Jazzie's eyes grew glassy with tears. 'Y-yes. I s-saw him l-leaving that d-day.'

'But why?' Janie asked mournfully. 'Why'd he do that?'

Jazzie blinked and the tears coursed down her cheeks. 'I d-don't know. He n-never said.'

Jazzie's tears set Janie to crying again. Taylor just held them, shifting so that her bleeding thigh was closer to the van's open door when Ford returned with a first-aid kit. He hunkered down beside her, applying bandages quickly and efficiently. Clenching her jaw, she focused on the two little girls and not the throbbing pain.

Ford rocked back on his heels when he was finished. 'That should hold you till the medics get you to the ER. There's no exit wound, so they'll have to remove the bullet.'

Jazzie had been watching Ford work and now lifted her face, horror in her eyes. 'I'm s-so sorry, Miss Taylor. He hurt you b-because of m-me.'

'I'll be fine,' Taylor assured her. 'Right, Mr Ford?'

Ford flashed a confident smile. 'Absolutely.'

But Jazzie didn't smile back, shuddering instead. 'He s-said that he k-k-k . . .' She scrunched her eyes closed and spit the word out. '. . . *killed* you because I t-talked to you.' She was shaking so hard that her teeth chattered, but she pushed on, determined to speak. 'I t-told him at f-first that I d-didn't tell you anyth-thing. B-but he . . . he . . .'

It was then that Taylor noticed the bruise darkening Jazzie's face. 'He hit you. That sonofa—' She bit off the curse, swallowing hard when tears filled her eyes. 'It's okay, Jazzie. It doesn't matter what you told him. It's okay. Mr Ford, is there a cold pack in the first-aid kit?'

Jaw clenched and hands trembling with rage, Ford placed the cold pack on Jazzie's face so very gently that Taylor wanted to cry some more, but she got control of herself.

'You protected yourself, honey,' she told Jazzie. 'Exactly what you should have done.'

Jazzie shook her head. 'He s-said he'd hurt J-Janie,' she said, her eyes imploring Taylor to understand. To forgive her. 'Sh-she's t-too little.'

Baby girl, you're breaking my heart. 'You had to protect Janie. I understand. It's okay.'

But Jazzie needed to talk, needed to get it out, so Taylor let her. 'So . . . so I l-lied. I t-told him that I t-told you everything. He took a r-rifle and said you were g-going to be d-d-*dead*.' Again she forced the word out. 'He c-came b-back and s-said you *were* d-dead.'

The thought of Gage terrorizing this child made Taylor's blood boil. 'He *tried* to kill me. But did you see his shoulder wound?'

The girl nodded, grimacing. 'He m-made me clean it for him. It was r-really gross.'

'Well, I did that. I put that hole in his shoulder. He shot my dad and he shot at Mr Ford, too. Mr Ford was wearing a vest like this' – she tapped her own vest – 'so it only hurt him a little. He hurt my dad badly, though. So I shot him to make him stop.'

'G-good,' Jazzie said harshly. Then her face fell. 'You were so b-brave.'

Taylor rested her cheek on Janie's head and met Jazzie's dark eyes. 'So were you, Jazzie. You saved your sister. I'm so *proud* of you.'

Jazzie laid her head on Taylor's shoulder. 'N-not brave. I w-was so scared. I r-ran away from him. You r-ran *to* him.'

Taylor made her lips curve, even though her leg burned like hellfire. 'I was scared too, just now, and don't you think I wasn't. But my dad always told me that being scared and still doing the right thing makes you even braver.' She realized that she'd just referred to both Clay and Frederick as her dad and it hadn't felt weird at all. The smile she'd forced became genuine. *Thanks, Dad. Both of you.* 'You did the right thing today, Jazzie. Even though you were afraid. When you remember all the bad things he did, you need to remember how brave you were. Whenever you look at Janie, remember that you saved her. You could have run away all by yourself, but you *saved* her. That makes you a very good, very brave person.'

Taylor looked up to find Ford smiling fiercely with approval. 'Perfect,' he mouthed, making her chest tight with pride, but Jazzie's small, grateful smile was her true reward.

'What about Aunt L-Lilah?' Jazzie asked. 'Is she okay?'

'She was okay when we talked on the phone about an hour ago.' Taylor wasn't sure what would happen to the woman. She'd withheld evidence and interfered with an investigation. Lilah might suffer legal consequences. But for now she was okay, so Taylor hadn't lied.

'What about our grandma?' Janie asked.

'He said she was asleep in the park,' Jazzie added. 'He said he gave her medicine to make her sleep. That she wasn't dead.'

Taylor sighed. 'Grandma's not so good, guys. She was in the hospital last I saw her.'

'She t-took us t-to him,' Jazzie said. 'But I th-think he tricked her.'

'I think you're right.' Taylor's stomach picked that moment to do a hard roll. She'd been successfully ignoring the little lights flickering in front of her eyes, but the black spots began to grow and clump together, filling her field of vision. 'I need to be quiet now or I'll be sick all over us, and nobody wants that.'

Ford spread his hand over her uninjured thigh, settling her with his touch. 'Girls, we called an ambulance for Miss Taylor, so in a minute or so you two will need to come with me or Agent Novak. Can you do that?'

Both girls regarded him solemnly. Janie nodded before Jazzie did, but neither balked when he opened his arms and picked them up. 'Miss Maggie is at the hospital.' He got in the van and sat on the bench seat, a child on each knee. 'She'll stay with you until Miss Taylor is feeling better, okay?'

'Okay,' Janie said, but she sounded doubtful. 'W-will Miss T-Taylor still be our t-teacher?'

'You betcha,' Ford promised.

'I will,' Taylor confirmed, making her voice sound a lot stronger than she actually felt. 'I'll be good as new before you know it. You'll see.'

Twenty-three

Baltimore, Maryland,
Sunday 23 August, 11.35 P.M.

'How y'doin?' Ford asked for the millionth time as he gently pushed Taylor's wheelchair down the hospital hall toward the room where Clay rested. She'd just been released from the ER with stitches in her leg and the order not to put any weight on it for a few days.

'Not too bad,' she said honestly. Getting the bullet removed had hurt, despite the painkillers the ER had given her, but thankfully the sharp pain had lessened to a dull throb.

Clay needed to be left alone to sleep, but he'd sent word to the ER through Stevie, insisting that Taylor come up as soon as she was released. He needed to see her, Taylor understood. To prove to himself that she was really okay.

Which she was, except for the throbbing in her leg. And the last remaining worry churning in her gut. True to his word, Novak had arranged for her hometown sheriff to check on her dad, but the sheriff had found no one at home and none of the ranch hands knew where Frederick Dawson had gone. Absently she patted the pockets of the newest pair of scrubs she'd been given. The first pair – on loan because her jeans had been covered in Clay's blood – had been cut away to clean and dress her wound.

No phone, she remembered with a wince. She wasn't having a great day when it came to pants or to phones. The burner Alec had loaned her had fallen out of her pocket – probably while she'd been running from Gage Jarvis – and Detective Fitzpatrick had promised he'd ask one of the patrolmen to try and find it. 'Have you

399

heard from Fitzpatrick about my phone?' she asked Ford.

'Nope, sorry. I'll call him once we get to Clay's room.'

Which might be *never* at the rate they were going. She looked over her shoulder and up at Ford's face, a picture of concentrated carefulness. He was rolling her along at a pace slower than a snail's. 'Um, you can push a little faster,' she said, and watched him scowl. 'I'm not going to break and I would like to see Clay before he's released.'

'He'll be here at least another week,' Ford said seriously.

'I know.' She made her voice tart, hoping that teasing him would take her mind off her dad. Both of her dads. 'But we won't get to his room till the week after that at this rate.'

'Ha ha,' he deadpanned, but he quickened his pace a little. He was at least as fast as a snail now. 'They said not to jar you. Quit complaining and enjoy the ride,' he added mildly.

She did as he asked, but breathed an extra-loud sigh of relief when they reached Clay's room. 'Finally.'

'Smartass,' Ford said without heat.

'Granny driver,' she shot back.

'I got you here in one piece, didn't I?'

'A significantly *older* piece,' she allowed.

He pushed her into the room and locked the chair's wheels. 'Are you always such a backseat driver?'

'Depends. Do you ever approach the speed limit?'

Stevie was sitting at Clay's bedside. 'Jesus, you two bicker like . . .' She laughed. 'Like us.'

Clay lay against the pillows, pale, but smiling, and Taylor felt a portion of her worry settle. She'd needed to see him too. To prove to herself that *he* was okay. 'You're looking pretty good there, Pops.'

He rolled his eyes. 'Do not call me Pop, and especially do not call me Pops. I'd rather be called by my name than any paternal nicknames that have two p's.'

'How about "Papa"?'

'I'll consider it.' Squinting, he crooked his finger. 'Come closer. Ford's got you parked in the next county.'

'Everybody's a critic,' Ford grumbled, but he complied, pushing her until she could grab hold of the hand Clay held out.

Clay squeezed her hand hard. 'I understand you two had another adventure all on your own.'

'Yeah, but we're okay.' She pointed to her thigh with her free hand. 'They had to dig the bullet out and they only gave me lidocaine. I think that earns me an ice-cream cone. Double dip, even. Calories be damned.'

Not letting go of her hand, he pointed to his own thigh. 'They had to splice some arteries from my other leg. I think that earns me the whole damn gallon. But I'll share with you.'

Her heart stuttered at how close they'd come to losing him. 'I'm so glad you're okay,' she whispered shakily.

'Same goes.' Clay cleared his throat. 'But you two took Gage down. Nice work.'

'And saved the kids,' Stevie added. 'Novak is singing your praises, even though he still says he told you to stay in the van.'

Ford pulled one of the chairs closer to the bed and sank into it. He looked drawn and tired. Taylor didn't want to think about how she looked.

'Deacon's gotta cover his ass with Joseph,' Ford said, waving his hand dismissively.

'Sometimes you gotta break the rules,' Clay said.

Stevie huffed. 'Sometimes? Clay, you never met a rule you've ever liked.'

'And that's why you love me,' he said, satisfied.

Stevie's face softened as she brushed a trembling hand over his hair. 'Among other reasons, yes.'

Clay let go of Taylor's hand, lowering his arm to his side with a wince. She hadn't realized that their holding hands had hurt him. 'I'm fine,' he said before she could say a word. 'Stevie told me how you worked with Alec to catch Gage. Also nice work. Don't make it a habit.'

Taylor held up her hand, palm out. 'I swear on a stack of bibles. My crime-solving days are *way* past over. I'm even tearing up my Nancy Drew fan club card.'

Ford was looking around the room. 'Where *is* Alec? I thought he'd be here with you.'

'He and Cole went to get Cordelia,' Stevie said. 'We kept the news from her until Clay woke up and the girls were found safely.'

'She would have worried herself sick otherwise,' Taylor said, and Stevie nodded.

'Exactly. She already wants to see Jazzie and Janie. She's got plans for a sleepover to cheer them up. I told her they'd need some time to process before the cheering-up stage.'

The thought of the girls having fun at an ordinary slumber party made Taylor smile. 'Hopefully not too much time. They need to be little girls again. Especially Jazzie.'

'Where are they?' Clay asked. His eyes had slid closed and he looked like he was fighting the need to sleep.

'You can only stay a little longer,' Stevie mouthed.

'I heard that,' Clay said mildly, eyes still closed. 'You're not as discreet as you think.'

Stevie kissed his forehead. 'Fine. But you do need your rest. I need you up to speed so that you can do my chores while I'm hanging over the toilet every morning.'

That made Clay smile. 'Understood. And understand that our baby will call me Daddy. Taylor better not try to teach him – or her – to say "Pop".'

'I ain't promisin' nuthin',' Taylor drawled, then sobered. 'Except that I'll be an awesome big sister. You can count on that.'

His chest rose and fell on a contented sigh. 'Thank you,' he murmured roughly, then cleared his throat. 'I believe I asked where the girls are now.'

'They were with Maggie, but now they're with Social Services,' Ford told him, 'because Lilah was taken in for questioning. Deacon didn't think Joseph would charge her with hindering the investigation, so the girls should be back home with her soon.'

'But she'll need to find someone new to help her with them,' Taylor added sadly. 'Eunice died about five minutes after we left to follow Denny.'

Ford rubbed his forehead wearily. 'Turns out Eunice was on

medication for Parkinson's. Gage gave her a sedative in the park so that he could take the girls without a fight. He didn't know it would react with her meds, but that seems to be what happened. That was what set Denny off, making him attack Gage.'

Taylor glanced at him in surprise. 'How do you know that?'

'One of the doctors told Joseph about the medication interaction, but Jazzie told me on our way to the hospital about Denny attacking Gage. You'd already gone in the ambulance. She says her uncle busted through the door, angry that his mother was in the hospital. Our Photoshopping wasn't as good as we hoped and Denny saw the IV tube. Jazzie said he still thought Gage had sent the photo. Then Gage figured out that we'd tricked Denny and he called him a moron. The two of them fought and Gage pulled out his gun and shot him.'

'And?' Clay asked. 'What happened to Denny?'

Taylor winced. 'He died in surgery. And yes, I know we didn't kill him directly,' she said to Ford when he made a growling sound. 'I know that Gage pulled the trigger.'

Ford folded his arms over his chest. 'Twice.'

'Right.' She sighed. 'But Denny wouldn't have been there if we hadn't tricked him.'

Clay lifted his hand only enough to crook his finger again. 'Come here.'

Taylor leaned in. 'What? What do you need?'

'To smack you with a rubber chicken,' he said grimly. 'Those girls were there because *Denny* aided his brother. Gage managed to elude the police for weeks because *Denny* helped him. *Denny* broke into the prosecutors' database and stole confidential information. He does not deserve your pity or your guilt.'

'Thank you,' Ford said fervently.

Taylor glared at them both. 'Can I at least feel sorry for his wife?' she asked.

Clay nodded. 'Yes, that you may do.'

'Thanks, *Pops*,' she said, then sighed. 'Missy is emotionally wrecked. She had no idea that Denny had broken into the prosecutors' server using her password, and she didn't know he was helping Gage. Poor woman. Daphne's sitting with her until the family gets there.'

Stevie sighed. 'I feel for her. Losing Paul nearly broke me, and he died being a hero. She'll have to deal with grief and shame as well. Luckily she has the kids to keep her sane. I'm not sure I would have survived if I hadn't had Cordelia to keep me busy.'

Clay reached out for Stevie's hand and brought it to his lips. 'I'm very glad you did,' he said, then turned back to Ford and Taylor. 'What else? Tell me quickly, because I'm gonna need another dose of the morphine soon.'

'Jazzie said that Gage told her he wasn't her father,' Ford told him. 'That he wasn't Janie's dad either. That her mother cheated and that was why he left.'

'Did he tell her why he killed her mother?' Stevie asked.

Ford shook his head. 'No, and Jazzie didn't witness that part, thankfully. Her mother was dead when she found her, and Gage was searching for money in the coat closet. She heard him coming and hid behind a chair. Gage might tell Joseph why he killed his wife, but he's such an asshole that I kind of doubt it. I meant Gage was the asshole, not Joseph,' he clarified dryly, and Clay's lips twitched. 'Although Mom thinks they might be able to negotiate more details in return for a protected prison cell. Gage was a defense attorney for a long time and he didn't win all of his cases. There'll be some disgruntled former clients in that jail with him, and he'll do serious time.'

'Even without the murder of his wife, they've got him on . . . What else do they have him on?' Clay frowned, his eyes closed again. 'Denny's murder and the attempted murder of the three of us. And the murder of his mother, even though some lawyer will try to call it manslaughter. Plus the murder of those three people in the alley yesterday morning.'

'One of them being a cop,' Stevie added coldly.

'He kidnapped the girls,' Taylor added.

'And assault, robbery and the theft of at least three cars,' Ford said. 'JD told me about this when you were getting stitched in the ER, Taylor. A man matching Gage's description robbed a man at an

ATM late last night at gunpoint, hit him in the head with the butt of the gun, then left him in his car, unconscious. One of the cars Gage stole belonged to the dealer he killed yesterday. He took two others when he was fleeing after shooting Clay.'

'He will never get out of prison,' Stevie said with satisfaction.

Ford nodded. 'Mom's practically salivating over the case. She says it'll be a slam-dunk. But I think that's everything, Clay. You should rest now.'

Taylor put her hand over Clay's. His face had grown more drawn as the minutes ticked by, and she found she just needed to touch him. 'Should we stop at the nurses' station on our way out and ask someone to come in with that morphine?'

He lifted a self-dosing pump from the folds of his sheet. 'I've got it. I'm just holding off till Cordelia gets here. She needs to see me awake.'

'Then we'll get out of your hair.' Taylor pushed herself out of the wheelchair, balancing on one foot so that she could lean over the bed railing to kiss his cheek. 'Bye, *Pops*. Rest now. I'll be back tomorrow. I promise.'

He smiled weakly. 'You're a brat, you know that?'

She rested her forehead against his. 'I think I come by it genetically.'

He snorted. 'Don't make me laugh. It hurts.'

'Okay, but first I want you to admit that Pops is growing on you.'

'I admit nothing. You're just trying to wear me down.'

'Damn. I'm not gonna be able to get anything past you, am I?' She kissed his forehead. 'See you later.' When she started to straighten, Ford was there, easing her back into the chair. Her butt had just touched down on the seat when she heard the voice that made her remaining fears settle to rest.

'Excuse me. I'm looking for Taylor Dawson.'

Her shoulders sagged and she choked back the sob that rose in her throat. He was here. He was okay too. 'I'm here, Dad. Right here.' She'd started to rise out of the chair to greet him when she saw the look on Clay's face.

Raw, abject fear. In a blink it was almost gone, his expression the

405

partly stern, mostly neutral one he presented to the cameras.

She rose, balancing on one foot again to lean over the bed's rail. 'Hey,' she murmured. 'Don't worry. It'll be fine. I can love you both, you know.'

He nodded, his jaw even more taut than it had been a minute before. 'Yeah, I know. But if you need to go back, I'll understand.'

'Relax. I'm not going anywhere for a while.' Using the rail for balance, she turned to smile at the man who'd been her father for most of her life. Frederick hung back in the doorway, the look on his face similar to the one Clay had worn. Abject fear. Then he, too, hid it away, showing what she'd always considered his court-room face. She reached out her hand. 'I've been so worried about you all day. You weren't answering your phone.'

Frederick slowly crossed the room, his eyes taking in the other faces before returning to hers. 'I've been on planes all day, trying to get to you.'

Because he'd been afraid that she'd choose Clay and Baltimore over him and California. She had to smooth this over somehow or she'd be a turkey wishbone forever. But that could wait a minute or two. 'You didn't check your phone?'

He flushed. 'I had it in airplane mode most of the time and forgot to switch it back on.' He stopped at the foot of the bed. 'We circled Baltimore for over an hour, waiting to land. I turned it on as soon as we did and saw all the missed calls, but you didn't answer your phone then.'

'I lost it. Actually, I lost two phones today.' She pointed to her leg. 'I've had a busy day.'

'I heard. Someone found your phone – a Detective Fitzpatrick – and told me that you'd been shot.' He pressed the heel of his hand to his chest. 'My heart almost stopped.'

So did Taylor's, just hearing him say it. 'I'm okay,' she assured him. 'Barely a scrape.'

Behind her, Clay sighed in exasperation. 'For God's sake, Taylor. You had a bullet in your leg. Do not lie to the man and tell him it was barely a scrape.'

Taylor looked over her shoulder to find Clay's eyes closed and his face pinched in pain. 'All right. I was shot. The bullet missed anything major. They dug it out, stitched me up, and told me to stay off the leg for a few days.' She gave Frederick her most engaging smile. 'Now are you going to come and hug me, or do I have to hop over there on one foot?'

Ford moved the wheelchair and Taylor met her dad halfway, falling into his arms and hanging on. He squeezed her so hard that she could barely breathe. 'Don't scare me like that, not ever again,' he whispered into her hair. 'For a moment I thought you were dead. The detective's next words were that you were okay and in the ER getting treated, but between "shot" and "okay" I thought I'd lost you.'

She rubbed her cheek on the lapel of the wool sport coat that had to be burning him up. But he smelled like home and horses and the pipe smoke he'd always favored, and she inhaled deeply, letting the scents fill her up and calm her down. 'Nope. You're stuck with me. Seems like I'm hard to kill.'

'Don't joke,' Frederick said on a rush of air. 'It's not funny.'

She pulled back and patted his cheek. 'No, it's not. I'm sorry. And now I have to sit down, because I'm still light-headed.' From behind her, Ford took her arm and lowered her to the chair. She took a breath and lifted her chin. 'Okay. So . . . introductions. Don't be weird about this, people.'

'Why would we?' Clay murmured. 'Because this isn't weird at all.'

That made them all laugh. 'Okay. So, I'm Taylor,' she said slowly, pointing at herself. 'But you all knew that. This is Ford Elkhart. Don't get riled up, Dad, but he and I are a thing.'

Ford's eyes widened almost comically.

'What?' Taylor asked, surprised. 'We aren't a thing, or you didn't think I'd tell him?'

'The second one. At least not straight off.' Ford visibly composed himself, holding out his hand and straightening his spine. 'Nice to meet you, sir.'

Frederick's brows crunched as he shook Ford's hand. 'What kind of a thing?'

'We don't know yet,' Taylor said. 'I'll let you know when we figure it out. This is Stevie Mazzetti-Maynard, former cop and now wife and business partner to this guy here in the bed, who I'm sure you've guessed is my birth father, Clay Maynard. Everyone, my other dad, Frederick Dawson.'

Clay turned to Stevie. 'Help me sit up. I'm not doing this flat on my goddamn back.'

Stevie gave Taylor a look that promised retribution if Clay were to be hurt from whatever words were likely to be exchanged, but she did as he asked, using the buttons to raise him to a slightly less prone position.

Clay scowled at his wife. 'That's not sitting up.'

'It's as sitting-up as you're going to get, so deal with it,' Stevie snapped, then met Frederick's wary gaze. 'He's been through hell. Do *not* upset him.'

Frederick leaned back on his heels, his apprehension *and* irritation clear. 'So noted. Ma'am.'

'Dad,' Taylor murmured. 'Do not suddenly become a lawyer again after all these years. You're much nicer as a rancher. You've told me so yourself.'

Frederick looked embarrassed. 'All right. I'm sorry. You're right, Mrs Maynard. I'm very tired and I'm ... emotionally not myself.'

'Join the club,' Clay said wryly. Drawing a breath, he looked up and met Frederick's eyes. 'Thank you,' he said, his sincerity unmistakably pure. 'Thank you for taking care of my daughter, for protecting her all these years, even though I wasn't the enemy you thought I was. You've been the father you didn't need to be.'

Visibly stunned, Frederick froze for a long moment, and then his shoulders slumped, his expression changing to one of regret. 'I'm so sorry,' he said. 'I would never have kept her from you if I'd known the truth.'

'I believe you. She loves you. She says you're a good man and that's enough for me. For the record, I won't try to keep her here if you'll be okay with her visiting whenever she can. I know she's made a life with you. I know she loves you.'

Frederick's whole body now sagged and he gripped the bed rail for support. 'I didn't think . . . I never expected . . .' He swallowed hard, overcome. 'We'll figure something out. I thought . . .'

'You thought you'd come here and find that I'd brainwashed her into staying?'

'Something like that, yes,' Frederick admitted. 'That's why I rushed out here. God knows you'd be in the right. I have no way of making this up to you.'

'Not your fault,' Clay said wearily. 'Nothing to make up. You sacrificed a helluva lot to keep her safe from a threat you believed to be real. And you were smart enough about it to keep me chasing my tail for way too many years,' he added ruefully.

'Plus he taught me how to shoot,' Taylor inserted.

Clay's mouth turned up at the corners. 'Can't forget that. She saved my life today. So thank you for that as well.'

Frederick let out a slow breath. 'It sounds like Taylor has quite a story to tell me.'

Clay's lips curved. 'You don't know the half of it. It's nice to meet you, Frederick.'

'Likewise,' Frederick said, extending his hand. 'It's good to finally, truly know you.'

Taylor breathed her first truly easy breath in . . . it had been so long that she couldn't remember when. *Maybe never.* And God, did it feel good.

Clay started to lift his hand to shake, but he didn't have the strength. 'I'm not at my best today.' He closed his eyes. 'Tomorrow we can arm-wrestle for her.'

Frederick chuckled, but it sounded strained. 'Rain check on the handshake, then.'

'And now it's time for Clay to rest,' Stevie said firmly. 'Please don't be offended, but you all need to leave. *Now.*'

Obediently they filed into the hall, Ford pushing Taylor's chair and her dad following behind. 'I saw a waiting room at the end of the hall,' Taylor said. 'They have machines with soda and munchies, and I'm suddenly *starving*. I'll answer all your questions there. I promise.'

409

'And then I need to find a hotel, a shower, a real meal and a bed. In that order.'

'No, sir,' Ford said. 'We've got plenty of room at the farm. That way you can see where Taylor's been working, too. Just to put your mind fully at ease.'

'Thank you, son. I'll take you up on the invitation.'

Taylor looked up to find her dad smiling at Ford, and the last little bit of worry faded away. 'Where are Daisy and Julie?' Daisy was always home on the weekend, and Julie rarely left the property at all due to the mobility issues caused by her cerebral palsy. Their absence had only added to Taylor's earlier concern. 'One of the FBI agents on this case sent the sheriff to the house, but nobody was home.'

'They're staying with the Larsons.'

'Ah, that makes sense. They're a family we knew from the homeschool group,' she told Ford. 'Mrs Larson used to be a nurse, so she can care for Julie if anything comes up.'

They reached the waiting room and Ford parked the wheelchair.

'I'm dry as a bone from the air on the plane,' Frederick said. 'I'll get us something to drink and eat and then you can tell me a story.'

Ford sat next to Taylor while her father went to the vending machine. 'So we're a thing?' he asked with a small smile.

'Yes.' She gave him an uncertain look. 'Unless you don't want to be. If it makes you nervous, I underst—'

'Taylor, hush. I want to be.' He laughed quietly as he took her hand. 'And I'm not even the least bit nervous. I think if we can survive this weekend, we can survive nearly anything.'

'Even a long-distance relationship if I go back?'

'If it's meant to be, we'll find a way.'

Taylor raised her brows in challenge. 'His back is turned. Kiss me quick.'

Ford laughed, but he did as she asked. Except it wasn't that quick and her father had to clear his throat to separate them.

Ford pulled back like she'd burned his lips, his cheeks red as fire, but Taylor just smiled up at her dad. 'I told you that we're a thing. You gotta expect a little of that.'

'I'll get used to it,' Frederick muttered. 'Maybe.' He took the chair next to Ford and handed them bottles of water. 'So, Ford, I read that you're an engineer.'

Taylor laughed. 'Smooth, Dad. Real smooth.'

'Give me a break, kid. I'm still a greenhorn. Daisy hasn't met anyone yet.'

Taylor snorted inelegantly. 'That she's told you about.'

Frederick's eyes grew wide. 'What?'

But Ford interrupted them. 'Wait. How did you know I was an engineer?'

'There was Wi-Fi on the plane. I figured I'd better familiarize myself with the folks on your farm, since that's where my girl is working.' He pulled a folded envelope from his pocket. It was covered with names connected by lines and arrows. 'I took notes and made a family tree of sorts, so I think I can follow along with your story.'

Taylor shook her head. 'Oh no, Dad. You're gonna need a *much* bigger envelope.'

Twenty-four

Baltimore, Maryland,
Monday 24 August, 5.45 P.M.

Clay leaned back against the pillows of his hospital bed, closed his eyes, and let the breath seep out of him. It was quiet. Finally. He'd had a steady parade of visitors throughout the day, progressing up in their level of elegance from barn clothes to tuxedos and sequined dresses as the clock ticked closer to Holly and Dillon's big event.

But they were all gone now, even Stevie, who'd sat at his side all day long, but who was now at the church with Cordelia, the prettiest little flower girl of all time. Not that he was biased in the least, of course. The wedding was due to start within the hour, and he'd watch it via Skype, but he had a few minutes to close his eyes and simply rest.

He must have dozed off, because he woke with a jerk to the light touch of a hand on his shoulder, his fists clenched and his abs burning as he tried to lurch up to sit.

The hand gently pushed him back to the mattress. 'Sshh. It's okay.' The voice was soft and feminine and it soothed him. 'It's just me, Becky, your nurse. I need to take your vitals, but then you can go back to sleep.'

'Sorry.' Clay focused on slowing his pulse back to normal. 'Military habits die hard.'

'I figured as much,' she said, and he heard the smile in her voice. 'A lot of vets wake up jumpy and disoriented. Cops, too.'

412

'Been there,' he grunted. 'Done both.'

'I know. Marine Corps, served in Somalia, came back to join DCPD, then went off on your own to start a personal security firm.'

He opened his eyes to look up at her. Fortyish with a sweet smile, she'd given him excellent care all day, even though he suspected he was not the best patient. Okay, he knew he wasn't, because Stevie had told him so. Multiple times.

'How did you know all that?' he asked.

'Your dad told me.'

Clay rolled his eyes. 'He brags.'

'Sounds like he's got a right to. I also heard it from your little girl. Cordelia, right?'

His lips curved. Cordelia had been by twice, once to bring him some pictures she'd drawn 'especially for him', and the second time to model her flower-girl dress. 'Right.'

'She's a cutie,' Becky said. 'I may have also heard it from your business partner, you know, the pregnant woman with the black belt. And from the young man who said he'd manage your networks for you for free, but I'm not supposed to tell you that because he has bills to pay.' She said all of this teasingly as she took his blood pressure and temperature and checked to make sure all the tubes in and out of his body were still connected.

'The young man is my . . . well, kind of an adopted son. Alec. He's my IT guy. He came in to set up the computer so that I can see the wedding.' He patted the PC that Alec had left propped up against his hip so that he could reach it easily.

'Kind of adopted, huh? Then you're both lucky to have found each other. You have a lot of people who care about you, Mr Maynard, and each one said something like "Oh, he'll be fine."' She dropped her voice to sound gruff. '"He's a former Marine. A little thing like a bullet can't keep him down."'

Clay laughed and Nurse Becky looked pleased with herself. 'You were a good sport today,' he said. 'Thanks for taking those photos for us.' He picked up his phone from the side table and scrolled through his pictures. Stevie had taken most of them, but Nurse Becky had snapped a few when Stevie hadn't been in the room or was in the photo herself.

'It was my pleasure.' She leaned over the bed rail to peek at the screen. 'That guy was a charmer,' she said, pointing to the photo of Dillon, dressed in his barn clothes, with his arm around Clay's shoulders.

Dillon had been his first visitor, stopping by long before visiting hours officially began.

'He's the groom.'

'Oh, I know. We made the mistake of telling him that visiting hours hadn't begun so he'd need to come back later. He told us that he couldn't because it was his wedding day and that he had chores to do before he married the girl of his dreams. But that he had to see his friend first. I saw his bride when she dropped by later. They're both very sweet. '

Holly had come by in her wedding gown, just so Clay could see. 'I was supposed to be one of the groomsmen. Holly brought me my boutonnière so that I could wear it when I watch the wedding on Skype. I'm going to give a speech at the reception if the technology cooperates.'

'Ask one of us to help you with the boutonnière. We don't want you stabbing yourself with the pin and needing more stitches.'

He winced. 'That would suck.'

'Indeed it would. Oh.' She tilted his phone to see it better. 'What a handsome couple.'

Clay paused on the photo Stevie had taken of Taylor and Ford on their second visit. The first time they'd stopped by had been that morning. Ford was bitching because Taylor wouldn't stay out of the barn and Taylor was bitching back that she could at least clean tack from the wheelchair. They'd come alone, having left Frederick Dawson back at Maggie's house, still sleeping off his cross-country trip from the day before.

The second time they'd visited, they'd been in their wedding clothes. Ford wore a tux, because he too was a groomsman, and Taylor had sparkled in a glittery dress she'd borrowed from Daphne. 'That's my daughter,' he said proudly.

Who'd found him after he'd searched for her for so many years. He still couldn't quite believe it. The daughter who'd saved his life and risked her own to rescue two little girls. His pride was very well-placed.

'She's stunning.'

'She's also a very good person.'

'Then you have as much of a right to brag on your daughter as your father had on you.'

'Thank you,' he said quietly. He hadn't had a lot to do with the person Taylor had grown up to be. That was all due to Frederick Dawson. Clay was just glad the man was willing to work with them so that he could have time with her too.

'You're welcome.' She straightened his sheets, chatting as she did so. 'There's quite an age difference between your two girls.'

'Fourteen years,' Clay agreed. 'And my wife and I have another on the way.' It gave him a thrill just to say the words out loud. *And I get to be the daddy this time. How this kid turns out will be on me.*

Becky beamed. '*Mazel tov!* Now I have to get back to work. Ring if you need anything.'

'I will.' Clay relaxed back into the pillows, letting himself daydream about all the things he'd be for his child. All the things his own stepfather had been for him. Gratitude welled up within him, stinging his eyes and thickening his throat.

A light knock on the door pulled him back before he melted into undignified tears. He had a second to school his features before opening his eyes to see Frederick Dawson standing in the doorway, holding a small paper sack in one hand and a shoebox in the other.

'Bad time?' Frederick asked.

Clay motioned him in. 'I'm kind of talked out, but you're welcome to join me.'

Frederick sat in the chair beside him and put the shoebox on the floor. The paper sack he continued to hold. He proceeded to say nothing at all. And that was okay. The two of them shared a comfortable silence until Clay's curiosity got the better of him.

'What's in the sack?'

415

Frederick pulled out a black bow tie. 'Taylor sent this. It goes with your tux for the wedding.' He chuckled. 'She thought you could wear it with your hospital gown. Said it would make you look classier.'

Clay huffed a tired chuckle of his own. 'Little twerp,' he said affectionately, reaching for the tie. He laid it on the table next to the boutonnière.

'She always has been.' Frederick fell silent again, then sighed. 'I've meant to come and see you all day, but I've been putting it off. I was actually hoping you'd be asleep, or that the nurses would run me off for visiting out of hours.'

Clay frowned. 'Why? I thought we settled things last night.'

Frederick's laugh was bitter. 'No. We didn't. We made nice because Taylor was watching us with her big dark eyes that . . . are just like yours.' He hung his head, his shoulders slumping. 'We haven't begun to settle anything, because my saying I'm sorry is just a drop in the ocean.'

'I thought we agreed that this wasn't your fault,' Clay murmured.

'Maybe it wasn't. Or maybe I shouldn't have listened to Donna when she told me the horror stories about her abusive ex. Maybe I should have done a little goddamn due diligence before I ripped my family away from Oakland, forced Taylor to change her identity, and moved to a ranch in the middle of nowhere. Maybe I shouldn't have believed Donna at all.' He buried his face in his hands, shaking his head. 'And maybe I just wanted to be the hero.'

'Maybe,' Clay said quietly, thinking about the terrible price the man had paid for his unquestioning acceptance of Taylor's mother's lies. Frederick had lost his oldest daughter. And Donna *still* hadn't told the man the truth.

How could you, Donna? How could you have been so cold? So utterly bereft of any conscience? Lacking in soul?

Clay knew that he might never learn the answer to those questions. But he might be able to give this man some comfort. 'As I recall, Donna could be quite persuasive. When she came on to me in high school, I believed her when she said it was over between her and her ex. I believed her when she said she was pregnant and that

416

it was mine. Turns out those last two were the only honest things she did say. When she wanted to go back to her ex-boyfriend, she told me that she'd miscarried, and I believed that too. I gave her a divorce without a fight. Don't you think I've second-guessed myself for that over the years?'

'You were young.'

Clay sighed. 'I think we need to accept that Donna was a very good liar. She could pinpoint a weakness and exploit it. You wanted to be a hero. I was – quite honestly – very relieved when she wanted a divorce. I wasn't even twenty years old. I didn't want a wife, and given time and half a world's distance, I'd already realized that I didn't want her.'

'You're saying we both believed her because we wanted to.'

'Exactly. You're going to have to forgive yourself, Frederick. I hold no grudge against you. Do I wish you'd come to me and asked if I really was a fucking bastard? Well, yes. Duh,' he said, and Frederick laughed sadly. 'But I would have told you "no", because nobody admits to shit like that. You still wouldn't have believed me. I had very few friends then. Certainly not the network that I have now. My best references were my mom and stepdad. They believed me. But Donna's parents believed *her*. So you would have had no real reason to believe the truth even if you *had* asked.'

'I know you're right. But forgiving myself is going to take some time, I think.'

Clay shrugged. 'I ain't goin' anywhere.'

Frederick laughed again, then returned to being pensive. 'There are so many things I wish I could do over, but – God forgive me – having Taylor with me all these years isn't one of them. If I'd known the truth, if I'd known you were really a good man, I'd have still fought you for custody, even if her mother hadn't been in the picture.'

'After knowing her for three days, I wouldn't blame you one iota. It would have been horrible for her, split between two coasts, so I probably would have moved to California. I didn't have roots then. Not like I do now.' And he was so grateful for each and every one of those roots. 'Not like you do now, either.'

417

Frederick shook his head. 'I'm not so sure. Don't mention this to Taylor, but I've been thinking of selling the ranch. My health isn't what it used to be, and it's getting harder and harder to keep up with the work. I've got several neighbors who've expressed their interest in my holdings. God knows, moving to civilization would be better for my youngest daughter. I met Holly and Dillon today and they told me about their community center and all the activities they do. The jobs they hold. Damn, Dillon even drives. Now, my Julie doesn't have Down syndrome and her needs are different, but, man, what they have? *That's* what I want for Julie. And my middle daughter . . . Daisy's been ready to fly the coop for a long time. She only stayed to be Taylor's shadow.' His smile was melancholy. 'She wants to go to Paris and paint. I want her to be happy. I want all my daughters to be happy.' He met Clay's eyes. 'Including the daughter I've had on loan from you. What would you say if I relocated?'

'You'd move?' Clay asked, surprised. 'Here?' He hadn't considered that.

'Maybe. Why not? I'm not a poor man, and when I sell my land, I'll make more than enough to buy a small house here. Maybe one that's outfitted for my youngest.' He tilted his head, wonder creeping across his face like a sunrise. 'I have options. I haven't had options since we went into hiding.'

'It's a big move, all the way across the country,' Clay said cautiously. 'You could get services for your youngest in any big city in California just as easily as here.'

'Yes, but Taylor won't be in California. She'll be here.' The man smiled again, and this time it wasn't melancholy or bitter. It was bright and hopeful. 'Why wouldn't she be here? If we were to move, why not move her close to her other family?' He made a worried face. 'And the boy, too. I mean, I like Ford. He seems like a stand-up guy. But she's my baby.'

Clay laughed even though he understood. 'He's a good man, Frederick. You don't have anything to worry about with Ford Elkhart. This thing of theirs may be nothing more than a summer romance, but if it's more . . . well, I couldn't ask for a better son-in-law.'

'Then I guess I can't either.' Frederick picked up the shoebox and fidgeted with the lid. 'I have a question. Maybe the answer will help me make sense of all of this. Of you.'

'Then ask.'

'Why are you being so understanding? Why aren't you calling her Sienna? Why have you accepted all of this so easily? Why don't you hate me?'

'That's four questions,' Clay said mildly. 'But I'll answer as best I can. Easiest first. I did call her Sienna on Saturday, but it's only a name. That it was the name her mother gave her without my input made it easier to let it go. Plus, in my mind, Sienna was that terrified little girl who screamed when she saw me standing outside her schoolyard. Taylor is the daughter who sought me out. I'm good with the name change.'

'Okay,' Frederick said slowly. 'That makes sense.'

'Good. As for the first and third questions, they're really the same thing. I could be angry about the twenty-three years I lost, or I could treasure the time we have from today on. I'm picking the happier option. Angry, bitter people end up alone, and I was alone for too long.'

Frederick nodded. 'All right. I guess I can only hope I'd make the same choice were I in your shoes. And the last question?'

'Why I don't hate you?' Clay closed his eyes. 'I've been in law enforcement to some degree for all of my adult life. I know what victims look like. You are a victim, same as me. Maybe you should have looked harder for the truth, but you believed your wife. Husbands are supposed to be able to believe their wives. You were the best husband you knew how to be. You were also the very best father you could be, and now Taylor is a smart, capable woman with a beautiful heart. I don't know that I could have raised her to become any better of a person. I can't hate you. But I might start if you don't put this issue to rest.'

Frederick sighed, long and low. 'It's an extraordinary gift, this kind of forgiveness. I can only say thank you.'

'I learned from a good man,' Clay said simply. 'My biological father was *not* a good man and my mother left him when I was only three. She worked hard to feed me, so hard she rarely went out. Rarely had fun. Then she met Tanner St James, and our lives changed. Tanner loved my mother. He loved me. I wasn't a burden and I wasn't an obligation. I wasn't some other bastard's kid. I was his *son*. He was the dad he didn't have to be, just like you were for Taylor. Every good thing I've learned about being a man, about being a father, I learned from him. So if you need to thank someone, thank my dad.'

Frederick's swallow was audible. 'I will,' he whispered. He picked up the shoebox and handed it to Clay. 'I can't give you the years back, but I can give you these.'

'These' were photos. Dozens and dozens of photos, all of Taylor. Infant pictures, toddler. First day of kindergarten. Christmas pictures, birthdays. Each photo was neatly labeled on the back with the date and the occasion. His daughter's life, right here in this box.

Clay's eyes teared up. 'My God,' he whispered. 'Look at her. She's beautiful.'

'I sat down with Donna two months before she died,' Frederick said quietly, 'and we put all the pictures on the kitchen table. She identified each picture and I labeled the back. I didn't want her to pass without me having a proper record of Taylor's growing-up, especially since I didn't know her when she was really small.'

'This . . .' *This* was what Clay had missed. Her first lost tooth, her gap-toothed smile. Riding a horse. Reading to her youngest sister.

Donna had stolen his daughter's childhood, but at least he had these pictures. And Frederick had brought them before he'd known that Clay hadn't brainwashed her or guilted her into staying. The man had come planning to make amends, no matter what. 'Thank you,' Clay whispered, overcome. 'Just . . . thank you.'

He looked through the photos, drinking in each and every one until his phone started to chirp. Reluctantly he put them back in the shoebox. 'That's my alarm,' he said, setting the laptop on his good thigh. 'It's wedding time.' He signed in to Skype and only had to wait a minute for Alec's call.

Alec's face appeared on his screen. 'You there, Pops?'

Clay growled at him. 'You do not get to call me that.'

Daphne's face appeared next to Alec's, and she was grinning. 'Sugar, *everybody*'s calling you that. You'd better get used to it.' She frowned a little, studying him. 'You look tired.'

'I am tired. I did just get shot yesterday, you know.'

'We know,' Alec said shortly. 'We're going to have a talk about protective body armor for your legs.'

'But later,' Daphne chimed in before Clay could object. 'It's time to get these kids hitched. Where's your bow tie?'

Clay held it up. 'I can't put it on myself. I'm too tired.'

Alec smirked. 'Told you so,' he said to Daphne.

Daphne rolled her eyes. 'Spoilsport,' she said.

'Heck, if I'd known being shot could have gotten me out of wearing a tie . . .' Alec said.

'Forget it,' Clay snapped. 'No more of my kids get shot, okay?'

Alec's smirk turned to a smile that lit up his whole face. 'Okay.'

'I can help with the tie,' Frederick said, taking it out of Clay's hand and ignoring his glare.

'I didn't know you were there, Freddie,' Daphne said.

Frederick winced, and Clay guessed that 'Freddie' was not his favorite nickname. 'We've been visiting.' Frederick neatly fixed the tie around Clay's throat. 'There.'

'Nice,' Daphne crowed. 'Thank you, Freddie.'

Clay tapped the tie. 'This I might not be able to forgive,' he said sourly. He handed the boutonnière to Frederick. 'Might as well go for the whole shooting match.' And he rolled his eyes as his new partner in fatherhood pinned the flower to his hospital gown.

'Holly will be happy to see you wearing it,' Daphne said softly. 'Bye for now. Gotta take our seats. If you want to see Taylor, she's sitting behind the back row in her wheelchair.'

Alec positioned his laptop behind the altar. 'Hope this works. Bye, Pops.'

Clay found he had to laugh. He muted the sound at his end and settled back to watch.

421

'I know Holly is Ford's step-aunt,' Frederick said, 'and that Dillon works in the barn, but why are they having a wedding on a Monday night?'

Clay turned 'step-aunt' over in his mind and realized that Frederick had it right. He'd never thought about how everyone was related to everyone else. 'Because Holly's sister and brother-in-law are caterers with a bakery and Dillon's folks run a diner. One's doing desserts and the other's doing dinner.' He sighed. 'It'll be barbecue, and I'm missing it.' He'd endured hospital meals before and would again, but the thought of seeing all that delicious food, even on the computer, made him grouchy. 'Both businesses do most of their sales on the weekend and are closed on Monday. Holly's sister probably could miss one day of sales, but Dillon's folks aren't wealthy. So . . . Monday.'

Frederick blinked. 'That makes sense, too.'

'You sound surprised.'

'I am. I expected everything to be complicated. But it all seems to be working out.'

Clay nodded, content. 'Sometimes it does.'

Baltimore, Maryland,
Monday 24 August, 8.40 P.M.

It had been a lovely wedding, Taylor thought as she wheeled herself toward the hospital lobby's elevator. She'd been capable of wheeling herself yesterday, too, but Ford had needed to keep his hands busy.

Busy hands. Oh my. She grinned a little secret grin. Because after they'd gotten back to Maggie's house and had her dad settled in a guest room, Ford had pushed her chair out to the barn, where Ford's hands had been very busy indeed. Nothing major. Just some serious cuddling.

Which Taylor couldn't wait to do again. And they would once the reception was over and Ford had returned to Maggie's. She knew he didn't actually live there full time and would at some point go back to his real home, wherever that was. But hopefully he'd stay long enough for them to figure out what this thing between them really was and what it might become. Hopefully the partygoers at the reception wouldn't dance all night, because Ford would be too tired to do any cuddling and that would be a real shame.

Taylor had waited for the cutting of the cake so she could bring a slice to Clay. She'd said her goodbyes to the bride and groom and then Ford had pushed her chair to the curb and hailed her a cab. He'd understood that she wanted to get back to sit with her father. It hurt her to think of Clay all alone while the rest of them partied and celebrated. Ford had wanted to come with her, just to make sure she arrived safely, but she'd had to draw the line right there. She needed to do some things for herself, because he wouldn't always be there. He had a life too.

'Taylor, wait.' Stevie was walking across the hospital lobby, leaning heavily on her cane. 'Hold the elevator, please.'

'Are you okay?' Taylor asked when Stevie slumped against the elevator wall.

'I'll be fine with some sleep and maybe an ice pack.' Stevie pressed her fist into her lower back with a grimace. 'I've just been on my feet too much today and I danced too many dances with Cordelia at the wedding reception. My old injury still gives me fits when I overdo it.'

'And I'm sure the pregnancy doesn't help that.'

'No.' Stevie's lips curved. 'But worth it.'

'The wedding dancing or the pregnancy?'

Stevie grinned. 'Both.'

'It was a beautiful service.' Elegant, but not over the top. Classy. 'I liked the mix of traditional and modern music.' JD's wife and her friend had played all the standards for the prelude and processional, but Dillon and Holly had each picked a song to be sung by two of the volunteers from their community center during the service itself. The two singers had done a wonderful job, although one of them had teared up midway through his song. The bride and groom had stepped in, lending their voices until their friend got control of his. Of course that had had everyone in the church in tears. It had been incredibly sweet.

423

Stevie's chuckle was affectionate. 'I wasn't surprised by "Love Story", because every girl wants to be Taylor Swift, right? But I've never heard of "Standing Outside the Fire" being played at a wedding.'

'Actually Ford told me that it was Dillon who picked Taylor Swift.'

Stevie's mouth fell open. 'You're kidding!'

'No. Ford said that it was partly to poke at Joseph for trying to scare Dillon away from Holly early on.' Because the song had a Romeo and Juliet theme. 'Apparently Joseph caught them . . . you know. On the living room couch. Ford says Joseph's never quite recovered, and Dillon was terrified of him for months.'

Stevie made a face. 'I can see how that might have got them off to a rocky start. But Joseph loves him now, so they obviously worked that out.' Her forehead bunched up. 'So the Garth Brooks song was Holly's pick? Why?'

Taylor had known why the moment the man had begun to sing, and she'd been crying long before the singer had. 'It's because of the music video. It's about a high-school kid with Down syndrome who wants to try out for the track team. Mom is supportive, but Dad is scared he'll get hurt. When the kid runs the race, he falls and bloodies his face, but it's Dad who runs out to the track and makes sure the boy crosses the finish line – all on his own.'

Stevie's lips quivered and she sucked in a breath. 'Damn. I'm glad I didn't know that during the ceremony. I would have been a sobbing mess.'

'I'm glad I was sitting in the back row because I *was* a sobbing mess. I always think of my sister when I hear that song. Julie really wants to have a life. More than what she's able to have back home. It's too small a town to have the same services that Holly and Dillon have.' Taylor sighed. 'Anyway, it was a beautiful ceremony and Holly was just . . . glowy. It was like she was so happy she couldn't keep it all in.'

'She was,' Stevie said fondly. 'And Dillon was so nervous.'

'So was Clay when he gave that little speech over Skype at the reception.'

424

Stevie laughed a little. 'He's been obsessing about that speech since Holly asked him to do it, months ago. I'm glad Alec thought of Skype.' She frowned again. 'Or was it you? Yesterday is like cotton candy in my head.'

'It was me, but that doesn't matter.' It did, actually. It meant that Stevie cared about giving her credit for ideas, which meant her father's wife might be starting to warm up to the adult child who had popped up out of nowhere. 'But Alec set it up.'

'Alec's a good kid,' Stevie said. 'He and Ford helped Holly and Dillon fix up their apartment. It was kind of shabby, but it was all Dillon could afford.'

'Alec and Ford respected Dillon's pride,' Taylor said quietly.

'Exactly. The apartment's close enough to Holly's sister's house that her sister can take Holly into the bakery on days when the weather's too snowy for Dillon to drive.'

'They'll be able to be independent and have privacy. That's so nice.' Privacy for a new couple was critical. Taylor knew that even though she had little experience with relationships. For now, anyway. If she and Ford ever got past second base, they'd need privacy too.

Stevie stopped to sit in a chair set against the wall, breaking into Taylor's concentration.

'Are you okay?' Taylor asked for the second time in fifteen minutes.

'Just tired. This hospital is too damn huge, and of course Clay's room is at the opposite end. Go on ahead and I'll catch up.'

Taylor didn't say yes or no. She simply stayed where she was, silently waiting until Stevie was ready to get up. Clay would want her to make sure his wife was okay. In the meantime, she wanted to know if there was such a thing as privacy in her new world.

'Stevie, where does Ford live?'

Stevie blinked at the topic change. 'He used to have an apartment in the city, close to the university, but now that he's graduated and working fulltime, I'm not sure where he'll live. Maybe with Daphne until he gets a place of his own. Why?'

'I just realized I didn't know.'

425

Stevie's eyes narrowed slightly. 'You're thinking of living with him?'

'Oh no, not right now. I just met him. And I'll be able to live at Maggie's until my internship is over next month.'

'And then?' Stevie asked evenly.

'You're asking me if I'll stay.'

'Yes, I am.'

'I'll definitely stay until Clay's back to full health, at least. He'll try to go back to work too soon. I can help out there so that he doesn't feel the stress.'

'Are you asking for a job, Taylor?' Stevie asked, not unkindly. 'Working with our firm?'

It was Taylor's turn to blink. 'No. At least I don't think so. I never even thought about it. All I meant was that I could do paperwork, answer the phone. I've done the books for the ranch since my mother died, so I can do that for Clay. Just basic stuff. I don't think I want to do what you guys do. I don't want to shoot people.'

Stevie's lips twitched. 'Well, we don't shoot people all that often. We try never to do so, in fact. If you don't want to work for us, what *do* you want to do?'

Taylor opened her mouth to say she didn't know, then realized that she did. 'I don't want to shoot people,' she repeated. 'I want to put them back together. I want to do what Maggie does. I'm going to ask her for a job after the internship. She's got empty stalls and I can train any new horses she brings in. We could double the number of counseling slots and eliminate the waiting lists. Kids like Jazzie and Janie shouldn't need to wait for help.'

Stevie pushed to her feet using the cane as leverage, smoothed the grimace of pain from her face and turned it into an encouraging smile. 'I like that plan. I don't think you'll have to twist Maggie's arm to make it so.'

'I have to get licensed first, though, which requires I get my masters. That'll take two years. I was signed up to go to grad school in California, but classes start in early September. I won't be ready to leave then. So I'll lose at least a semester. Hopefully Maggie can wait.'

'You could go to school locally.'

'I could.' She'd considered it. 'I still might, if there's time.'

'Which brings us back to the question of housing. Where will you live when your internship is over?'

Taylor hesitated. 'Clay mentioned something about you guys having an extra room. Just until I can find something I can afford. I can help around the house. Work for my keep. I can take Cordelia riding and do Clay's heavy lifting, since he won't be able to for a long time and you won't be able to in a few months. You really shouldn't be lifting anything now.'

'Okay.'

'Okay to which thing?' Taylor asked, wary of Stevie's easy acceptance.

'Okay, I won't lift heavy things, and okay, you can have the spare room. You don't have to work for your keep, Taylor. You're family. We want you to stay with us, but we want it to be what you want too. And once you're back in California, you'll have a room to come back to when you want to visit.'

'Thank you. I'll be a good guest, I promise.'

'I wouldn't have thought anything different. Ah,' Stevie sighed. 'Finally.'

They'd made it to Clay's room, possibly at a slower pace than Ford's snail's crawl yesterday. *Poor Stevie. If she's this bad now, what's she going to be like when she's carrying a whole baby?* Taylor was seeing bed rest in the woman's future, which meant Clay would have even more to do – and even more to worry about.

She couldn't go back to California. Not yet. The extra time she could spend with Ford was only a very nice side benefit.

Except . . . Stevie and Clay had so many people who loved them, who would help them. *Frederick has only me.*

She wouldn't be able to stay indefinitely. That much was crystal cl—

'Shit,' she hissed, wheeling herself into the room as quickly as she could, because the laptop she'd loaned Frederick was sliding off his lap. She retrieved it just in time, setting it on her own lap.

Both of her fathers were sound asleep, Clay in the hospital bed

427

and Frederick slumped in a chair, his head back at an unnatural angle. *You're gonna regret falling asleep like that*, she thought. She looked over her shoulder at Stevie, who was carefully making her way to the more comfortable of the two chairs situated at Clay's bedside.

On the nightstand was Clay's laptop and phone, and a shoebox that Taylor recognized from home. The very sight of it made her eyes burn, because she knew what it meant. Sitting on its lid, precisely arranged, were the boutonnière and the bow tie. Holly had gotten such a kick out of the fact that Clay had gone to the trouble of wearing them. Taylor imagined that Clay had gotten a far bigger kick from the contents of the shoebox.

Stevie was frowning at the box. 'What's in it?' she asked softly.

'Pictures,' Taylor whispered. 'He keeps all of our photos in shoeboxes. Each of us girls has one. That's my box. I decorated it the year he adopted me and changed my name. Dad – I mean Frederick-Dad – brought with him.' Her heart twisted, but it was a nice kind of twist. 'He wanted Clay to see the years he'd missed. It was the best he could do.' She turned to look at Frederick's face, the face she'd loved for so long. 'How can I leave him? How can I make this kind of a choice?'

'You might not have to,' Clay muttered grumpily before Stevie could say a word. 'You two really have to learn sign language or something. Your whispers are loud enough to wake the damn dead.'

Taylor kept on whispering, hoping to at least not wake Frederick. 'What do you mean, I might not have to?'

'Look at your laptop. It's okay.'

Warily Taylor lifted the laptop's lid. And drew a fast, harsh breath. 'He wrote emails to the neighboring landowners.' She looked up at Clay, trembling so hard it was a wonder her teeth didn't clatter. 'He's selling the ranch.'

Stevie's eyes widened. 'Just like that?'

'He'd been thinking about it for a long time,' Clay said quietly. 'He said if he moves away from the ranch, he might as well move here as anywhere else. He can make some money selling the property, and get his youngest daughter the services she's been

428

needing.' He rolled his head to meet Taylor's eyes, his weary but so kind. 'He loves you, Taylor. So much that he's going to uproot himself to keep you from having to choose. I don't know how your mother managed to snag him, but he's a hell of a guy.'

Taylor's heart was racing, and she found she'd pressed her hand to her breastbone in a feeble attempt to make it slow down. Frederick wasn't going to make her choose. She looked at him, love flowing out of her heart so hard that it hurt her chest. Her hand shaking, she switched to the browser window he'd left open.

And then she smiled. 'Doesn't Grandpa live in a place called Wight's Landing?'

Clay's eyes twinkled. 'He does, in a house right on the beach. Has a dock and everything.'

'Looks like Dad found a house there too. He's got it bookmarked. It's right on the water. It's got a dock as well. And a boat.'

'He's already called a realtor and made an appointment to see it. Dad's taking him out there tomorrow, first thing.'

'We had a weekend cottage on the beach when we lived in Oakland. He told me once that was the only thing he missed from his old life. He loved living on the water.'

Stevie's lips trembled. 'Now he might be able to again.'

Clay frowned at her. 'Are you crying? Again?'

'Hormones,' Stevie snapped. 'Shut up.' But she said it lovingly, if that was possible. 'Everyone was bawling at the wedding. I fit right in.'

Taylor was still blown away. Frederick Dawson had sacrificed for her, and now he was about to do so again. 'But I'm gonna let him,' she murmured.

'Let him do what?' Clay asked.

'Let him sell the ranch and move here, even though it's another sacrifice. Does that make me selfish?'

Clay's smile was gentle. 'No, honey. But for what it's worth, I don't think you could stop him. He's been thinking about this for some time.'

Ford. I need to tell Ford. She found her phone and texted him. *Call me when you can. Good news.*

His answer came back immediately. *Turn around.*

She turned and found him in the doorway, breathing a little hard, still wearing his tux, although he'd unfastened the tie so that it hung around his collar. He looked . . . rakish. Good enough to eat. 'You came! I thought you'd dance all night.'

'Dillon and Holly threw me out. They said I was too gloomy after you left and I was bringing their party down.' He glanced at the still-snoring Frederick. 'I have a car, so I can drive us all back. What's your news?'

She opened her mouth to tell him, but Clay held up a hand. 'Are you going to get all, you know . . .' He made a face. 'Kissy?'

Taylor nodded. 'Probably.'

He waved his hand toward the door in a shooing motion. 'Then take it outside, kid.'

'Privacy. Right.' She deftly turned the chair around and glided past Ford so quickly that he had to turn on his heel to follow her and nearly stumbled.

'You're really good at wheeling that thing yourself,' he accused as he followed her.

'Yep. I spent four months in a chair after a horse rolled over me and broke my pelvis. I have biceps of freaking steel.'

'Your horse . . . You broke your pelvis?'

'Yeah. It's fine now. All screwed back together. I set off the metal detector in LAX, and if I have kids, they may need to be delivered by C-section. Otherwise, everything is in perfect working order.' She lifted her brows as she said this. 'Got it?'

He actually blushed. 'Got it.'

'Good.'

Baltimore, Maryland,
Monday 24 August, 9.00 P.M.

They made it to the waiting room in half the time it had taken the day before, and Ford lowered himself into a chair very carefully, wincing at the sudden tightness of the tux pants. He did not want to have to explain a rip or, God forbid, a stain when he returned the damn monkey suit. That would be beyond embarrassing.

Taylor frowned. 'Did you hurt yourself at the reception? Dammit, I was afraid you'd reinjure your leg. Do we need to go down to the ER?'

'No, that's not the problem.' The thigh that had been shot had been throbbing all night, but didn't hold a candle to the throbbing in his groin. 'If you must know, thinking about all your *perfectly working parts* has me hard as a rock.' He stretched his leg out and adjusted himself.

She grinned, pleased with herself. 'Poor baby.'

'Yeah,' he groused, but it was all for show. 'You go ahead and laugh. I'll make you pay.'

'Please and thank you?' she said hopefully.

He laughed. 'Tell me this good news that'll make us all kissy.'

'Dad may be selling the ranch and moving to Wight's Landing.'

She'd just blurted it out, leaving Ford blinking in her wake. 'Wow. That was not what I expected.' He sat up straighter, a slow smile blooming. 'It's much better than I expected. He's not going to make you choose.'

'I know,' she whispered. 'He'll be close enough to visit and far enough away to let me have a life. And Julie can get the care she needs and maybe one day she'll have a wedding too.'

Ford couldn't help it. He lunged forward, palmed the back of her neck and pulled her into a kiss that left them both breathless. 'He gave us time.'

'He did. Now it's up to us to figure out what we want this thing between us to be.'

He held her face in his hands. 'I know what I want it to be. I want what I see everyone around me finding.' He kissed her again, this time hard and fast – stamping her as his. 'I want a family and a home and someone who chooses me.'

So many emotions flickered in her eyes. 'I don't know how I would have chosen between my two fathers, but . . . once we knew we were a real thing, I would have chosen you over both of them, Ford.'

His eyes burned. 'I know,' he whispered. 'But I'm so damn glad that you didn't have to.' Frederick Dawson had given them the gift of the time to see where their road led without any of the pressures of a long-distance relationship, and for that Ford would be forever grateful. 'If you'd had to choose, you would have left part of your heart behind. And I want that heart whole, Taylor. Just in case you ever decide to give it to me.'

She smiled at him so sweetly. 'For an engineer, you sure have pretty words.' Then she lifted her brows, her sweet look gone sly. 'So now that we've covered my news, did you have anything in mind as you were driving to see me?'

His grin was very wicked. 'Yes, but we can't do *that* here. I do, however, remember you asking me for something yesterday. You're not about to hurl, right?'

She laughed. 'No.' Then laughed again as he reached into the wheelchair and scooped her up, lowering them both back into his chair. She fit in his lap perfectly, nuzzling her cheek against his chest, making a purring sound. 'Just like I remembered. Pretty damn impressive.'

He rested his cheek against the top of her head and exhaled quietly, content for now to simply hold her. They'd sat in easy silence for a minute or two when Taylor started to laugh softly. 'What?' he asked.

She pulled back far enough for him to see her cheeky grin. 'I'm just wondering what we're going to do for fun next weekend. Skydiving? Lion-taming? Lying down on a bed of nails? Cliff-diving in Mexico? Oh, I know – we can take out a cartel or two while we're there.'

He huffed a chuckle and kissed the tip of her nose. 'I have a better idea. How about a nice *quiet* ride to my clearing after your sessions are done? We can pack a picnic and a pair of binoculars for birdwatching.'

The look on her face was priceless – surprised disappointment that she tried to cover with a very manufactured acceptance. 'That . . . birdwatching sounds fun. But just one pair of binoculars? I don't get my own?'

He rested his forehead against hers and tried not to smile. 'Taylor.

Sweetheart. Birdwatching is just a cover story in case anyone comes along and catches us doing what we'll *really* be doing.'

Her eyes widened and her lips curved. 'Ohhh.' She returned to her snuggling position. 'I like that idea a whole lot more.'

He tightened his hold on her, pretty sure this was the happiest he'd ever been. 'I was really hoping you would.'

About Karen Rose

Author photo: © Deborah Feingold

Karen Rose was introduced to suspense and horror at the tender age of eight when she accidentally read Poe's *The Pit and the Pendulum* and was afraid to go to sleep for years. She now enjoys writing books that make other people afraid to go to sleep.

Karen lives in Florida with her family, their cat, Bella, and two dogs, Loki and Freya. When she's not writing, she enjoys reading, and her new hobby – knitting.